"Christy Award winner Whitlow's (*The Trial*) experience in the law is apparent in this well-crafted legal thriller. Holt's spiritual growth as he discovers his faith and questions his motives for hiding his secret is inspiring. Fans of John Grisham will find much to like here."

—*Library Journal* on *The Confession*

"Whitlow writes with the credence of a legal background and quite adeptly incorporates intrigue, romance, and redemption in its many forms into his book. Recommend to young adults and older readers with a penchant for unexpected twists and unanticipated outcomes."

—*CBA Retailers + Resources* on
The Confession

"Whitlow has weaved a well-constructed and engaging mystery with a crisp, concise style of storytelling, authentic, gritty characters and a well-defined plot. Strong tension and steady pacing add to this stellar read."

—*RT Book Reviews*, 4-1/2 stars, on
The Confession

"Whitlow intertwines legal drama with spiritual highs and lows in an intensely exceptional read."

—Dale Lewis, Novel Crossing, on
The Confession

"Readers will find plenty to love about this suspenseful novel as they watch its appealing main character juggle personal, professional, and spiritual crisis with a combination of vulnerability and strength."

—*CBA Retailers + Resources* on
The Living Room

". . . an intensely good read."

—Booklist on *The Living Room*

"In *The Choice*, Robert Whitlow crafts a moving tale of a mother's love for her unborn children cast against the specter of the culture wars. Fans of Whitlow's courtroom drama will not be disappointed, but here too the human drama of which we all become a part takes center stage. Every page entertains and inspires. I dare you to put this book down. Heartrending and triumphant, Whitlow at his best."

—Billy Coffey, author of *Snow Days* and
Paper Angels

"Whitlow captures the struggle of many women trapped in the battle over abortion in a truly sympathetic and affecting way."

—Booklist on *The Choice*

"Author Robert Whitlow combines Grisham's suspenseful legal-thriller style with the emotional connection of a Hallmark made-for-TV movie."

—CBA Retailers + Resources on *Water's
Edge*

". . . a solid, suspenseful thriller."

—Booklist on *Water's Edge*

A HOUSE
DIVIDED

Also by Robert Whitlow

The Confession
The Living Room
The Choice
Water's Edge

The Tides of Truth Series

Deeper Water
Higher Hope
Greater Love

Mountain Top
Jimmy

The Alexia Lindale Series

Life Everlasting
Life Support

The Sacrifice
The Trial
The List

A HOUSE
DIVIDED

ROBERT
WHITLOW

THOMAS NELSON
Since 1798

NASHVILLE   MEXICO CITY   RIO DE JANEIRO

Published in Nashville, Tennessee, by Thomas Nelson. Thomas Nelson is a registered trademark of HarperCollins Christian Publishing, Inc.

Thomas Nelson titles may be purchased in bulk for educational, business, fundraising, or sales promotional use. For information, please e-mail SpecialMarkets@ ThomasNelson.com.

Library of Congress Cataloging-in-Publication Data

Whitlow, Robert, 1954-
A house divided / Robert Whitlow.
pages ; cm
ISBN 978-1-4016-8888-2 (softcover)
I. Title.
PS3573.H49837H68 2015
813'.54--dc23
2015006803

Printed in the United States of America

15 16 17 18 19 20 RRD 6 5 4 3 2 1

*To those who never stop believing, who never
quit praying, and who faithfully offer practical
help to those who have lost their way.*

Two are better than one because they have a good return for their labor. For if either of them falls, the one will lift up his companion. But woe to the one who falls when there is not another to lift him up.

ECCLESIASTES 4:9–10 NASB

ONE

Corbin Gage shifted in the front pew and rubbed the large spot on his neck that his razor had missed. The stubbly gray hairs rose up against his fingers in sharp protest. He furtively cast his eyes toward his daughter, who sat to his right. There was no hiding his external or internal flaws from Roxy. Clutching a wad of tissues, she stared straight ahead as the minister finished his eulogy.

Everyone stood as the pallbearers picked up the casket and carried it slowly down the aisle. Corbin pressed his lips tightly together. His son, Ray, did the same. After the casket passed, Corbin felt a tug on his sleeve and glanced down into the face of his eight-year-old grandson, Billy.

"Pops," Billy said.

"Not now," Ray said to his son, raising his finger to his lips.

"Gran isn't really in there, is she?" Billy persisted, his eyes looking up at Corbin.

If under oath on the witness stand, Corbin would have pleaded the fifth. Instead he simply shook his head.

"I didn't think so," the little boy said.

Corbin patted Billy on the shoulder as the family followed the casket down the aisle. Sometimes innocent ignorance was better than dogged doubt.

The church cemetery was across the street. Two sheriff's deputies wearing white gloves halted traffic in both directions as the mourners crossed. It was a bright fall afternoon, and after the retreat of summer's muggy humidity, the air smelled fresh and clean. The flower beds in front of the cemetery were an explosion of late season color. Corbin saw the flowers, and his mind went back twenty-five years to Kitty and a group of women pulling weeds from the beds. One of the first groups Kitty joined when she returned to church with Ray and Roxy in tow was the garden committee. Bringing beauty to her surroundings was at the core of her being. Yet despite her patient efforts and best intentions, the weeds of Corbin's life had proven infinitely more stubborn than crabgrass or dandelions.

A mound of freshly dug red clay marked their destination. Corbin stood a few feet behind his children. The ten years since his divorce from Kitty disqualified him from closer proximity.

While the minister offered a few final words, Corbin stared at the ground and moved a red clod of dirt from side to side with his foot. Glancing up he saw Ray's wife, Cindy, put her hands around Billy's shoulders to steady him as the boy leaned forward to peer into the hole where the casket would soon be lowered into a steel vault.

The minister finished and people began to slowly move away. Several spoke to Corbin as they passed. Whatever their secret thoughts, today they showed him kindness. He nodded and mumbled a brief response. Once the crowd cleared, the workers released the straps holding the casket and lowered it into the ground. Ray and Roxy turned around. Their eyes were red. Billy was holding Cindy's hand.

"Mama, can I ride over to Gran's house with Pops in his truck?" Billy asked his mother.

"Honey, we're not sure he's—"

"I'm coming," Corbin interrupted. "But I won't stay long."

"Okay," Cindy said slowly. "Don't stop anywhere in between."

Corbin gave his daughter-in-law an icy stare and put a hand on Billy's shoulder. The little boy was thick and muscular, and people who saw pictures of Corbin at the same age as Billy swore grandfather and grandson looked like twins.

"We'll be there before you and Ray," Corbin said.

Ray, Cindy, and Roxy recrossed the street to the large parking lot beside the church.

"I parked behind the cemetery," Corbin said to Billy.

"Are you sad about Gran dying?" Billy asked.

"Of course I am."

They walked toward the back edge of the cemetery. Dead leaves crunched beneath their feet.

"Everybody was crying but you and me," the boy said. "Why is that?"

"People are different that way. We're all going to miss your gran. If you feel sad later, it's okay to cry."

"Is that what you'll do?"

"Maybe."

They reached Corbin's truck. He'd grown up in rural Georgia, where every male worth his jeans and boots drove a pickup. Thirty-seven years as a lawyer in the northeastern part of the state hadn't changed his opinion about the only true masculine mode of transportation.

A large man with big, powerful hands, Corbin had a full head of gray hair, thick eyebrows, and dark brown eyes. Within seconds of combing his hair, a large shock usually drifted down over his forehead.

"Buckle your seat belt," he said to Billy when they got into the white truck.

"I always buckle my seat belt. I don't want you to go to jail."

"Who told you they'd put me in jail if you didn't fasten your seat belt?"

"Daddy said he persecuted a man who didn't buckle in his son."

"Prosecuted. And the man probably did something else wrong, too, like not being a safe driver and causing a wreck."

"Have you had any wrecks?"

"A few minor things we call fender benders. Nothing serious. Nobody ever got hurt."

The most embarrassing accident happened two years before. Late one Friday afternoon Corbin backed into a light pole outside The Office, a local tavern. Startled by the sudden impact, he put the shifter in drive, stepped on the gas, and sideswiped a parked car. Fortunately the deputy called to the scene didn't administer a Breathalyzer test.

"Good thing you didn't pull into the street, Mr. Gage," the deputy said.

Corbin had represented the man's mother years before when she was wrongfully terminated from a job.

"Yeah, I'll get the truck towed to Garrison's," Corbin said as he sucked on a peppermint. "The wrecker driver can take me home."

"Yes, sir. That's a good idea."

As soon as the truck was repaired, Corbin had sold it and bought a new one. Colonel Parker, Corbin's former mentor and law partner, claimed it was bad luck to drive a vehicle that had been wrecked.

It wasn't far to the house where the family would gather. Corbin stopped at one of Alto's twelve traffic lights. He waited almost a minute for the light to turn green. In the meantime two cars passed through the intersection.

Willow Oak Lane was a short street that ended in a cul-de-sac. Corbin and Kitty bought the rambling white house three years into their marriage and nine months after Corbin obtained the largest jury verdict in a personal injury case in the history of Rusk County—1.2 million dollars for the estate of a young wife and mother killed when her car was struck from behind by a logging truck. The insurance company's lawyer argued that the woman didn't turn on her blinker and slowed down too quickly before turning off the highway, thus making it impossible for the driver of the truck to avoid hitting her. He also threw in a few barbs about the diminished economic value of the woman's life because she didn't work outside the home. Corbin had called a mechanic for the trucking company as a witness. He testified that the brakes on the truck weren't properly fixed because the owner of the company had more business than his limited fleet could handle. A grim-faced jury shocked the courtroom when they announced the verdict. Corbin collected an attorney fee of $400,000 and used most of his after-tax income as a down payment on the house. He promised Kitty an even fancier house for a future that never came.

There were several cars parked in the driveway. Women were carrying dishes of food across the yard. Corbin pulled alongside the curb and stopped in front of a For Sale sign placed by the real estate company that was selling the house to pay Kitty's massive medical bills.

"There will be a lot to eat inside," he said to Billy. "That's what people do when someone dies. They bring food so the family won't have to cook."

"Will I have to try stuff I don't like?"

"Nobody except your mama will be paying attention to what you eat. If you want to try something new and don't like it, just find me and put it on my plate."

The broad flower beds across the front of the house were weedy, which made Corbin sad. Congestive heart failure had taken Kitty's life and, before it killed her, sapped her strength like a constant drain on an already weak battery.

"Your gran loved flowers," he said as much to himself as Billy. "And tomatoes."

Corbin smiled. Billy was right. Before she got sick Kitty had become interested in heirloom tomatoes and cultivated multiple varieties in a fertile spot behind the house. The high acidic content in the local soil grew great tomatoes, and when a vine started producing fruit, she'd leave a message for Corbin at his office. He'd stop by after work and, without disturbing her, go around back and pick a few for a simple supper.

The cordiality toward Corbin that had marked the funeral continued inside the house. He received greetings and condolences as he moved from room to room. Women from the church and neighborhood were arranging food in the kitchen. Someone had brought in a long plastic table for desserts. Corbin didn't like sweets, but he saw Billy making a beeline toward a massive, multi-layer chocolate cake.

"Not yet," Corbin said, grabbing the boy by the shoulder. "You know better than that. Get a plate of regular food and show it to your mama when she gets here. She'll let you know when you can get dessert. I'll be in the green bedroom."

Corbin piled a plate high with more than he wanted and walked down an unused hallway that had a slightly musty smell. He pushed open the door to the master bedroom with his foot and went inside.

Instantly he knew he'd made a mistake.

TWO

After the crowd at the grave site cleared, Ray and Cindy left the cemetery and got into their six-year-old Honda. They'd bought it shortly after Ray passed the bar exam on his second try and landed a job at the district attorney's office.

Cindy flipped down the visor and fluffed her short blond hair.

"Is Dad going to drop Billy at the house and leave?" Ray asked.

"He said he would stay awhile, but I wouldn't be surprised if he cuts out immediately." She returned the visor to its place. "Do you think he listened to anything the minister said?"

"He heard it, but who knows if it got beneath the surface. He had to know the part where Reverend Adams talked about Mom praying daily for those she loved had Dad's name written across it in billboard-size letters."

"And our names."

"And Roxy."

"And Billy."

"Yeah." Ray nodded. "She's left a huge hole."

Cindy reached over and patted Ray's arm. "You're her son. Everyone knows your father isn't going to lead this family. It's up to you now."

Ray glanced in the rearview mirror and saw his sister's new

BMW behind them. "Roxy's following us at the moment, but I don't see that continuing."

"You know what I mean."

Ray wasn't sure he did.

"Did you talk to Roxy about the estate?" Cindy continued.

"For a few minutes after everyone left the funeral home last night. There's not much to discuss. Mom had been drawing down a ton on the reverse mortgage before she got sick, and the hospital lien will eat up the rest of the equity she had left."

"Did Roxy say anything about all the money your mother gave her to go to college and law school debt free?"

"No."

Cindy shook her head. "If your father had been paying a decent amount of alimony all these years—"

Ray held up his hand. "Please don't go there right now."

"Sorry. I shouldn't have said that."

"Even though there isn't anything to divide between us except the stuff in the house, Roxy will be a stickler about every detail. She'll drive me crazy trying to control everything. I bet she changed the floral arrangement on the casket six times before she was satisfied. I thought Mrs. Langford was going to cry."

"She can't help it," Cindy said. "That's how she's wired."

Ray glanced sideways. "Be sure you remember that when she starts demanding all the pieces you want from the house, including the hand-painted serving bowl."

"Your mom knew I loved that bowl," Cindy protested. "She told me in front of everyone last Christmas that she wanted me to have it."

"Do you want me to remind Roxy of that if it comes up?"

Cindy faced forward and pursed her lips. "I'm not going to be petty, but part of your being a leader will be keeping your father and sister from running over you."

Cars stretched along the entire cul-de-sac and down both sides of the street. Kitty had been a bright light in the community, and the outpouring of support at her death was living proof.

"There's Dad's truck," Ray said. "But I bet he's slipped off by himself somewhere."

Ray pulled into the driveway and onto the grass beneath a large pin oak tree whose leaves were turning yellow. "Facing a houseful of well-meaning people is going to be hard," he sighed as he turned off the motor. "I'd rather be alone too."

"People deal with loss differently. And I want to support you."

Ray glanced at his wife, then reached out and squeezed her hand. They knew about loss. Cindy had suffered the late-term miscarriage of a little girl before Billy was born and another since his birth.

"We'll go through this together," he said, "just like everything else since you maneuvered your way in front of my lab table in ninth-grade biology."

Cindy smiled. "You've told that story so many times you believe it's true."

"Yeah, I'm like the guys at the jail who convince themselves they weren't really present when the crime occurred."

"Well, you did get in trouble with Mr. Jenkins for staring at the back of my head instead of doing your work."

"Your neck looked way better than the frog we were dissecting."

Ray leaned over and gave Cindy a quick kiss on the lips. She touched the side of his face with her hand.

"I loved your mom, and I love her son," she said.

"I know."

"And she loved me," Cindy said. "That's the greatest gift she could ever give. And no one can take that away from me."

It had been almost a decade since Corbin entered the master bedroom. So long that he'd forgotten about the picture hanging on the wall opposite the bed—a large, framed wedding photo made to look like an oil painting. He started to back out of the room, but he was already trapped by the memory of the afternoon in May that everyone in attendance thought was pregnant with promise.

Kitty's eyes shone with bridal joy. Corbin's sheepish look was a by-product of the hangover from a last-minute bachelor party held the previous night—the one at which moonshine whiskey of an unknown but potent proof rendered him unconscious and suffering from amnesia from 11:00 p.m. until he woke up the following morning with a splitting headache, still wearing his rehearsal clothes.

Today Corbin didn't think about the long-ago headache. He took in every detail of the picture, especially the intertwining of his fingers with Kitty's. He shut his eyes for a moment and tried to remember what that casual, yet intimate, closeness felt like. With his thumb he rubbed the ring finger on his left hand and touched again the empty place that had been home to his wedding band for twenty-nine years.

He opened his eyes and sighed. No longer hungry, he put the plate of food on a dresser, sat on the end of the bed, and put his head in his hands. There was a knock on the door.

"Come in," he said, wondering who'd tracked him down the deserted hallway.

It was Branson Kilpatrick, a lifelong resident of Alto who owned a small lawn care business. Corbin had incorporated Branson's business and represented his son, Tommy, when the young man injured his leg in a motorcycle wreck.

"Hey, Branson," Corbin said, getting to his feet.

Branson glanced at the photo, then quickly turned his gaze to Corbin. "Sorry, Corbin. I didn't mean to disturb you, but I didn't get a chance to come by the funeral home last night, and I wanted to give you my condolences before leaving. Like everyone else, I'll miss Kitty."

Corbin reached out and shook Branson's hand. "I appreciate that. She thought the world of you. And thanks for taking care of the yard after the—" Corbin stopped. He didn't want to mention the word *divorce* in the presence of the picture.

"It's what I do," Branson said awkwardly then stared at the floor. "I wish I'd been able to keep up the flower beds."

"It's okay."

The two men stood in silence for a moment.

"Well, I'd better get going," Branson said. "I guess you heard about my little grandson getting cancer. He's seeing some kind of specialist later this afternoon, and his mother wants my wife and me to be there too."

"I didn't know about your grandson," Corbin replied. "Is that Samantha's boy?"

"No, Tommy's boy, Mitchell."

"I'm real sorry to hear about that. How old is he?"

"Just turned five. He's got that stuff the doctors call non-Hodgkin's lymphoma. No matter what they name it, cancer is bad and I hate it. My daughter-in-law doesn't have any family close by, and she's leaning heavily on me, especially since Tommy lost his job at the fertilizer plant."

"What happened to his job?"

"They're running a bunch of new product over there, but like everyplace else, robots are replacing people. Tommy just missed the cutoff to save his job by a few months of seniority. You know what they say about it raining and pouring. That's what we've been going through—" Branson paused. "I'm sorry. Your family's loss is the reason we're here today."

"No, no." Corbin waved his hand toward the picture. "Kitty was always thinking about the other person. Let me know how Mitchell gets along. Tommy too."

Branson left. Corbin looked again at the portrait. Kitty's bright smile never had lost its luster. In the picture, her eyes seemed filled with secret knowledge. Corbin shook his head. He hated it when he slipped into a delusion while drinking, and he didn't want to start while sober. He picked up his untouched plate and left the room.

———

Of course Ray had parked on the freshly cut grass. To Roxy her brother's action was indicative of his careless outlook on life and constant need for guidance and supervision.

At twenty-nine Roxy was two years younger than Ray, but ever since she was old enough to stand up and start giving orders, she'd made it her life mission to whip him into shape. As a ninth grader, her knowledge of grammar and composition exceeded that of her brother, so when he came to her with red ink–stained papers, she bailed him out. The same thing happened the following year in an upper-level Spanish literature class. Roxy felt guilty allowing Ray to plagiarize her papers for most of his translations, but he was desperate, and she had a soft spot for his weakness that he exploited.

The codependency that marked their childhood and teenage

years faded as they passed through their twenties. Now they rarely talked on the phone and only saw each other when at their mother's house.

So far Ray had avoided most of their father's worst habits, but in Roxy's opinion, he didn't have many good ones of his own. He'd returned to Alto after law school because he had no other options and married Cindy, his high school sweetheart, because she was the easy choice.

Parking on the street, Roxy made sure she left room to maneuver her car in case a vehicle pulled in behind her. She got out of the car and straightened the jacket of her black suit. She'd bought the suit at Nordstrom to wear at meetings when her law firm's pharmaceutical clients came to Atlanta. After today, she resolved, she would put it at the back of the walk-in closet in her renovated townhome and not wear it for at least a year. It would be a private way to honor her mother's memory.

She reached into her pocket to make sure she had a few fresh tissues. She rarely cried, but an encounter with something or someone in the house today was bound to trigger a few tears. She walked briskly down the street. Her slender legs and well-shaped calves were the pistons that propelled her as a long-distance runner. Petite like her mother, Roxy had started running as a tiny but determined seventh grader and hadn't stopped while earning a BS in chemistry with honors from Georgia Tech and then serving on the staff of the law review at Emory Law School. Once, after a couple of drinks, her father had asked if she was running away from Alto. Roxy's look answered him.

Now, with her mother's death, her childhood link to Alto was severed. As executor, Ray would take twice as long as necessary to close out the nearly bankrupt estate, but once that was done, Roxy could let the eighty miles between Alto and Atlanta turn into eight hundred.

She reached the front door of the house, took a deep breath, and went inside. The house contained a mixture of contradictory memories. The clash between chaos and order during her childhood had caused her to build walls that she still vigorously protected. Her greatest regret was that her father waited until after she left home for college to abandon the marriage. She still reacted sharply when she heard about couples "staying together for the sake of the children."

Ray and Cindy were standing in the living room talking to a neighbor. Roxy avoided them and went into the kitchen, where she surveyed the solemn row of casserole dishes full of calorie-laden Southern comfort food. She picked up a carrot stick from a vegetable tray and slipped into the laundry room to eat it.

Knowing she couldn't hide in the laundry room forever, Roxy finished her carrot and returned to the living room, determined to make the next few minutes as positive a memory as possible. She approached Ray and Cindy and touched her sister-in-law on the arm.

"I need to talk to you," Roxy said. "In private."

"What's wrong?" Cindy asked.

Roxy steered her down the hallway toward the master bedroom. Her father was just coming out of the room with a plateful of food.

"Uh, forgot," he muttered as he passed by them.

Roxy didn't bother to reply. She led Cindy into a small den across the hall, then turned to face her sister-in-law.

"I want to thank you for all the time you spent with Mom when she was in and out of the hospital over the past few months, and I couldn't be there. It meant a lot knowing you were with her."

"You're welcome," Cindy said, her eyes opening wider. "She was a wonderful lady."

Roxy pointed to a shelf lined with decorative objects. "Take the hand-painted serving bowl home with you today. I know she wanted you to have it."

"Are you sure?"

"Yes, it doesn't fit the décor of my townhome. And it will look great on the sideboard in your dining room or on the table as a centerpiece with fresh fruit." Roxy paused. "Tell you what, I'll think about where it should go and let you know which option is better."

THREE

The crowd at the house had thinned by the time Corbin scraped his remaining food into the garbage bin in the kitchen and left through the back door. He was proud of himself for staying as long as he did.

Billy was in the backyard sitting in the limbs of a sweet gum tree. He saw Corbin and waved. "Pops, I found some nails sticking out of the tree!"

Corbin limped slightly as he made his way across the expanse of soft grass to the tree. After standing up for several hours, his right knee often ached from a high school football injury.

"Is your leg hurting?" Billy asked when Corbin reached the tree.

"Yeah, it's thinking about the Dawson County game when I had to play both offense and defense because one of the other boys had the flu. I'm not up for tree climbing today."

Billy laughed. It was one of the most wonderful sounds in Corbin's life. The boy stood and balanced on the limb.

"The nails are up here," he said, reaching with his hand. "I can feel five of them."

Corbin shielded his eyes with his hand. "That's where I built a tree house for your daddy. Eventually the boards rotted and fell to the ground, but the nails stayed. One side of the floor was attached to that limb."

Billy looked down at Corbin. A gentle breeze made the remaining leaves on the tree rustle.

"The floor?" he exclaimed. "I want a tree house up this high."

"It was a lot closer to the ground back then. I wouldn't build a house higher than your daddy could fall from and not break a bone." Corbin paused as memory of the sharp debate with Kitty about child safety resurfaced. "But it was plenty high. It had walls all around it and a rope ladder that was like the cargo net on the playground at your school."

Billy tapped his foot against the limb that supported him. "Could we build a new one?"

Corbin shook his head. "Not in this tree. Now that Gran is gone, her house is going to be sold so another family can live here."

He could see the disappointment in Billy's eyes. "Hey," he said. "Why don't we go fishing at Braswell's Pond on Saturday? It's been over a month."

Billy's face brightened. "Will you ask my mama?"

Corbin glanced over his shoulder at the house. He didn't want to go back inside. "She's busy right now, but I'll call her later. And hey . . . don't mess up your good clothes."

Billy touched his dark blue pants. "I scraped my knee and made a tiny hole, but I brushed it off. She'll never notice."

Corbin winced at the tiny seed of deception. By the time he was a teenager, his own mother had known little of his secret life.

"Tell her anyway," he said. "I gotta go. See you later."

"Bye, Pops. I love you."

"I love you too."

Corbin walked around the side of the house. He couldn't remember the last time he'd heard those words from Ray or Roxy.

He made it to his truck without having to talk to anyone else and didn't look in the rearview mirror as he drove away.

———

Ray and Roxy sat together at the kitchen table—Ray facing down a massive piece of double chocolate cake and Roxy nibbling a stick of celery. Ray rolled a mouthful of chocolate around in his mouth for a few seconds before chewing.

"This cake should be illegal," he said. "It's more potent than the bootleg shots Dad and his buddies get from the back steps of the kitchen at Red's."

"You shouldn't joke about it," Roxy replied. "That stuff is dangerous."

"I wasn't joking," Ray replied. "At least he seemed sober today. Maybe it was his way of honoring Mom's memory. She never gave up on him even if everyone else did. I just hope he doesn't do anything that gets him disbarred or hurts someone."

"Do you know how often he's drinking?"

"Not exactly. We eat lunch occasionally, but never at Red's. I know he keeps a bottle or two of bourbon in his office, and once he gets home . . ." Ray paused. "He's always asking if I've heard anything from you. You should call him more often."

"It's always so awkward. Did you notice the huge spot on his neck that he missed with his razor? It was embarrassing."

"Yeah, he'll show up in court with a couple of days' growth sprouting out all over. The local lawyers are used to it, and the judges don't seem to care."

Roxy shook her head. "Has he given up trying to talk you into joining his practice?"

"Are you kidding? He brings it up all the time. He's rattling around there by himself with less and less to do. Janelle spends most of her time talking on the phone to her cronies." Ray glanced over Roxy's shoulder to make sure they were alone. "And I'm 99 percent sure I'm going to get an offer any day from Simpkin, Brown, and Stamper. I've met with them twice. They need another litigator. Nate Stamper watched the last felony case I tried and was very complimentary."

"Really?" Roxy raised her eyebrows. "Congratulations. Their office is an architectural eyesore, but by Alto standards, they practice at a high level."

"It's not downtown Atlanta." Ray gave his sister a dry look. "But they represent the fertilizer plant, the electric co-op, both local banks, a bunch of insurance companies, and anyone in town with significant personal assets. Plus they serve as county attorneys. They scoop off all the cream and leave the other firms to fight over the crumbs. I bet Mr. Simpkin makes as much as some of the senior lawyers at your firm."

"It's possible," Roxy admitted. "I've heard the partners complain that big corporations don't roll over and pay legal fees without pushback like they used to. And the ladder above me is pretty crowded. I'll have to stay another five or six years before I have a realistic shot at making partner. And even then . . ."

It was a rare show of vulnerability for his sister.

"Hey, I'm sure you'll catch the eye of the right people," Ray said in a softer tone of voice. "Remember you didn't lose a single cross-country race your senior year."

"Until the state meet," Roxy replied. "Then I barely broke the top thirty. The legal market in Atlanta is like the state meet."

"There's always a place for you here with Dad."

"That's not funny either," Roxy said flatly.

"No," Ray admitted. "It's not."

—

Corbin drove four blocks to the center of town. Downtown Alto clustered around the courthouse square. In front of the courthouse a stone monolith erected by the state historical commission in the early 1900s memorialized the county's Confederate war veterans. On the other side of the courthouse was a large brass plaque identifying the town as the birthplace of a man who became lieutenant governor of Georgia during the unbroken era of Democrat-dominated politics from 1870 to 1970.

Corbin stopped at the intersection next to his office. The single-story gray stone building became a law office when Jesse Parker, Esq., bought it and began practicing law in Alto during the Great Depression. Known in his later years as Colonel Parker, the crusty lawyer brought Corbin into his practice and taught him the tangible and intangible essentials of being a small-town attorney. The pithy sayings that forced their way past Colonel Parker's tightly clenched teeth remained the guideposts of Corbin's life.

When Colonel Parker died, Corbin bought the building but out of respect didn't move into the senior partner's office for six months. Somehow it didn't seem right to immediately displace the man whose presence had so totally dominated the wood-paneled walls for decades. When he finally did move into the office, Corbin displayed on the credenza a black-and-white photo taken the day Colonel Parker presented him to the court at his swearing-in ceremony. The photo still looked over Corbin's shoulder.

Leaving the center of town, Corbin entered a less prosperous area. Most of the textile mills that once thrived in the area had been located on the south and east sides of town, and the houses near them were simple, wood-framed structures with tiny rooms.

Next Corbin passed the chicken processing plant. A single con-
fused chicken had managed to escape and was walking across the
asphalt parking lot. Corbin knew its reprieve was temporary.

The sprawling facility that housed the Colfax Fertilizer
Company wasn't visible from the road, but a large, colorful billboard featuring pictures of a vibrant green, healthy soybean plant
and an enormous ear of yellow corn announced where to turn. It
was time for the day shift workers to leave, and a line of cars was
backed up waiting to turn onto the roadway.

Across from the Colfax sign was a billboard that trumpeted
the merits of the Fishburn Law Center in Gainesville. For twenty
years Stan Fishburn's bald head and smiling face had awkwardly
graced the advertising landscape as he trolled for legal business.
And Fishburn didn't limit his marketing efforts to billboards.
Everyone in Rusk County who received a speeding ticket or was
involved in a car wreck received a thick packet of information in
the mail that included a colorful brochure and testimonials from
satisfied clients. Fishburn maintained an office in Alto staffed by a
slick-talking male paralegal who wore expensive suits and never told
prospective clients he wasn't a lawyer. The Fishburn firm siphoned
off many potential clients who would have otherwise hired Corbin,
whose practice depended on representing people injured due to the
negligence of others. The net effect was like a six-inch hole in the
bottom of a barrel. Water drained out faster than it could be poured
in.

A half mile down the road, the houses were more spaced out.
Corbin slowed and turned onto Cascade Drive, a road that mean-
dered up a low hill past a few modest houses, then ran along the
crest of the ridge. When life had held more promise for the future,
Corbin bought two acres on top of the ridge, where he built a redbrick duplex to lease out as a rental property. His accountant at the

time told him it wasn't a good business decision, but Corbin liked the view. It served an unforeseen purpose when Corbin left Kitty and needed a place to live.

He pulled his truck into the carport on the right-hand side of the building. There was an identical carport on the opposite side. The other unit had been vacant for over a year, and Corbin wasn't seeking a tenant. In the distance to the west he could see the glint of the late afternoon sun on Braswell's Pond. He turned and looked in the direction of Willow Oak Lane. It was about three miles to Kitty's house as the crow flies.

He got out and ran his hand along the back gate of his truck. Even though he'd been living by himself for ten years, the duplex seemed lonelier today, and he didn't want to face the silent house.

Kitty's passing seemed to lie like a somber blanket across the whole county.

FOUR

Corbin walked into the office promptly at nine o'clock the following Monday morning. Janelle Griffin, his longtime secretary, glanced up in surprise and quickly hung up the phone.

"I didn't expect to see you," she said, adjusting the half-frame glasses that rested on the end of her nose. "I thought you'd—"

"No, I didn't spend all weekend drowning my sorrows," Corbin interrupted, answering the question he knew she was thinking but was afraid to ask.

"It was a beautiful service," Janelle sniffed. "I thought Reverend Adams did a fine job, and the flowers on the casket were gorgeous. Roxy looked nice, more like her mama every time I see her. And afterwards, everyone was saying how much Kitty—"

"Stop!" Corbin held up his hand. "I can't talk about it this morning."

Janelle's tongue was a runaway train, and this morning Corbin halted it in its tracks. She gave him a wounded look.

"I know how you feel without your saying anything," Corbin said. "And I appreciate it. What's on my calendar?"

"Nothing." Janelle plucked a tissue from a box on the corner of her desk. "As I said, I didn't think you'd be here. It was hard enough for me to get out of bed and drag myself down here."

Even on a good day Corbin could only take Janelle in small doses. And this wasn't a good day. He moved past the secretary's desk and toward the privacy of his office, then turned around when the beep for the front door sounded. A young woman in her twenties with short dark hair and wearing faded blue jeans came into the reception area.

"Yes?" Janelle asked.

"Is this Mr. Fishburn's office?"

"No. That's on the other side of the square next to Langford's Florist."

"May I help you?" Corbin asked, taking a step toward her.

"Are you a lawyer?" the young woman replied.

"Yes, I'm Corbin Gage."

Out of the corner of his eye, Corbin could see Janelle frown. The young woman hesitated.

"Uh, will it cost me anything to talk to you? The letter I got from Mr. Fishburn said I could meet with a lawyer for free."

"That's the way I do it too," Corbin replied smoothly. "Only I'm actually here. Mr. Fishburn spends his time in Gainesville, and if you go to his office here in Alto you'll meet with a paralegal, not an attorney."

The young woman's eyes widened. "Oh, I didn't know that."

Corbin stepped to the side and motioned with his hand toward his office. "Come in and have a seat." With a glance at Janelle, who still had a disapproving look on her face, Corbin ushered the young woman into his office.

"Would you like some water or coffee?" he asked.

"Coffee would be nice," she replied. "With cream if you have it."

"Sit in either of the chairs in front of my desk," Corbin said, then stuck his head back out the door. "Janelle, would you fix a cup of coffee with cream?"

"You shouldn't steal a client like that," his secretary responded in a stage whisper.

Corbin stepped over to her desk. "She's not his client and we both know the type of representation she'd get from Fishburn's outfit. I'm doing her a favor."

"Are you sure about that?"

Corbin's eyes narrowed. "Just get the coffee. Bring me a cup too. Black, of course."

Corbin's office was a spacious room with walnut bookcases lining two walls and in the middle a large wooden desk with an inlaid leather top. The bookcases were reminiscent of the days before computer research, when lawyers used the printed word and relied on their own legal reasoning more than software-assisted analysis. Corbin's six-year-old computer rested on the credenza behind his chair. A full-length leather sofa rested against one wall. The combination of wood and leather gave the room a comfortable, relaxing feel and smell.

"What's your name?" he asked as he made his way around the desk to a high-back burgundy chair.

"Millie Watson."

Corbin reached for a blank yellow legal pad. "And your address."

"It's 4428 Harris Street."

Corbin jotted down the information. "Near the fertilizer plant?" he asked. "Do you know Branson Kilpatrick, or maybe his son, Tommy? They live in that area."

"They live one street over. I know Larissa better than I do Tommy."

"Larissa is his wife, right?"

"Yes, sir."

Janelle came into the office and handed Millie her coffee. She set Corbin's cup on the edge of his desk, slightly out of reach.

"Thanks, Janelle," Corbin said. "Please hold my calls while I talk to Ms. Watson."

Janelle rolled her eyes and left the room. Corbin waited until the door closed behind her.

"What did you want to talk to a lawyer about today, Ms. Watson?"

"Bankruptcy," Millie replied. "Only I don't know if I should do it now or wait until later."

Corbin exhaled and kept the disappointment from his expression. Bankruptcy cases were filed in federal court in Gainesville. He had never been interested in developing a consumer debtor practice, and it was way too late in his career to begin. He cleared his throat.

"I didn't know the Fishburn law firm was handling bankruptcies," he said.

"Yes. I'm not sure how they found out I was behind on my medical bills, but I got a letter telling me they could help me wipe them out or set up a plan to pay what I can."

"That's either a Chapter 7 or Chapter 13 proceeding," Corbin said, then stopped. He had nothing to offer Millie, but it didn't seem right to escort the young woman out of his office before she'd had a chance to take a few sips of coffee. "What got you into financial trouble?"

"Mostly medical bills for my son. He's just started treatment and will need a bunch more before he's finished. Then my husband got nine months in jail on his second DUI charge and lost his job at Colfax, and I haven't been able to get on Medicaid for me and the kids."

"Are you working?"

"No. One of my daughters is in kindergarten; the other is two. My son was in second grade before he got sick. He just turned seven. He has the same kind of cancer as Larissa's little boy."

Corbin sat up straighter in his chair. "Non-Hodgkin's lymphoma?"

"Yes. Mitchell was diagnosed before Josh. Larissa's been telling me how expensive the treatment is going to be." Millie's eyes suddenly filled with tears. "But I have to do what I can, don't I? He's in the hospital right now, and the doctors are treating him, but I'm wondering if there's more that could be done if he wasn't a charity case. On top of everything else, I'm getting calls every day from all the places where he's had X-rays, scans, and tests. It's way more than I can handle."

The young woman covered her face with her hands. Corbin opened a drawer of his desk and retrieved a partially collapsed box of tissues. He put the box on the front edge of his desk, where it tilted oddly to the right. Millie grabbed two tissues and wiped her eyes.

"If I file bankruptcy, will the doctors hear about it and put it in Josh's chart?" she asked.

"No, they'll do what they think best for your son." Corbin used his most soothing tone of voice. "The ones I know focus on the patient, not the payment."

"But the hospital will find out. The woman who's been calling me has been so hateful."

An image of Billy hooked up to machines pumping chemotherapy into his body shot through Corbin's mind.

"I'm very sorry about what's going on in your family," he said, "but I'm not a bankruptcy lawyer. For that type of problem, I'd recommend Barry Morgan. He practices here in Alto, and I know he'll give you good advice and charge a fair fee."

Millie wiped her eyes.

"Let me call Mr. Morgan for you," Corbin offered.

He picked up the phone. To his relief, Barry said he'd be able to see Millie immediately, and Corbin delivered the news to her with a smile.

"Mr. Morgan's assistant will talk to you first and take down your information, which will help the lawyer give you the best advice. Do you have a list of your creditors and how much you owe each one?"

"Yes, I filled out the forms that Mr. Fishburn's office sent me the best I could."

Corbin stood and they returned to the reception area, where Janelle eyed the young woman closely.

"Thanks for talking to me," Millie said.

"You're welcome. I see Branson Kilpatrick from time to time, and I'll ask him how Josh is doing."

Janelle spoke as soon as the front door closed behind the young woman. "What did she want? She didn't look like she'd been hurt."

"She's been hurt all right," Corbin replied. "But nothing I could help her with."

———

Some women love chocolate. Roxanne Gage had a long-standing love affair with caramel. She took a sip of caramel-flavored coffee as she merged her car onto the interstate and quickly reached cruising speed. Roxy justified her addiction by pretending it was a form of superfuel that gave her an added burst of energy, and she always kept a few cellophane-wrapped squares of the brown candy in her purse.

Her cell phone buzzed and her boyfriend's face popped into view. Peter was an IT engineer with a master's degree from Johns Hopkins. He had a lanky frame and closely cut brown hair and had completed three triathlons in the past year. They'd met on a popular running trail near Piedmont Park in Atlanta. Beginning a conversation while trying to catch their breath had been a unique way to start a relationship.

"Where are you?" Peter asked.

"On my way back to Atlanta. I'm going straight to the office."

"I've been thinking about you a lot. I wish you'd let me be there with you for the funeral. How was it?"

Roxy hesitated. Where to begin?

Perhaps sensing her predicament, Peter asked another question. "Maybe I should have limited that to 'How was your father?'"

"The good news is that except for one evening, he was sober for four days and nights. And when he drank, he crawled into the cave of a duplex where he lives. I went over there to drop off some shirts he'd left at Mom's house. The next day I'm not sure he even remembered that I'd been there."

"That's rough."

"It's nothing new. My brother is worried he may do something stupid and lose his license to practice. The elephant in the room is what we're going to do when he becomes completely incompetent. As much as I want to get away from Alto, I won't be able to run away from that."

"I'm sorry," Peter replied. "What's happening for you at work today?"

"I'm not exactly sure. Mr. Caldweller has blown up my phone with texts and e-mails over the past twenty-four hours. He sent me three messages while I was at the funeral."

"Didn't he know where you were?"

"He has a short-term memory problem for anything except what he wants his staff to do for him."

Roxy shifted lanes to pass a slow-moving truck hauling a load of chickens in crates. Peter filled her in on his work world and then said, "Hey, I've got to run. Have a meeting in a couple of minutes."

"Thanks for calling. I really needed to talk to a normal person. My family is so dysfunctional I'm surprised you want to stay with me."

"I'm only sticking around until I can beat you in a 5K."

"That's not happening." Roxy laughed. "Just don't throw me in the lake for a long swim or prop me up on a bike and ask me to ride for an hour and a half. I'm a one-trick pony."

"And a beautiful one."

Roxy suddenly wondered if she should have let Peter come to Alto. With him at her side, maybe she could cope better with her broken family.

"How about dinner tonight?" Peter said.

"I'd love it unless I have to work late at the office."

"Sneak away."

Roxy felt the familiar tug-of-war between her heart and her head. "I'll let you know," she said.

FIVE

Corbin propped his feet up on his desk and opened the latest issue of the *Georgia Bar Journal*. As usual he turned first to the list of lawyers who'd recently died. Almost every month the magazine recorded the passing of an attorney Corbin knew personally or against whom he'd had a case at some point in his career.

Once he'd been having lunch with Colonel Parker when the subject of mortality came up.

"Do you know the two questions a lawyer asks when one of his comrades at the bar dies?" his mentor asked.

Corbin knew the colonel was using him as the straight man. "No, what?"

"What did he die from?" Colonel Parker said, rubbing the side of his nose. "And who got his cases and clients?"

When Colonel Parker died from a massive stroke, it was Corbin who took over his cases and clients. Unfortunately the older man's practice had been withering for several years, and most of the remaining apples on the tree were the size of persimmons.

The old-fashioned phone on Corbin's desk buzzed, and he picked up the receiver. "Who is it?" he asked.

"Lori at Judge Ellington's office," Janelle replied. "The judge wants you to come right over to the courthouse and meet with someone."

Corbin dropped his feet to the floor. "Somebody probably showed up *pro se* and needs a lawyer," he said. "Print out a blank contingency fee contract and medical release form. Oh, and do a contract for an hourly case too. I'll be right out."

"Are you going to talk to Lori?"

"Yeah, I was getting ahead of myself."

"She's coming through."

Corbin waited until the red light on his phone blinked, then he pressed the receive button. "This is Corbin Gage."

"Did Janelle tell you why I called?"

"Yes, do you know what kind of case it is?"

"No, I'm not sure what the judge has in mind. He's on the bench and sent one of the bailiffs back to tell me to contact you."

"Okay, I'll be there in five minutes."

Corbin hung up then hovered by Janelle's desk while she slowly tapped the keys on her computer. "Did you find the right forms?" he asked.

"You know I can't get anything done when you're standing there leaning over my shoulder like a hungry vulture."

"All right, all right."

Corbin went to the bathroom and inspected himself in the mirror. His face was clean shaven today, but his eyes had a perpetually runny look that he couldn't do anything about, and the skin on his face sagged from his broad cheekbones. He pushed his hair away from his forehead and straightened his tie. At least he had a full head of hair, and his voice remained strong and vibrant.

He returned to Janelle's desk. "Ready?"

"Right there." She pointed. "Do you have any business cards in your wallet?"

Corbin patted his hip pocket, then picked up the papers. "These are dated last year," he said.

"Oh, I need to redo the form." Janelle held out her hand. "It won't take but a second."

"No," Corbin replied. "I can cross it out and change the year if I need to. But fix it by the time I get back."

"Suit yourself."

Ignoring the tone of Janelle's answer, Corbin opened the front door of the office and stepped onto the sidewalk. Normally there wasn't enough traffic in downtown Alto to create any pollution. Only when the wind blew strongly from the south did odors from the chicken processing plant and Colfax cast a pall over the center of town.

The light at the corner was red for pedestrians, but Corbin didn't see any cars coming and jaywalked across the street. Turning left he walked up the sidewalk to the courthouse and up the broad steps, worn down by the shuffling of countless feet over many decades. As he reached the top of the steps, he felt his shirt pocket for a pen that wasn't there. He'd have to borrow one from someone inside.

The main courtroom was on the first floor and occupied the left half of the building. Also on the first floor were the clerk's office and the deed room. On the second floor were the district attorney's office, the probate judge's chambers, and the office suite used by the sitting superior court judge. Two judges served the circuit: James Ellington, who was three years older than Corbin, and Dexter Perry, age forty-one, and formerly a partner at Simpkin, Brown, and Stamper. Judge Perry never referred a potential client to Corbin.

Corbin walked into the rear of the courtroom, a large, square space with a slightly sloping floor intended to improve visibility for people sitting in the gallery. This morning there were ten or twelve people scattered across the pew-like seating. The floor creaked beneath Corbin's feet.

Judge Ellington was on the bench. His black robe contrasted with his wavy white hair. It was a criminal call calendar, and standing in front of him was Ray, and next to him Nate Stamper, an ambitious young partner at the Simpkin firm. Seated at the defendant's table was Guy Hathaway, the local plant manager for Colfax. Hathaway was a tall man in his fifties with a sharp nose, thinning brown hair, and the demeanor of a sphinx.

The judge saw Corbin and motioned for him to come forward and have a seat in the front row. Ray glanced over his shoulder, and Corbin caught his son's eye, then made the motion of clicking an imaginary pen with his thumb. Ray gave him a puzzled look, then nodded, took a pen from his pocket, and handed it to him.

"Mr. Stamper," the judge said. "I'll hear from you first."

Nate Stamper, wearing an expertly tailored blue suit and red tie, stood and spoke in a respectful tone of voice.

"Your Honor, the imposition of a criminal fine in this case is neither supported by the law nor warranted by the evidence. The cease and desist order you issued last week is an ample remedy, and my client is in the process of complying with the order as we speak. The cleanup and abatement operations should be finished within a reasonable time period."

"I would expect nothing less, if Mr. Hathaway wants to avoid the possibility of being held in contempt of court," the judge replied sternly. "What is the State's position on the fine?"

Ray shifted his shoulders before he spoke. "The State is satisfied with Colfax's response to the order you issued last week at the conclusion of the bench trial. It would be redundant to impose a criminal sanction for the release of pollutants without a showing of criminal intent on the part of authorized representatives of a corporate entity. For this reason—"

"Redundant?" the judge interrupted. "What's redundant about requiring a corporate defendant to pay a statutory fine intended to deter misconduct in the future? The legislature made provision for a fine of $2,500 per day that a prohibited discharge of a pollutant substance takes place. You gentlemen will recall that in my findings of fact I determined that the respondent's violation of the statute continued for at least ninety days, which, if each day is considered a separate act, would warrant imposition of a fine in the amount of—"

The judge paused, waiting for Ray to provide the number.

Corbin realized his son hadn't calculated the amount of the potential fine. The drowning of millions of brain cells in alcohol hadn't deprived Corbin of a lifelong ability to perform basic math calculations in his head.

"Two hundred twenty-five thousand dollars," he said in a court-room whisper that carried all the way past the lawyers to the judge.

Stamper turned and glared at Corbin. Ray looked slightly embarrassed.

"Thank you, Mr. Gage," the judge replied.

Stamper stepped forward and spoke in a more forceful tone of voice. "Your Honor, if the assistant DA isn't seeking the imposition of a fine, my client requests that none be assessed. Mr. Gage is here to represent the interests of the citizens of Alto and Rusk County."

"It's true that Mr. Gage is an assistant DA," the judge answered drily. "But it's also true that I'm the judge. And I'm going to treat this as a single occurrence and impose a fine of $2,500, payable to the clerk of court within thirty days of today's date."

Stamper pressed his lips together tightly and glanced at Mr. Hathaway. Corbin couldn't see Hathaway's reaction.

"Do you want me to prepare the order?" Ray asked.

"Yes, with findings of fact that conform to my ruling from the bench last week."

"Send it over to me for review," Stamper said to Ray, who nodded. The defense lawyer packed up his briefcase and left the courtroom without looking in Corbin's direction.

"Do you want me to call the next matter?" Ray asked the judge. "It's a bond forfeiture motion."

"I want to talk to the other Mr. Gage first," the judge replied.

Ray returned to the prosecution table, and Corbin approached the bench. The judge put his hand over the microphone in front of him.

"I expressed my condolences to Ray before the calendar call," the judge said in a low voice. "I'm sorry I wasn't able to make it to the funeral. My wife and I had a prior commitment out of town."

"I understand," Corbin said, shifting his shoulders just as Ray had done moments before. "And I appreciate the sentiment. Lori said you wanted to see me?"

"Yes, there's a man and woman sitting on the third row who've received an eviction notice from their landlord."

Corbin turned and saw an older man in overalls sitting next to a short woman with her hair pulled back in a bun.

"They came to my office asking for an appointed lawyer. I would have sent them to the legal aid office, but the man mentioned he'd hurt his back when he fell because the landlord wouldn't fix a rotten step."

"I'll be glad to talk to him," Corbin said. "Is the jury room available?"

———

Still stinging from Judge Ellington's rebuke about his lack of zeal in seeking imposition of a large fine against Colfax, Ray watched his father go into the jury room and close the door.

The decision to drag Rusk County's biggest employer into court hadn't originated at the DA's office in the first place—it was the result of an investigation and report issued by a state environmental official in Atlanta. A lawyer with the attorney general's office reviewed the report, contacted Steve Nelson, the local DA, and gave him the option of pursuing the case or cooperating with a government lawyer who would drive in from Atlanta to head up the prosecution.

If the attorney general's office hadn't been involved, the matter could have been handled with a phone call. But with the state official looking over their shoulders, a behind-the-scenes resolution wasn't an option. No one in Rusk County wanted a hotshot lawyer from Atlanta cruising into town with an agenda to generate a bunch of negative publicity by busting the county's largest employer, even if it was an industrial polluter. Steve assigned the potentially controversial case to Ray, whose first call had been to Simpkin, Brown, and Stamper.

It was quickly apparent that Colfax couldn't challenge the findings, so Nate Stamper and Ray had agreed to a bench trial at which most of the facts were stipulated and a cease and desist order drafted in advance. The attorney general's office was satisfied because the excessive discharge of harmful by-products from the fertilizer plant would stop. And Colfax was glad it could keep a low profile and avoid negative publicity. The only hiccup turned out to be the imposition of a small criminal fine. Ray knew it would be hard to keep that tidbit out of the local paper. At least he'd been able to do his job without jeopardizing his future employment possibilities.

He finished the last matter on the calendar, and Judge Ellington left the bench. Ray was packing up his catalog case when the jury room door opened and his father emerged, reaching his right hand into different pockets of his trousers and suit.

"Here it is," he announced triumphantly as he pulled a business card from an inside pocket of his suit jacket. "Last one. I'll send you a copy of the letter I'm going to serve on your landlord. He'll probably hire a lawyer, and we'll go from there."

"Thank you so much, Mr. Gage," the woman said. "I was worried we'd be on the street."

"This may take several months to work itself out, which should give you time to find another place if your landlord refuses to make this one habitable."

The couple slowly walked up the aisle. Corbin stayed behind with Ray.

"Who owns the property?" Ray asked.

"Harold Dickens."

"I'm not surprised. Is it one of the row houses on Baxter Street? They ought to bulldoze all of them and start over."

"True, but this one is going to be brought up to code if he wants to rent it, and Dickens will have to notify his premises liability about a personal injury claim. By the time I'm finished, Mr. and Mrs. Bowater should be back on their feet."

"Contingency fee?"

"The poor man's key to the courthouse."

"Is that one of Colonel Parker's sayings?"

"He quoted it, but it wasn't original with him." Corbin handed the borrowed pen back to Ray. "Do you want to grab a bite for lunch?"

Ray hesitated. He had deadlines crowding his calendar in several cases and had planned on grabbing a pack of crackers from the vending machine in the break room. He pulled up the retractable handle for the case containing his files.

"I can't," he said. "I have a backlog of work and have to prepare orders in the cases Judge Ellington heard this morning."

"Especially the one in which you were afraid to stand up to Nate Stamper and Colfax?"

Ray's jaw tightened. He didn't need to be lectured by his father about the administration of justice. "Yeah, that will be the first one."

"I guess I'll head over to Red's," Corbin replied. "I've been craving some of his beans."

Corbin turned and walked up the aisle toward the rear of the courtroom. As Ray watched him go, he offered up a quick prayer that his father wouldn't order anything except beans and cornbread.

He doubted that his silent request went higher than the courthouse ceiling.

SIX

I t was almost ten when Roxy pulled into the parking lot of Frank and Donaldson. Her office was one of twenty crammed together in an L shape on the rim of the twenty-first floor of a thirty-story office tower in north Atlanta surrounded by a cluster of similar thirty-story office towers. Seven spacious partner offices and conference rooms A through F took up the rest of the space along the walls, with the support staff corralled in the middle. Frank and Donaldson was an international law firm with over three hundred partners, fifteen hundred associates, and thousands of nonlawyer employees spread across the globe. The twenty-seven attorney Atlanta branch was one of the firm's smallest. Lawrence Frank and Fitzhugh Donaldson, the two men who founded the firm in Philadelphia in 1880, would never have imagined their names on brass nameplates from New York to New Delhi.

Each associate attorney's office had a narrow window, a sleek glass-topped desk, a chair for the lawyer, and a chrome side chair in case someone needed to sit down for a brief chat. Roxy had added a potted palm to the corner of her personal space. The view out the window provided a distant hint of green in spring. A stainless steel sign on her door read *Roxanne P. Gage—Attorney-at-Law*.

She savored the last morsel of a caramel as she shared the

elevator with a young man who worked for the firm but whose name she couldn't recall. She thought he was in accounting and billing but didn't want to embarrass herself by asking. They stood in silence until the elevator door opened.

"Have a good day, Roxanne," the young man said as he held the door open for her to exit.

"You too," Roxy replied, knowing her failure to use his name was a dead giveaway.

"I'm Vince Pearson," the man said, following her out of the elevator. "We talked about kayaking during the firm holiday party at the Keystone."

"Of course," Roxy said. "You told us about the trip you took last summer on the Kenai River in Alaska. You work in billing."

"Yes, and you don't hear from me because the details you provide for your time are among the best in the firm."

"Thanks," Roxy said, feeling even worse that she hadn't remembered Vince's name. "Do you have any trips planned this year?"

"Montana. We're going to kayak all over, but I'm especially looking forward to the action on the Swan River."

They turned to go separate directions.

"See you later," Vince said.

Roxy watched him walk away for a few seconds and silently repeated his name to herself while imagining him in a lime green kayak. She reached her office and turned on her computer. The first photograph that popped up in her rotating series was a candid shot of her mother looking up from the flower beds in front of the house in Alto.

"Roxy!" A male voice interrupted her thoughts.

Mr. Caldweller stood in her doorway. Tall and studious with rimless glasses, the lawyer looked like a tenured English professor but acted like a football coach in the middle of a losing season.

"I've delayed a meeting all morning until you got back," he said in a New England accent refined at Yale Law School. "The alpha team in the Boren Pharmaceutical case will be in conference room F in two minutes. Bring your analysis of the defendant's chemist with you. I'm flying to Chicago tomorrow to consult with our shadow expert and want to make it count."

"Yes, sir."

Roxy's fingers flew across the keyboard to access the file. There was no time to reread what she'd written after poring over the technical data for two days the previous week; she hoped she had better recall of the insights she recorded than she did about kayak-loving Vince from accounting.

According to Colonel Parker it was a good day when a lawyer either settled a case or took on a new client. With the signed contract from Mr. and Mrs. Bowater in his coat pocket, Corbin had turned a bad day into a good one.

There were several locally owned restaurants within a three-block radius of the courthouse, among them a diner that featured hamburgers cooked on a grill top and a Greek restaurant that served gyros, shawarmas, and three kinds of hummus. Corbin could make a meal of red pepper hummus and several pieces of pita bread. But Red's Restaurant was across the street from the Greek place.

Corbin opened the door and was greeted by the blast of arctic air that made the place a haven in the heat of summer but too cool in the winter. The owner, Mike "Red" Britton, was in his usual place, guarding the cash register by the front door.

"Booth or counter?" asked the potbellied man with a fringe of stubborn red hair still clinging to an otherwise bald scalp.

"Booth."

Red looked down the row of booths on the right side of the restaurant. "Number five just came open. Grab it."

The booths were upholstered in red plastic. Red-themed artwork hung from the walls. Above Corbin's head was a reproduction of the famous Audubon painting of a northern cardinal. A neighboring booth displayed a photograph of a red barn with a black roof and the words *See Rock City* painted in white.

Sally, a wiry middle-aged woman with tired wrinkles lining her face, came up to him with a notepad in her hand. "What'll it be?"

"Mountain water, no ice," Corbin began. "I'll chase it with red beans and rice and cornbread."

"Onions on the beans?"

"Yep, I don't have to go to court this afternoon."

Sally left and Corbin rubbed his temples with his fingers. He leaned out of the booth and looked toward the rear of the restaurant as Sally disappeared through a swinging door. Regardless of the day of the week, a select group of Red's customers could order a double shot of moonshine by the glass. Sally reappeared with a small plastic glass in one hand and a larger glass in the other. Both contained clear liquids. She set them down in front of Corbin.

"It'll bite you," she said in a slightly hoarse voice.

Corbin took a cautious sip from the smaller of the two glasses. The harsh burn of the alcohol scorched its way down his throat. Sally was right. The day's batch could double as paint thinner. He licked his lips and took another sip. The second swallow's journey was less traumatic than the first and fueled a warm glow in Corbin's stomach. He sighed. Although of unknown proof, the alcohol content of the liquid in the glass was enough to have a rapid impact, especially on an empty stomach.

Red had three moonshine suppliers, all reputable distillers in Rusk

County with stainless steel rigs, who prided themselves on the consistent quality of their nontaxed brew. Corbin took a third, larger sip, then followed it with a drink of water. Sally returned with his food.

"Have you tasted this?" he asked Sally.

"I stay away from the beans and onions," she replied.

"I mean the hooch."

"This batch came from Beanpole. He was bragging about the size of the bead, so we all had a tiny taste when it was delivered after breakfast. That was it for me. I have to work all day, and I prefer something fruity."

A simple test for alcohol content involved shaking a jar of moonshine. The size of the bubbles that appeared and how quickly they popped revealed the proof. Some moonshiners infused their liquor with apples or pears for folks like Sally. Corbin was a purist.

"How big were the beads?"

"About the size of the dime Grover Ledbetter left as a tip after making us recook his bacon for breakfast."

"I'll do better than that."

"Thanks." Sally smiled. "I'm spending the extra money in my head already."

Corbin took a bite of the food. Beans and rice at Red's were the result of a seasoning process that transformed ordinary pinto beans and white rice into tiny trucks of flavor. Bits of smoked pork and an explosion of spices created a savory dish. The onions provided a final wallop of taste.

Corbin took tiny sips of whiskey while he ate. He didn't want to enter the fuzzy world of semi-intoxication that would make it necessary for him to return to his office and take a nap on the sofa. When there were two swallows of moonshine left, he held the glass a few inches above the table and swirled the liquid around. He wished he could have seen the dime-sized bead.

"Corbin?" A female voice interrupted his thoughts.

Corbin looked up into the face of Maryanne Christopher, the executive director of a local nonprofit organization that helped people below the bottom rung of the economic ladder. Maryanne was a sturdy woman in her forties with curly brown hair and blue eyes that could both pry money out of a reluctant donor's wallet and welcome a man without a coat off the street to shelter on a cold winter day.

"May I join you?" she asked. "I didn't get a chance to talk to you the other day at the funeral."

An Ohio native, Maryanne had retained her Midwestern accent and preference for sugarless tea even after fifteen years in Alto.

"Uh, sure," Corbin replied. She sat down across from him, and Corbin moved the glass of moonshine closer to his side of the table.

Sally came up to them. "Would you like something to drink?" she asked Maryanne.

Maryanne glanced at the two plastic glasses in front of Corbin, and a puzzled look crossed her face. Corbin's hands were beneath the table, and his fingers tapped together nervously.

"Unsweetened tea, please," Maryanne replied. "And a bowl of vegetable soup."

Corbin picked up his glass of water and took a sip. He couldn't remember seeing Maryanne in Red's before.

"I stopped by your office, and Janelle said to try here," Maryanne said in answer to his silent question.

"I'm a creature of habit," Corbin replied. He was glad he was eating onions, which should mask the odor of alcohol on his breath.

"Kitty told me that too," Maryanne replied crisply.

Corbin glanced past Maryanne as Jimmy Broome, the owner of a local auto parts store, came into the restaurant and approached their booth. Jimmy didn't drink, and normally Corbin wouldn't have any interest in talking to him, but today Corbin looked long-ingly at him, as if the man were his best friend. Jimmy offered his condolences on Kitty's death and moved on.

"You may not know it," Maryanne continued, "but Kitty helped the ministry out of a financial jam several times over the past few years. I thanked her, of course, but I should have thanked you too."

"Not necessary," Corbin said, holding up his hand. "What Kitty did was her doing. All the credit goes to her."

Sally returned with the tea and bowl of soup. Maryanne bowed her head for a silent prayer. While the woman's eyes were closed, Corbin quickly dumped the rest of the moonshine into his water glass. Red's secret stash of booze wasn't the best-kept secret in Alto, but so far knowledge of its existence had remained hidden from anyone interested in stopping it. It helped that the local sheriff was Red's first cousin.

Maryanne finished her prayer and looked up. "The last conversation I had with Kitty took place a few weeks ago, shortly after she went into the hospital. She held my hand and asked me to tell you something, but not until after she was gone. Do you want to know what she said?"

Corbin felt a lump rise in his throat. He wasn't sure he wanted to hear a voice from a grave that was barely covered with soil.

SEVEN

Roxy's meeting with Caldweller's alpha team about the Boren litigation lasted four hours.

"Where is the analysis of chlorazine's interactions with other drugs in your memo?" Caldweller asked her impatiently as he scrolled through the document. "It's not organized in a way that's particularly helpful to me."

"Part C, subpart F. I put it there because I think you'll benefit from letting him walk you through the background chemistry—"

"That's advice I don't need from you."

"Yes, sir."

Caldweller turned to another associate and asked a question the lawyer couldn't answer.

"Why are you working on this case if you can't help me?" Caldweller growled.

Roxy watched impassively. Rebukes and put-downs were standard practice at the firm. She never secretly exulted in someone else's failure, because her own shortcomings, real or manufactured, would soon be identified. When she came to work for the firm, Roxy thought she had a hide as thick as a rhinoceros, but she quickly learned that her emotional calluses were softer than a little girl's palm. However, she now appreciated the professional reasons behind the firm's abrasive atmosphere. After surviving the meetings with the partners in the conference rooms, the attorneys weren't intimidated by vicious adversaries or antagonistic judges. Caldweller's reputation for toughening people up made him both hated and respected.

When the meeting ended, Roxy closed her laptop and prepared to return to her office. No one in the room had mentioned her mother's death. She glanced at her watch. At least two more hours of work to do before she could rendezvous with Peter.

"Roxy, stay a minute," Caldweller said.

Roxy flinched. If a new urgent task landed on her desk, she might not get away from the office before midnight. Caldweller didn't speak until everyone cleared the room.

"I wanted to take you with me to Chicago," the senior partner said. "You're ready to take your place on the front lines in this type of case. But when your mother passed away, I thought you should have time to get back into the flow of life. That doesn't happen as quickly as some people assume. My mother died when I was in my early thirties, and it took months before I came to a place where my thoughts were more happy than sad."

"I appreciate that," Roxy said, searching her boss's face for confirmation of his sincerity. "A lot."

"Take a day or two off if you need it," he continued. "But not too much. Within your niche of technical analysis, no one in the office can do exactly what you do better than you."

It was a stunning compliment. The collective IQ of the law firm rivaled that of any comparable group in the city.

"Thank you," Roxy managed.

"Of course, give me as much notice as you can."

"Certainly."

Caldweller stood and resumed his usual imperial demeanor.

"No time away for the next two days while I'm in Chicago, though. I want you on twenty-four-hour call in case I wake up in the middle of the night with a thought I need to run by you. Also, I may put you on a conference call with our expert if it seems beneficial to the discussion."

"Yes, sir."

Roxy returned to her office, stared at her plant, and wondered about the implications of Caldweller's compliment. Nothing at Frank and Donaldson happened by accident. Everything was calculated.

Corbin sat in silence. To ask Maryanne to repeat Kitty's dying request would somehow bind him to it. Maryanne kept her blue eyes focused on him and waited.

"You should eat your soup before it gets cold," he said.

Maryanne picked up her spoon, dipped it into the soup, and raised it to her lips. Corbin's inner tension rose higher and higher. Maryanne and Kitty were members of a women's prayer group, and he was certain there'd be a religious component to Kitty's request. Corbin didn't like to be preached to, at, or about. He felt a rumbling rage boiling up inside him that the mellowing effect of the fiery moonshine couldn't quench.

Not wanting to say something he might regret, he glanced past Maryanne at Red, who was still standing behind the cash register. There was nothing to stop Corbin from bolting from the booth, paying his check, and returning to the safe isolation of his office.

"Okay, tell me," he blurted out.

Maryanne placed the spoon beside the bowl and took a sip of tea. "She told me to tell you that she believed in you and for you."

"For me?" he asked after a few moments passed. "How does that work?"

"I'm not sure, but she grabbed my hand and squeezed it tight when she said it."

Corbin visualized the scene in the hospital, then shrugged his shoulders to shake off the depressing image. "Kitty and I got along better after we divorced than when we were married," he said.

As soon as the familiar words rolled past his lips, Corbin wanted to take them back. "I mean, it was all so complicated," he continued lamely.

"I'm sure it was in your mind," Maryanne said. "I'm not so certain about her."

Corbin had heard enough. "Thanks for tracking me down," he said without meaning it. "I need to get back to the office."

He slipped out of the booth. Standing up, he felt slightly light-headed and rested his hand on the table.

"Are you okay?" Maryanne asked.

"Yeah, blood pressure dropped."

He made his way to the cash register and paid for his meal and drink.

"How was your water?" the owner asked.

"Not for the uninitiated," Corbin replied.

"Don't go dropping those fancy words on me, Corbin." Red shook his head.

Corbin leaned in closer. "Beanpole needs to back off the sugar a little bit and go with bread yeast."

"I agree." Red nodded. "He's trying too hard to ratchet up the proof just to prove he can."

Corbin handed Red an extra twenty. "For Sally."

Red put the bill in a mason jar with the waitress's name on it.

Normally giving one of the waitresses a large tip made Corbin feel good. Today, it didn't.

———

District Attorney Steve Nelson was five years older than Ray. He'd received his appointment as DA not based on his expertise as a trial lawyer, but because his uncle knew the governor. Ray handled the more serious cases.

"Ray!" Steve called out as Ray passed in the hallway.

Ray stopped and entered the DA's office.

"What happened in the Colfax case? Did the judge go along with your recommendation?"

Ray told him about Judge Ellington's ruling. As a public official, the DA didn't want to ruffle the feathers of the most politically powerful entity in the county. Virtually everyone in a management position with the local Colfax facility lived in Rusk County, and their support was crucial to any politician. They contributed money as a block and voted the same way.

"Were any reporters present?" Steve asked anxiously.

"No, I stuck it at the end of the calendar. Cecil Scruggs from the newspaper was there earlier in the morning for entry of the plea in the Davidson voluntary manslaughter case, but he left as soon as the judge sentenced the defendant."

"Did he accept our recommendation in that one?"

"Yeah, he gave him twelve years, followed by ten on probation."

"That's newsworthy. Maybe you should follow up with a phone call to Scruggs to see if he'd like an official comment about the Davidson plea."

"Will do."

Steve wrinkled his nose and grabbed a tissue from a large box on his desk. The DA had bad allergies and would loudly blow his nose during a closing argument by a defense lawyer or the cross-examination of a key witness. It wasn't something that could be considered contempt of court, but it did create awkward tension in the courtroom.

"I hate being bullied by a bunch of tree huggers from Atlanta into prosecuting a case against a local business that issues more paychecks every Friday than any employer within twenty miles," Steve said. "The stuff they dumped is used by farmers on crops all over the country. Where is the criminal intent in that?"

"I agree, but at least it's over. I'll prepare a report for the attorney general's office and emphasize that the judge issued both a cease and desist order and a fine. That should satisfy them."

"Good work." Steve nodded. "I don't know what I'd do without you."

Ray hesitated. He hadn't told Steve he was talking to Simpkin, Brown, and Stamper. For now he decided to keep his mouth shut.

Ray's office had a high plaster ceiling and narrow tall windows only seen in older buildings. The glass in his windows was distorted by changes over time and made the trees on the courthouse lawn look slightly crooked. He had a small wooden desk. On the credenza behind his desk were a photo from his wedding day and a picture of Billy as an infant when he left the hospital.

The phone on the edge of his desk buzzed.

"Branson Kilpatrick wants to see you," said Sue, the office receptionist. "He doesn't have an appointment, and you haven't had lunch yet. Do you want me to—"

"No, he was a big help to my mom. I'll talk to him."

Ray stepped into the reception area. The stoop-shouldered owner of the landscaping business was standing beside Sue's desk.

In his hand he held a cap with the name of his business printed on the front. Branson's clothes smelled of recently mowed grass.

"Hey, Branson." Ray shook his hand. "Come on back." He led the way to his office. "What can I do for you?" he asked as he closed the door.

Branson coughed into his sleeve and cleared his throat. "I tried to make it to court this morning but got caught at a job. One of my regular workers was out sick, and I had to run a mower."

While Branson spoke, Ray quickly ran down the docket in his mind and tried to identify a case that might be of interest to the small business owner.

"Which case were you interested in?" he asked.

"The one against Colfax, about the chemicals they dumped on the tract of land that drains into the Cheola watershed. My boy, Tommy, and his family live near Colfax on Harris Street. They're not on city water out there and noticed last year that their well water had a peculiar odor and odd taste."

"It should be better soon if what Colfax did had a negative impact on the water table, which I seriously doubt. The company stopped spraying residue on the field last week. There wasn't any evidence of a real problem, but they agreed to stop it anyway."

"What kind of residue was it? I know they've been putting pesticides in some of their newer brands of fertilizer. I have to be careful with that stuff in my business. I make my boys wear gloves when they put it out and warn customers to keep their kids and pets inside for at least twenty-four hours."

"I don't remember the exact names of the chemicals," Ray said, trying to sound more authoritative than he was. "But it wasn't full strength. It had to do with by-products of the manufacturing process that won't kill anything. You know, most of the bag contains filler."

At the hearing Ray had simply presented the data collected by the experts in Atlanta and let the judge make up his mind. The information in the DA's office file may as well have been written in hieroglyphics.

"Well, I guess getting them to stop is the important thing," Branson said. "Thanks for taking that on. It's not everyone who'll tangle with Colfax."

"You're welcome," Ray responded, slightly embarrassed. "I'm just doing my job."

"I'll let Tommy know. His family is going through a tough time right now, with his little boy having cancer and all."

"I'm sorry to hear that. It's worse when a young child gets sick."

"Yeah, it's got us all torn up." Branson stood up. "Thanks for seeing me."

After Branson left, Ray swiveled in his chair and saw the picture of Billy. If Billy had cancer, Ray would be torn up too.

EIGHT

Corbin received a pleasant surprise in the afternoon mail—payment of a fee he'd billed six months earlier and given up hope of collecting. He held the check up in the air triumphantly as he approached Janelle's desk.

"Look what dropped down from heaven," he said with a smile. "Jarvis Kemp paid the $2,500 he owed me for representing him in a condemnation case."

"If you'd taken it on a contingency, you'd have been paid three times that much," Janelle sniffed.

"And he would have hired someone else to represent him. Jarvis may not have gone to school past the sixth grade, but he knew all he needed was a lawyer willing to pull together a higher appraisal and then rattle a sword in front of the Simpkin firm. Even if we'd gone to trial, I think the chances of getting him more money for that piece of hardscrabble land would have been less than 50 percent. If the moon had red clay it would look like Kemp's property."

"Do you want me to deposit the check today?"

"Yes, even though I'm sure it won't bounce."

Because Corbin owned the little building, his overhead costs were ridiculously low, and he'd been able to survive even though his practice sputtered much of the time. Janelle hadn't received a raise in five years and had long since quit dropping hints. Corbin figured she knew she'd have to work harder and learn new technology if she abandoned him for another job. So he put up with her surly attitude, and she accepted a noncompetitive salary.

Thirty minutes later she brought the Bowater file into his office and placed it on his desk with the completed dictation on top. "Somebody needs to help that couple," she said. "That place sounds awful."

"It is. Would you swing by and take some pictures on your way back from the bank? I'll let them know you're coming."

Janelle stared at him for a moment, then shook her head. "That's not funny."

"Maybe not," Corbin admitted. "But I'm going to have to hire someone to take a look at the problems and estimate the cost of repair."

"How about my nephew Stanley?" Janelle asked, brightening. "He's been doing remodeling work for quite a while."

Corbin vaguely remembered Stanley as a clean-cut young man who might be able to express himself decently in court if the case ended up in front of a judge.

"Yeah, he'll do. Give him a call and coordinate a time with the clients."

Corbin picked up some papers and began to read them. Janelle didn't move.

"What else?" he asked.

"What are you going to pay Stanley to be your expert witness?"

"Oh, he's an expert witness now?"

"It looks that way to me."

Corbin was irritated, but he liked Janelle's suggestion. "Less than I would if he had a degree in structural engineering from Georgia Tech, and more than if all he knew was how to frame up a house that somebody else laid out."

"And how much is that? I don't want to get him involved and then end up being embarrassed when—"

"Twenty-five dollars an hour," Corbin replied as he felt his face get red. "With a maximum fee that I'll set once I figure out how hard Dickens is going to fight. And in case you forgot, you write the checks around here. He'll get paid."

"That's fair," Janelle said as she retreated in victory toward the door. "I'll call Stanley this evening and get him over there within the next day or so."

"With a camera. And he has to buy his own film."

"Nobody uses a film camera."

"You know what I mean. He needs to print out photos I can use in court." Corbin dismissed her with a wave of his hand.

A headache that had danced around the edge of his brain before lunch crept back. He rubbed his forehead as he made a few small changes in a letter with a red pen.

"Do this as quick as you can," he said, taking it to Janelle. "I want to sign it and go home."

By the time Janelle brought back the letter, Corbin's headache had moved from the fringes and become a throbbing drumbeat that would only get louder if ignored. He signed the revised letter without reading it and left the office.

Several times during the drive home the road twisted to the west, causing Corbin to squeeze his eyes shut for a few seconds to avoid the harshness of the setting sun. Once, the sound of a horn from an approaching car forced him to open his eyes and swerve to the right. He made it home and pulled a bottle of bourbon from a cupboard in the kitchen. Pouring the clear brown liquid into a tumbler, he sat at the kitchen table and downed it in two swallows. That drink was quickly followed by others. He fell asleep on the couch in the living room, and when he groggily opened his eyes at

3:30 a.m., he was still wearing his clothes. He stumbled into the bedroom, put on pajamas, and fell into bed.

———

Roxy left her townhome at 5:50 the next morning and locked the front door. She slipped the house key into a tiny pocket in the front of her running shorts, then performed a few stretching exercises while holding on to an ornate cast-iron fence that extended the entire length of her block. She loved the cool feel and texture of the black fence, which was decorated with black magnolia flowers and replicas of the tree's large, broad leaves. Limber as a gymnast, she switched positions and rested her right leg against the railing and touched her knee with her forehead.

The fence wasn't old, but in Roxy's mind it captured the essence of the antebellum South when Atlanta was a railroad terminus for steam engines carrying women wearing hoop dresses and fancy petticoats. Roxy's ancestors weren't wealthy landowners. Her father's forebears were farmers and blacksmiths, and her mother's family were middle-class French shopkeepers who immigrated to America in the 1880s.

Roxy ran at a slow pace down the sidewalk. Piedmont Park opened its gates at six, and she liked to time her arrival precisely at the time the park opened for the day. During the warm-up portion of her run, Roxy took in all the details of her surroundings. Each season had its unique sights and fragrances. With the arrival of early fall, every breath of cool air was refreshment to her lungs.

She reached the park and headed to one of the large open fields. On Saturdays and Sundays the area would be crowded with people, but this early in the morning she only shared the space with fellow joggers and a few people walking their dogs.

Roxy reached the field and quickly accelerated. Her feet flew across the wet grass, leaving nothing but tiny marks in the dew. She pushed hard all the way to the end of the field, then slowed down and ran in a horizontal direction for a couple hundred yards. This was followed by another sprint of several hundred yards. Called interval training, the alteration of sprinting with short rest breaks was designed to increase her overall speed during long runs. She enjoyed ramping up her heart rate, letting it drop, then ratcheting it up again. The high caused by the massive release of endorphins was as addicting as a bag of caramels. Only when her muscles cried out in fatigue and her breathing became labored did she turn toward home.

It was 7:10 when she reached the iron railing in front of her townhome and repeated her stretching exercises. Inside the house she grabbed a bottle of water from the refrigerator. Her phone, which was on the small table in the kitchen where she ate her meals, vibrated, and Mr. Caldweller's name popped up.

Corbin took a stiff drink of bourbon as soon as he woke up, then stayed in the shower for a long time. Still bleary-eyed from the previous night, he stopped for breakfast on his way to the office. The twenty-four-hour restaurant no longer allowed smoking, but the cook produced enough overdone toast to give the air a burnt smell. Corbin chased his earlier whiskey with a cup of black coffee while he waited for a plate of sunny-side-up eggs, hashed brown potatoes, and dry wheat toast. He ignored the bustling activity in the restaurant as he read the morning news on his phone and waited for his food.

"Can I join you?" a male voice asked.

Corbin looked up. It was Max Hogan, the bald-headed owner of a payday loan business and pawnshop next door to a tattoo parlor. Max's arms were a living canvas.

"Sure." Corbin gestured for Max to sit down. "I haven't seen you for weeks. How have you been?"

Max got the attention of a waitress and ordered a cup of coffee before answering. "Sober," he replied.

"What?" Corbin asked.

"No more liquor for me," Max answered. "I completed a twenty-eight-day alcohol rehab program at a facility in Gainesville a couple of weeks ago, and I'm going to a group that meets at Hopewell Methodist Church."

"Oh," Corbin replied. He braced himself for what he knew would follow.

"Yeah, I'm going to at least one meeting every day, sometimes two," Max said. He smiled. "Corbin, you look like I just told you I had lung cancer and was on my way to the hospital for a last-ditch dose of chemotherapy."

"Max, I'm not an everyday drinker," Corbin began. "And I've only been on one binge in the past few weeks."

Corbin stopped. He'd passed out the night before and needed a drink to kick-start his day, but that didn't qualify as a binge unless he kept drinking throughout the day.

"No need to go there," Max replied. "I've said the same thing many times, and I know exactly how you feel and what you're thinking. It's not an accident I'm here this morning. I saw your truck in the parking lot and pulled in. You're one of the first guys I wanted to track down as soon as I felt strong enough."

For over twenty years Corbin and Max had shot pool, watched sports on TV in smoky bars, and laughed at bad jokes made funny by booze. This was the first time Corbin could remember Max trying to stop drinking. He wouldn't have tolerated most folks who invaded his personal space at 8:00 a.m. to preach sobriety, but Max was different. They had a long history.

"I understand," Corbin replied. "And I'm happy for you if that's what you want. But don't try to twist my arm. I've been tapering back since Kitty got sick."

"That's the other reason I stopped to see you," Max said. "I wanted to tell you how sorry I am that she passed. I know how much you cared about her."

In moments made vulnerable by booze-induced candor, Corbin had poured out his heart to Max about his marriage. He couldn't deny what he'd said then was true.

"Yeah."

Max patted his multicolored forearm. "And if I wanted to twist your arm, I could jerk it clean off with this."

"Don't get cocky," Corbin said as he tightened his right bicep and tapped it with his finger. "I have bullets left in my guns."

Max grinned. "We talk tough for a pair of old guys."

The waitress arrived with Corbin's food. Max didn't order anything, but accepted Corbin's offer of a piece of toast. He asked a few questions about the funeral, then checked his watch.

"I'd better get going."

Corbin swallowed a bite of eggs mixed with hash browns. "One last thing," he said slowly. "Why did you enter the twenty-eight-day program? What happened?"

"Family intervention," Max replied. "My brother and his wife came in from Albuquerque, and my kids piled into town. There were fifteen people sitting in my living room when I got home from work one Friday night. They had everything set up at the treatment facility. They cried, I cried. It was just like you see in reality TV shows."

"Okay."

Max stood up. "Are we still friends? Or does the only thing connecting us come from inside a bottle?"

"Is that something they taught you in rehab to say to your old drinking buddies?" Corbin asked aggressively.

"Would it make a difference? I'm the one standing here."

Corbin paused for a moment. "No. We're still friends."

"Thanks." Max reached out and touched Corbin on the shoulder. "And no, they didn't teach me that in rehab. They warned me to stay away from guys like you for at least six months."

NINE

R ay returned to the house after walking Billy to the bus stop and poured a second cup of coffee.

"You didn't wait with him?" Cindy asked when she came into the kitchen.

"He didn't want me to. He reminded me he's in the third grade."

"And one of the youngest boys in his class," Cindy answered. "Was Sammy Baldwin at the bus stop? He's been picking on Billy recently during the ride home from school."

"Yes, and the last thing I did was to make Billy let Sammy out of a headlock. From what I saw, you may be getting a call from Josie Baldwin complaining about our son. Billy may not turn nine for another month, but he's a big, strong kid."

"Your dad plays rough with him. I don't like it when they wrestle. That's probably where Billy learned how to put someone in a headlock."

Ray didn't respond. Trying to defend Corbin, even if the charges weren't justified, was a case he had no chance of winning in front of Cindy, who had been in an unusually negative mood for several days.

"I saw him in court yesterday," Ray said.

"How did he look?"

"Decent. He'd shaved and probably taken a shower. And his mind was sharp enough that he gave me a hard time about the way I handled an environmental case against Colfax."

"Why would he care about that?"

"He believes what Colonel Parker told him about contingency lawyers being the champion of the common man. Going after something big, whether it's an insurance company, a corporation, the government, or a cheapskate landlord, is in his blood as much as the booze."

"Well, all of those are things I'm thankful you didn't inherit from him," Cindy sniffed. "And I don't think that's being disrespectful. Colfax gave my father a great job, and we wouldn't have a nice place to visit in Brunswick if he hadn't been paid well enough to retire on the coast."

She closed the door of the dishwasher and pushed Start, then turned around. "What's your day like today?"

"A bunch of office stuff. Nate Stamper handled the case for Colfax yesterday. He was upset because Judge Ellington didn't go along with the deal we'd worked out before the hearing, so I may see if he's available to grab a bite to eat." Ray paused. "And find out where they are on putting together a job offer."

"If Steve finds out you're meeting Nate for lunch, will that make him suspicious?"

"It might," Ray admitted. "But the more I think about it, the more I want to make the move to the Simpkin firm. If I stay at the DA's office, we'll never take a vacation at the beach unless it's with your folks. And I read an article the other day about the cost of a college education in ten years. It will be crazy expensive if Billy goes to a private school."

"What about a bigger house for us?" Cindy asked, leaning against the kitchen counter. "Two bedrooms isn't enough."

Ray looked at her, startled. "What do you mean?"

His wife had grown up in a frugal family and was an expert coupon clipper. New house fever was a surprising new ailment.

Cindy smiled shyly. "You didn't ask me what I'm going to do today."

"Uh, go house hunting?"

"Not yet." She shook her head. "I'm going to the doctor first."

Ray looked alarmed, then the expression on his face changed. "You're not—?"

"I am," Cindy interrupted, beaming. "I took a home test while you were walking Billy to the bus stop, and it was positive!"

Cindy almost jumped into Ray's arms, and he held her close.

"That's great, honey," he said, "but don't you think we need to manage our expectations until—"

"No!" She pushed him away fiercely. "I'm not going to allow fear to ruin this for me! It's been six years since we lost the last baby, and I'd almost given up hope for another."

"All right then!" Ray said, holding up his hands. "I'm glad too."

"We're going to pray and believe," Cindy replied with determination. "And if it's a girl we're going to name her Kitty!"

———

Roxy placed the water bottle on the table as she continued to hold the cell phone to her ear.

"You're sending me to Chicago?"

"That's right. I've been up most of the night with the worst pain I've ever felt. I saw an ENT doc at the hospital a couple of hours ago, and she says there's no way I should get on a plane. Both ears are infected, but it's worse on the right. If I wasn't on strong pain meds, I wouldn't be able to talk to you now, so don't waste my time."

"Yes, sir."

"Christine transcribed my notes from yesterday's meeting and will send them to your phone. She'll e-mail your ticket information. The flight leaves at 9:45. The meeting with Dr. Sellers begins at noon."

Roxy glanced at the clock. It was a thirty-minute ride from the nearest MARTA station to the airport. Whether she could make the flight would depend on how fast she could get through security and navigate the massive concourses to the correct gate.

"Will Christine let Dr. Sellers know I'm going to meet with him?"

Mr. Caldweller didn't answer. Roxy glanced down at her phone. Either the call dropped or her boss had ended it. She didn't call him back. If Mr. Caldweller wanted to reach her, he would. Her next step was clear.

She had to get ready to leave for the airport a lot faster than she'd sprinted across the grassy field at Piedmont Park.

———

Corbin unlocked the door of the office. Janelle wasn't there, and he checked the answering machine. Mr. and Mrs. Bowater wanted him to call them ASAP.

"This is Corbin Gage," he said when Mr. Bowater answered the phone. "I faxed a claim under the lease and for your personal injuries to Mr. Dickens yesterday afternoon."

"We know," Mr. Bowater replied in his country twang. "He came by while we were eating supper and told us if we filed a lawsuit against him he'd make sure no one in Rusk County would rent a place to us."

Corbin sat up straighter in his chair. "My letter explicitly prohibited him from direct contact with you. He was supposed to get in touch with me."

"Uh, maybe you should talk to my wife. She's the one who answered the door. I was lying down because my back was bothering me."

Corbin fumed while he waited for Mrs. Bowater to come to the phone. Courage wasn't a common commodity in people used to economic oppression. He could visualize Harold Dickens standing on the porch delivering his threats to a cowering Mrs. Bowater.

"Hello," Mrs. Bowater said in a voice that trembled slightly.

"I know Mr. Dickens came by and tried to intimidate you," Corbin began, "but I want to reassure you and your husband that I'm going to—"

"He said you were a drunk," Mrs. Bowater interrupted. "Is that true?"

"No," Corbin replied. "And I could sue him for slander for saying that in an effort to pressure you into backing off your legitimate claims."

"And he agreed to fix up the house this week if we dropped you as a lawyer. Otherwise he's going to tell everybody that we're troublemakers and bad tenants."

"Mrs. Bowater, let me do this the right way."

"Can you guarantee the judge will make him fix this place up?"

Corbin hesitated. "No lawyer can *guarantee* exactly what will happen, but I wouldn't have taken your case on a contingent fee basis if I didn't think we could win. Remember, I don't get a cent unless Dickens or his insurance company pays you. And this isn't just about repairs on the house. There are also the injuries your husband suffered when he fell because of the leaks Dickens didn't fix."

"Medicare will pay the doctor bills, won't it?"

"Yes, but not for pain and suffering."

"We don't care about that. Before he left I told Mr. Dickens we'd give him a chance to make things right before getting a lawyer involved. We believe that's the honest thing to do."

Corbin knew he was defeated. Dickens was both savvy and sneaky. He knew how to intimidate and manipulate simple folks like the Bowaters.

"I've got your card in my pocketbook," Mrs. Bowater continued. "If we need you we'll give you a holler."

The call ended, leaving Corbin steamed. He slid open the bottom drawer of his desk and took out a bottle of bourbon. There wasn't much more than an ounce of amber liquid left. He drained the last drops of whiskey in a single gulp. The front door beeped.

"I'm in here!" he called out irritably.

In a few seconds Millie Watson eased her face into view. Corbin quickly moved the bottle from his desk to the floor beside his chair and stood up.

"I should have called," Millie said, her eyes wide.

Corbin could tell by the look on the young woman's face that she'd seen the whiskey bottle.

"It's okay," he said with a wave of his hand, not exactly sure what he meant by the words. "What can I do for you?"

"I met with Mr. Morgan, and he's going to help me file for bankruptcy. When I told him about Josh's cancer, he asked a bunch of questions, then said I should come back to you and talk about filing a lawsuit."

"A lawsuit?"

"Against Colfax."

Corbin reached up to straighten his tie, only to discover he didn't have one on. "Uh, come in and have a seat," he said. "And close the door."

Millie hesitated.

"Or leave the door open. It doesn't really matter unless someone else comes into the reception area."

Corbin saw Millie cautiously glance at the spot where the whiskey bottle had rested on his desk. She sat on the edge of a chair across from him.

"What exactly did Barry tell you?" he asked.

"Just that the stuff they make at Colfax could have caused Josh to get cancer. When I told him about Mitchell Kilpatrick having the same disease, he said you were the kind of lawyer to look into it."

"Branson Kilpatrick and I have been friends for years. He mentioned Mitchell's illness to me the other day."

Corbin tapped his legal pad with his pen, then told Millie about the court hearing he'd witnessed the previous day. While he talked, the morning fog that had clouded his mind lifted.

The young woman's eyes widened as she listened. "Mr. Morgan didn't say anything about that."

"He didn't know. The prosecutor and the lawyer for Colfax wanted to keep it quiet. I just happened to be over at the courthouse."

It hurt to link Ray to a conspiracy of silence, but it was the truth.

"All I want is for Josh to get the best medical treatment available so he can beat this cancer. But I don't have money to pay a lawyer," Millie said.

"These kinds of cases are handled on what's called a contingent fee."

Corbin repeated the familiar litany about percentage payment of any recovery as attorney's fees in personal injury cases.

"The first step would be a preliminary investigation prior to filing suit."

"So you'll look into it?" Millie asked.

Toxic tort litigation against a large corporation wasn't in the same legal universe as a premises liability claim against a scuzzy landlord like Harold Dickens. Corbin glanced at the picture of his swearing-in ceremony. He'd been young then and full of fight. Now he wasn't so sure.

TEN

Roxy stood in front of a long mirror in the women's restroom at O'Hare and applied a fresh coat of lipstick. She'd made it onto the plane in Atlanta seconds before the doors closed, then spent every spare moment on the one-hour-and-fifty-five-minute flight poring over the information needed to question Dr. Sellers. Her brain was crammed with data about buttressed generics, polymorphs, targeted proteins, and enzyme-binding agents.

She took a taxi from the airport to an office on LaSalle Street. Roxy loved the vibrant feel of downtown Chicago and felt energized by its sprawling hustle and bustle. She barely had time to boot up her laptop when a door opened and a stocky, black-haired man in his late fifties, wearing an open-collared shirt, blue jeans, and cowboy boots, opened the door.

"Ms. Gage?" he asked in a Texas drawl.

"Yes."

"Your office called and told me you'd be coming instead of Mr. Caldweller."

Dr. Willard Sellers looked like he'd be more at home on a ranch than in a chemistry lab. Roxy followed the chemist down a narrow hallway and into a conference room barely big enough for four people. His laptop was open on the table.

"Do you have my curriculum vitae?" he asked.

His educational and professional qualifications, including academic papers published in scientific journals, ran to twenty pages. Roxy had identified five papers of particular interest and reviewed them in detail for Mr. Caldweller in her memo.

"Yes, I do. And before we do anything else, I'd like to ask you about the article you published last year in the *American Journal of Chemistry* about enzyme-binding agents."

The chemist's eyes perked up. "Okay."

Because Dr. Sellers was a shadow expert, Roxy's meeting with him was, under the law, nothing more than a conversation at a cocktail party. He would never testify in the case or prepare a formal report. However, his opinion was important because it would help Roxy's firm decide what to ask in-house or outside experts and develop strategies for cross-examination of witnesses used by the plaintiffs. Everybody in high-stakes litigation utilized the practice.

She placed a recording device on the table. "Let's go," she said.

Getting a scientist like Dr. Sellers to talk about a peer review paper was easy. Even though the particular article wasn't directly relevant to the lawsuit, it was a recent work and helped Roxy set the tone for the type of interaction with the chemist she hoped would be most beneficial. Over the next three hours they transitioned from topic to topic.

"Let's take a break," Dr. Sellers suggested after he finished a particularly long explanation about the chemical interactions of compounds in the drug that was subject to the litigation.

"Sure."

The chemist stood to his feet and stretched. "You've done your homework," he said. "You've read my CV. What's on yours?"

"Undergraduate degree in chemistry from Georgia Tech, followed by law school at Emory. I've been with Frank and Donaldson for five years."

"You remind me of a graduate student who interned with me last year and now works in the petrochemical field."

Two hours later Roxy rubbed her forehead in fatigue. She had a much clearer idea of the small holes in their case and how to fill them.

"What have I forgotten to ask you?" she asked.

Dr. Sellers thought for a moment. "About this," he said.

As Dr. Sellers laid out a problem she'd not considered, but which created a huge risk for the law firm to be blindsided, Roxy grew more and more nervous. None of the internal documents from their client had tipped her off, but now she saw that they should have. If Mr. Caldweller had been in the room, he would have bored holes with his eyes through Roxy for not seeing it and giving him a heads-up. She tried to keep her voice nonchalant for the sake of the recording.

"I see—thanks for clarifying that," she said.

"Glad to do it," Dr. Sellers said.

She turned off the recorder. "Wow, I really mean it," she said, sitting back in her chair. "I didn't realize the significance of the interaction between those two compounds. It was in the information we received, but—"

"I see things like this from time to time," the chemist interjected. "The company hopes they can bury a problem in the midst of a data dump and takes a chance no one will identify its relevance."

"Which is why I'm glad I got to talk with you."

Dr. Sellers checked his watch and made an entry into his computer.

"I have to get ready for another of these meetings tomorrow. This is supposed to be a vacation week, but I work harder consulting than I do teaching or in research."

"What's the general subject of your next consult?"

"Medical claims for exposure to phenoxyacetic acid herbicides, particularly 2,4-dichlorophenoxyacetic acid. There are ancillary questions related to organophosphorus insecticides. I've not written about this area professionally, but I've studied it for years. I grew up on a family farm wondering if the stuff my father and uncles used to kill weeds and insects might not be good for us, either. Dichlorodiphenyltrichloroethane was a great bug killer."

"DDT."

"Right. And we know how that turned out."

"Which side hired you?" Roxy asked.

"Defendants."

———

Janelle arrived at the office five minutes after Millie Watson left. In the meantime, Corbin put the empty whiskey bottle in a plastic bag and deposited it in a large bin behind the building. There was a foul taste in his mouth left over from his drinking the previous night, but he didn't have any toothpaste at the office. He made a mental note to buy some—and another bottle of bourbon. Reentering the office, he found Janelle talking to a tall young man with a dark mustache and goatee.

"Good morning, Corbin," Janelle said cheerfully. "You remember Stanley, don't you? He put off a remodeling job so he could get right on the Bowater matter. I told him you were in a hurry to nail down the problems—no pun intended. Anyway, he has his camera and is ready to go as soon as you tell him what you want him to do."

While Janelle chattered away, Corbin tried to decide whether he should pay Stanley for missing a job to investigate a remodeling case that wasn't going to happen. When the secretary stopped talking, Corbin stepped forward and shook Stanley's hand.

"Well," Corbin said, drawing out the word as long as possible, "there's not going to be a Bowater case."

Janelle's face fell. "What happened?"

"You know I can't discuss that. Even if a case doesn't pan out, the discussions I have with prospective clients are confidential."

"It's okay," Stanley said before Janelle could respond. "I'll be on my way. I appreciate you thinking about me."

"Wait a minute," Janelle said. "You lost a job so you could do this—"

"Naw, I'll give them a call as soon as I leave here. I'm not going to charge Mr. Gage if I don't do anything."

Corbin's opinion of Stanley was rising faster than a hot new stock.

"Tell you what," Corbin said. "I have some roof shingles that need to be replaced at my duplex. Would you be interested in taking a look at it and giving me a bid?"

"Sure."

"I'll call you."

"You'd better," Janelle interjected.

After Stanley left, Corbin turned to his secretary. "Something way bigger than the Bowater case has come up this morning," he said, and told her about his conversation with Millie Watson.

By the time he finished, Janelle's mouth was hanging open in shock. "Are you kidding or crazy?" she managed. "When was the last time you looked in the mirror? Do you think you're a character in a TV show? I mean, that type of case . . ."

"I wouldn't turn it into a class action," Corbin replied defensively. "But if I could sign up both children and join them as plaintiffs in the same lawsuit—"

Janelle spun around, put her hands over her ears, and began walking rapidly toward the women's bathroom.

Returning to his office, Corbin stood in front of a small mirror with a gilt frame that Colonel Parker had bought for the firm. The first thing he noticed was his eyes. They were so bloodshot that Max Hogan probably didn't have to ask if Corbin had been on a recent binge. The skin beneath both eyes was sagging more than he'd noticed before. He needed a haircut but he'd done a decent job shaving and only missed a tiny place under his lip. It barely showed. He rubbed it and noticed that his fingernails were seriously past due for a trim. Going to his desk, he rummaged around in a drawer until he found a pair of clippers. He was snipping his fingernails over a circular metal trash can when Janelle appeared in the doorway.

"Corbin, how long have I worked for you?" she asked.

Knowing it was a trick question, Corbin hesitated. "Nineteen years?"

"Twenty-one."

"I knew it was a long time," Corbin began. "You know how things run together—"

"And I've earned the right to tell you the truth," she interrupted. "You're in no shape to take on big-time litigation like this. It wouldn't be right for you to start something you can't finish. What did Colonel Parker used to say about not strapping on your gun unless there's a bullet in every chamber of the magazine? It would be criminal for you to ask these folks to trust you."

As Janelle listed his inadequacies, Corbin didn't get angry. His secretary knew the magnitude and scope of his faults as an attorney better than anyone.

"How will you feel when the case gets dismissed and you have to think about two sick little boys and their families who believed you were going to help them?" she continued. "I'd be worried about you too. When the black bear of booze and depression jumps on your back and you don't show up for two or three days at a stretch, there's no way I can cover for you."

Janelle paused to take a breath. Corbin scratched his chin with the newly trimmed fingernails on his left hand.

"You're right," he said. "I'll call Millie Watson and tell her I'm not the lawyer who should evaluate the case. This might even be too much for Foxcroft and Bartlett, but they're the best plaintiff lawyers in the area. I'll send her over to them so they can check it out."

Janelle's shoulders slumped. It wasn't a victory pose.

"I'm sorry, Corbin," she said, "but I had to speak up before you did something that could hurt a lot of people."

"Okay, okay." He held up his hand. "You've won. So you should shut up before you unconvince me."

Janelle snapped her mouth closed and returned to her desk.

Corbin sank down in his chair.

And desperately wished he'd brought a bottle of whiskey from home to replace the one he finished earlier.

ELEVEN

G ood morning, and thanks for calling Simpkin, Brown, and Stamper," announced the perky receptionist with the British accent.

"This is Ray Gage at the DA's office. I'd like to speak with Nate Stamper, please."

While he waited on hold, Ray tried to imagine the former London resident pronouncing his name. Hiring a secretary from the UK had created a buzz in the legal community and bolstered the perception that Simpkin, Brown, and Stamper was a cut above the other firms in town.

Nate came on the phone. "Hey, Ray. I did an hour of damage control with Guy Hathaway after we got back from court yesterday. He couldn't get it through his head that the judge had the power to disregard your recommendation and impose a fine. I tried to convince him you did all you could."

"And I hope you told him a $2,500 fine is a lot better than a $225,000 fine."

"No, because then he would have gone off about your father jumping in and mouthing off to the judge about how big the fine could be. I hate to say it, but your old man needs to realize it's time to close up shop and spend more time fishing and—"

Nate stopped. Ray suspected the rest of his sentence had to do with alcohol.

"That's up to him," Ray replied. "His name is the only one on the door. But I called because I wanted to bring a proposed order."

"Just scan and send it as an e-mail attachment. I'll redline any changes and shoot it back to you."

Ray cleared his throat. "How are things going with my résumé? I'm 100 percent ready to make a move, and there's no place I'd rather end up than with your firm."

"It's on the agenda for our partners' meeting in a couple of weeks. We get together at Mr. Simpkin's lake house the first of every month. I know how I'm going to vote, but Simpkin and Brown still have a few questions."

"What kind of questions?" Ray asked, then immediately regretted it. No smart lawyer asked a question to which he didn't already know the answer.

"Leave that to me," Nate replied smoothly. "They know the firm has to bring in fresh blood if it wants to continue. When the governor appointed Dexter Perry to the bench, we had to divvy up his litigation files, which overloaded everyone's docket. And as Simpkin gets closer to retirement, someone is going to have to serve his clients and help fund his buyout with ongoing revenue."

Mr. Simpkin had the best trust and estate practice in town. He'd grown rich collecting the percentage of large estates allocated for attorney fees in wills he drafted for clients.

"I'm a trial lawyer, but I'm looking forward to learning about a trust and estate practice."

"Yeah, that's the last thing we'll pry from Simpkin's bony fingers. It's an unbelievable gravy train, but he's a menace to his clients and himself if he gets within a hundred yards of the courthouse in a litigation matter. That's how I'm going to sell you to him, and I think he'll see that passing that part of his practice off to someone else will be a relief."

"Whatever works for the firm. I'm a team player."

"Great. Send over the order in the Colfax matter as soon as we hang up."

"Will do."

The call ended and Ray took a deep breath. Simpkin, Brown, and Stamper currently had four partners and two associates. Ray would be at the bottom of the pecking order, which meant any work the other lawyers didn't want to handle would be dumped on his desk.

One of his first priorities would be to wiggle as close to Nate as he could and slip under his umbrella. Nate was a rising star, and Ray could try to link himself to the young partner's success. The salary range Nate had mentioned at their second meeting would mean a 30 percent increase over Ray's pay at the DA's office. He might not be able to afford a BMW like Roxy, but he could set Cindy free to start looking for a bigger house.

Steve Nelson interrupted Ray's daydream. "Ray, could you come into my office for a minute? I need to talk to you."

———

Corbin grabbed a pack of peanut butter crackers from the stash in his credenza.

"Don't forget your appointment at two o'clock," Janelle said as he walked through the reception area toward the rear door. "You missed the last one and it took a lot of persuasion from me to convince the new client to reschedule."

Corbin had failed to jot down the meeting in the old-fashioned Day-Timer he kept on his desk.

"I know about it," he said grumpily. "What's he want?"

"The guy bought a new car that's been in the repair shop so much you told him he might have a case under the lemon law."

"Oh yeah. Is he bringing all the invoices?"

"I asked him to."

Corbin drove to the cemetery and stopped beneath a maple tree whose few remaining leaves were hanging on precariously. Fall was his favorite season; he liked the cool mornings and bright colors.

The cemetery was deserted. A few graves were decorated with flowers. Most were as barren as Corbin's heart. He walked slowly between the new and old markers to the fresh mound of reddish earth that marked Kitty's grave. The flowers from her funeral were fading fast. Corbin took out the pack of crackers and put one in his mouth. He chewed it slowly. Kitty had loved peanut butter crackers.

Before he put another cracker in his mouth, a wave of aching sorrow and regret rose up within him. Tears rushed into his eyes, and he was barely able to wipe them away with the back of his hand before they escaped. A second wave followed immediately upon the heels of the first. Giving up, Corbin didn't try to deny them. Standing like a statue at the foot of the grave, he let the tears run down his cheeks and fall from his face to the earth at his feet. When his vision cleared, he glanced down and saw where they had watered a tiny circle of soil. He touched the place with his shoe, and it disappeared. His grief came and passed without leaving an earthly mark.

Corbin took a deep breath and sighed. He didn't feel better, but he felt lighter. And he knew what he'd experienced was a beginning, not an end. He took out a cracker and placed it on the earth over her grave. It wouldn't stay there long. A bird or squirrel would discover it with delight.

Which would make Kitty happy.

After finishing his appointment with the new client, Corbin called Cindy. "Could I take Billy fishing for an hour or so at Braswell's Pond after school?" he asked.

"Where are you now?" Cindy replied.

"At the office."

"Have you been there all day?"

Corbin tried to fight back resentment. He hated it when Cindy cross-examined him about his whereabouts. He gritted his teeth for a moment before answering.

"Except for a few minutes during lunch when I went to Kitty's grave," he replied in a steely voice.

"And you'll come straight here to pick him up—"

"Then swing by my duplex to change clothes and hook the boat to my truck," he interrupted. "That's the plan."

"Okay. What time should I expect you?"

"Doesn't Billy get off the bus around a quarter to four?"

"Yes."

"Then I'll be there at four."

Corbin hung up before Cindy could say anything else. He stayed in his office with the door closed until it was time to leave. When he came out, Janelle was typing a letter. She took the ear-buds from her ears.

"I'm taking Billy fishing and won't be back today," Corbin said.

"That's good." Janelle smiled. "You'll enjoy that much more than getting bogged down in a huge lawsuit."

"You made your point earlier."

"Did you call Millie Watson and refer her to Foxcroft and Bartlett?"

"No, I'll do it tomorrow."

"I could do it for you today," Janelle volunteered. "I know it goes against your grain to pass on a case. I could set up an appointment for her in Gainesville."

"What would you tell her about why I'm not going to take the case?"

"Nothing that will make you seem like a coward."

"A coward?"

"No, no," Janelle replied quickly. "That's a poor choice of words. I'll emphasize the truth—that a lawsuit like this will require a ton of resources."

The woman made him want to reopen the debate. He took his hands out of his pockets and brushed his hair off his forehead.

"What time are you picking up Billy?" she asked quickly.

"Uh, four o'clock."

"Then you'd better get going. It's 3:52."

Muttering to himself, Corbin left the office.

TWELVE

Corbin's spirits rose at the sight of Billy sitting on the front steps of the house with his fishing pole and tackle box beside him.

"Hey, Pops," the boy said when Corbin got out of the truck. "What are we going to use? Plugs or worms?"

"That's up to you," Corbin replied. "You're the captain of this voyage."

Billy opened his tackle box and took out a lure that was still in its packaging. "I want to try this one!" he said. "I looked it up on the Internet and watched a video on how to use it. They had a camera underwater and filmed bass going after it."

"Sounds good," Corbin said. "Where's your mama?"

"Inside."

Corbin opened the front door and called into the house. "Cindy! I'm here!" He waited a few seconds. "Do you know where she is?" he asked Billy.

"I think she's in the bedroom."

"Run inside and tell her I'm picking you up. I don't want her to wonder where you are."

Billy left, and Corbin inspected the new lure. He had serious doubts that the garishly colored rig had a chance of attracting a fish.

"Mama said it's okay for me to go," Billy said when he returned. "She's not feeling good."

"What's wrong with her?"

"I don't know, but she's glad you're getting me out of the house so she can rest."

Billy picked up his fishing pole, and Corbin grabbed the tackle box. They stashed the pole and box in the narrow space behind the truck's seat.

"Don't tell me to buckle up," Billy said as he climbed into the cab. "I do it automatically."

"Automatically?"

"Yeah, that's another way to say I'm going to do something without being told."

As Corbin backed out of the driveway, Billy launched into the details of a softball game that took place during PE class.

"Coach Henry let me be the pitcher," Billy said. "It's slow pitch, and the best way to do it is to throw the ball high in the air so it's coming down from the sky when it crosses the plate. Then, even if the batter hits it, the ball won't go very far. I got the hang of it real quick and struck out a bunch of kids."

"How did you do at the plate?"

"I struck out once and got a single the second time. Do you think you could take me to the baseball field and throw me some balls to hit?"

"Sure. Would you rather do that instead of fishing?"

Billy gave Corbin an incredulous look. "Pops, are you kidding?"

"I guess I am."

They reached Corbin's house. A small aluminum boat with a ten-horsepower motor rested on its trailer, covered by a blue tarp.

"Take off the tarp while I go inside and change clothes," Corbin said.

When he returned, wearing blue jeans and a short-sleeved shirt, Billy greeted him with the gas can in hand.

"It's almost empty," the boy said. "I can pick it up with one hand."

Corbin refilled the container from a bigger one he kept in a storage shed behind the house.

"Pops, do you think you should see if the motor starts before we get to the pond?"

"I cleaned the spark plug, but it wouldn't hurt to make sure. Do you want to pull the rope?"

Billy hesitated. "No, I can't do it as hard as you can."

Corbin pulled out the choke on the engine. After a couple of stout yanks of the rope, he pushed it in and tried again. The engine sputtered to life, and Corbin quickly killed it. He placed his fishing tackle in the truck bed.

"Let's go," he said.

It was a five-minute drive down the hill and along the main roadway to the turnoff for Braswell's Pond. As is the case with many small lakes, the pond was dominated by big fish that devoured most of the fry before they grew large enough to fend for themselves. Corbin paid the owner a yearly fee that gave him the right to fish as much as he wanted. The only stipulation was one Corbin would have kept anyway—a strict catch and release policy for the bass.

"Who do you think we'll hook up?" he asked Billy as the truck rolled to a stop beside the gently sloping bank.

"I want Judge Ellington," Billy said, referring to one of the biggest bass in the murky waters.

"That would be fun," Corbin replied, "but I haven't seen old Mr. Murdoch in a while. I think he needs some exercise on the end of my line."

After catching them multiple times, Corbin could identify individual fish by their markings and scars. Rupert Murdoch, named in honor of the media mogul, was a craggy bass with a torn dorsal fin and a distinctive black line on the right side of his jaw.

"Rupert Murdoch hangs out over there, doesn't he?" Billy asked. He pointed to an area where thick grasses grew down into the water.

"Yes, and there's an old tree beneath the water there, just waiting to reach out and snag our lures."

Corbin unhitched the trailer and rolled the lightweight boat to the edge of the water. "Hop in," he said as soon as the boat's stern was wet. "I'll hand you the gear to stow."

The older man and the young boy worked as a team transferring poles and tackle boxes along with a small cooler. Inside the cooler was a mason jar filled with the same kind of mountain water dispensed from the rear of Red's Restaurant.

Billy knew where everything went in the boat. Corbin released the winch and let the craft settle into the water. Grabbing a rope attached to the bow, he tied it off to a wooden post so the boat wouldn't drift off with Billy alone at the helm. Corbin quickly moved the truck and trailer out of the way in case another fisherman came along.

"Stay seated!" he called out to Billy, who was standing up in the boat.

"I'm getting my life jacket," the boy replied.

"Wait for me! We'll do it together. The water is only about five feet deep there, but I don't want to have to fish you out."

"I know how to swim," Billy protested, but he sat down on the middle seat.

Corbin returned and climbed aboard. He reached under a seat and handed a life jacket to Billy, who put it on.

"Where's your life jacket?" his grandson asked.

Corbin stuck his hand under the seat again, but it came up empty. He resisted the urge to swear.

"It must have blown out during the drive over here," he said, annoyed. "If I fall in you're going to have to jump in and save me."

Billy's face grew serious.

"I'm kidding," Corbin said quickly. "When was the last time I fell in the water?"

"Uh, you got wet putting the boat in the pond the other day."

"That's not what I'm talking about. Let's go."

Corbin crouched low to keep the boat from rocking as he walked its length to the motor. Squatting down, he pulled the rope to start the engine. It sputtered but didn't fire. He tried again, and it failed to catch. Corbin took a deep breath.

"Do you need to choke it?" Billy asked.

"Yeah, I forgot."

The engine fired up after Corbin increased the richness of the mixture. Puffs of bluish-gray smoke shot out of the exhaust for a few moments. Corbin opened the throttle, and they headed toward the center of the pond.

"This is way better than rowing!" Corbin shouted over the sound of the engine.

Billy, his hands clutching the seat, faced forward and didn't turn around. When they reached the middle of the pond, Corbin shut off the motor and let them drift toward the bank.

"I don't want to spook Mr. Murdoch," he said.

Billy swung one leg over the bench and straddled it. He squinted against the late afternoon glare of the sun in a way that reminded Corbin of Ray. The boat came into the target area. Corbin picked up his homemade anchor, a cement block tied to a thick rope, and gently lowered it over the side of the boat. Using a fishing knot, Billy tied his new lure onto the end of his line.

"Pops, will you check it to make sure it's on good?" He held out his pole toward Corbin, who cradled the lure in the palm of his hand and pulled against the monofilament fishing line.

"That's a good knot. You're ready."

Sometimes they fished at the same time, but Corbin enjoyed watching Billy more than he did fishing himself. Billy flipped the bail on the open-faced reel and cast the lure about forty feet in front of the boat in the direction of the shore.

"Nice," Corbin said. "Count to twelve and start working it. I don't want the first cast to end up in a limb on the sunken tree."

Billy counted in Spanish.

"Show-off," Corbin said with a smile. "What would you have done if I told you to count to fifty?"

"We've only learned to twenty. But one of my homework assignments was to count while doing something at home before class tomorrow."

"Well, you can tell your mama you did your Spanish homework."

Largemouth bass are aggressive eaters that savagely attack prey. Billy worked the lure with a series of gentle jerks coupled with turns of the reel until the lure bumped into the side of the boat.

"Try it again," Corbin said. "And count to fifteen before starting your retrieve."

Over the next ten minutes, Billy patiently worked several depths and angles without getting a bite.

"I like your new lure, but let's try something else," Corbin suggested.

"You take a turn," Billy said. "I want you to fish too."

"Okay. Are you thirsty?"

"Yeah."

Corbin opened the cooler and handed Billy a bottle of water, then unscrewed the top of the mason jar and took a swig of moonshine. It wasn't as harsh as Beanpole's latest brew. Corbin licked his lips. He started to take another drink, then decided against it. He screwed on the top and returned the jar to the cooler. His fishing pole was already set up with a lure, and with a flick of his wrist he sent it flying. It entered the water with a plop. Corbin counted to ten in Spanish, got crossed up, and finished to eighteen in English. He began his retrieve. After two quick jerks followed by a brief pause, the fish bit.

"Fish on," he said as the pole bent sharply.

Billy watched as the fish changed directions beneath the water. "Is it a big one?" he asked.

"It's not Mr. Murdoch," Corbin said as he kept the tip of his pole high in the air above the water. "He goes down deep and shakes his head back and forth. This guy is running all over the place."

As soon as he spoke, the fish took off on a run. Corbin let it go. "Do you want to play him?" he asked Billy.

"No, Pops, he's yours."

The fish tired quickly and Corbin brought him to the side of the boat. Billy scooped him up with a net. Corbin grabbed the bass by the bottom of its mouth, which made it go limp, revealing the cavernous mouth that gave the species its name.

"I'm not sure we've met him before," Corbin said. "He's a juvenile who's survived. What do you want to call him?"

"Sammy."

"Why Sammy?"

"He's a boy at my bus stop. He was picking on me until I jumped on him the other day and held him on the ground. I didn't hit him or anything. I used the wrestling move you showed me."

Corbin wanted more details about Billy's altercation with Sammy, but the fish demanded their immediate attention. He turned it so they could inspect it.

"What do you see about Sammy that makes him stand out?"

"He's missing a piece of his back fin."

Corbin took a closer look. Sure enough, there was a notch in the fish's caudal fin.

"Yeah, maybe that happened when another fish jumped on him and held him underwater."

Billy laughed. Corbin lowered the bass into the pond, and it swam off. During the next hour and a half, Billy caught two fish and Corbin hooked one. None of the fish deserved a name. In between fish, Corbin continued to sample the beverage from the mason jar. Eventually there was only an inch or so left.

"Let's go to the far end of the pond before we call it an afternoon," he said as the sun dipped below the western hills.

"Okay," Billy replied, picking up his pole. "Do you feel bad?"

"No," Corbin answered. "Why?"

"Your voice sounds different."

Corbin cleared his throat. He didn't think his speech was slurred. He steered the boat to the place where a small stream that was part of the Cheola watershed entered the pond. Corbin cut the engine and let the boat drift.

"Pops," Billy said, pointing, "do you see that fish?"

Corbin followed the boy's hand and saw a slow, swirling movement in the water. "Yeah, let's check it out."

Corbin kept an old aluminum oar in the bottom of the boat in case the motor died or he wanted to move the boat a few feet. He dipped the oar in the water and directed them toward the fish. It was an enormous bass, moving across the surface like a submarine coming up for air.

"Don't spook it," Corbin whispered. "Get the net and hand it to me."

Corbin carefully laid down the oar and took the net from Billy.

The boat silently slid near to the fish. Corbin held the pole attached to the net up in the air with his hand, then scooped it down in the water beneath the fish.

"You got it!" Billy cried.

It took both of Corbin's hands to lift the heavy fish out of the water. The bass lay on its side in the net.

"That's Mr. Murdoch," Corbin said. "See that dark streak down his jaw? He's the only big fish in here with that marking."

"Why did he come down here?" Billy asked. "What's he eating?"

Corbin carefully picked up the fish from the net. It was limp in his hand. "Something's wrong," he said. "I think he came here to die."

"No, put him back," Billy said. "He'll swim off."

Corbin returned the fish to the water, but instead of swimming, it turned on its back and floated. Corbin shook his head.

"Pops!" Billy called out. "There's another one!"

Sure enough, about twenty feet away a smaller fish was floating on its back. Corbin paddled the boat over to it. Nearby there were other dead bass of various sizes.

"I need to tell Buck Braswell about this," Corbin said. "Something's attacked his fish. It could be a parasite outbreak."

As Billy stared silently at the dead fish, Corbin regretted that he'd personalized the bass in the pond. The fish weren't pets, but he'd made them seem that way to his grandson. He started the boat's motor, and they rode in silence to the take-out spot.

When they reached the bank, Corbin unsteadily moved to the front of the boat. Holding the bow rope in his hand, he tried to make the transition directly to the bank. Suddenly his left foot slipped and his right leg went into the water. The right side of his face crashed into the top edge of the boat.

Everything went black.

THIRTEEN

Pops!" Billy called out.

Corbin blinked his eyes and grabbed the side of the boat with his hand, but it slipped off. He tried again and managed to pull himself upright. He lunged toward the bank and fell onto his back. Stunned, he still managed to keep the bow rope in his hand.

"Are you okay?" he heard Billy ask.

Corbin touched the side of his face. His fingers came away red. "Yeah," he managed. "But it looks like I've got a little cut on my face."

He touched the sleeve of his shirt to the wound. When he saw how much blood it soaked up, he pulled a clean handkerchief from his pocket and pressed it against the cut.

"Can you get out on your own?" he asked Billy, who was looking at him anxiously from the front of the boat.

Billy jumped from the boat onto the bank and came over to him.

"I need to put some pressure on this cut for a few minutes, then I'll get the boat onto the trailer," Corbin said.

"Should we call my dad?"

"No, no. We can take care of this. You hold on to the rope while I tend to this scrape."

Corbin lay on the grass and kept the handkerchief pressed tightly against the cut. He felt light-headed, but he wasn't sure if it was from the blow to the head or the moonshine. He closed his eyes and inwardly kicked himself for bringing the mason jar along on the fishing trip. It wasn't the first time he'd done so, but it was always a bad idea. He blinked open his right eye. Billy had a tight grip on the rope attached to the boat.

"All right," Corbin said. "I'm going to sit up and see how I feel."

He hoisted himself up and hoped the light-headed sensation wouldn't return. "I'm ready to get us out of here and take you home," he said.

"What do you need me to do?"

Corbin looked at the boy. The obvious concern in Billy's face and voice deeply touched him. If Corbin hadn't already emptied his reservoir of tears at Kitty's grave, he would have choked up.

"Just hold the rope while I get the trailer."

Corbin struggled to his feet and stood still for a moment to make sure he could stand. Everything seemed to be working as it should. He lowered the handkerchief from his face, but the sudden flow of blood forced him to return it. The pressure from the handkerchief didn't seem to be slowing the bleeding as much as it should. He made his way to the truck and got in.

Corbin checked himself in the rearview mirror. There was a gash beneath his right eye that made him look like he'd been in a bare knuckle prizefight. The area around the eye would begin turning black over the next few hours. He needed to get Billy home.

Holding the handkerchief against the cut with one hand, he used the other to turn the steering wheel as he backed the trailer close to the boat. Billy stood on the bank. Corbin attached the bow rope to the winch and let Billy turn the handle that pulled the lightweight boat onto the trailer. It was the first time Corbin had allowed the boy to operate the winch, and Billy did it exactly as he'd seen Corbin do it many times before.

"Good job," Corbin said. "Hop in. I'm going to take you home. I can unhook the boat and trailer later."

Corbin turned onto the main roadway. He lowered the handkerchief, now completely soaked in blood, and checked his face again in the mirror.

Wide-eyed, Billy watched. "Pops, that looks terrible. Do you think you need to go to the hospital?"

Corbin couldn't deny that the cut was deep. Blood still seeped from the wound. "I want to take care of you first."

"There's a boy at school who's in the hospital. He has cancer," Billy said. He turned his face toward Corbin. "What is cancer? I know it's bad, but I don't understand why it makes someone get sick and die."

Corbin kept the pressure on the cut with one hand and drove the truck with the other. His brain was foggy, but talking to Billy helped.

"Uh, it's when a part of the body won't stop growing." Corbin paused as he tried to think of a simple way to explain the disease. "When this cut on my face heals up, my body won't keep making skin to cover the place that's damaged. It'll stop. Cancer doesn't stop. It keeps on getting bigger and takes away nutrients from healthy parts of the body. Have you studied cells in science class yet?"

"No."

"That's the best I can do right now. There are different kinds of cancer that work against the body in different ways." They reached the edge of town, and Corbin slowed to a stop as a light turned from yellow to red. "Who's the sick boy?"

"Josh. I don't know his last name. He's in Mrs. Ott's class."

"Josh Watson."

"Yeah. One of the girls in my class said all his hair was going to fall out because of the medicine the doctors will give him. Is that true?"

"It depends on the treatment, but it often happens. Usually the hair grows back."

Billy was quiet for a moment.

"Some of the kids in his class are going to visit him at the hospital," Billy continued. "I'd be afraid to go. I don't want to catch cancer."

"It doesn't work that way."

"How did he get it?"

Corbin gripped the wheel tightly with his one hand as he turned onto the street where Ray and Cindy lived. A thought suddenly crossed his mind.

"Maybe from the same place that made the fish at the pond sick."

Roxy had to wait over an hour for her flight to leave Chicago. She considered calling Mr. Caldweller to give him a preliminary report, but decided not to for a couple of reasons. First, she didn't know if the senior partner would feel well enough to talk, and second, she didn't want to rely on her memory to relay the information. She listened to part of the interview and began preparing a written summary on her laptop. She continued the process on the plane, but halfway through the flight to Atlanta fatigue hit, and she closed her eyes for a quick power nap.

As she reached the platform for the MARTA station at the airport, Peter called.

"Where are you?" he asked. "I called your office, and all they would tell me is that you weren't available."

Roxy told him about her sudden trip.

"That's intense," Peter replied. "I bet you're exhausted."

"Yes, but I'd like to see you."

"I'll pick you up at your station and take you out for a salad."

"Perfect."

Roxy crossed her legs and glanced out the window as the train rocked slightly back and forth on the rails. She and Peter had known each other for over a year and dated for nine months. The relationship began with a common interest in running, but Peter soon nudged her to talk about other things. At first this made Roxy uncomfortable, and she accused him of being nosy, but his persistent interest in her as a person finally won her over. As a computer geek, a large part of his brain was even more scientific than hers, but he possessed a significant dose of intuitive empathy.

The train eased into the station. Peter, a broad smile on his face, stood on the platform wearing the khakis and collared shirt that were the business casual uniform at his office. A shade over five foot ten with dark hair and brown eyes, he had the slender, deceptively strong body of a triathlete.

Roxy gave him a quick kiss on the lips. "Thanks for picking me up," she said. "After the day I've had, I'm glad to have someone take care of me."

During the short walk to the car, Peter filled her in on his day. An IT troubleshooter, he spent most of his time grinding out solutions to problems. His company worked in teams, but each analyst spent a lot of time alone. That made him more ready to talk in the evenings than Roxy, who often needed to unwind from intense interpersonal interaction.

"Did you get in a workout this morning?" he asked as they reached his car, a small hybrid.

"Yes. I was still trying to catch my breath when Caldweller called and told me I was going to Chicago."

Peter backed out of the parking space. The music that filled the car sounded unfamiliar.

"What are you listening to?" she asked. The song had a peaceful, pleasant sound.

"Christian worship," Peter answered as he turned down the volume. "Noah from work suggested I download it. I went to church with him and his wife last Sunday while you were in Alto."

Roxy was surprised. Peter had never expressed an interest in religion. She'd stopped going to church when she left home for college.

"Why were you interested in going to church?" she asked.

"I wasn't, but he took me to a place in Buckhead that was way more interesting than I thought possible."

"Are you going back?"

Peter glanced sideways at her. "Yes, and I'd like to take you with me."

Billy ran into the house with his fishing pole in his hands. Corbin wanted to leave without saying anything to Ray or Cindy, but he knew that wasn't an option. He couldn't let Billy report the accident.

Ray appeared in the front door before Corbin reached the steps to the house.

"You're a mess!" his son exclaimed.

"Yeah, I need to go home and take care of this cut."

"No, no. Come inside. Billy said you may need to go to the hospital, and I agree with him."

Cindy joined Ray at the door and put her hand to her mouth in shock. Ray took hold of Corbin's arm and guided him to the guest bathroom. Cindy and Billy followed close behind. They crowded into the small space. Cindy took a clean washcloth from the towel rack.

"I don't want to mess up a nice washcloth," Corbin said.

"Don't be silly," Cindy replied. "Billy, wait in the kitchen."

"I've already seen it," the boy protested.

"And once is enough," Cindy responded. "Go!"

Billy skulked away. Corbin lowered the handkerchief and replaced it with the slightly damp washcloth.

"You're going to need stitches," Ray said when he saw the cut. "It's hanging open."

"It stings a little bit, but the bleeding is way down."

Cindy watched with her lips pressed tightly together for a moment, then spoke. "How did it happen?"

"I slipped while taking the boat out of the water and hit my face against the gunwale."

"Why did you slip?"

Corbin looked in the mirror and saw Cindy's eyes. "The grass was wet," he replied tersely.

"Any other contributing factors?" Cindy asked. "Isn't that what a lawyer would ask?"

Corbin didn't respond, but rinsed out the cloth and returned it to his face. He needed to get away from his daughter-in-law's accusing eyes.

"Okay, I'll go to the hospital," he said.

"I'll drive you," Ray said.

"Will they do a blood test at the hospital?" Cindy asked. "You know, the kind that shows if there is alcohol in your system."

Corbin turned around and faced her. "Billy is fine," he said, raising his voice. "The first thing in my mind was taking care of him. He's home safe and sound. Isn't that enough for you? You don't have to turn this into some kind of inquisition."

"Dad, go easy with Cindy," Ray interrupted. "This has been a hard day for us too."

"Why?" Corbin asked.

"I lost my job."

FOURTEEN

W hat?" Corbin asked.

Ray looked at Cindy, who shrugged. "He'll find out eventually," she said.

"I'll tell you on the way to the hospital," Ray said.

He got an old but clean shirt from his closet and handed it to his father, who remained in the bathroom. He and Cindy stepped into the bedroom.

"You know what he's going to want you to do," she said as soon as they were alone.

"Yes, and now is as good a time as any to let him know that's not an option."

Cindy ran her fingers through her hair and set her jaw. "And you've got to talk to him about Billy. Nothing horrible happened today, but I could tell he'd been drinking the second he came through the door. This was Billy's last fishing trip. Mixing operation of a little boat with alcohol is dangerous enough; getting behind the wheel of his truck and driving is worse. I know he'll pitch a fit, but we can't take a chance. If Billy got hurt I'd never forgive myself."

While he listened to Cindy gather steam, Ray tried to come up with a reason not to impose a total lockdown on Corbin's independent relationship with his grandson, but he couldn't. Cindy was right.

"Do you want me to tell him that too?"

"I don't know if it has to be done tonight. But we can't go on like this. I'm not going to change my mind."

Ray emerged from the bedroom and found Corbin and Billy sitting at the kitchen table. Corbin still had the washcloth pressed against the cut on his face. Reddish-blue discoloration was beginning to creep up toward his eye.

"I'm thirsty," Billy said, and got up to get himself a glass of water. "Do you want one too, Pops?"

"No, thanks."

"Did you drink all the water you had in that jar?"

"Uh, no."

Ray glanced over his shoulder to see if Cindy had heard Billy's question, but she hadn't come out of the bedroom.

"Why does a bruise look red before it turns black?" Billy asked Ray. "Pops doesn't know."

"Uh, I think it's because the blood under the skin is red and turns black as it dries."

Corbin reached over and patted Billy on the arm. "You did great taking care of everything at the pond when I slipped and fell. I'm proud of you."

"Okay," Billy replied, lowering his eyes for a moment. Then he looked up. "I keep thinking about those dead fish. Are you going to tell Dad about them?"

"Maybe, but we have other important things to talk about too."

Ray led the way from the house. They got into his car, and he maneuvered it around Corbin's truck.

"So why did you lose your job?" Corbin asked.

"Steve found out I was talking to Simpkin, Brown, and Stamper about going to work with them and wasn't willing to keep me employed while we worked out the details. The way he reacted makes me suspect he already had someone in mind for my position and was just using this as an excuse to get rid of me."

"I thought you were going to join me."

"I know that's what you want, Dad, but it wouldn't work," Ray said, keeping his eyes on the road.

Corbin was silent for a few moments. "Have you signed an employment contract with Simpkin?" he finally asked.

"No, we're working out the details."

"Then it's not settled." Corbin nodded. "Who do you think Steve has in mind to replace you?"

"My guess is a young lawyer from Pittman, Brett Dortch. You probably don't know him; he's only been out of school a year or two."

"That's not a smart political move for Steve. When reelection time rolls around, he's going to need support from the whole district." Corbin glanced at Ray. "Would you consider running against him? You could beat him."

"No and no."

"That would be way better than selling your soul to the Simpkin firm," Corbin grunted. "I can't believe you'd want to work for Darryl Simpkin. He's always been such a pompous—"

"Stop it," Ray cut in. "I'm taking you to the hospital. This isn't going to turn into a debate about the merits of Simpkin, Brown, and Stamper."

"Colonel Parker couldn't stand him either," Corbin continued, undeterred. "Before he hooked up with Carl Brown, Simpkin worked for a lawyer named Brookline who moved down here from Pennsylvania. A real sleazy character. We had several cases against him. I'll never forget one case—"

Ray tuned out his father's voice. He'd heard all these stories before. Despite years of alcohol abuse and his current state of intoxication, Corbin could still remember details of long-ago insults and slights. They neared the hospital.

"So you see that you really ought to join forces with me," Corbin concluded. "I'm not giving up. The practice isn't what it used to be, but the foundation is there, and with the trial experience you've gained at the DA's office, we could turn it into something special. I'd be willing to cut back my draw to ease the transition—"

"Do you take a regular draw?" Ray interrupted. "I thought you were struggling to pay your overhead."

"That was several months ago. I've gotten in some fees and plan on getting everything back on a sound footing."

Ray pulled into a parking spot near the emergency room doors. He could hear the sound of an ambulance approaching.

"Let's get your face stitched up before we talk any more about my future. Keep the pressure on that cut."

Ray led the way across the parking lot as the ambulance, its lights flashing rapidly, approached.

"I wish I had some business cards to hand out," Corbin said. "I could prove that all the people who've accused me of being an ambulance chaser are right."

Ray managed a slight smile. "At least the blow to your head didn't destroy your sense of humor."

They reached the triage desk. Ray listened as his father answered the intake worker's questions.

"When was the last time you had a tetanus shot?" the young woman asked as she typed in Corbin's responses on a keyboard.

"Uh, more than five years."

"And what medications are you taking?"

"I'm on pills for high cholesterol, blood pressure, and a problem I have with my stomach."

"What kind of problem do you have with your stomach?" Ray asked. "I didn't know anything about that."

"Acid reflux. Nothing serious."

The woman continued down a long litany. "Have you consumed any alcohol during the past twenty-four hours?"

"Twenty-four hours?" Corbin repeated.

Ray spoke up. "Would that include what he drank last night or just what he's consumed since noon today?"

The woman's eyes got big. "Uh, let's stick to today."

Corbin cut his eyes toward Ray before he answered. "I had a couple of drinks this afternoon. Like I told you, I slipped and fell while trying to bring in my boat."

Ray wanted to elaborate on his father's affinity for bootleg liquor and mention Billy's presence on the fishing expedition. The ER was a place people came for emergencies, but the young woman at the computer wasn't the right person to referee a family feud.

"We'll get you back to an examination room as soon as possible," the woman said. "Would you like a fresh piece of gauze to hold against the cut?"

Corbin lowered the white washcloth that was now mostly red. "Yeah, that would be nice."

The woman left her station to fetch the gauze.

Corbin turned to Ray. "I know you're upset about losing your job," he said, "but it's not right for you to hound me in front of that girl. It came across as petty."

Ray didn't respond. The woman returned with a rolled-up piece of gauze. The two men sat beside each other on beige vinyl chairs with an extra chair between them. Corbin pressed the gauze against his cheek and closed his eyes for a moment.

"I'm dizzy," he said. "Maybe I've lost more blood than I thought."

"Or drank too much 'water' from the mason jar."

"It was mostly empty when I put it in the cooler," Corbin replied. "I had Billy with me and wouldn't drink more than a sip or two."

"Is that how you want me to sell it to Cindy?" Ray responded tersely. "Honey, don't be too hard on Dad. A sip or two of moonshine with his grandson in the boat is fine. And it doesn't increase the risk of a car wreck during the drive home."

"She needs to lighten up."

"Really? Mom didn't let me get in the truck with you if she knew you'd been drinking. Why would you expect us to do anything different?"

Corbin closed his eyes for a few seconds. His right eye was getting puffier and puffier.

"There's nothing I like more than spending time with Billy," Corbin said slowly. "And I'm worried you and Cindy are going to cut me off from him. I'll do better. I promise."

Ray sighed. His father didn't know Cindy's scissors had already come out of the drawer.

The young doctor who came in to stitch up Corbin's face mentioned that he hoped to become a plastic surgeon.

"Then I'm glad you can practice on a cadaver like me," Corbin said as the physician prepared to inject a numbing agent. After the shot, Corbin added, "I take all that back. I think you should be a veterinarian."

Ray watched as the doctor carefully closed the wound. Regardless of the cause of the injury, Ray felt sorry for his father. The doctor finished and applied a bandage over the wound.

"Nice job," Ray said to the physician. "When will the results of the blood test be available?"

"Within a couple of days."

"Is it a full spectrum test?"

"Don't answer that, Doc," Corbin cut in. "My son doesn't have a health care power of attorney, and I'm leaving all my estate to his sister."

It was dark outside when Ray and Corbin left the ER.

"Do you want me to drive you home? Cindy and I could bring your truck to your house in the morning."

"No, I'm better now that I have use of both hands." Corbin pulled down the car's sun visor and inspected himself in the tiny mirror. "I'd better come up with a better story than slipping in wet grass."

They reached Ray and Cindy's house.

"Let Billy know I'm going to find out what killed those fish at the headwaters of the pond," Corbin said when he got out of the car. "I bet it has something to do with the pollution coming out of Colfax. That pond is part of the Cheola watershed, and I'm going to look over the file in the case you prosecuted against the company."

"The whole case was shipped back to Atlanta per Judge Ellington's final order. All that's left is the accusation and the orders. Anyway, I doubt there's a connection. It was a limited discharge on a field. There wasn't any dumping directly into the water system."

Corbin touched the bandage beneath his eye. "Yeah, if you think that's true, you won't have any problem believing I got this cut brushing my teeth."

Roxy and Peter left the MARTA station and ate supper at a small Mediterranean restaurant with an outdoor dining area. They both ordered salads and an aromatic soup made with pureed carrots and spices.

"This is what I needed to cleanse my soul." Roxy sighed as she lowered the spoon from her lips.

They ate in silence for a few moments. Roxy's phone, which was resting beside her plate, vibrated. Hoping it wasn't Mr. Caldweller, she glanced down to read a text message.

"It's from Ray," she said, looking up from her phone. "My dad hit his head on his fishing boat and had to go to the hospital for stitches."

She quickly sent a message asking about the severity of the cut, then waited for the reply.

"Ten stitches," she said, then added, "Oh no."

"What?" Peter asked. "Did he have a concussion?"

"It's not him. Ray lost his job at the DA's office."

FIFTEEN

Corbin made it home, then leaned his head against the back glass of the truck for a few seconds. His cheek was throbbing as the local anesthetic wore off. Getting out of the truck, he unhooked the trailer and returned the boat to its place beside the carport. He ran his finger along the gunwale. The metal was smooth as when the boat left the factory. It was the sheer force of the blow that had opened the gash.

Inside the house he took the jar of moonshine from the cooler and vigorously shook what remained of the clear liquid. It had a good bead. He placed the jar on the kitchen counter and stared at it as if expecting the jar to speak. Instead he talked to it.

"If I have to choose between you and Billy," he said, "there's no contest."

Unscrewing the metal top, he took a whiff of the slightly sweet-smelling liquor, then slowly emptied it into the sink. Moonshine was probably better for cleaning pipes than for pouring down his throat.

The following morning Corbin carefully removed the bandage. Not surprisingly, the whole right side of his face was swollen and discolored. After taking a shower and carefully shaving, he rummaged around his medicine cabinet for material to make a fresh bandage. He found an oversize adhesive bandage that fit nicely over the cut.

Because his face looked so rough, he spent extra time trying to make sure the rest of him was presentable. He even put on a newer tie without any food stains on it.

Roxy called as he was driving to work. "Ray told me what happened," she said. "Are you staying home today?"

"No. I'm a lawyer, not a pro football player."

"Does your head hurt?"

Corbin couldn't deny he had a headache. "Yes, but . . ."

"It could be due to a hangover," she said.

"I was banged up from hitting the boat, not the bottle."

"I wish I could believe you."

On the heels of his concern about losing access to Billy, Roxy's words hurt more than they normally would.

"You'll be glad to know I dumped my hooch down the drain when I got home from the hospital," he said in an effort to impress her.

"You got rid of all your liquor?"

"Just the moonshine and I'm going to cut back on the other stuff."

"I hope you're serious. If not, it's a cruel joke."

Corbin stopped at a red light. Like Cindy, Roxy was as accusatory as a prosecuting attorney, but this morning Corbin wanted to hear her voice even if her words were harsh.

"Are you working on any interesting cases?" he asked.

"What?"

"I asked about your caseload."

"Oh, I'm busy."

She told him about Mr. Caldweller's rare praise for her job

performance. She was still talking when Corbin reached the office. He stayed seated in the truck to continue the conversation.

"That's good," Corbin lied.

In reality he shared Colonel Parker's lifelong disdain for lawyers who represented huge, amoral companies. But Roxy was, after all, his daughter, and he wanted her to succeed.

"Thanks. While you were in the fishing boat with Billy, I was interviewing a shadow expert in Chicago, a chemist. We hired him to help us get a better handle on a big pharmaceutical patent case."

"Shadow expert?" Corbin asked. "What's that?"

As he listened to Roxy's explanation, Corbin realized how out of touch he was with high-stakes litigation.

"Yes, he's also an expert in pesticides and herbicides," Roxy continued. "He grew up on a farm in Texas."

Corbin sat up straighter in the seat of the truck. "Does he testify for plaintiffs or defendants?"

"Probably for whoever pays him. In our case we're the plaintiff trying to protect a patent."

"What about the one involving pesticides?"

"The defendant, I think. We didn't go into detail about it."

Corbin's thoughts stayed with the chemist. "Last week Colfax pleaded guilty to a criminal charge of pollution."

"You're kidding," Roxy said. "Colfax? Evidence of a guilty plea would expose them to all kinds of liability if there's ancillary damage to a private party."

Corbin took a deep breath. "Yeah, and someone contacted me about a claim."

"What kind of claim?"

Corbin quickly laid out what he knew about the two boys with non-Hodgkin's lymphoma. He felt a surprising degree of nervous excitement as he talked.

"The mother of the older boy is the one I talked to the other day," he finished. "Her son goes to school with Billy. Getting Branson Kilpatrick to meet with me about his grandson should be easy, and I could file the two cases together."

"Who's going to finance the litigation?" Roxy asked sharply. "The out-of-pocket costs could quickly reach six figures."

Corbin swallowed. It was hard to accurately guess the litigation expenses, but his rough estimate had been much lower.

"I guess part of it would fall on me. Branson could probably pony up some money, but not at that level."

"I think you should steer clear of it," she said matter-of-factly. "It's way out of your league. This isn't a fender bender in front of a grocery store with a client who has a sore neck and goes to her chiropractor."

The excitement drained out of Corbin as quickly as air from a punctured balloon.

"Maybe you're right," he sighed. "Janelle said the same thing. I asked her to schedule an appointment for the mother of the older boy with Foxcroft and Bartlett in Gainesville."

"That's no good. Do you want me to locate a firm in Atlanta willing to meet with them? A lawsuit for a couple of kids with cancer has emotional appeal, but there won't be a claim for lost wages. That's what drives up the value in a way a jury can sink its teeth into. Future medical expenses won't work because of the statutory insurance offset if there's health coverage in place and the Medicaid lien deduction for the woman who's on the verge of bankruptcy."

Listening to Roxy break down the case so succinctly increased Corbin's respect for her more than any compliments she'd received from her boss.

"Yeah, if it's not too much trouble, send me a few recommendations."

"Sure, I'll research it this morning. Oh, and Dad . . . don't pester Ray about coming to work for you. I know you don't like Simpkin, Brown, and Stamper, but let Ray find his own way. He needs to come out of your shadow."

"How's he been in my shadow?" Corbin asked, startled.

"Come on, Dad. You got him the job at the DA's office because you were drinking buddies with Jimbo Sanders. Who else was going to hire Ray after he failed the bar exam the first time?"

"Steve Nelson kept him when he took over from Jimbo."

"Because Nelson barely knew the way to the courtroom himself. Even Ray is more qualified to try a case than he is. At the Simpkin firm, Ray will get a chance to be trained by lawyers who've been successful by Alto's standards for years. That's what he needs to give his career a boost."

"I'm at the office," Corbin said, trying not to blow up at the blatant insult to his mentoring ability. "Gotta go."

Still fuming, Corbin stormed into the office. Janelle was on the phone and looked up as he entered. Her mouth dropped open and her eyes bugged out when she saw him, and she quickly ended the call.

"What happened?" she asked.

"Roxy," Corbin replied. "She really knows how to push my buttons."

"Roxy hit you in the face?"

Corbin touched the bandage on his cheek. "No, no," he said. "I slipped taking my little fishing boat out of the water yesterday afternoon and hit the gunwale. I went to the ER and left with ten stitches in my cheek. But I was just on the phone with Roxy, and something she said ticked me off."

"Uh, okay." Janelle nodded in a way that didn't signal she completely understood.

Corbin pressed his lips together. "Did you set up an appointment for Millie Watson with Foxcroft and Bartlett yet?"

"Yes, I talked to Mr. Bartlett yesterday afternoon, and he seemed very interested. He told me the firm handled a case involving contaminated chicken feed with similar issues."

"Chicken feed? How is that similar? We're talking about people getting sick, not chickens."

"I didn't cross-examine him," Janelle sniffed. "Anyway, her appointment is this morning. I called Ms. Watson, and she told me to tell you thanks again for meeting with her."

"Whatever," Corbin sputtered as he turned away and went into his office.

———

Ray and Cindy sat at the kitchen table drinking coffee after Billy left the house to catch the school bus.

"At least I don't have to rush out and get ready for court," Ray said as he took another sip.

"It's really hard for me to see a bright side to this," Cindy replied.

"I know," Ray said forlornly. "I should have shut my door before talking to Nate. It was a stupid move on my part, but Steve's reaction was way out of line. That's what makes me suspect he wanted to get rid of me anyway."

"Are you sure you didn't do something wrong?"

Ray put down his cup. "That sounds like something Roxy would ask me."

"Sorry." Cindy got up and put a piece of bread in the toaster.

"I'm craving anything I can slather with strawberry jam. I ate a peanut butter and jelly sandwich for lunch yesterday, and you know I'm not a huge fan of peanut butter."

Ray rinsed his cup at the kitchen sink and put it in the dishwasher. He felt Cindy's arms around his waist and put his hands on top of hers.

"I've got your back," she whispered in his left ear. "Also, if you ever compare me with Roxy again, I'm going to bite off your ear."

Ray laughed and turned around to kiss her.

"No more Roxy comparisons," he said. "I promise."

"Are you going to check on your dad?"

"I don't know. An evening trapped in the ER with him was enough father-son time for a while. I'll check with Janelle later in the day and see how he's doing."

"And don't forget we're going to have to talk to him about Billy," Cindy said. "As much as I want them to have a good relationship, there have to be limits."

"I said enough last night to get him thinking."

"To mean anything, those thoughts had better turn into actions."

Corbin slammed shut the door of his office and plopped down in the chair behind his desk. He needed a drink. He pulled open the lower drawer, then remembered he'd finished off the bourbon the previous day right before Millie Watson showed up. He closed the drawer and continued to fume about Roxy, Janelle, and everyone else lined up against him.

He glanced down at the legal pad on top of his desk and saw the information he'd taken from Millie. Underlined at the top of the sheet was the young woman's cell phone number. He stared at it for several seconds, then picked up the phone.

"Millie," he said when the young woman answered the phone. "This is Corbin Gage. Have you left yet for your meeting with Mr. Bartlett?"

"No."

"Great. Don't go to Gainesville. Come see me instead."

"What about Mr. Bartlett?"

"I'll take care of it. What time can you be here?"

"Uh, about thirty minutes. But it's not just me. The Kilpatricks are coming too."

"Even better. Bring them with you."

"But . . . you can see us right away?"

Corbin glanced down at his calendar. It was depressingly empty.

"Yes, I'll be able to work you in as soon as you get here."

He hung up the phone. Colonel Parker would never let a big case escape to another lawyer. Corbin canceled the appointment in Gainesville. Then he set down the phone and reality set in.

The responsibility for helping two cancer-stricken boys and their families was about to wrap itself around his soul.

SIXTEEN

C orbin lay low in his office and didn't tell Janelle what he'd done. Normally he'd ask her to prepare contracts and medical release forms for the clients to sign at the initial meeting. But he'd reached his limit of pushback from the secretary. He wasn't going to let her roll her eyes again and pretend to be protecting him. So instead he did some quick reading on the Internet about possible links between fertilizer and cancer.

There were as many divergent opinions as there were experts to give them. Rather than discouraging him, this made Corbin confident there might be a case. One of the major hurdles in toxic tort litigation is surviving a defendant's motion for summary judgment designed to end a lawsuit before it has the chance to reach a jury. Differing opinions about causation create issues of fact that juries, not judges, have to decide.

The phone on his desk buzzed.

"Why are all these people here to see you?" Janelle asked in an intense whisper. "There's not an empty seat."

"I'll be right out," Corbin replied.

He straightened his tie and pressed down one corner of the bandage covering the cut on his face. Walking into the reception area, he didn't have to look at Janelle to know she was scowling at him.

"Good morning," he said to the group. "Just to let everyone know, I cut my face yesterday while dragging my fishing boat out of Braswell's Pond. I'd been fishing with my grandson. Let's talk in the conference room."

The conference room was on the opposite side of the reception area from his office. Because he was avoiding Janelle, Corbin hadn't prepared it for the meeting. There were several law books on the table and sheets of paper strewn about. He began to clear off the table.

"Sit anywhere you like," he said. "Does anyone want a cup of coffee or glass of water?"

Millie asked for a coffee with cream and sugar, Branson wanted a black coffee, and Branson's son, Tommy, requested coffee with sugar. Corbin scribbled the orders on a legal pad.

"Are you going to charge us anything to meet with us?" Larissa asked nervously in a slow Southern twang.

"No, no," Corbin reassured her. "And the drinks are on the house too," he said with a smile. "This is a time for us to get together and talk a bit about what's going on with the boys and a possible connection between their illness and Colfax. I'll ask a few questions, listen to you, and let you ask me anything you want. You're under no obligation to hire me. I've known Branson for many years, and he can vouch for me."

Corbin left the conference room with the drink orders. He marched across the reception area toward Janelle with the sheet of paper in his hand.

"Don't start," he said as her mouth opened. "Here are their drink requests. Is there a pot of coffee brewing?"

"Yes," Janelle replied crisply. "But no decaf."

"Uh, I think everybody wants regular."

Janelle glanced at the sheet of paper. "What about Branson's daughter-in-law?" she asked.

"Sure, get her one too. It'll do her good. She's nervous."

"She should be," Janelle replied.

Corbin ignored the dig and spun around on his heels. Back in the conference room, he sat at the head of the table.

"Let's get started," he said. "First, is it okay if we meet as a group? I'm sure there are facts common to both situations, but you have to consent to a joint meeting."

The Kilpatrick clan quickly agreed.

"It's okay with me," Millie said. "But do I need to ask my husband?"

Corbin remembered that her husband was in jail for a DUI. "As Josh's mother you can act on his behalf," he assured her.

He began collecting information and was busily taking notes when Janelle appeared with the coffee.

"This is my legal assistant, Janelle Griffin," Corbin said as she distributed the drinks. "We've worked together for over twenty years. She answers the phone, and if I'm not available she can take a message. I try to return all calls within twenty-four hours."

Janelle rolled her eyes then left the room, taking her negative vibe with her.

"How do you feel about going up against Colfax?" Tommy asked. "They pretty much run this town."

"I've never represented Colfax and never will, no matter what they offer to pay me," Corbin replied. "And everyone walks into the courthouse through the same door."

Corbin then told the group about the criminal case he'd observed and the dead fish in Braswell's Pond. When he finished, Millie Watson was wiping her eyes with a tissue, and Branson Kilpatrick scowled with barely concealed fury.

"That's horrible," Millie sniffled. "If the poison they're

dumping in the water is killing fish, then think about what it's doing to my Josh—"

"I'm not telling you about that to upset you," Corbin said in a reassuring tone of voice. "It may not be related, but enough circumstantial evidence can lead to a causal connection. In virtually every case like this, the key is opinion evidence from expert witnesses."

"It's a good thing nobody from Colfax is in this room," Branson said, biting off his words. "I'm not sure I could hold myself back."

Corbin had never seen Branson so mad. But if Billy were as sick as Mitchell, Corbin would feel the same way. However, he didn't want the meeting to overheat with emotion.

He kept his voice calm. "As I said, we'll have to hire scientists who can review the evidence and tell us if what Colfax did made the boys sick."

"Who's going to pay for that?" Tommy asked.

"We'll have to talk about it. No attorney fees are charged in a case like this unless money is paid by the defendant company or its insurance carrier, but the out-of-pocket costs of litigation are ultimately your responsibility."

"I don't like the sound of that." Tommy shook his head. "I looked at the website for the law firm we were going to see in Gainesville. They didn't say anything about us having to pay for anything, and they claimed to know a bunch of experts who worked specially with them on cases."

"I guarantee you they would tell you the costs of litigation are handled differently from attorney fees," Corbin replied.

"You paid for me to see a doctor when I busted up my leg in the motorcycle wreck," Tommy said. "And you didn't charge me for the doctor's deposition until we settled up with the insurance company. What's changed since then?"

Corbin pushed his hair away from his forehead. Tommy was

right. When Corbin had represented him almost a decade earlier in the personal injury case, it made sense to advance the cost of a medical evaluation and deposition because it significantly increased the potential return.

"I remember that, but this is going to be on a much bigger scale, and we could be looking at thousands and thousands of dollars to do this right."

"That's a deal breaker for us," Tommy said. "We don't have that kind of money."

Millie Watson just looked bewildered.

Backed into a corner, Corbin could feel the opportunity to handle the cases slipping away. He waited for Branson to speak up, but the landscaper remained silent.

"Tommy, I tell you what," Corbin said. "Because I've known you and your family for so many years, I'll agree to advance the cost to investigate the cases. All I'll need is a signed contract hiring me as your lawyer and agreeing to pay me back if it turns out we have a case and win. The same goes for Millie."

Tommy looked skeptical. "Dad, what do you think?" he asked his father.

"I'm mad enough about what's happened to do something I'd regret, and I think Colfax should be held responsible. But none of us has any extra money to spend on a lawsuit. Corbin, if you're willing to take on the company, then I'd recommend they let you do it. But you're going to be on your own financing this thing. It's like when I bid on a landscaping job. When I set a price, I have to follow through even if there are a bunch of rocks I didn't know about hiding beneath the surface. There are going to be rocks down this road, and you're the one who's going to have to deal with them."

Any hope that Branson would help defray the litigation costs was gone, leaving Corbin caught like a bass on a treble hook. This was a huge decision, one that could ruin him financially. He put his hands together on the table in front of him.

"Branson, you remember Colonel Parker, don't you?" he asked.

"Yeah, sure."

"He used to say a lawyer afraid to take a risk to help a client should hang up his shingle and sell life insurance."

Corbin made eye contact with each person in the room. "I'll fund the case," he said. "You deserve someone who's willing to fight for your boys."

Roxy slipped her cell phone into her purse. Maybe the blow to her father's head had done some good. Convincing him not to take on a high-risk, prohibitively expensive litigation against Colfax hadn't been as hard as she expected. The bigger challenge would be forcing him to realize he needed to let Ray loose so he could fly on his own. The thought that her brother might end up trapped in the same office as their father sent a shudder down her spine.

She got off the elevator. Her first stop was the desk of Mr. Caldweller's legal assistant.

"How's he feeling?" she asked.

"Ask him yourself. He's been here for over an hour, buzzing me every five minutes wanting to know if you've arrived yet." The light on the assistant's phone lit up. "That's him," she said.

"Tell him I'm on my way."

Roxy made her way to the senior partner's office, a long room that featured an expansive plate glass window with a panoramic view. Mr. Caldweller was typing on his keyboard when she appeared in the doorway. He motioned for her to enter.

"Good morning," she said when he turned his chair away from his computer. "I'm glad you're doing so much better."

"Antibiotic injections are miracle drugs. Once it hit, I came out of the cave in a hurry."

"That's great. I remember once—"

Caldweller interrupted her. "I checked my inbox this morning and didn't see a memo from you about your meeting with Dr. Sellers. I need it ASAP. I've scheduled a conference call with the client for ten o'clock. It's the only time we could get all the decision makers on the line at once."

"I'm still working on it," Roxy replied numbly. "It's number one on my to-do list."

Caldweller gave her a steely look. "Are you suggesting I cancel the meeting and tell the client it's because my associate didn't do her job?"

"I wrote part of it while waiting for the plane in Chicago and during the flight. I didn't know you'd need it so soon . . ."

"And you didn't finish it when you got home? What about first thing this morning?"

Roxy felt trapped. To unwind the previous night, she'd stayed up and watched TV for over an hour. And of course she'd gone for her usual early morning run before coming into the office.

"I should have done it," she said. "There's no excuse."

"It's a question of priorities, isn't it?"

"Yes." She looked at her watch. Just past eight. "What if I have something on your desk by quarter past nine, then debrief you from nine thirty until time for the call? Will that work?"

"It's going to have to. And it had better be good. I don't want to dodge a question."

"Since I met with the expert, do you want me to participate?"

"No. You'll find an assignment on your desk that I want you to work on for the rest of the day."

Roxy walked rapidly to her office, where she took thirty seconds to see what the new job involved. If Caldweller expected her to complete it before leaving the office, it would be a long, long day.

Summoning every available brain cell into action, she dived into the memo for the ten o'clock conference call—thankful as always for her machine-gun speed on a keyboard. Locating a law firm to help the people with the claim against Colfax dropped off her mental radar.

———

There was lightness in Corbin's steps as he left the office and walked down the sidewalk. As people and cars passed by, he savored the secret knowledge that he was about to unleash a legal maelstrom that would rip from one end of the community to the other. Those who'd written him off as a washed-up old plaintiff's lawyer would have to reassess his premature demise.

His feet headed in the direction of Red's Restaurant, but when he reached the corner to cross the street, he hesitated. He wanted to celebrate, but guzzling a glass of mountain water didn't seem the proper way to do so. He needed to be mentally sharp. Turning around, he retraced his steps to a soup and salad place where Kitty had liked to eat. As he munched on a fresh cucumber, he wished he could tell her about the new case. She would have approved—of both the case and his choice of eating place.

SEVENTEEN

Ray tapped the steering wheel with his fingers as he drove to his lunch meeting with Nate Stamper. He saw his father enter the soup and salad place and honked the horn, but Corbin was already through the front door.

Ray continued past the city limits to the Rusk County Country Club, a nine-hole golf course with a small restaurant in the club-house. Ray had only eaten there a handful of times. He parked beside Nate's new Lexus and went inside.

Nate was coming out of the bar with a mixed drink in his hand. "Do you want anything?" he asked, raising his glass.

"No, thanks." Ray would have welcomed a soothing glass of wine, but he'd promised Cindy he'd never drink during the workday.

"Thanks for agreeing to get together on short notice," Ray said, trying to sound casual. They sat down at a table for two. "Before we talk about anything else, I wanted to pass along some news directly before you hear any rumors."

"Is it about you getting fired?"

Ray swallowed, but his mouth was dry. "I knew word would get out quickly, but not that fast. How did you find out?"

"A client told Mr. Simpkin but didn't have any details. What happened? Tell me you didn't make a huge mistake."

"No mistakes. Steve gave me the boot because he found out I was talking to you about a job. He considered it a breach of loyalty."

Nate grunted. "I think that's just an excuse to bring in someone else."

"I agree. Anyway, I wanted to see if we could move up the timetable for the transition to your firm. I know you said the partners would discuss it the first of the month—"

"And you'd like to be able to tell your wife you have a job and won't have to file for unemployment," Nate cut in with a smile.

"Yeah." Ray gave a nervous laugh.

A waitress took their lunch order, but Ray kept his eye on Nate, who took a sip of his drink.

"I figured that's why you wanted to talk," Nate said. "So I huddled with Simpkin and Brown before driving over here."

At that moment, a man with a booming voice hailed Nate from across the room and came over to their table. The man launched into a story about a round of golf the two men had played a few weeks earlier. Apparently they'd lost a hundred dollars to their playing partners because Nate missed a three-foot putt on the final hole.

"My five-year-old could sink that putt eight out of ten times," the man said. "You choked, big-time."

"And who hit a nine iron twenty feet over the green from forty feet away two holes earlier?" Nate countered. "If we'd halved that hole, my putt wouldn't have meant anything."

"You still owe me a drink," the man said.

"And you haven't paid my legal fees for the lease I prepared for that piece of commercial property you own on Hixson Street."

"The check is in the mail."

"Right. I'll hold my breath till it comes." Nate motioned toward Ray. "Charlie, this is Ray Gage. He's worked at the DA's office for several years and will be joining our firm as soon as we iron out the details."

Ray looked at Nate, who had a big smile on his face.

Charlie extended his hand. "Nice to meet you," he said. "I'd rather be Nate's law partner than depend on him to sink a putt."

"Next time we'll see who makes the money shot," Nate said.

Charlie moved away.

"Does that mean I have the job?" Ray asked, just to be sure.

"With Charlie as your witness." Nate patted Ray on the shoulder. "It wasn't a hard sell. Simpkin and Brown knew we needed to snatch you up. We'll prepare a written employment contract after our monthly meeting. I think you'll be pleasantly surprised at the starting salary."

Roxy didn't have time for lunch. She nibbled raw carrot sticks at her desk, then popped a caramel into her mouth for dessert. As soon as the caramel dissolved, she replaced it with another. It created a bulge in her cheek that she quickly hid when Mr. Caldweller appeared in her doorway.

"How was the phone conference?" she asked as she maneuvered the caramel into the center of her mouth.

"Satisfactory," Caldweller answered. "You dodged a bullet and saved us from getting blindsided by our own client. The head of R&D wasn't happy when he realized some of his own people had tried to bury data. Our shadow expert in Chicago earned his fee on that point alone."

"What is the client going to do about it?" Roxy positioned the caramel so it wasn't a threat to stick to her teeth.

"Give us greater flexibility to work out a settlement. We'll put up as hard a front as we can for the other side, but when it comes to crunch time they know it will be better to pay for a few more months of exclusive distribution of the drug than try to shut the door on release of the generics. The money side will be more an accounting function than a chemical one, and since we know the case won't go to trial, I'm going to let you take a more active role in the litigation."

Roxy's eyes opened wider. The senior partner could jerk her from the basement to the penthouse so fast it made her head spin.

"Uh, if you think I'm ready—"

"You're ready to do what I tell you to do. Once the CFO realized we're not going to go to trial, he wants to keep a lid on legal fees. You bill at less than half my hourly rate."

"Yes, sir."

"I dictated a memo to the e-file that you should read. We're going to request mediation before discovery is completed."

"Won't that tip the other side off to our willingness to settle?"

"Not if we raise a stink in discovery and set it up to informally address discovery issues. We'll designate a former judge as mediator, then float the idea of settlement at the mediation without looking too eager."

Roxy doubted she could finesse a move like that and sell it.

"I'll handle the mediation," Caldweller said as if reading her thoughts. "Your job is to be as aggressive as you can be in discovery so I can look like the good guy at the mediation."

Roxy burst out laughing. Fortunately the caramel had shrunk enough that it didn't come shooting out of her mouth. Caldweller glared at her for a moment, then a grin creased his face.

"Okay," he said. "You've made your point."

Roxy covered her mouth with her hand as Caldweller's grin grew.

"That's the kind of story you can tell when I retire," the senior partner said, pointing his finger at her. "Until then I want to maintain my image."

Roxy wiped her eyes and took a deep breath. "I have no doubt about your ability to do that, sir."

Corbin finished lunch and returned to the office. He made a couple of phone calls, then spent the rest of the afternoon behind closed doors researching different courses of action against Colfax. Forty years removed from law school, he felt like a first-year student wrestling with a hypothetical case study developed by a sadistic torts professor. Strict liability, negligence, hazardous substances, trespass, public nuisance, fraudulent concealment, and other concepts ricocheted around inside his head.

He jotted down notes and drew arrows from one thought to another, but when he looked at what he'd done an hour later, he wasn't sure why some of the arrows existed. What he wanted was a theory that would make the company strictly liable for injuries caused by its actions, bypassing the need to prove negligence. If Colfax introduced a substance inherently dangerous to public health into the environment, and the dangerous substance made the boys sick, Corbin would automatically get a chance to make a plea for justice and compensation in front of a jury. He read cases about asbestos, benzene, cigarettes, and hazardous waste. But until he knew exactly what Colfax dumped onto the land, he wouldn't know which path to take.

At five o'clock he leaned back in his chair and rubbed his hands against his temples. He was getting a headache that would only worsen if he didn't do something about it. Not sure if Janelle was still around, he buzzed her desk.

"Yes," she answered.

"Are you still here?"

"Unless you fired me and forgot to tell me, I work for you."

"And usually leave around four thirty."

"I've been busy."

Corbin went into the reception area. Janelle was surrounded by stacks of papers.

"What's all this?" he asked.

"Medical records. I faxed release forms to the local doctors and drove over to pick up copies so we wouldn't have to wait for them to be mailed. Of course, the hospital records and information from the out-of-town specialists will be delivered in the usual way from a copy service. They should be here next week."

Corbin picked up a sheet of paper. It was an office note from Mitchell Kilpatrick's pediatrician. The report was filled with unfamiliar medical terms that Corbin knew would have to become part of his vocabulary.

Janelle continued. "I'm starting an index for each boy. There's no way we can keep this much stuff straight without continually organizing it. Did you know there are three main types of non-Hodgkin's lymphoma that affect children?"

"No," Corbin replied. "And both boys had better have the same kind. Otherwise, there may not be a link between the disease and a chemical exposure."

"Are you sure about that?"

Corbin hesitated. "Not really. I don't know enough to say anything with certainty. I've spent all afternoon trying to wrap my head around the different legal theories. My brain can't ramp up as fast as it used to."

"I have a solid theory about that," Janelle said.

"Keep it to yourself."

"One thing you do want to know," she said.

"What's that?"

Janelle touched the thickest stack of the records in front of her. "The boys are getting treatment, but there may be options out there that require more money or better health care coverage. Lymphoma can be aggressive. If you want to help these folks, you're going to have to act fast. What did you tell the families was the goal of the litigation?"

"To make Colfax pay damages if its actions caused the boys to get sick. You know the company is going to do everything it can to get the cases dismissed and then drag them out as long as possible."

"If that happens, you could end up with wrongful death cases."

Corbin's headache worsened. "Go home," he said. "I'm ready to leave too. These records will be waiting for us tomorrow."

Corbin locked the door of the office. He needed a stiff drink. On his way out of town he passed the Hopewell Methodist Church, the place Max Hogan mentioned as the location for a local AA meeting. There were several cars in the parking lot, and Corbin recognized Max's vehicle. Jimmy Broome, the auto parts store owner, was walking across the parking lot. Corbin didn't slow down.

Later that night Corbin was dozing in the recliner in his living room after a steady diet of bourbon on the rocks for supper when his phone vibrated. It was a text message from Roxy, identifying three law firms as good candidates to evaluate possible litigation against Colfax. He fumbled with his phone and deleted the message.

The following morning Corbin had a pretrial conference in front of Judge Perry in a car wreck case. Hung over, he arrived at the office ten minutes before he was supposed to be in court.

Janelle scolded him as soon as he walked through the door. "In all the hoopla yesterday, did you forget about the Anderson case?"

"Maybe," Corbin answered grumpily, "but I remembered when I saw your cheerful face."

"At least it's good for something. I'm finishing up the proposed pretrial order."

Corbin went into his office and picked up the thin file. His client had suffered a whiplash injury in a rear-end collision but only missed ten days from work and had less than two thousand dollars in medical expenses, mostly tests to rule out a more serious problem. He returned to Janelle's desk.

"Judge Perry likes to do his own orders," Corbin said.

"That's why I copied the one he issued in the Johnston case a few months ago. Maybe he'll sign this because it looks familiar. You know he'll chew you out if you don't have something prepared, even in a little case like this."

"Little? Don't start agreeing with the insurance company's lawyer."

Janelle wrinkled her nose. Corbin turned toward the door.

"Corbin," Janelle called after him.

He turned around. "What?"

"Is there a reason you're wearing one brown sock and one blue?"

Corbin glanced down. He scooted his pants down a fraction of an inch so they covered more of his shoes. "If I'm able to get this case settled, I'll buy extra pairs of both colors."

"That won't solve the root problem!" Janelle called after him as he walked out the door.

It was a pleasant morning, and the fresh air helped dispel some of the stupor from Corbin's brain. Inside the courthouse he immediately began fielding questions about what happened to his face. He quickly developed a stock reply.

"Got it fighting a monster bass at Braswell's Pond while fishing with my grandson," he said. "The fish won."

Judge Perry and Judge Ellington conducted pretrial conferences in their offices, not the courtroom. Corbin entered the waiting area and repeated his fishing story for the judge's secretary, a plump woman who formerly worked for Jimbo Sanders in the DA's office. As soon as he finished, a young lawyer with a square jaw and shortly cropped brown hair rushed through the door.

"I'm Henry Byram," he said, slightly out of breath. "I'm here for the pretrial conference in Anderson v. Cochran."

Corbin extended his hand and introduced himself. Hope of resolving the case evaporated when he saw that the insurance defense firm had sent an attorney who barely looked old enough to be a law school graduate.

"Where's Jack Granville?" Corbin asked.

"He's number two on the docket for a federal case in Atlanta."

"Do you have authority to settle the case?"

"Yes."

"The judge is ready," the secretary interrupted.

"We'll talk afterwards," Corbin said, and led the way into Judge Perry's chambers.

Upon graduation from law school, Dexter Perry came to Alto to work for Simpkin and Brown, and also cut his teeth as an insurance defense lawyer. He and Corbin had been on opposite sides of at least twenty cases over the years. Corbin found Perry to be a sneaky lawyer who interpreted his obligation to his client as justification to see how close he could get to deceit without crossing the line into outright lying. Perry brought his defense bias with him to the bench. Corbin much preferred Judge Ellington, who at least often made both sides of a case mad.

Judge Perry raised his eyes when he saw the bandage on Corbin's face. Corbin quickly repeated his story.

"Is your grandson okay?" the judge asked.

"Yes, he's a trouper."

The lawyers sat down. Because he represented the plaintiff, Corbin spoke first.

"Judge, as you can see, this is a personal injury case, and I've prepared a standard pretrial order," he said. He placed the order on the edge of the desk and handed another copy to Byram.

"Discovery is complete," Corbin continued. "We're going to call our medical witness to testify at the hearing."

"The chiropractor?" the judge asked.

"Yes."

"Then we'd like the chance to depose him in advance of trial," Byram responded.

"They've had nine months to do that," Corbin answered. "Dr. Hannah was identified in our responses to their interrogatories, and they've known he provided treatment to the plaintiff."

While he talked, Corbin could sense Byram shifting nervously in his seat. The young associate wouldn't want to return to Atlanta and inform his boss they were going to have to cross-examine the chiropractor without the benefit of a deposition.

"Your Honor," Byram began.

"No need to respond, counselor," the judge cut in. "I'm going to let you depose Dr. Hannah. How much time do you need?"

"Four months," Byram replied.

"I object." Corbin raised his voice. "This case is set for the trial calendar next month."

"And won't be prejudiced by the delay," the judge answered. "I'll grant the defendant's request and include it in the pretrial order. Any other depositions?"

"We'd like to retake the plaintiff's deposition," the defense lawyer said.

"On what grounds?" the judge asked.

"Newly discovered evidence."

"What kind of evidence?" Corbin asked, turning in his chair.

"Surveillance video," Byram replied smugly.

"You haven't supplemented your responses to my interrogatories and identified that type of information," Corbin shot back.

Byram handed Corbin some papers. "Here."

Corbin quickly read a generic description that revealed nothing beyond the name of a private detective.

"Then I'd like to depose the private detective," he said to the judge.

"Certainly, but only after the defense retakes your client's deposition. This further supports the need to bump the case down the trial calendar. Anything else?"

"Not from the defendant," Byram replied.

"No," Corbin groused.

The lawyers stood up to leave.

"Mr. Gage, please stay for a minute," the judge said.

"I'll wait for you in the hallway," Byram said.

The young lawyer left, and the judge spoke.

"I found out this morning that Ray is going to leave the DA's office and work with Simpkin, Brown, and Stamper. He's turned into a fine trial lawyer, and I'm sure you're proud of him."

Corbin knew that from Judge Perry's point of view, Ray's going to work with the judge's former firm was a big step up. He managed a crooked grin.

"We'll see how it goes. Ray has worked hard and tried a lot of cases. I never would have fit in—" He stopped.

"No, you wouldn't," the judge said. "But I think he'll do great."

Corbin turned to leave.

"Any chance of settling this case?" Perry touched the file on his desk.

"We're going to discuss it now."

"Good. Let me know what happens. If you can't resolve it, I'll have the pretrial order signed by the end of the day."

Corbin stepped into the hall. He could see a mixture of pity and disrespect in the young lawyer's eyes. "What do you have?" he asked, pressing past Byram's youthful arrogance.

"If we don't settle and have to take these additional depositions, there won't be an offer. We'll take our chances in court."

"Which is where I've lived for the past four decades," Corbin replied flatly.

"I can offer forty-five hundred, which includes the medical lien. You'll have to take care of that."

It was barely on the verge of acceptable, but the cost of taking the depositions would eat into Mr. Anderson's possible recovery.

"I'll talk to my client and let you know," Corbin said.

"The offer is only on the table until five o'clock tomorrow," Byram said. "Then it's automatically withdrawn."

"Is that supposed to scare me?" Corbin replied.

Byram blinked his brown eyes, and Corbin knew he'd caught the young lawyer off guard. He couldn't resist needling him a bit more.

"Oh, and be sure to tell Jack Granville you came up here and thoroughly intimidated me. Will you do that? Then ask him to tell you about the case we tried to a verdict about fifteen years ago. He'll remember it." Corbin turned and walked away.

The formerly refreshing air outside the courthouse did little to dissipate the steam coming out of his ears as he waited to cross the street. He was irritated at Henry Byram, but also miffed at himself for letting the young lawyer get under his skin. He would need to do a better job of keeping his emotions in check in the Colfax litigation.

But what upset Corbin more was the judge praising Ray's decision to join forces with Simpkin, Brown, and Stamper. Judge Perry was right about the development of Ray's ability as a trial lawyer, but both he and Roxy were wrong that Ray should throw away his talent working for someone like Darryl Simpkin. Corbin's relationship with his son wasn't what it should be, but he still had an obligation as his father to try to keep him from making a huge mistake.

Corbin pulled out his phone and called Ray.

EIGHTEEN

Roxy stared out her office window. She and Ray had just finished one of their more honest discussions about their father, a conversation that was long overdue.

"You've made the right decision about what's best for Billy," Roxy said after Ray explained what he'd done. "Just because Dad didn't put up a fight, don't get blindsided if he comes at you from another angle. He's cagy."

"I don't know. You should have seen the look in his eyes at the hospital. He was hurt in more ways than one."

"That's what I'm talking about. He'll mess with your mind. He's never honestly looked in the mirror, so when he tries to manipulate everyone around him, he doesn't feel guilty about it. Mom never could separate the image of who she wanted him to be from the reality of who he was."

"And she never stopped hoping and praying for him. Who's going to do that now?"

"Not me. I used to lie awake at night worrying about him getting drunk and killing someone, but I had to stop because it was out of my control. Now I don't expect anything from him, so I can't be disappointed. Make your decision and stick to it. Protecting Billy from danger isn't an option. Cindy is 100 percent right."

"I guess so."

"Oh, and I told Dad the other day to stop pestering you and let you find your own way as a lawyer."

"You talked to him?"

"After I found out he'd cut his face. For us it was a good conversation. I told him it would be great if you went to work for the Simpkin firm and warned him not to jump in and micromanage your career. I also told him to steer clear of a crazy lawsuit he was thinking about filing against the fertilizer company. For once he seemed to listen."

"It still hurts to think—"

"Hold steady," Roxy cut in. "Living in Alto you can't avoid him like I can, but you need to transition to as healthy a relationship as possible. Using the word 'limits' with him is perfect. It sounds harsh, but it's the truth."

"Yeah, you're right," Ray replied slowly. "As usual."

"Let's talk again soon."

Roxy replayed in her mind what she'd said to Ray. As the child of an alcoholic, she knew the desire to control as much of her life as possible was based on the emotional chaos she'd experienced growing up. A troubled childhood could either destroy a person or make her stronger. She'd chosen the path of survival and strength. But that didn't help her shake the memory of the sorrow that never left her mother's eyes. Kitty had been too sweet a soul to suffer such deep disappointment.

Corbin ignored Janelle, went into his office, and closed the door. He stared at a picture on his credenza of Billy holding a long stringer of fish. One Saturday they'd happened on a bunch of bream huddled together at the shallow end of Hackburn's Lake, their other favorite fishing spot. Billy pulled the fish out of the water as fast as Corbin could bait the hook. Corbin cut off thin filets, rolled the fish in cornmeal, and fried them in hot oil. The sweet meat tasted better than candy.

There was a light knock on Corbin's door. He didn't respond. Janelle should have been able to tell from his body language that he wanted to be left alone. There was another knock, and then the door opened and Ray appeared.

"I got your call," he said. "How's the eye?"

"What do you think?" Corbin replied, touching the bandage.

"The bruising is worse. Has there been any bleeding?"

"No. Come in and have a seat."

Although they'd meet for lunch occasionally, it had been months since Ray had visited the office. Corbin glanced around and regretted the mess he'd failed to clean up.

"There's something I need to talk to you about," Ray began.

"I already know. Judge Perry couldn't wait to congratulate me about your move to Simpkin, Brown, and Stamper. You'd have thought you won the lottery. Have you signed an employment contract yet?"

"No, but the offer is solid. Nate Stamper confirmed it yesterday. All we need to work out are the specific terms."

"Then it's not finalized."

"In my mind it's set," Ray said, looking directly into Corbin's eyes. "I know what you think about it and why you feel that way. But it's my life, my career, and my family."

Corbin shifted in his chair. "But I thought we were going to talk seriously about the possibility of you coming in with me. The potential you could earn in a contingency practice is way more than what you're looking at grinding it out by the hour over there."

"Potential isn't what I'm interested in, Dad. I want security, and a chance to learn."

Corbin leaned forward. "Colonel Parker was the finest trial lawyer in this circuit, and he passed everything he knew along to me. I admit that I've not applied myself as much as I should have the past few years, but if you were in the office it would be like fresh wind in my sails."

"I don't want to hurt your feelings." Ray shook his head. "But that's not happening. Not now, not ever."

"Is this you talking or Cindy?"

"It's my decision. She agrees."

Corbin glanced down at the floor for a moment, then looked up with obvious disappointment in his eyes. "I had to try."

"I know, and I appreciate the opportunity even though I'm not going to take it."

Corbin swiveled sideways in his chair.

"One other thing," Ray said. "I need to talk to you about Billy."

"What about him?"

"You saw this coming the other night in the ER. We're going to put limits on your time with him. I know you love him, but we can't risk a situation where your drinking puts him in danger. It was bad enough that you got hurt, but what if something had happened to him?"

"He wasn't in any danger."

"You drove him to our house after you'd been drinking on the boat. That's not going to happen again."

"I was fine."

"No, you weren't, Dad. I'm not saying you slipped and fell because you were drunk, but you were impaired. It was obvious to me at the hospital, and I bet your blood alcohol content would confirm it."

Corbin wrinkled his brow and pushed his hair away from his face. "Is this your idea of punishing me?" he asked in a husky voice. "I've made plenty of mistakes in my life, but my relationship with Billy isn't one of them."

"Are you even listening to me?" Ray asked in exasperation. "All I'm saying is there are going to be limits. If something happened to Billy while he was with you, it would devastate you."

"He broke his arm when Cindy took him to the playground."

"Come on. You know what I'm talking about."

"What kind of limits?"

"Cindy and I will talk it over with you later."

"I can imagine how that conversation will go," Corbin grunted. "Anything else you want to say to beat me down? You won't listen to my advice about your legal career, and you don't give a rip about my relationship with my grandson."

"That's it for now," Ray said testily.

Corbin watched his son's broad back disappear through the doorway. A few seconds later Janelle appeared.

"What do you want?" he asked.

"Are you going to tell me what happened in court?"

"That's not important. I just talked to Ray, and he's not going to let me see Billy on my own."

"What?"

Corbin pushed his hair out of his face with his hand. "That's not totally accurate, but it feels like it to me. He and Cindy are going to limit my ability to see Billy. They're worried he might get hurt when we're together."

"Oh . . . it's because . . ." Janelle hesitated.

Corbin, who was staring at the top of his desk, glanced up at her. "Yeah, they're trying to make my drinking into a bigger deal than it is. I've never gone too far when I've been with Billy, and

I never would." He touched the bandage on his face. "This was caused by wet grass, nothing else, but they're using it as an excuse."

"I'm sorry," she said, clearing her throat. "Maybe Billy could come over here every so often after he gets out of school. You could spend time with him in your office, reading a book or playing a game."

"With you as a chaperone?"

"If that's what it takes," Janelle replied with an edge to her voice. "Look, I'm trying to help. If you want to mope around and feel sorry for yourself, that's your choice."

"I can count on you to turn a feather into a sharp stick," Corbin said bitterly. "I'll probably end up standing alone outside the fence while he plays ball or sitting by myself in the school auditorium watching him in a play."

"You should have been doing that already. Corbin, you decide in your head what you're going to do in a situation, and that ends any discussion. That's the way you act with Ray, me, anybody. If you were a little more flexible, people would appreciate it."

"I've been getting more than my share of free advice lately."

"Which should tell you something."

Corbin pointed to the Anderson file that he'd dropped on his desk. "I have a lowball offer to settle, but before I call the client, get on the phone with the hospital and the chiropractor's office and see if you can convince them to reduce their liens by half. Remind them that if I don't collect anything they won't get a dime. I want the client to get something out of this." Corbin paused. "And I need to make enough to buy a pair of socks that match."

NINETEEN

Once the lingering effects of any hangover passed, mid- to late morning was Corbin's most productive time of day. Concepts that had been fuzzy the previous afternoon came into clearer focus. He quickly concluded there was only one way to proceed against Colfax—file a multicount complaint that alleged liability under every possible legal theory, then use discovery to separate the wheat from the chaff. He hoped there would be a few kernels of wheat left after the sifting was complete.

Under the notice pleading rules it wasn't necessary to lay out exactly what the company did wrong, but Corbin wanted to include enough specific information to convince the company that he'd been investigating it. He went out to Janelle's desk.

"Who do you know that works at Colfax?" he asked.

"Uh, that would be half the people with jobs in Rusk County."

"I need an employee willing to nose around and provide information about what they dumped on the land near our client's property."

"I'm not sure about that. Maybe Tommy Kilpatrick has a contact who would help."

"Good idea." Corbin turned on his heel and returned to his office. When he called Tommy's number, Larissa answered.

"This is Corbin Gage. Is Tommy available?"

"We talked about the lawsuit until late last night," Larissa said, ignoring his question. "Could we end up owing money if we lose? Or have to pay Colfax's lawyer bills? If that happened I know we'd have to file for bankruptcy like Millie, which would make it hard for Mitchell to get the treatment he needs. There's no way, we're—"

"No, no," Corbin cut in. "As long as we have any kind of argument that Colfax is responsible for Mitchell getting sick, there's no chance you'd get hit with attorney fees."

"That's not what Tommy saw on the Internet."

Corbin rolled his eyes. The World Wide Web was great for some things, but it was a headache for lawyers whose clients mined it for dubious data used to second-guess what their attorney told them.

"Print it off if you want and bring it into the office the next time we meet, and I'll explain why that's not likely or even possible. May I speak to Tommy now?"

"All right," Larissa said slowly. "I'll fetch him."

Tommy came on the line, and Corbin told him what he wanted to find out.

"Yeah, I can ask a buddy to pull the material safety data sheets from the drums of chemicals that may have been involved. The only thing is he won't know for sure if that's what they broadcast on the ground."

"It's a start."

"Okay, I'll send him a text message as soon as we hang up."

"Warn him to be careful that no one knows what he's up to. Don't mention we're filing a lawsuit."

"He'll want a reason."

Corbin thought for a moment. "Tell him it's because your water tastes funny and you want to have it tested to see if there's anything in it that came from the plant. That's the truth because we'll have the groundwater analyzed as part of the litigation."

Corbin ended the call, and Janelle buzzed him.

"Mr. Anderson is on the phone."

"Were you able to make any progress knocking down the medical liens?"

"Yes, with the chiropractor. He'll take 60 percent. The woman at the hospital has to get back to me."

"Okay."

After Corbin explained the options to the client, he agreed to settle.

"Take it," Anderson said. "The insurance adjuster who called me after the wreck wasn't going to give me anything, so I'll be tickled to get a check."

"Oh, you'd be interested to know the insurance company sent someone out to spy on you."

"Yeah, I knew they was snooping around. No strangers come down our road without us knowing about it. A man and woman in a car with heavy tint on the windows parked near the garden while my brother was hoeing. I bet they took a bunch of pictures of Sammy. People mix us up all the time."

The news made Corbin pause. He could let Henry Byram or his boss argue that the client wasn't injured and produce a video as proof. When the jury realized the investigator filmed the wrong person, it could bust the case open. It was the type of evidence that produced courtroom laughs that translated into verdict dollars. Corbin explained it to his client.

"That might be fun for you, Mr. Gage, but I'm glad we don't have to go to court. I wasn't looking forward to it."

"Okay, we'll see what we can do with the bill to the hospital. That will have an impact on what you clear."

"Do your best. I appreciate all the help you've given me. No one else was willing to take on my case."

"That describes a lot of what I do," Corbin replied.

After Janelle left for the day, Corbin stayed at the office working on the Colfax complaint. But in the back of his mind was the message he'd listened to on his phone inviting him to supper the following evening with Ray, Cindy, and Billy. He knew the invitation wasn't about fried chicken and creamed corn. He was a convict waiting to hear his sentence. Checking his watch, Corbin had an idea how he might enhance a plea for mercy.

Getting in his truck, he drove away from the center of town, but instead of accelerating once he reached the city limits, he slowly approached the Hopewell Methodist Church. Again there was a handful of cars in the parking lot, including Max Hogan's older model sedan. Corbin put on the blinker of his truck and eased into the space beside it. He turned off the motor but didn't move. What seemed like a brilliant strategy while sitting in his office had turned daunting during the three-minute drive to the church.

Like everyone, Corbin was familiar with the famous introductory line for AA participants: "My name is _____ and I am an alcoholic," and the standard response, "Hi, _____." He was aware of the existence of a twelve-step plan for recovery that included reference to a "higher power," the "God of your understanding," or something like that, but he couldn't name a single one of the steps if someone pointed a gun to his head.

Corbin didn't consider himself an alcoholic, because he could go several days without drinking. He only drank because of the mellow state of mind it brought him. As he sat in his truck he felt the twinge of a headache, which reminded him that he also drank to ward off headaches. And he frequently drank alone. And he drank when he started to feel shaky on the inside. And he drank when he felt depressed. And he drank because it made him feel more alive. And he drank to ease an inner pain that nothing else could touch. He paused. And he knew that many people in his life considered his drinking a problem. Otherwise he wouldn't be eating supper with Ray and Cindy in twenty-four hours to find out how they were going to restrict his contact with Billy.

Corbin looked at his reflection in the rearview mirror of the truck. His right eye was bruised; his left eye slightly runny.

He thought about Kitty.

Death was more final than divorce. When Kitty was alive he could always do something nice for her to let her know he cared even though he'd messed up their marriage. Pay Branson Kilpatrick's bill for cutting the grass and putting out extra fertilizer on the plants; ask her to make a list of things that needed to be done around the house and take care of them while she was out running errands on Saturday mornings; buy her a gift card for her favorite dress shop and leave it peeking out from the edge of the mat in front of the door. He'd write notes, especially after he'd had a few drinks, begging for her forgiveness, none of which he ever gave her. Now there was no way to touch her, even from a distance.

He knew Kitty would want him to go inside the church. She'd want him to do it for himself. She'd want him to do it for Billy. She'd want him to do it for her. Corbin tightly gripped the steering wheel with his hands, but in his heart he knew it was time to let go.

He opened the door of the truck.

The following morning Corbin sleepily turned off the alarm clock. On the nightstand beside the clock was a copy of *The Big Book of Alcoholics Anonymous*, cowritten in the 1930s by Bill Wilson, one of the founders. Corbin stayed up late flipping through the book to get an overview of the program and how it worked. He slowed down to read a few personal stories about men who'd battled serious alcohol addictions.

The cut on his face was beginning to itch, and he let warm water run over it to ease the discomfort while taking his shower. He gently patted it dry and reapplied a bandage. The cut didn't really need to be covered, but the black stitches stuck out at odd angles and would attract more unwanted stares than a white cover. He brewed a pot of strong coffee and took two painkillers. He'd not drunk any alcohol when he got home from the AA meeting and needed medication to combat the aggressive headache that began before he left for the office. He toasted a bagel and spread cream cheese on top of it for breakfast. He glanced longingly at the liquor cabinet in the corner of the kitchen, but instead of pouring a shot into his coffee, he chewed the bagel as a form of sensory distraction.

As he shut the door to leave for the office, Corbin remembered that he'd not replaced the liquor bottle he kept in the bottom drawer of his desk. He let his hand rest on the doorknob as he debated whether to go back inside and get one. He even visualized which one he'd take, a twelve-year-old Tennessee bourbon with a black label. His feelings brought him face-to-face with the first of the Twelve Steps—the admission that he was powerless over alcohol and his life had become unmanageable.

When he'd heard the step read by the woman who led the meeting, Corbin had relaxed. The definition indicated a degree of domination by alcohol that didn't describe his life. But now in the light of a new day, the first step seemed uncomfortably relevant. If he went inside the house and grabbed a bottle for the office, it would be an admission of the power of alcohol over his life. He abruptly turned away.

Corbin was in a foul mood. The medication had dulled his headache, but it still lurked at the edge of his consciousness. Janelle hadn't arrived yet and he mumbled and grumbled as he brewed another pot of coffee. Going into his office, he pulled open the bottom drawer and stared at the empty space. Irritation at Cindy rose up inside him. Just because his daughter-in-law came from a conservative, religious family steeped in a judgmental outlook was no reason for her to arbitrarily control Corbin's relationship with Billy.

Thinking about Cindy's father, Corbin remembered that he'd retired from Colfax. Shuffling through his notes and research, Corbin tried to channel his negative energy into his lawsuit against the company. An hour later Janelle buzzed him.

"Good morning," she said when he answered.

"What's good about it?" Corbin replied gruffly.

"Sorry to disturb the bear in his den," Janelle snipped. "Tommy Kilpatrick is on the phone. Do you want to talk to him?"

"Yeah, put him through." Corbin turned to a blank sheet of paper in a legal pad.

"I talked to my friend at the plant," Tommy said. "He has several material safety data sheets, including one for a chemical that he's sure was included in the material dumped on the ground near my property."

"Do you have the sheets?"

"Yes. It's a bunch of stuff with long names I can't pronounce.

When I worked there all I did was meet my production quota. I didn't try to understand the technical stuff, but my friend says they're developing a product designed to fertilize crops and kill weeds at the same time. When he mentioned it, I remembered it being discussed at a meeting before I was laid off."

"A fertilizer and an herbicide," Corbin said.

"Yeah, one of the bosses said it would cost less than the two products sold separately and could be applied by a farmer in one application, which would save a bunch of time and fuel expense. Carl—oh, don't write down his name, okay?"

Too late. Corbin immediately made a note. He could always subpoena Carl without revealing why he'd selected him.

"Go ahead," Corbin said.

"My buddy is going to see if he can find out anything else and let me know. Carl is a low-level guy in research and development; he hauls the drums around for the chemists who create the formulas. That's why he knows a little bit about what's going on. He coached Mitchell's T-ball team last summer."

Corbin thought for a moment. "Until the final mix is set, are there runs of product that can't be marketed?"

"Sure, and that stuff has to be thrown away. Also there is by-product from normal manufacturing that is waste material. I have no idea what's in that. Some of it gets trucked out, and I'm not sure where it ends up."

"Would Carl know about that?"

"I doubt it."

"Okay, how soon can you get me the material safety data sheets?"

"This morning. I have to come to town for a job interview. I'm trying to get on as a supervisor at the chicken plant."

Corbin cringed. Even supervisors at the chicken plant didn't earn enough to support a family.

"I've got to latch on with a company big enough to accept Mitchell on their health insurance," Tommy continued. "That cuts down on my choices."

"I understand. I'll be here."

The call ended and Corbin took two more painkillers. The bottle warned that the maximum dosage in twenty-four hours was eight capsules. At his current rate Corbin would swallow sixteen pills by the end of the workday. He massaged his temples with his fingertips as he turned toward his computer. Pulling up what he hoped was the correct phone number for the branch of the attorney general's office in charge of criminal prosecutions for environmental offenses, he squinted to better focus as he punched in the number.

TWENTY

"W"ill I have to file a request under the Open Records Act to examine the file?" Corbin asked the paralegal he finally reached after wading through three lower levels of administrative barriers.

"Not if you are willing to come to Atlanta and examine it at our office."

"Can I make copies of anything I think relevant to my investigation?"

"For a fee. We'll have to make the copies. A clerk can assist you."

It was less red tape than Corbin had anticipated.

"Okay," he said. "I'd like to set up a time to come later this week if that's possible."

"Just a minute."

There was a long silence on the other end of the line. Corbin began to fidget.

"What is your name again?" the woman asked when she returned.

"Corbin Gage. I'm a lawyer in Alto."

"Are you Raymond Gage?"

"No, that's my son. He's the assistant DA who handled the case here in Rusk County."

"Why don't you get what you need from him?"

Corbin didn't want to say that his son was angling for a job and didn't want to upset the law firm representing the defendant.

"Uh, he sent the entire file back to you."

"Okay. Since I talked with you, I'd like to be here when you come. That will make things smoother."

"I appreciate that." Corbin relaxed. "How about Thursday afternoon?"

"No, Friday afternoon is better for me."

"What about next Monday?"

"I'm out of the office all next week."

Corbin didn't want to face Friday afternoon traffic in Atlanta, but there seemed to be no other option. "Then Friday it is."

"Come to the waiting area on the third floor of the judicial building around four o'clock and ask for Melissa Thompson."

"See you then."

The call ended and Corbin got up to stretch. He went out to the reception area to tell Janelle about the appointment in Atlanta, but she wasn't there. Her computer was dark, and her desk didn't show any signs of recent activity. Corbin suddenly wondered if she'd quit without notice. He opened the middle drawer of her desk. All it contained were paper clips and pens. The two side drawers of the desk were locked.

Corbin walked tentatively into the rear of the office. The secretary wasn't in the break room or the storage room where they kept supplies. The bathroom door was open and the light turned off. He opened the door at the rear of the office. Janelle's car was gone.

Corbin stormed back into the office. He was on the verge of filing one of the biggest lawsuits of his career and didn't have time to hire a new secretary. Finding and training a replacement would be a huge hassle. His headache forced its way to a spot behind both of his eyes with such pressure that it made him nauseous.

He rested his hand on Janelle's desk, then checked his watch. Red's opened in ten minutes, and Corbin would be the first customer in the door. He desperately needed a cool glass of mountain water. He imagined the first searing drink of moonshine and shut his eyes in an effort to drive back the pain of the headache.

A voice interrupted his dark fantasy.

"Are you okay?" Janelle put her purse on her desk.

"Where have you been?" Corbin exploded.

"The office supply store," she replied, her eyes opening wide. "We were almost out of paper for the copy machine, and there were a few other things I needed."

Corbin shook his head and pushed back his hair with his hand. "I thought you'd quit," he mumbled.

"Quit? Why did you think that?"

"You weren't at your desk." Corbin motioned with his hand. "And you didn't tell me you were leaving on an errand."

"And you were in such a bad mood this morning you thought I couldn't stand working here another day and walked out without notice?"

"No. Uh, yes."

"Sit down," Janelle commanded, eyeing him. "You look terrible. You're not having chest pains, are you?"

"Just a splitting headache."

Janelle reached for her purse. "I have some pretty strong stuff in here. Two of them usually knock out—"

"I've tried that already," Corbin replied, taking a deep breath in an effort to regain control. "And thanks for not quitting."

"You're welcome. Unless you do something crazy, I'll give you at least two weeks' notice."

Corbin turned back toward his office. Before he reached it, the front door opened and Tommy Kilpatrick entered. Corbin gathered himself in an effort to look normal.

"How's the eye, Mr. Gage?" Tommy asked.

"Getting better every day. But I've got a terrible headache."

"A knock on the head can do that. I got a concussion when I was playing football in high school. It's no joke."

Corbin didn't want to compare headaches. "Do you have the MSD sheets?" he asked.

Tommy handed him a thin stack of the labels that had been affixed to containers of chemicals.

"The one my buddy believes was part of the stuff dumped on the ground has a Post-it sticker on it."

Corbin saw the yellow slip peeking out to the side.

"I'll look them over. I'm going to the attorney general's office in Atlanta on Friday to inspect the file that formed the basis of the criminal prosecution. I'm sure the state hazardous material inspectors went inside the plant and compiled a list of chemicals."

"Okay. I'm on my way to the chicken plant for my job interview."

"Good luck," Corbin said with a forced smile.

Tommy left and Corbin handed the MSD sheets to Janelle.

"Make copies of these for the file. I don't want to sort through a bunch of sticky labels."

"Will do. Are you sure you don't want some of my meds?"

"I'm sure."

As soon as the clock signaled 11:00 a.m., Corbin was out the door of the office and walking rapidly down the street to Red's. The restaurant closed between the breakfast and lunch shifts and reopened an hour before noon. Corbin was the first customer for the midday meal.

"Hungry?" Red asked.

"And thirsty," Corbin said, looking past the owner toward the kitchen.

"Uh-oh," Red replied, lowering his voice. "I was supposed to get a fresh shipment this morning, but Beanpole didn't show up. I called his house, and his wife said he was in the middle of a big run and couldn't get away to make the delivery."

"Don't you have any left over from yesterday?" Corbin asked, trying to keep the panic out of his voice.

"No, we sold it out the back door to a customer who was having a big party on the lake last night. Sorry, but I'm cleaned out."

Corbin wanted to swear at Red, but the sincerity on the restaurant owner's face stopped him. "All right." Corbin sighed. "I guess I'll eat."

"The usual?" Red asked. "I can put in the order for you."

"Yeah, but light on the onions. I've got a horrible headache, and my stomach is shaky."

Corbin slipped into a booth, leaned his head against the cool vinyl, and closed his eyes. He couldn't understand why his brief ride on the alcohol abstinence wagon was so rough.

"Here you go," a voice said.

Corbin opened his eyes to see Red setting down a steaming hot bowl of beans and rice. Beside the bowl was a plastic glass half full of clear liquid.

"What's this?" Corbin asked, his hopes rising.

"Not what you wanted, but I think you'll find it to your liking."

Corbin picked up the glass and sniffed the contents. It was odorless. He took a sip. "Vodka?"

"Yep. If you'd prefer it mixed with orange juice, I've got some in the fridge."

While Red spoke, Corbin took two more sips. The clear liquor had a bite, but it was more like a nip from a miniature poodle than the German shepherd–size chomp delivered by brew from moonshiners like Beanpole.

"No," Corbin said as he let himself begin to relax. "This'll do."

By the end of the meal, the glass and Corbin's bowl of beans were both empty. His headache retreated from the entrenched position it had taken up behind his eyes, but it remained crouched at the edge of his brain. He took his ticket to the cash register and handed Red a twenty.

"I didn't see my special beverage on the tab," he said, "but I hope this will take care of it."

Red took the money and gave Corbin change based on the cost of the beans and rice only.

"I said to keep it," Corbin insisted.

"No." Red shook his head. "It's on me. I could tell how much you needed a shot. Has it been a rough morning?"

It took Corbin a couple of seconds to remember what he'd done before leaving for the restaurant. "Uh, no. I mean, no fires to put out at the office. I just—"

Corbin stopped. The only explanation that came to mind was from the first step of AA—he couldn't resist the pull of alcohol. The need for a drink had compelled him down the street like a man dragged behind a horse, and his will was powerless to stop it.

Corbin bolted from the restaurant.

———

Occasionally Roxy and Peter would meet for lunch. Arranging their schedules to accommodate a midday meal was a logistical challenge, but Peter was persistent. Roxy arrived early at the French-themed eatery that served some of the most delicate yet flavorful sauces in the city. A waiter passed by with a veal dish swimming in what Roxy guessed was a sauce velouté. She followed the waiter with her nose.

"Don't overwork your olfactory receptors," a voice said.

She turned to smile at Peter. "I bring every part of me to this place," she said.

Peter leaned over and kissed her.

"Thanks for driving the extra distance to meet me here," Roxy said.

The maître d' seated them at a table for two in a secluded corner at the rear of the restaurant. There were fresh flowers in the middle of the table.

"I wish I could call in sick for the rest of the afternoon and stay right here." Roxy sighed and took a sip of glacier water.

"Rough day?"

"Mr. Caldweller dumped responsibility for a big case in my lap, and it's going to take the rest of the week before I see the bottom of my to-do list."

The waiter took their order. Roxy ordered the veal dish that caught her attention earlier. Peter selected the quiche of the day.

"Is your father getting over his injury?" he asked after the waiter left.

"I guess so. I've not talked to him again. But a bigger blow is coming when Ray and his wife restrict his access to my nephew, Billy."

"Because of your father's drinking?"

"And the fallout caused by it. It's a shame in a way, because Billy is the only person who brings him any happiness. But actions have consequences. Isn't that the way it works in the IT world?"

"I'd like to meet your father," Peter said.

Roxy, who had taken another sip of water, choked and barely managed to swallow. "Why?" She coughed into the back of her hand.

"You met my parents when they were in town from Florida last month. Isn't that supposed to be part of the process of getting to know each other better?"

Roxy eyed Peter suspiciously. "I'm not sure. It's hard for me to imagine you sitting down with my father and talking about anything that you're interested in."

"We're both interested in you."

Peter's simple statement stunned Roxy. Tears rushed to her eyes. She grabbed the linen napkin from her lap and quickly raised it to her face.

"Peter," she said from behind the napkin.

"I'm sorry," he said. "I mean, I know you and your dad aren't close, but I didn't want to upset you—"

"Oh, it's not that," Roxy replied with a sniffle. She gave a slight shake of her shoulders to compose herself. "It's the thought that my father should care about me the same way you do. We've only been dating for nine months, but you've shown me more kindness and respect than I've received from any other man, including him, in my life. Thinking of that, along with my mother dying, just—"

She again raised the napkin to her face. This time she wasn't able to banish her tears with a shrug of her shoulders. When she finally lowered it, she saw that Peter's eyes had welled up too, and that set her off again.

"I never cry," Roxy said when she regained her composure. "I must look like a mess."

The waiter arrived with their food. With professional detachment he ignored the obvious flood of emotion that had swept over the two people at the table.

"He probably thinks you broke up with me," Roxy said after he left.

"Or finally beat you in a 5K race."

She laughed louder than his joke warranted. Peter reached across the table and took her hand. Her lips trembled.

"Please," she said. "Be careful what you say. It won't take much to reduce me to a puddle."

Peter looked into her eyes. He opened his mouth, hesitated, then released her hand. Roxy let out the breath she'd been holding, suddenly sorry she'd squelched him.

Peter picked up his fork and cut off a small piece of quiche. "Do you want the first bite?" he asked.

On her way back to the office, Roxy tried to unravel the reason for her sudden inability to control her emotions. She'd shed a few tears at her mother's funeral, but nothing like the explosion at the restaurant. At least Peter didn't freak out when she started bawling. She'd never considered herself an overwrought female. Her cell phone vibrated. When she saw the identity of the caller, she almost swerved into the curb.

TWENTY-ONE

Corbin leaned back in his chair and propped his feet on his desk. Due to either repeated doses of pain medication, his midday shots of vodka, or a combination of the two, his headache was gone. And with its departure Corbin's attitude had improved immensely. He felt almost euphoric.

"Dad?" Roxy asked in an odd tone of voice.

"Yes, are you in the middle of something?" Corbin replied.

"Peachtree Street on the way to the office after meeting Peter for lunch. Why are you calling?"

"I'm coming to Atlanta on Friday and thought I might swing by and see you. I've not been to your office in years, and I'll need a place to hang out until traffic clears. I-75 will be a parking lot until seven. I even thought we could grab a bite to eat if you don't have plans."

As her father chattered away, Roxy stopped at a red light. She held the phone away from her ear and stared at it.

"Are you okay?" she asked.

"Yes, the day started out rough, but I'm feeling much better now. The cut on my face is healing faster than you'd expect for a man my age. It seems the people who predicted my early demise are dead wrong."

Corbin laughed at his joke. Hearing the sound, Roxy knew for a fact that her father had been drinking. She shook her head and prepared to turn down his request. But her conversation with Peter at the French restaurant stopped her. She knew he would pester her until he had a chance to encounter Corbin Gage for himself.

"Would it be okay if Peter joined us for dinner?"

"Yeah, of course. I'd like to meet him." Corbin paused. "He hasn't asked you to marry him, has he?"

"No," Roxy said, rolling her eyes. "But I met his parents a few months ago when they were in town, and he'd like to meet you. We can get together at my office and go someplace from there. What time do you think you'll get here?"

"Around five thirty. I'm not exactly sure when I'll finish at the attorney general's office."

"Why are you going there?"

"Background research on a case," Corbin replied cryptically. "What's the address for your firm again? I haven't been there since—"

"The first month I started. You brought Mom to show her my office."

Corbin was silent.

Roxy took a left turn into the firm's parking area. "Are you ready?" she asked.

"For what?"

"The address of the office."

"Oh, right. Give it to me."

Corbin spent the next two hours working on the first draft of the complaint in the Colfax litigation. His handwriting was barely legible, even to himself, but seeing the rough paragraphs unfold was exciting. As he scribbled, he imagined the reaction the lawsuit would have on the upper-level management of the company at their Richmond, Virginia, headquarters. Until the recent prosecution initiated by the attorney general's office, Colfax was used to having its way in Rusk County.

There was a knock on his door, and Janelle popped her head in. "How's your headache?" she asked.

"Much better. I'm putting together the complaint in the Colfax case. I don't want to include too much detail in the complaint, just enough to let them know I have bullets in my gun."

"I'll be interested to see if you do. Are you going to include both boys in the same case?"

"Yes, and let the defense try to separate them. They won't be able to make a stab at that until I've cracked open some doors during discovery and found out what sort of skeletons are in the closets."

"Impressive." Janelle raised her eyebrows. "This started out as a bad day, but you've turned it into a good one."

Corbin checked his watch. "I only hope that continues with Ray and Cindy. I'm eating supper over there tonight, and I know they're going to hammer me about Billy."

"Remember what I said about letting him come to the office and—"

"Yeah, yeah." Corbin cut her off with a wave of his hand. "But it's his father who needs to come here, not an eight-year-old boy. I don't want to stick Billy in the conference room playing games on a smartphone."

"Does he have a phone?"

"No, but he has one of those electronic gadgets. He knows not to drag it out when we're together. I'd throw it in the pond."

"No, you wouldn't."

"You're right, but if you give a kid something real and exciting to do, he doesn't have to waste all his time and energy on one of those things."

"Okay. I'm out of here in five minutes unless there's something else you need me to do."

"No, and thanks again for not quitting."

Janelle shut the door.

Corbin leaned back in his chair. The restorative high he'd experienced after his trip to Red's was slipping away and he felt tired. He considered going home for a quick drink or two before heading to supper, but didn't want to risk it. Instead he propped his feet on his desk and closed his eyes for a nap.

He awoke with a start and glanced at the time. He was already ten minutes late for supper.

———

Billy ran into the kitchen from the backyard and opened the refrigerator door.

"I'm starving," he said as he took out a jug of milk. "Lunch at school today was gross. Can I fix a sandwich and drink a glass of milk while we wait for Pops to get here? I promise I'll still eat my supper."

"You can wait," Cindy replied with a glance at Ray, who was sitting at the table reading the local newspaper.

"Daddy?" Billy appealed to his father.

"How hungry are you?" Ray asked, lowering the paper. "Describe it for me."

"Huh?"

"Tell me what it feels like to be starving."

Billy paused for a moment. "It feels like the juices in my stomach are eating away at my insides." He gestured across his midsection. "There is a pain that starts here and goes over to this side. I think that's the part being eaten from the inside out."

Ray turned to Cindy. "I think we should let the boy drink a glass of milk. I don't want to see stomach juices coming through his shirt. It will ruin my appetite."

Cindy took a glass from the cabinet and set it on the counter.

"I expect you to be that descriptive when you have to write a paper for English class in high school," she said as Billy filled the glass to the brim.

Billy lifted the glass to his lips and didn't lower it until a third of it was gone. "Ah," he said. "This milk has a good bead to it."

"What did you say?" Ray and Cindy both asked at the same time.

"When Pops really likes his water, he says it has a good bead to it."

Cindy looked at Ray. "Do we have any doubt about the need to have this talk with him?"

"Not a bit."

The doorbell sounded.

"I'll get it." Billy bounded out of the room.

"Are you going to tell him what Billy just said?" Cindy asked.

"It's not on our list, but we can add it."

Corbin and Billy entered the kitchen.

"And I want to show you the fort I'm building against the fence in the backyard," Billy said to Corbin.

"After supper," Corbin replied. "I'm starving."

"Me too," Billy replied.

"Sorry I'm late," Corbin said to Cindy as he brushed his hair out of his eyes. "I was working late at the office and time slipped by on me."

"Was that before or after your nap?" Ray replied.

Corbin grinned and held his hands out in front of him. "I'm busted, Mr. DA. Put on the handcuffs."

Cindy had prepared fried chicken, mashed potatoes, green beans, and creamed corn. Corbin's eyes got bigger when he saw the meal.

"Let me make a better apology for being late," he said. "If I'd known you were going to all this trouble, I'd—"

"Save it, Dad," Ray interrupted. "Let's eat."

The table in the small dining room had seating for six. Ray sat at one end with Corbin at the other.

"Can I pray?" Billy asked.

"Sure," Ray replied.

Billy bowed his head and closed his eyes. "God, thank you for this food. And don't let Judge Ellington die like Rupert Murdoch. Pops and I want to catch him. Amen."

"You've been thinking about those fish?" Corbin asked Billy.

"Yeah. Can we go on Saturday? I have a soccer match in the morning, but maybe we could eat lunch on the boat. I really like it when we—"

"Let's talk about that later," Cindy interrupted as she passed the platter of chicken to him.

Corbin didn't speak during the rest of the meal; however, that didn't keep him from finishing off one plate and loading up another. Ray and Cindy kept the conversation going by asking Billy questions. Finally the boy turned to his grandfather.

"Pops, are you feeling okay? You sure are quiet."

"It's my heart," Corbin said. "It hurts."

"Dad—" Ray started.

"Not like Jamie Campbell's grandpa," Billy interrupted in alarm. "His heart hurt and he had to go to the hospital. After he got home he couldn't do anything."

"Pops's heart is fine," Ray said. "Remember, he got checked out at the hospital when his face was stitched up. The doctor said his heart was okay, isn't that right?"

"Yeah," Corbin said to Billy. "I meant that I'm feeling kind of sad today, but it's nothing for you to worry about."

By the expression on his face, Billy didn't seem convinced.

"Has your stomach given up on the idea of eating your insides?" Ray asked his son.

"Yes, sir," Billy replied in a subdued voice, with another worried glance at Corbin.

"Are you finished?" Cindy asked the boy.

"Yes, ma'am. But you said we were going to have peach cobbler with ice cream for dessert."

"We are, but only after your supper has a chance to settle into that huge hole that was in your stomach. Go to your room and complete the math problems Ms. Patterson sent home."

"But I want to show Pops my fort."

"We can do that when you finish," Corbin replied. "Obey your mama."

Billy left the table and the adults sat in silence until they heard the door to his room close. Ray leaned over to the sideboard for the sheet of paper he and Cindy had prepared to guide the painful conversation. However, Corbin spoke first.

"Before you issue a ruling from the bench or read from the order you prepared, you should know I went to an Alcoholics Anonymous meeting at Hopewell Methodist Church last night."

"You went to an AA meeting?" Ray asked, his mouth dropping open.

"Yes, and got a copy of the Big Book written by the guys who started it. I fell asleep last night reading stories about men who stopped drinking through AA. A lot of them didn't get help until they experienced some kind of personal crisis connected to alcohol. For me, I can't think of a bigger catastrophe than losing my time with Billy. I realized you were serious about your threat the other night at the hospital and knew I had to do something to win back your trust. Max Hogan is the one who invited me to the meeting and can verify I was there."

"I thought it was supposed to be anonymous," Cindy said suspiciously.

"It is. There were other people there you might know, and I won't give out their names. But Max and I have been drinking buddies for years, and he wouldn't care. Ray knows him."

Cindy pointed to the sheet of paper in Ray's hand. "And you think going to a single AA meeting is going to change our minds about what we need to do to protect Billy?"

"Of course not. If I weren't eating supper with you tonight, I'd be at an AA meeting at the mental health center on Calhoun Street. All I'm asking is that you don't do anything drastic. Put me on probation or whatever you want to call it until your fears are put to rest."

Ray scratched his head. "Dad, that's great. I never thought you'd admit you had a drinking problem, much less do something about it. I wish Mom . . ." He stopped.

"That's what got me out of the car at the church last night. I thought about her and what she'd want me to do. I hate to admit it, but I was afraid to go inside. But the people were nice, and nobody put any pressure on me to say or do anything."

"Wait a minute." Cindy held up her hand. "I thought you had to admit you're an alcoholic and agree to stop drinking to be a member of AA."

"You're a part of AA when you show up," Corbin replied. "They don't keep a membership roll."

"But you have to admit to a drinking problem," Cindy persisted. "Isn't that one of the Twelve Steps?"

"Yes, and I do have a problem," Corbin said slowly. "That's what convinced me to go to the meeting."

"Hey, I'm going to celebrate what you've done and encourage you to follow through," Ray said, glancing at Cindy. "I heard about Max Hogan getting help. Didn't he go through an inpatient rehab program?"

"Yeah, he's a huge believer in AA. That's where he's focusing his attention."

"Would you consider a twenty-eight-day program?" Cindy asked.

"I don't want to be locked up. All I need is support and encouragement. And I can't be away from the office for a month. My practice is picking up, which is another motivation to curb my drinking. I've got to be alert and focused." Corbin turned to Ray. "I identified a lot with one of the men in the AA book who drank as a form of self-medication because he was depressed. That's true for me, so I'm going to make an appointment with Dr. Fletchall to see if there's something mild he can give me to help stabilize my mood."

"I don't know." Cindy shook her head. "This is awfully sudden. I mean, one meeting doesn't make me comfortable—"

"Here's what I ask," Corbin cut in. "I'll start coming to more of Billy's activities with you. Just don't cut off my chances to hang out with him one-on-one. What kind of message is it going to send to him if I tell him I can't take him fishing or for hikes in the woods?"

Ray looked at Cindy. "What do you think?" he asked.

Cindy pressed her lips together tightly for a moment and tapped the sheet of paper on the table between her and Ray. "I think we ought to stick to what we discussed earlier," she said, then turned to

Corbin. "But if you will promise not to drink a drop of liquor before or during your times with Billy, I guess we can see how it goes."

"Absolutely," Corbin said quickly.

"And you promise to continue going to the AA meetings and keep Ray up to date on how you're doing. In a way it's none of my business, except for the impact on Billy."

"I hear you loud and clear," Corbin replied.

"What's an AA meeting?" a voice asked.

The adults turned and saw Billy on his hands and knees in the hallway peeking around the corner.

"How long have you been there?" Ray demanded.

"Just a minute," Billy replied defensively. "I solved all my math problems and checked them to make sure they were right."

"We were working out the details for a fishing trip on Saturday," Corbin said. "I'll come watch your soccer game, then we can take off for the pond. Oh, and we'll have lunch on the boat too."

"It's a soccer *match*, Pops," Billy said.

"Right. I'm learning new stuff all the time."

After he finished his tour of Billy's fort, Corbin left the house and got in his truck. He shut his eyes for a moment. He'd pleaded his case to a two-person jury and won. Well, maybe *won* was too strong. He'd avoided summary judgment, but the final verdict was still in doubt.

It had taken every ounce of his willpower to hold it together in the house. Toward the end of the meal his hands began to tremble involuntarily, forcing him to keep them hidden beneath the table. Ray and Cindy would have labeled the shakes *delirium tremens*, a charge Corbin doubted he could refute.

He backed the truck out of the driveway. Shortly before reaching the Hopewell church, he slowed in front of The Office tavern. The parking lot was nearly full, and he recognized several vehicles. Corbin hadn't visited the popular watering hole since before Kitty's death. After being absent for such a long period, he knew he'd be greeted with enthusiasm by the regulars and rewarded with free beer purchased by his friends. He'd done the same thing for others many times. He felt the familiar craving for a drink rise up from the core of his being.

He pulled in and stopped next to the light pole he'd hit late one Friday afternoon.

Through the truck's windshield Corbin watched the bright neon signs that decorated the front of the bar, and the Budweiser sign blinking in an explosion of flashing light. He contrasted the fear he felt outside the church before the AA meeting with the pleasant pull to join the party.

Corbin glanced down. The light from the pole illuminated the passenger seat floorboard. A glint of something shiny caught his eye. He leaned over and picked it up. It was Billy's new fishing lure that hadn't made it back into the boy's tackle box. The garish colors of the lure were as bright as the neon signs and more likely to attract the interest of a young boy than convince a fish to strike. Corbin held the lure in his open palm for several moments, then laid it gently on the seat. Turning on the truck's engine, he carefully pulled away from the light pole. Like a wily old bass, he wasn't going to be tempted by neon colors.

At least not tonight.

TWENTY-TWO

Corbin continued his evening battle with the bottle by watching a movie and going to bed early. The stress and tension of the day had worn him out emotionally, and it didn't take long for his body to catch up. He didn't wake up feeling refreshed, but at least his headache was gone. The bruising on his cheek was less purple and more yellow. When he arrived at the office, Janelle was there.

"Are you feeling better today?" she asked when he entered the reception area through the rear of the office.

"No headache, if that's what you mean," Corbin replied.

"And how did it go with Ray and Cindy?"

Corbin didn't want to get into a detailed conversation with his secretary about the personal issue and regretted venting to her in the first place.

"They're going to work with me," he replied cryptically. "What's on the agenda for today?"

"You have a deposition at the Simpkin firm at 10:15. I put the file on your desk so you can review it."

Corbin arrived five minutes early for the deposition. Simpkin, Brown, and Stamper was located in a twenty-year-old brown brick building. It was a utilitarian structure with a row of boxy offices for the lawyers on the left side of a long hallway and support staff on the opposite side. Depositions were held in one of the firm's two conference rooms, neither of which had windows to the outside.

As he waited for an associate attorney, Corbin wondered which office would be Ray's new home. It didn't really matter because all the spaces, even those occupied by the partners, were the same size. Corbin shook his head. It was a desperately depressing work environment, without an ounce of flair.

The deposition continued right through the lunch hour, and when Corbin finally said, "No more questions," it was the middle of the afternoon. The Simpkin firm's client owed fifteen hundred dollars to their lawyer for time spent watching Corbin talk. Best of all, Corbin had gotten what he wanted, a pattern of fraud regarding the valuation and sale of antique furniture owned by an estate.

The adrenaline was still flowing as he drove back to his office. He walked briskly into the reception area.

"Where have you been?" Janelle asked.

"Taking a deposition."

Janelle pointed at the clock on the wall. "You left at ten this morning. It's three o'clock. Are you sure you didn't take a detour to one of your watering holes?"

"They had plenty of water at the Simpkin firm," Corbin replied. "At least they're not stingy with that. Any calls while I was gone?"

"Yes, the important one was from Millie Watson. Josh's most recent blood work wasn't good, and the oncologist is recommending a more aggressive form of treatment. Millie was in tears. I told her I'd request the updated medical records."

"Getting that complaint filed is number one on my to-do list," Corbin said. "But I want to wait until I've had a chance to review the information at the attorney general's office before pulling the trigger."

Janelle was silent for a moment.

Corbin rubbed his hands together. "I just busted a crooked appraiser who was buying antiques below market value from nice old ladies. I think I'm ready to force Colfax to change the way it does business before other little boys get sick and die."

———

Roxy played out several possible scenarios for her father's visit to the firm, most of which ended badly. Her biggest fear centered around possible contact with Mr. Caldweller. Thankfully the senior partner was scheduled to be out of the office for a late afternoon social event with a client. Roxy checked her watch, popped a caramel into her mouth, and continued to stare out the window.

A male voice interrupted her. "I assume you're meditating about a litigation matter and will bill your time to a legitimate classification code," Mr. Caldweller said.

"No, sire," Roxy replied.

"What did you say?" Caldweller asked, raising his eyebrows.

Roxy suddenly realized her slip. "I'm sorry. I don't know why that came out 'sire,'" she replied sheepishly.

Caldweller nodded. "I like it, but it would engender an EEOC claim if I insisted on everyone using it. I understand your father is stopping by the office for a visit. He's a lawyer, isn't he?"

"In Alto."

"I'd like to meet him, but I've got to leave for cocktails with some executives from the Castille Group who are in town for the golf tournament."

"That's okay," Roxy said with relief.

Caldweller paused. "It's going to be a large gathering. Would you like to bring your father? The company's corporate counsel is going to be there, and I'd like her to meet you. They've sent us business to beta test the firm, and I want to give them the best impression possible of our staff."

Roxy's heart jumped into her throat. The idea of taking her father into a room full of free liquor would be an invitation to disasters far worse than any she'd considered.

"I'm flattered, but no, thanks," she said. "We're going to dinner with the man I'm dating."

"An associate who can maintain a social life," Caldweller replied. "Impressive. Just make sure you have the memo in my inbox first thing Monday morning on the issues I asked you to research in the Roxboro case."

"It's at the top of my list for tomorrow."

———

Corbin cinched his tie up closer to his neck. Normally by this time on a Friday afternoon the tie would be off, along with his shoes. He'd selected his nicest suit because he wanted to make a good impression at the attorney general's office and avoid his daughter's ire. Roxy considered criticism of his slovenliness both a right and a duty.

The receptionist at Frank and Donaldson eyed Corbin in a way that made him wonder if he'd not properly straightened his tie. He touched it again to make sure and brushed his hair out of his eyes.

"I can see the family resemblance between you and Roxy," the young woman said.

"You're kidding," Corbin responded. "Roxy is the spitting image of her mother."

"Maybe, but she has your jaw and some of your mannerisms."

Before Corbin could unpack what unfortunate mannerisms he

might have passed down to his daughter, Roxy came into the room and quickly inspected him.

"Come on back," she said.

"Have a nice tour," the receptionist said to Corbin, then she turned to Roxy. "Seeing you beside your father is so much fun."

Roxy gave the woman a puzzled look before entering the security code for the office suite.

"What did she say to you?" Roxy asked as she led the way past cubicles occupied by busy people who didn't look up as they passed.

"That you have my jaw, and we share mannerisms. I have no idea what she meant."

"Neither do I," Roxy said as she brushed her hair back in a way similar to her father. "They've moved me to a different office since you were here. I have a window now." She slowed down and gestured toward a door. "That's Mr. Caldweller's office."

Corbin casually stepped through the open door.

"Don't go in," she said quickly.

"Why not? Is it under video surveillance?"

Roxy glanced over her father's shoulder at Mr. Caldweller's enormous desk and private sitting area.

"That's a good question," she said. "I don't know."

"What about your office?"

"That's a better question. The IT department keeps a log of every click we make on the computers, but it would be weird if someone is watching me every time I blow my nose or touch up my makeup."

They continued to walk side by side. The hall was wider near the partner's offices.

"I installed a camera so I can keep an eye on Janelle," Corbin said.

"No, you didn't," Roxy replied. "But she ought to have a peephole drilled through your wall so she can tell when you're propping your feet on your desk and taking a nap or pulling open the bottom drawer where you stash a fifth of whiskey. Ray and I found your bottle one day when you left us alone. You were supposed to be watching us after school, but you weren't there."

"There's no whiskey in my drawer now."

"Only because you finished the bottle. Right?"

"Not exactly. I've been to two AA meetings this week."

Roxy stopped and faced him. "Are you serious?"

"Yes."

She led the way into her office.

"The view's not bad," Corbin said, glancing out the window. "You see more green than I would have suspected."

Roxy sat in the chair behind her desk. "I like it. Are you going to tell me why you went to AA?"

Corbin was prepared to rehash his presentation to Ray and Cindy but suddenly doubted his ability to pull it off in front of Roxy. She might have his jaw, but she had Kitty's eyes, and Ray had never successfully fooled those eyes.

"Why do you think I'd go to AA?" he asked defensively.

"Because Ray and Cindy threatened to cut off your alone time with Billy."

"You know about that?"

"And totally agree with them. Drinking and your grandson don't mix. If your dabbling in AA is a pretext, it won't last."

"Who said it was a pretext? Ray?"

"No, but it would be terribly wrong for you to deceive him and Cindy in an effort to manipulate the situation. You've always had the power to jerk Ray in the direction you want him to go."

It was a harsh indictment.

"I want what's best for Ray and Billy," Corbin said in a subdued voice.

"Then prove it by your actions over time."

Corbin opened his mouth to further defend himself, but the cold look in Roxy's eyes stopped him. Though similar to Kitty's, his daughter's eyes lacked any hint of the compassion that had marked her mother's countenance. Corbin desperately missed Kitty's eyes. He suddenly became teary. Roxy stared at him.

"Are you about to cry?" she asked.

"If I did you'd think I was faking it," Corbin said, standing up and wiping his eyes. He cleared his throat. "Coming to see you was a mistake. Tell Peter I couldn't stay for supper. I'll find my own way out."

If Roxy said something as he left, Corbin didn't hear her. He blinked his eyes to clear them as he quickly retraced his steps. He didn't slow down or respond when the chatty receptionist wished him a good evening. Roxy's harsh judgment was a cruel bookend to Ray and Cindy's threats to his relationship with Billy.

Once in the elevator Corbin pressed the button for the ground floor and leaned against the wall. He wished the elevator would malfunction and drop twenty floors in a pain-ending free fall.

TWENTY-THREE

A nd then he stormed out without giving me a chance to explain myself," Roxy said to Peter. They sat across from each other at the coffee shop she'd substituted for the nice restaurant where Peter had wanted to take her and her father.

Peter sipped his latte.

"Well?" Roxy asked. "What do you think?"

He lowered his cup and stared for a moment at the brown liquid. "Do you care what I think?"

"Of course I do!" Roxy exploded, then quickly looked around to see if anyone had noticed her outburst.

"First, I'm trying to put myself in your father's skin," Peter responded in a calm tone of voice. "When I do that—"

"You don't want to go there," Roxy interrupted. "And how can you possibly imagine what that would be like? My father's brain is a mix of alcohol-diminished brilliance and diabolical subtlety."

"You're right." Peter held up his hands. "I won't go there."

They sat in silence. Peter took two more sips of his latte. Roxy vigorously stirred the hot chai tea she'd ordered.

"Okay, tell me about your deep identification with my father's psyche," she said.

"I'm not claiming anything like that, but it's obvious he wanted to see you. He could have finished his business and gone straight back to Alto. And based on what you've been feeling, there are obviously issues you need to work through with him."

Roxy stared incredulously at Peter for a second. "You make it sound like we had a disagreement over the color of the dress I wore to the high school prom."

"Who took you to the prom?" Peter sat up straighter in his chair. "You should have waited to date until you met me."

Roxy managed a slight smile.

Peter leaned forward and cradled her hand in his. "Look, you're right. I have no idea what it's like growing up with an alcoholic parent. However, when there's a chance to fix something, we ought to give it a shot. If a software program doesn't solve a client's problems, we don't send them on their way and tell them to have a good life. We find out what it takes to make it right. I don't know the real reason why your father went to a couple of AA meetings or wanted to see you this evening, but something is stirring in him, and I think you should put as much effort into that as you are into twirling the plastic stick in your tea."

Roxy glanced down at the stirrer and took it out of her cup. Peter released her other hand.

"You don't know what you're asking me to do." She shook her head. "I left all that behind years ago, and with my mother's death I buried it deeper. It takes a ton of effort to talk to Ray. And with my father—" She stopped.

Peter leaned back in his chair. "I have a selfish reason for bringing this up," he said.

"What's that?"

"Because I don't want the woman I love to carry such a huge weight of past pain into our future relationship."

Once again unexpected tears rushed into Roxy's eyes. She

grabbed the tiny square napkin that came with her drink. Peter walked to the counter, grabbed another napkin, and put it down in front of her.

"And I'll keep doing that until there are no tears left to cry," he said.

"That's an odd way to say you love me," Roxy managed after a few moments passed.

"I'm not in this to impress you. Just to be with you."

Roxy's eyes reddened again. "I need more napkins, please," she said.

———

Ray sat in the waiting area of Cindy's ob-gyn. She'd asked him to drive her to the doctor's office so they could swing by a house she was interested in looking at on the way home. As none of the women's magazines on the table interested him, Ray called his father's office to let him know the time for Billy's soccer game the following morning.

"He's in Atlanta," Janelle said. "He had an appointment with a paralegal at the attorney general's office and then was going out to dinner with Roxy."

Ray was surprised by both statements. "Why was he meeting with someone at the AG's office?"

"Uh, you'd have to ask him the details."

Suddenly Ray suspected what his father was up to in Atlanta. He cupped his hand over the phone and spoke in an intense whisper. "Is he investigating the chemical spill by Colfax? I told him to leave that alone. Has Branson Kilpatrick been by to see him?"

"Ray, I shouldn't have said anything at all. Please don't let

Corbin know I slipped up. I let down my guard because it's you asking the questions."

"I won't bust you, but I can't believe he's thinking about tilting at that windmill. It would be terrible to get Branson's hopes up and then not be able to deliver any results."

"I told him the same thing. And it's not just Branson. There's another family with a sick child involved."

Ray exhaled. "Is he conducting a preliminary investigation or is he actually going to file suit?"

"I'd better not answer that either. Can we forget this conversation happened?"

Janelle's refusal to provide more information told Ray what he needed to know.

"Okay. I'll send him a text about the soccer game."

After the call ended, Ray sent the text to his father. A few minutes later Cindy emerged from the examination area with a bright smile on her face.

"Everything looks great," she said.

"Good."

"What's wrong?" she asked. "You look worried."

Ray stood up. "Nothing. I'm fine."

"No, you're not."

Cindy was worse than a persistent detective, but Ray didn't want to get trapped in a discussion about Colfax and childhood cancers.

"I called Janelle and found out my dad is having supper with Roxy in Atlanta."

"Really?" Cindy responded in surprise. "Let's hope they don't start a second civil war."

Corbin tried to leave behind his imaginary attempt at suicide by malfunctioning elevator as he walked across the parking lot to his truck. Roxy had needled him, and he'd reacted like a blubbering old man. He headed north on the expressway away from the city. Trying to force a relationship with her that she obviously didn't want was pointless. And he didn't really know what healthy interaction with his daughter would look like, or whether he even wanted to make the effort.

His cell phone rested in a holder attached to the lower left corner of the car's windshield. The phone vibrated and a text message from Ray popped up, notifying him about the time for Billy's soccer match. Corbin relaxed his grip on the steering wheel. He didn't have to wonder about the nature of his relationship with his grandson. And that was worth preserving.

The following morning Corbin left the liquor bottle in the kitchen cabinet and fortified himself with three cups of coffee. He drove to the soccer field, which was set up in the outfield of the Little League ballpark where Ray had played baseball when he was a boy. Billy, wearing a purple shirt and high-top purple socks, saw Corbin and ran over to him. The players on the opposing team were dressed in red.

"Hey, Pops," Billy said. "Thanks for coming."

Corbin rubbed the top of Billy's head. "What's the name of your team?"

"Purple Hurricanes. We're playing the Red Raiders. Alex Cross, who's in my class at school, is on their team." Billy pointed. "He's number eighteen."

Corbin saw a short boy with black hair.

"He's little, but he's fast," Billy said. "He plays striker, and I'm on defense."

"Where are your parents?" Corbin asked.

"I forgot to give Mama a note telling her it was her day to bring snacks and drinks for the team, so they went to the store."

"Did she get upset?"

"Yeah, but it wasn't like I did something terrible, like break something and lie about it."

A young man standing on the sideline held up his hand.

"That's Coach Stevens," Billy said. "I've got to go."

"Okay, I'll be cheering for you."

Billy paused. "You don't have to yell or anything. Just watch."

"Whatever you want."

The match started with both Billy and Alex on the field. Parents and family members clustered along the sideline. Corbin stood by himself and watched. Neither team seemed to have any set plays; the game plan apparently called for everyone to crowd around the ball. Every so often the ball would squirt out and a boy would kick it as hard as he could. It reminded Corbin more of rugby than soccer.

Once, while the ball was at the opposite end of the field, Corbin caught movement behind him and glanced over his shoulder to see Branson and Tommy Kilpatrick. A boy wearing a Red Raider uniform left them and ran up to the team coach. A younger boy with a ball cap on his head stayed behind, holding Branson's hand. Corbin walked over and greeted them.

"This is Mitchell," Branson said. "He's here to watch his brother play. Is Billy on the other team?"

"Yes," Corbin answered, but he kept his eyes on Mitchell.

He could tell the little boy was bald from chemotherapy, and his dark eyes were sunk back in his head. Corbin knelt down in front of him and extended his hand. "Hello, Mitchell," he said.

"This is Mr. Gage," Branson said.

Mitchell extended his hand. It felt as delicate as fine china. Corbin gently shook it. The boy kept his eyes downcast.

"He wanted to watch Kyle play," Branson said. "But he had a rough morning so we got a late start."

Corbin stood up. "I don't want to get in the way of that."

"Daddy, will you pick me up and take me?" Mitchell asked in a high-pitched voice.

Tommy scooped the boy up in his strong arms and headed over to the sideline. Corbin remained with Branson.

"Mitchell was already a bit of a runt before he got sick," Branson said, "so this has really knocked him backward. But on the bright side, he's spending so much time in the house that he's reading way better than Kyle did at age six. Larissa has really been working with him on the days he can't make it to school, and I think he's learning more from her than he would in a classroom."

"I don't doubt it."

Branson lowered his voice. "But the chemo treatments send him over the edge. I can't stay in the room and comfort him. It has to be either Tommy or Larissa. I don't think it hurts that much when it goes in, but he knows how bad he's going to feel later. It's rough."

Corbin told Branson about his trip to the attorney general's office in Atlanta.

"I haven't gone over all the data, but I'm confident there's enough to get me going with the lawsuit. There was also a reference to an anonymous report filed with the government by a whistle-blower at Colfax. I'll try to find out who that is as soon as I can."

"How will you do that?"

"I may ask Ray to contact one of the lawyers at the AG's office. As a prosecutor he's more likely to get an answer than I will."

Branson glanced over Corbin's shoulder. "Here comes Ray now. Let's ask him."

"I don't think now is the best time to bring it up."

Before Corbin could explain why he didn't want to say anything, Ray was standing beside Branson.

"Glad you could make it," Ray said to Corbin, then greeted Branson.

"I said I'd be here," Corbin replied.

"And we're going to turn you and Branson into soccer fans," Ray said. "What were the two of you talking about just now? You had your heads close together like a pair of bank robbers planning a heist."

"Your dad is representing us and another family in a lawsuit—" Branson began.

"Nothing has been filed," Corbin cut in. "Did you see Billy knock the ball away from the fast little player on the other team? That's Alex Cross. He and Billy are in the same class at school."

"Is that the lawsuit against Colfax?" Ray asked Branson. "I remember you coming by the other day to talk to me about the criminal charges against the company."

"There's no—" Corbin began.

"Hold on," Branson interrupted. "You were just telling me that you'd like to find out who turned the company in to the state EPA, and the folks in Atlanta are more likely to give Ray the inside scoop. It makes sense to me, seeing he's a government lawyer and works on the same side of things."

"Was a government lawyer," Ray corrected. "I've left the DA's office for private practice."

Corbin, who had been clenching his teeth, tried to relax and sound casual.

"How about it, Ray?" Corbin asked. "Would you do that for Branson? His six-year-old grandson is the one with non-Hodgkin's lymphoma. Tommy is holding him over there on the sidelines. He's the little fellow wearing the green ball cap."

"It's the hardest thing our family has ever gone through,"

Branson added, shaking his head. "And what made it worse is Tommy losing his job and benefits. I'm paying the premium under that COBRA thing so Mitchell can go to the doctor. But that's going to run out in a couple of months."

"And there's another little boy from the neighborhood with the same disease," Corbin continued, keeping his eyes on Ray. "What are the chances of that being a coincidence?"

"Is that the standard in court?" Ray asked caustically. "Proving that something might not be a coincidence?"

Corbin saw Branson glance back and forth between him and Ray with a puzzled expression on his face.

"There's no need for us to argue the case on the soccer field," Corbin replied testily. "If you decide you can help us out, it would be great."

"Yeah," Branson added. "I'd appreciate it a lot."

Corbin moved away toward the field.

———

Ray watched him go, then turned to Branson.

"I'll make the call but I'm not sure it will yield much. The important information is what the attorney general's office has in its file. Dad went to Atlanta yesterday to copy that."

"Right. He's working hard for us and the family of the other sick boy."

"You hired him?"

"Yep, we met with him last week at his office."

Ray watched his father walk down the sideline toward the end of the field where most of the action was taking place. He struggled with what else, if anything, to say to Branson.

"You say he's working hard?" He repeated the statement as a question.

"And you know what a bulldog he can be when he sinks his teeth into something." Branson lowered his voice. "At first I wasn't sure he still had enough fight left in him, but I trust him to let us know if he gets in over his head."

"Did you mention that to him?"

"Uh, no."

"Maybe you should. Just don't tell him I encouraged you to do it. He hates it when I stick my nose into his business."

"Really? He's always talked about you joining his firm someday."

"That's not happening, and he's upset about it."

"Tommy and I have had our moments," Branson said, patting Ray on the shoulder. "I wanted him to take over my business, but he likes to collect a regular paycheck. He went by the chicken plant this week looking for a job with benefits. Of course he has to do that so he can get on group insurance with a big company."

"Did they offer him a job?"

"He's waiting to hear."

Some of the spectators along the sideline began to cheer.

"Look at that!" Branson exclaimed. "Kyle's got the ball, and I don't think anyone is going to run him down!"

As they watched, Kyle deftly maneuvered past the goalkeeper and nudged the ball into the open net. Branson let out a whoop. Tommy turned around, saw them, and pumped his fist. Ray saw Mitchell's pale face beneath the brim of the ball cap. He knew dealing with a sick, possibly dying child would generate incomprehensible pressure on a family. They'd grasp at any straw in hope it would turn into a rope.

He looked at his father, standing by himself on the sidelines with his hands behind his back.

Ray doubted Corbin Gage had the ability to weave together anything that could hold up even a child as fragile as Mitchell Kilpatrick.

TWENTY-FOUR

Corbin made sure the boat was securely fastened to the trailer and climbed into the driver's seat of the truck.

"What do you think?" he asked Billy. "Has it been a good day?"

"Yeah." Billy nodded. "Did you send Daddy a picture of the fish I caught?"

"No, but I'll do it before we leave."

Corbin found the photo he'd taken with his phone. It was one of the largest bream he'd ever seen in Hackburn's Lake. The fish had put up a ferocious fight, expertly handled by Billy, who never lost his cool and reeled it in perfectly. Corbin stared again at the fish, which they weighed, measured, and released back into the pond.

"Man, that is an awesome fish," he said more to himself than to Billy. "A lot of fishermen as old as I am have never caught a two-and-a-half-pound bream."

"How old are you, Pops?"

"Sixty-two. I bet that seems ancient to you."

"Ancient?"

"Very old."

"Yeah, but you still go fishing."

Corbin started the engine and put the shifter in drive. An unopened jar of moonshine hadn't left its spot behind his seat all day.

"If your daddy or mama asks, make sure you tell them I drank water from the bottles we bought at the tackle shop, not from a mason jar."

"Okay. What are you going to do with the leftover crickets?" Billy asked.

"Do you want to set them free in your backyard? That way you can listen to them sing through the open window in your bedroom when you lie down tonight."

"I'd like that," Billy answered as he stared out the window. "And thanks for coming to my soccer match."

"You played great."

"Not really. I'm not that good at soccer. I have a problem making the ball go where I want it to when I kick it. I'm a lot better at fishing because you've taught me how to do it. Coach Stevens never played soccer. He's just a dad who agreed to help out."

Corbin pulled onto the main roadway and turned toward Alto. When they approached the Hopewell Methodist Church, Billy spoke.

"Is that the place where you go to your special meeting?"

"Who told you about that?" Corbin asked in surprise.

"Mama. She said it has to do with the AA club you joined. What kind of club is it?"

"It's for people who help each other with their problems."

"What kind of problems?"

Corbin drove for a few moments in silence. "Maybe you should ask your mama, since she brought it up. That way she can explain it the way she wants to."

"Does she go too?"

"No." Corbin smiled wryly. "And I doubt she ever will."

When they reached the house, Corbin moved stiffly as he got out of the truck. "You've worn me out," he said as he leaned over the side of the truck to take out Billy's fishing pole.

"Will you help me turn the crickets loose?" Billy asked.

"Sure."

Leaving Billy's fishing pole and tackle box on the front stoop, they walked around the side of the house into the backyard. Billy carried the wire mesh bucket that contained about twenty brown crickets.

"These are the lucky ones," Corbin said.

Billy turned over the bucket. A few crickets fell out, but most of them clung to the mesh.

"Shake it," Corbin said.

Billy shook the bucket but only dislodged one cricket.

"This isn't going to work," the boy said.

"Give it to me. They're going to take individual encouragement."

Corbin reached in and carefully caught a cricket without crushing it. He placed the insect on the ground. With all the hungry birds in the neighborhood, the cricket's life expectancy was probably a matter of hours, but Corbin didn't point that out to Billy.

"You get one," he said to Billy.

He watched as Billy gently pinched a cricket between his fingers and lifted it out. Taking turns, they released all the crickets. The back door of the house opened, and Ray came out.

"We're letting this group of crickets out of jail," Corbin said. "They survived our trip to the pond, and I decided it would be double jeopardy to keep them incarcerated."

"I saw the picture of the huge bream you caught," Ray said to Billy. "Did you use a cricket as bait?"

"No, I hooked him with a lure. Pops says a fish that big wants a big meal."

"And we're done," Corbin said, getting to his feet. "I need to be getting home. Between soccer and fishing, it's been a long day."

"Pops drank the water we bought at the bait shop," Billy said. "He didn't use a major jar."

"Mason jar," Corbin corrected.

"That's good," Ray replied. "Go inside and wash up. Supper will be ready in a minute. Your mama is fixing lasagna."

Billy ran into the house.

"Do you want to eat with us?" Ray asked.

"No, I only stayed to help Billy free the crickets." Corbin picked up the empty bucket.

"After seeing Branson's grandson at the soccer match, I understand why you want to help them," Ray said. "I told him I'd try to find out who reported Colfax to the state environmental authorities."

"Thanks."

"But if you're bound and determined to file the lawsuit, you have to associate another firm to help. Roxy did some checking, and you should give her a call and—"

"No," Corbin cut in. "I'm not going to be talking to Roxy, and I'd appreciate you not mentioning her to me. Good night."

Corbin turned around and retraced his steps to the front of the house.

"What happened?" Ray called after him.

Corbin paused and glanced over his shoulder. "I left Billy's pole and tackle box on the front stoop. Don't forget to put them away. And tell Cindy thanks for letting me take him. What Billy said about the bottled water was true."

———

Sunday morning was one of Roxy's favorite times of the week. Like most days, she went for a run, but she rarely arrived at the office until midafternoon. Today she left Piedmont Park and turned onto Eastside Trail. It was one of the first sections to open off the Atlanta Beltway, a comprehensive urban development project designed to unite the center city area with walking, running, and biking trails.

The weather and temperature were perfect, and Roxy ramped up to cruising speed, which meant she passed all the female and most of the male runners on the path. The unfettered freedom she felt when her feet tapped out a light, quick rhythm was an incredible natural high. She looped around at Irwin Street and returned to the park. After completing her short burst interval runs, she jogged to her townhome, where she was surprised to see Peter's empty car parked near her unit.

Roxy kept a spare key hidden beneath a fake rock in the bushes. Peter knew about the key, but when she checked, it was still there. Holding on to the iron railing, she stretched and looked up and down the street, wondering where he might be. As she finished he came around the corner, wearing khakis and a collared shirt and carrying a tray from a nearby coffee shop.

"What are you doing here?" she asked when he came closer.

"Bringing you coffee and the cheese Danish you like."

"But how did you know what time to get here?"

"Roxy, you're more predictable than the tides. I know within a few minutes when you'll be finished and cooling off."

"Does that make me boring?"

Peter laughed. "You have plenty of uncertainty in other areas of your life. You're allowed to have some routine too."

They walked up the steps into the townhome. Peter put the coffees and bag of pastries on the small round table in the kitchen.

"Why are you dressed for a business meeting?" Roxy asked.

"So I can take you to church."

Roxy had her back to him and was pouring a glass of water from a purifier on the counter beside the sink. She turned around.

"Church?"

"Yeah. We don't have to be there for over an hour. Will that give you time to cool off and get ready?"

Roxy glanced at the clock on her microwave. It would be hard to turn him down after he showed up with fresh coffee and her favorite pastry.

"Okay, I guess."

"We're going to meet Noah and Julie. Do you want your coffee now?"

"Yes, and I'll nibble the Danish."

Roxy left Peter reading a local magazine and sipping coffee in her living room. He spent so much time in front of a computer screen that she knew he liked to occasionally hold reading material in his hands.

This sudden interest in church baffled her. Unlike Roxy, Peter'd had no prior contact with organized religion. His parents lived for golf and bridge, with an occasional Caribbean or Mediterranean cruise thrown in for variety.

After taking a shower, Roxy stood in the doorway of her closet and tried to decide what to wear. Buckhead was the heart of old money, aristocratic Atlanta. So even though Peter wasn't wearing a coat and tie, she selected one of her nicer, conservative dresses. She walked downstairs to the living room.

"Wow," Peter said. "You're gorgeous."

"Thanks."

"But this isn't the kind of church where you have to dress up like you're going to a nice restaurant."

"Oh. Do you think I'll stick out if I wear this?"

"Yeah," Peter replied. "I mean, you look fantastic, but—"

"No, I get it. I'll switch to something else."

Roxy trudged upstairs to her bedroom and took inventory of

her wardrobe. It was not the kind of decision she'd expected to make on a Sunday morning. Finally she settled on a standby outfit of skinny jeans, ankle boots, and a deep red tunic.

"Perfect," Peter said when he saw her. "You wear that a lot."

Roxy stopped in her tracks. "Do I wear it too much?"

"No, it's good, and we need to go."

"Do I have time to warm up what's left of my coffee?"

"Sure. I made a pot if you want to top it off with home brewed."

They got into Peter's car. Roxy placed the full cup of coffee in a holder and fastened her seat belt.

"Don't drive like a maniac," she said. "If I spill coffee or get a stain on my clothes, I can't go."

"When was the last time I drove like a maniac?"

"When we were late for our dinner date with your boss and his wife. You ran two red lights and almost hit a truck backing into a loading bay."

"Okay," Peter admitted as he pulled out of the parking space. "Although I think one of the lights was still yellow."

They rode in silence for several blocks while Roxy sipped her coffee and nibbled on the pastry.

"How's the coffee mix?" Peter asked when he carefully slowed for a light as it turned from yellow to red.

"We should have gone back to the shop for a refill."

Roxy's level of frustration at the unexpected disruption of her Sunday morning plans steadily increased. She stared out the window as they passed the most exclusive shopping districts in the city.

Peter turned into a side street for a parking deck between two office towers. They waited in a line of cars to enter the deck.

"There's a church here?" Roxy asked.

"Yes, it meets in the lower level of the building to the left."

"I didn't see a sign or anything. Do they rent the space on Sunday?"

"Maybe. Like I said, it's different from my idea of a church."

"I don't want to go to anything weird."

"Noah's a computer nerd like me. Does that make him weird?"

"Probably."

"And Julie grew up in a little town in Alabama that sounds a lot like Alto."

"Exciting," Roxy said flatly.

A young man wearing a large orange vest with VOLUNTEER printed on it motioned for them to enter the deck. Roxy took a final sip of coffee as Peter pulled into a parking space.

"I hope this isn't as boring as the motion calendar I sat through last week in federal court," she said. "Our case was supposed to be called at ten thirty, and the judge didn't reach it until one o'clock in the afternoon."

She reached for the door handle. Peter didn't turn off the motor.

"Do you want to leave?" he asked. "I'll text Noah and tell him something came up."

Roxy pressed her lips together tightly for a moment. "No. You want to do this, and I shouldn't be a brat about it. I promise to put on my best Sunday morning church face and be as Southern nice as sweet tea to everyone I meet."

Peter chuckled. "That will be interesting."

As they joined the crowd leaving the parking deck, Roxy reached out for Peter's hand. She took it and squeezed it.

"Is that part of being Southern nice?" he asked.

"Only to you."

As Peter had promised, the people coming to the service were casually dressed. There were singles, young couples, families with small children, and a few older folks sprinkled in the mix like the first appearances of gray hair.

"There's Noah," Peter said.

When she saw him, Roxy remembered meeting him at Peter's office Christmas party. He was shorter and heavier than Peter. His wife, Julie, was about the same age as Roxy and very pregnant. Peter introduced everyone.

"When is your baby due?" Roxy asked Julie.

"Four weeks. And this may be one of the last times I get out. I'm having twins, and my doctor will probably confine me to the house until I deliver."

Roxy's eyes widened. "Is everything okay?"

"Yes, but I wouldn't want to miss the service this morning for anything."

"Let's go," Noah said.

Peter glanced at Roxy and raised his eyebrows. She ignored him. They followed Noah and Julie into a large room where chairs were set up for four or five hundred people. Over half the seats were already taken. A band was gearing up to play.

"We like to sit close to the front," Noah said to Peter. "Is that okay?"

"Sure," Peter answered without consulting Roxy.

They followed Noah and Julie down a center aisle. Julie had the distinctive waddle of a seriously pregnant woman.

Roxy touched her own rock-hard abdomen and wondered if she would ever be the incubator for a baby. They stopped four rows from the front and sat down.

Peter leaned over to Roxy. "The other time I came we sat on the second row."

"Thrilling."

"Southern nice, don't forget."

There was a lot of hubbub in the room as people clustered in small groups to talk and laugh. It was a different atmosphere from her mother's church in Alto, where little more than whispers preceded the service. The members of the band took their positions and began to play. Roxy sat down, but when everyone remained standing she got back up. The words to an unfamiliar song appeared on a screen. The congregation sang along with the band.

And Peter joined in on the chorus.

TWENTY-FIVE

Corbin spent Sunday morning at the office. Work was the only source of sporadic discipline and structure in his life, and he knew if he stayed home, he would end up sitting on the couch in the living room with a bottle in his hand, staring at the opposite wall. An alcohol-induced stupor had a certain level of attraction, but he couldn't get the image of Mitchell Kilpatrick at the soccer match out of his mind.

Laying out the information obtained from the attorney general's office, Corbin carefully went through each page, making notes on a legal pad. He wrote down the multisyllabic names of different chemicals, cross-checked the list against the material safety data sheets from the Colfax plant, then logged onto the Internet to determine if there were any other verified or alleged health risks associated with each chemical. It was a tedious but necessary process.

Shortly before noon, he wrote down an herbicide with the tongue-twisting name of 2,4-dichlorophenoxyacetic acid. A scholarly article popped up about pesticides and non-Hodgkin's lymphoma. Contained in the article was a reference to herbicides, including 2,4-dichlorophenoxyacetic acid. Known by its abbreviation, 2,4-D, it had been linked to a two- to eightfold increase in non-Hodgkin's lymphoma in studies conducted in Sweden, Kansas, Nebraska, and

Canada. Corbin's heart started beating faster. He tried to track down the studies mentioned in the article, but couldn't access them because he wasn't a subscriber to the sites where they appeared. At any rate, detailed analysis of the technical data would be a job for an expert witness who could explain everything to him.

"This could be it," he muttered as he printed off several pages of information.

Reading other materials available to the public, he quickly found himself in the midst of a debate between scientists defending the use of 2,4-D as a broadleaf herbicide and those who cautioned against its environmental impact. Academic passions flared and he learned that 2,4-D was one of the primary ingredients in the herbicidal cocktail known as Agent Orange that was used during the Vietnam war to deforest jungle where the Vietcong liked to hide.

Corbin leaned back in his chair. If he could land a Vietnam vet on his jury, the man might add personal horror stories to the testimony brought out in the courtroom. Emotion could influence a jury's deliberation as much as facts.

Corbin returned to his list of chemicals. It was midafternoon by the time he finished going through the information. The review left him with one major disappointment. The state EPA did not go after Colfax for its use of 2,4-D. Their complaint had to do with Dacthal and Endothall, two herbicides with a greater propensity to seep into groundwater than 2,4-D but with no known or alleged connection to non-Hodgkin's lymphoma. Dacthal, in large concentrations, could result in thyroid or liver problems, and Endothall seeping into well water could cause an upset stomach. One thing was clear. With unsurprising corporate arrogance, Colfax treated Rusk County as its own unregulated dumping ground.

Corbin was hungry. He'd been so engrossed in his work that he hadn't taken a break for lunch. He locked up the office but didn't know where to go. Dining options on a Sunday afternoon in Alto were limited.

Getting in his truck, he drove to a convenience store and bought a pack of crackers. He munched one as he passed the local mental health facility. In the parking lot he saw Max Hogan getting out of his car. Guessing there might be an AA meeting about to start, Corbin pulled into the lot.

—

"What did you think?" Peter asked Roxy as soon as the church service was over and people began moving out of their seats.

Roxy didn't want to put a damper on Peter's enthusiasm, but her mind had wandered while the young minister spoke about the Sermon on the Mount and contrasted Jesus's perspective on morality with the view of the Pharisees. The message had been less stuffy than the preaching at her home church in Alto, though, and she could tell Peter had been listening intently.

"It was fine," she replied.

"I'd heard of the Sermon on the Mount," Peter said when they left the room and entered a large lobby near a bank of elevators. "But I thought it was just the Beatitudes. I didn't know it filled several chapters of the gospel of Matthew."

Hearing Peter talk about the Bible as if it was a book he was studying for a college class sounded odd to Roxy's ears. They continued through the door that led to the parking deck.

"I didn't know that either," she said, "and I went to church a lot when I was growing up in Alto."

"Why did you stop?"

Roxy started to give him a flippant answer, but the words didn't come out of her mouth. They entered the elevator in the parking ramp, and Peter pushed the button for the level where they'd left the car.

"I'm not sure why I lost interest in religion," she said thoughtfully. "It might have been my desire to leave behind everything I could from Alto. When I packed my car for college, I didn't want to bring along anything that had made my life so painful."

"And what you experienced in your home church fell into that category?"

"Not really."

"Then why didn't you pack God in your car when you left home?"

Roxy bit her lower lip and hesitated for a moment. Peter deserved an honest answer.

"Because I didn't believe that God, if he existed, was interested in coming with me. Otherwise he would have answered my mother's prayers for my father."

———

Monday morning, Corbin thought about the AA meeting on his way to the office. Having been three times now, he was getting more familiar with the format of the gatherings, although each one was unique in its own way. The previous afternoon had been a speaker meeting, and a retired salesman who lived at Lake Lanier told the story of his struggle with alcoholism and subsequent four years of sobriety. It was a different verse of the same song played over and over in the Big Book, but for Corbin, hearing it from the lips of someone standing in front of him made it come alive. He thought there would be a time for questions and answers when the speaker finished, but the meeting ended abruptly, leaving Corbin wanting more.

"What brings you in so early?" he asked Janelle after he entered through the back door and poured a cup of freshly brewed coffee.

"I wanted to follow up first thing on the medical records we haven't received in the Colfax case. Sometimes it's easier to reach someone at the doctor's office before they get busy."

"I worked all day yesterday." Corbin told her about his research.

"I'm not following you," Janelle said when he finished. "Who believes this 2,4-D stuff causes cancer in little boys, and why didn't the EPA in Atlanta go after that if it's so dangerous?"

"The health risks are still a matter of debate among the scientists, and I didn't find any link to kids." Corbin stopped. "Which means I really don't know what I'm talking about until I hire someone to explain it to me."

"And who can lay it out to a jury made up of people who are as dumb as I am."

"Give yourself credit for a few extra brain cells. Your instincts are usually right."

"Including when I warned you against taking the Colfax case in the first place?"

"Except for that." Corbin sipped his coffee. "By the end of today, I want to have a complaint ready to file. Keep tracking down medical records while I dictate a first draft."

Ray was sitting in front of the computer in the corner of the bedroom checking the news when an e-mail popped up from Nate Stamper. Ray took a deep breath and clicked open an attached document. His heart rate picked up as a contract popped into view.

Employment agreements are often like stories that keep the reader in suspense until the very end. Ray waded through the expected boilerplate provisions about his obligation to perform his job duties to the best of his ability and a paragraph stating not to engage in any activity that might be in conflict with his work at the firm. There was a very detailed noncompete section. Courts and judges hate restraints against unfettered economic freedom, and Ray knew each sentence was the product of guidance handed down by appellate judges. He shook his head at a stipulation that the firm would own the rights to any legal works he wrote or published. Ray's expertise was as a trial lawyer, and there wasn't a market for anything he might put on paper.

The important sections didn't begin until page eight. He slowed down to make sure he understood the firm's health insurance options and how participation in the profit sharing plan worked for an associate attorney. Like Jacob in the Bible, he would have to wait seven years before he was fully vested and able to take all his profit sharing money with him if he left. Not that he would start a job with a plan on leaving. There was no better place for a lawyer in Alto, and he and Cindy were going to plant their roots deeper, not pluck them up. Ray advanced the screen to the next page. Finally a number appeared in the middle of a long paragraph: the amount of his base salary. When he saw the figure, Ray stopped and read it again.

"Yes!" he cried out, raising his arms in the signal for a touchdown.

A few seconds later Cindy appeared, looking bedraggled and pale. "What's going on?" she asked.

"Are you okay?" Ray responded.

"No, I just finished doing what pregnant women often do during the first trimester."

"Would you like some good news?"

"Yes."

"I got the employment contract from the Simpkin firm. And guess how much they're going to pay me?"

"I'm not in a guessing mood. Is it good?"

"Much better than good." Ray told her the terms of the offer. "As soon as you feel better, schedule an appointment with the real estate agent. You're getting a bigger nest."

"Fantastic," Cindy replied in a flat tone of voice. "And if that doesn't sound like I mean it, it's because my stomach is dragging down my heart and mind. Do you think you should get someone else to look over the agreement in case you missed something?"

"Who would I ask? My father? He knows less about employment law than I do. It's a long document, but simple enough for me to decipher. Besides, I trust Nate to make the best proposal possible."

"Okay, congratulations. I need to lie down for a few minutes, then I'll call the Realtor."

Ray signed the contract, scanned it, and sent it to Nate with a note reiterating his appreciation for the job and promising to be there bright and early Monday morning. The next stage of his life was set.

Wanting to tell someone, he took out his cell phone and called Roxy. He didn't really expect her to answer, but to his surprise, she did.

"I thought I'd leave you a voice mail," he began.

"Do you want me to hang up so you can call back?"

"No, no. I didn't want to interrupt something important."

"Normally I wouldn't have been able to take the call, but I'm in a conference room waiting for a lawyer to get here so we can take a deposition. His assistant claims he's stuck in traffic, but I breezed over here from my office, so I suspect he's lying. What's going on?"

Ray told her about the job offer. He hesitated before revealing the starting salary, but did anyway.

"The amount of compensation is supposed to be confidential," he said, "but I can tell you. Hey, would you be willing to look over the agreement as my attorney and make sure I didn't miss a red flag?"

"Have you signed it?"

"Yes, and sent it to Nate Stamper."

"It's better to get a lawyer's advice before you sign something."

"I know, but I was pumped up and excited. Anyway, I'm sure it's fine. I studied the important parts myself."

"Did you suggest any changes?"

"No."

"Then let's hope it's okay. Hey, I'm happy for you. That much money will stretch a lot farther in Alto than it does in Atlanta." Roxy paused. "Did you see our father this past weekend?"

"Yeah, he came to Billy's soccer match, then took him fishing. I don't think he drank while they were out in the boat."

"That's positive. Do you think his interest in AA is for real? Or is it a new form of manipulation because he's afraid of losing time with Billy?"

"Time will tell. And I heard from Janelle that he stopped off to see you on Friday, but when I asked Dad about it he told me to drop it. What happened?"

Roxy told him. "And I've been upset about the way I acted ever since," she finished.

Ray sat up straighter in his chair. It was a rare admission of fault from his sister.

"Do you want me to talk to him for you? It might take him a few days to calm down before I can bring it up."

"Whatever you think is best. After Mom's funeral I came back to Atlanta prepared to write him off."

"I don't blame you. A lot of what he did rolled off my back, but it didn't work like that for you. You absorbed it. Mom would pray. That was her outlet."

"It didn't do her any good."

"Not yet. But just because she's gone doesn't mean her prayers died with her."

Roxy was silent.

"Are you there?" Ray asked.

"Yes. It's just I've never thought about things like this before. Or talked about it. Peter is making me face things I've stuffed way down deep. I even went to church with him yesterday."

Ray almost dropped the phone. One of their mother's constant prayers was that Roxy would return to God's sheepfold, but his sister's heart was diamond hard.

"That's great," he said, trying to sound casual.

"But I'm not sure it's for me." Roxy paused again. "Opposing counsel has arrived. Gotta go."

The phone went dead. Ray lowered it to his desk. He had more surprising news to share with Cindy.

TWENTY-SIX

Corbin reviewed the complaint and declared himself pleased with his work. He'd located several toxic tort cases via computer research, and the work of the other attorneys helped him structure his opening salvo in a professional, organized way. Because he wasn't sure which theory of liability would eventually stick, he included several. One yellow brick road was all he needed to find his way to a huge recovery. He stepped out to Janelle's desk with the complaint in his hand.

"What did you think when you typed it?" he asked, holding up the stack of papers.

"You've worked harder on this than on anything I can remember in years," she replied. "It tells the story and lays out the claim pretty well."

"Thanks." A compliment from Janelle had to be earned.

"Have you made any progress finding an expert?" she asked.

"No, but I'm not going to file any interrogatories or requests for production of documents until I have one. The complaint puts Colfax on notice that I'm coming after them. I want my discovery questions to be more focused. And I'll have at least sixty days after I serve the complaint to find an expert. One of the cases I reviewed involved a claim against a chemical company. I'm going to get copies of what was filed and find out who the plaintiff used."

"Was it a Georgia case?"

"No, California."

This time Janelle rolled her eyes. "That means paying a bunch of money for travel, in addition to the expert's time analyzing the evidence," she said. "And it will be hard to convince a Rusk County jury to believe a guy who comes into court looking like he just got off a surfboard."

"Don't profile him yet." Corbin put the complaint on her desk. "Format the complaint in final form along with the service copy for the defendant."

Janelle picked it up and held it loosely in her hand. "Are you sure—" she started, then hesitated.

"Yes. As much as anything I've sent out of this office in the past twenty years. This is a righteous cause."

Energized, Corbin returned to his office and worked on several matters he'd put to the side while he focused on the Colfax case. Working on the big case seemed to give him the ability to focus on other matters as well. He felt more like a lawyer than he had for years.

A little later there was a light tap on his door, and Janelle entered.

"Okay, here it is," she said. "I advanced the filing fee since I assumed you weren't going to wait for the plaintiffs to pay it."

"Right. That's pocket change compared to the money I'm about to spend."

"Do you know the amount of reserve in your operating account?"

Corbin usually did little more than glance at the bank balance to make sure he had enough to keep going for another month. Janelle balanced the books and paid his personal and business bills. He tossed out a figure.

Janelle nodded, and he felt good—until she spoke.

"Cut that in half," she said. "The property tax on this place is due this month, along with your annual malpractice premium and a three-month deposit on your health insurance, which is up 20 percent over last year."

"Ouch."

"Yeah."

Corbin picked up the complaint, turned to the final page, and signed it. He returned it to Janelle.

"Like Colonel Parker, I'm not dwelling on past failures but pressing on into future triumphs."

"What about the newspaper?" she asked.

Corbin hesitated. The complaint would be public record as soon as he dropped it off at the clerk's office, but without a push from him it might never generate a newspaper article unless the case went to trial. Without publicity he wouldn't have to worry about disqualifying a potential juror who'd formed an opinion against the company. But he also wouldn't have the benefit of the pressure that public opinion would exert on Colfax. The company took great pride in its community image.

"I'll decide after the case is filed," he said. "I'll take the complaint to the courthouse myself."

"Today?"

Corbin checked his watch. It was just past four thirty. "Yes, so I can try to find out which judge is on deck."

Fifteen minutes later Corbin left the office and waited for the light to change before crossing the street. Since it was near the end of the day, he hoped the atmosphere would be sufficiently relaxed that he could engage in the time-honored practice of judge shopping.

New cases were assigned to either Judge Ellington or Judge Perry. In virtually every situation, Corbin preferred the crusty independence of the former to the subtle hostility of the latter.

"Good afternoon, June." He greeted the assistant clerk, a plain-looking young woman with mousy brown hair. "How's business?"

"Booming, if you like divorces," she replied.

"Is your husband still treating you like a queen?"

Several years before, Corbin had represented June's husband for injuries sustained in a car wreck. At Corbin's suggestion, the first thing the young man did with his settlement money was buy a legitimate diamond ring for June. The ring still sparkled on the young woman's stubby finger.

"Most days. What do you have for me today?"

"A complaint." Corbin leaned against the counter and tried to make out the images on June's computer screen. "Who's up to bat?"

The clerk's office would assign cases to the judges according to a rotating formula, three cases to Judge Ellington followed by three for Judge Perry, or some other system for the week or month. Knowing the code and each judge's status was highly desired information to the local bar.

"Mr. Gage, you know I can't tell you that," June replied.

"I wouldn't expect you to," Corbin replied smoothly. "But if you would pull this case for me, I'd really appreciate it."

He reached across the counter and handed her a slip of paper with a file number on it. June gave him a knowing look and smiled. As she got up from her chair, she turned her computer screen so it faced Corbin. He could barely make out the names of the last five cases that had been opened as active files. There were two with E after the number, followed by two with a P, followed by one with an E. The next case would be assigned to Judge Ellington. June returned with the file he'd requested.

"You dismissed this case two months ago," she said as she flipped through the folder.

"And I'm thinking about refiling before the statute of limitations runs out."

It was a true statement. Corbin had discussed the matter with the client while he waited for Janelle to finalize the Colfax complaint. He handed the complaint and filing fee check to June.

"Stamp this in for me, please."

The clerk looked at the style of the pleadings where the names of the parties appeared. It included the names of the boys, their parents, and Colfax as defendant. June's eyes widened.

"Yes, sir."

———

Two days later Ray and Cindy were having their morning time together at the kitchen table after Billy left the house for the bus stop.

"What's on your schedule today?" Cindy asked him.

"I'm going by the law firm to begin setting up my office, and I may try to see if Dad is available for lunch."

"Has he been to another AA meeting?"

"I don't know, but I'm going to suggest he reach out to Roxy. He's had almost a week to settle down, and I'd like to tell him the positive things happening in her life."

"Will he think going to church is positive?"

"Since it's Roxy, I think so. He knows how hardheaded and independent she is."

"Does he know where she got those traits?"

"Our family isn't very self-aware," Ray replied with a smile, "but if I can deliver the message that she's sorry for the way she acted when he came to Atlanta, it'll get his attention."

Cindy took a final sip of water. She'd sworn off caffeine for the rest of the first trimester.

"I told the Realtor I'd let her know if I'm up to seeing a few houses," she said. "I received an e-mail this morning about a place that just came on the market. It's a four-bedroom on Walker Street, not far from the intersection with Lafayette Place. I'm meeting the real estate agent there in forty-five minutes."

The area was familiar to Ray. It was an established neighborhood.

"Those are older homes," he said. "I thought you wanted something new."

"She claims this place has been totally modernized. And it's on one of the bigger lots in the subdivision, with a lot of mature trees."

"Let me know the address if you like it. I might run by before I come home."

After Cindy left for her meeting with the real estate agent, Ray called the law firm to make sure it was a good time to stop by and begin organizing his new office.

"This is Ray Gage. I'd like to—"

The British receptionist cut him off. "Nate Stamper told me to let him know immediately if you called or came by. Please hold."

TWENTY-SEVEN

"Let's take a ten-minute break," Roxy said. "I'm about halfway through my questions for the witness."

"No, we're going to proceed," came the crisp response from Eric Shoemaker, the older lawyer on the other side of the table. "Dr. Callahan has a limited amount of time available, and we're not going to prolong the deposition."

"I could use a bathroom break," interjected the female court reporter, raising her hand. "I had an extra cup of coffee on my way here this morning."

"All right, but make it five minutes or we're going to suspend questioning and excuse the witness," Shoemaker responded.

Roxy pulled out her phone and started her timer. "Should we coordinate our stopwatch apps?"

The older lawyer ignored her. Roxy and the court reporter walked rapidly to the restroom together.

"Thanks," Roxy said.

"I've seen him pull that stunt before." The court reporter smiled.

When everyone returned to the conference room, Roxy placed her phone on the table. "We have twenty seconds left in our break, but I'm ready to proceed if you are."

"It's your deposition," Shoemaker grunted. "Get on with it, and if you try to cover the same ground twice, I'm going to instruct the witness not to answer."

"And I'll file a motion for sanctions that will be waiting on you when you return to your office."

Contrary to popular belief, the most contentious aspects of a trial didn't occur in the courtroom, but during the long discovery process. Without a judge present to force the attorneys to behave as adults, petty hassles and groundless controversies frequently erupted. One of the most common tactics used by older lawyers against younger ones was raw intimidation. However, Roxy didn't hesitate to call an obstinate lawyer's bluff, and used belligerence as fuel for increased focus. Also, she knew that if she backed down, the chewing out she'd receive from Mr. Caldweller after he reviewed the transcript would be much worse than anything opposing counsel could dish out.

An hour later she scored a big point with the witness that caught the defense lawyer off guard.

"Objection!" Shoemaker shouted.

"On what grounds?" Roxy shot back. "You're limited to the form of the question, and your problem is with the answer."

Out of the corner of her eye, Roxy saw Heather Lansdowne, the younger lawyer who'd accompanied her boss to the deposition, cover her mouth to keep from laughing. He spouted a few words of legal-sounding gibberish that Roxy knew wouldn't hold up in front of a judge.

"Is that all?" she asked him when he finished.

"Subject to supplementation."

Roxy didn't revel in her momentary triumph. She had other important matters to cover. When she finished, the defense lawyer did a good job of trying to undo the damage. Roxy didn't get upset.

The ability to point out inconsistent answers in a deposition would quickly render an expert useless at trial. She doubted she'd see Dr. Callahan again. She finished the deposition an hour earlier than she anticipated.

"See, that didn't take too long," she said to Mr. Shoemaker.

The man didn't respond as he packed up his briefcase. His female associate cast a secret smile in Roxy's direction.

"Let's go," her boss said.

Heather lagged behind for a moment and made the motion of drinking from a coffee cup.

"Yes." Roxy nodded and handed her a business card.

Returning to the office, she passed the church she'd attended with Peter. It looked like a typical Atlanta office complex. Often what took place inside a building couldn't be discerned from its exterior. People were like that too.

Corbin finished reading the résumé of Dr. Vincent Westbrook, the expert witness who testified in the California chemical exposure case. Dr. Westbrook was certainly a seasoned courtroom warrior, having testified in over 120 tort cases. But the very scope of the chemist's experience made Corbin nervous. The defense lawyers hired by Colfax would comb the record in every one of Westbrook's cases in search of inconsistent statements or nuggets of testimony that could be turned into mountains of criticism. The more an expert testified, the bigger the target he became.

It was too early to call someone in California, so Corbin slowly typed a brief e-mail to Dr. Westbrook explaining the type of help he needed in the Colfax litigation. At the least Corbin might pick up a few pieces of free information via preliminary dialogue about the case. After sending the e-mail, he looked at an unopened stack of mail from the previous two days on his desk and buzzed Janelle.

"Come into my office and bring a steno pad," he said.

A few seconds later Janelle opened the door and hesitantly peered inside.

"Are you going to make me use my shorthand?" she asked. "I told you five years ago to let that die a natural death, and I haven't practiced since. Nobody within fifty miles of this office expects a secretary—"

"Calm down." Corbin held up his hand. "I just want you to take a few notes on what we need to do as I open the mail."

"Oh. Okay."

Janelle sat down and crossed her legs. Corbin picked up an envelope and sliced it open. Fifteen minutes later, they completed the task.

"That wasn't so bad, was it?" Corbin asked. "And it forced me to address things that might have gotten buried on my desk until they rose up to bite me."

"Okay." Janelle nodded. "What made you think about doing that?"

"Something I heard recently about making a searching and fearless moral inventory. Putting things off can be a problem for me, and I need to do something about it."

"Moral inventory? What's that?"

"Identifying and facing your problems instead of ignoring them."

Janelle's mouth dropped open. "You're doing that?"

"Starting with the mail."

Janelle shook her head as she left the office. She stopped and turned around. "Oh, Ray called while you didn't want to be inter-rupted. He'll meet you at Red's for lunch at noon. I told him your calendar was clear."

"Red's?"

"That's what he said."

Corbin walked past several booths until his son's face came into view. Ray was squeezing a lemon wedge into a glass of tea. Corbin slipped into the booth.

"I didn't know you liked Red's beans and rice," Corbin said.

"I don't. I'm getting a vegetable plate."

Sally took their orders. After she left, Ray remained quiet. Corbin shifted in the booth and placed his hands on the table.

"Has Steve Nelson hired your replacement?" he asked.

"I heard through the grapevine that Brett Dortch came in this morning," Ray replied in a flat tone of voice.

"Dortch? How long has he been practicing? Six months? He barely knows where the jury sits in the courtroom. He's going to have a hard time filling your shoes. Within three months Steve Nelson is going to wish he had you back running the felony trial calendar—"

"The Simpkin firm withdrew its offer," Ray interrupted.

Corbin's mouth opened, then immediately snapped shut. Ray glanced down at the table.

"Why?" Corbin asked.

Ray looked up into his father's eyes. "Because of you."

In a split second several thoughts raced through Corbin's mind in a rapid-fire moral inventory a lot more serious than procrastination in opening the mail. In the deepest part of his soul, he knew his conduct could, at times, be embarrassing to his family, but not to the level of costing Ray a job.

"I don't understand."

"Are you that dense?" Ray tapped the side of his head.

Startled, Corbin sat back in his seat. Ray had never been so blatantly disrespectful.

"The Colfax lawsuit," Ray continued. "The company hired the Simpkin firm to defend it."

"That's bogus." Corbin's eyes flashed. "They knew when they offered you the job that I could end up on the opposite side of a case. That's been going on for decades."

"Petty stuff"—Ray shrugged—"which could be ignored so long as I didn't work on the files. Colfax is the firm's biggest client, and my name can't be on the letterhead if your name is on pleadings against the company."

Corbin saw Sally across the restaurant and suddenly wished he could order a tall glass of "mountain water." He rubbed his temples as a headache began to creep up the sides of his skull.

"I'm sorry," he said.

"Is that all?" Ray asked.

"What do you want me to say? I can't dismiss the lawsuit."

Ray stared hard at him. "It probably wouldn't make any difference if you did, but I wish you hadn't been so blunt about it. It just reinforces my opinion that you really don't care about anyone except yourself."

Corbin felt backed into a cage of his own making. He ground his teeth together. "I could call Darryl Simpkin. He's a pompous, arrogant—"

"Don't go to the trouble," Ray cut in. "At this point Mr. Simpkin is convinced I'd be more of a liability to the firm than an asset, and there's nothing anyone can do to change his mind. A phone call from you would only make it worse."

Ray put his face in his hands.

Corbin stared at the top of his son's head. "Have you told Cindy?" he asked in a softer tone of voice.

Ray spoke to the tabletop. "No, she's out house hunting today."

Corbin winced. Sally brought their food. Corbin waited for Ray to say a blessing. Instead his son stuck his fork in a mound of mashed potatoes and slowly stirred in the brown gravy pooled on top.

"Aren't you going to pray?" Corbin asked.

Ray looked up. "What do you suggest I pray?"

They ate in silence.

———

Roxy was pleasantly tired when she walked through the door of her townhome. Some days she left the office with a sense there was more to do than when she'd arrived in the morning. Today hadn't been one of those days. It ended in a meeting with Mr. Caldweller and several other attorneys to discuss a new case transferred from the Houston office to Atlanta. Roxy waited with resignation to find out what the senior partner was going to pile on top of her already full plate. When he reached her, he paused.

"Roxy, I'm going to let you sit this one out," he said. "Unless you want to volunteer, of course."

Roxy hesitated. There would have been a time early in her career when she would have been afraid not to volunteer. "Thank you," she said. "I'd appreciate a pass."

"Done," Caldweller replied. "You're free to leave."

Roxy caught a hint of envy in the eyes of a couple of associates who'd not been given the opportunity to choose their fate. She left the conference room and took a deep breath of air free of increased responsibility.

As soon as she closed the front door, she kicked off her shoes and walked barefoot into the kitchen. Her cell phone vibrated.

"Did you just get home?" Peter asked.

"Are you stalking me? First you know when I'm finished running. Now this."

"It's just a guess based on when your assistant told me you left the office and my research into traffic congestion."

"That makes me feel better."

"The bad news is that I'm going to have to break our dinner date."

Roxy leaned against the kitchen counter. "Why?"

"I'm working the second shift because we need to talk to a client in Korea, and they won't be available until eleven o'clock tonight."

"Ouch. How long will the meeting last?"

"At least three or four hours."

"Can you sleep late tomorrow?"

"Yeah, our whole team is involved in this project. What time works for you tomorrow evening?"

"I won't know for sure until the afternoon." She told him what happened with Caldweller and the new case.

"That's cool," Peter answered. "He's beginning to figure out what I've known for months."

"What's that?"

"That you're awesome in every way."

Roxy knew Peter's compliments were genuine, but she still felt a nagging doubt whether they were really true. "I don't know—"

"No," Peter interrupted. "I won't be able to focus on this Korea project if I'm wondering whether you believe me."

"Okay, okay." Roxy licked her lips.

"Send me a text about tomorrow."

"Will do."

Roxy placed her phone on the counter beside the microwave. The more contact she had with Peter, the more she wanted. She heated up a leftover chicken and pasta dish from a restaurant meal and took it out to her patio. It was a pleasant evening with promise for a cool morning, perfect for running. She sat in a wrought iron chair painted a light cream color and propped her feet up on its twin. Taking out her phone, she checked her messages. There was one from Peter with a selfie. In the photo he had a big smile on his face as he held up a picture of her he kept in his office.

I'D RATHER BE HANGING OUT WITH THE REAL PERSON

Roxy smiled as a sense of thankfulness rose up within her. "Thank you, Lord," she murmured, then stopped.

The words had come out of her mouth without checking with her mind first. She glanced around the patio, not sure what she was looking for. Then she remembered where she'd heard them.

From her mother's lips.

Buried in her subconscious, the phrase had lain dormant, waiting for a perfect time to bubble to the surface. It was a simple response Kitty applied to things great or small that brought her a hint of joy. Roxy had heard the phrase while her mother knelt in the flower beds in front of the house on Willow Oak Lane, when she held the infant Billy in her arms, and many times in between. It was a quiet, gentle refrain that had lodged deep inside a secret place Roxy never visited.

Until now.

She looked again at Peter's selfie and decided he would probably like what she'd said. Sitting in the fading light of the patio, Roxy thought about being thankful.

And she looked forward to telling Peter in person.

TWENTY-EIGHT

Ray waited until Billy was asleep to break the bad news to Cindy. Her eyes widened, then filled with tears that silently ran down her face. She grabbed a paper napkin from a stack in the middle of the kitchen table.

"Well," she said. "I didn't really like the house on Walker Street anyway. It wasn't my style."

"And we still have a house payment on this place. I'm not sure—"

"No!" Cindy raised her hand to stop him. "That's not what I need to hear. I realize what losing this opportunity means to us, but to hear you say it like that is too much for me right now."

"Sorry."

Cindy put her hand on her abdomen. "The tiny person in here has the perfect home, and I'm going to pray we'll have one for all of us by the time he or she comes out to meet us."

Ray didn't point out the obvious hurdle—that he not only didn't have a job with the Simpkin firm, he had no job at all.

Cindy continued with increased determination in her voice. "And if you have to work with your father for a while until something else comes up, I won't stop you."

"What?" Ray asked, shocked. "It's his fault this happened."

"And he owes it to you to help us out. Didn't that thought cross your mind when you were eating lunch with him?"

"No," Ray answered truthfully. "It didn't. I was hard on him."

"He deserved that too. Look, I can tolerate you working with him on a temporary basis, so long as he matches the salary you've been making at the DA's office."

Ray's head was spinning. "Should I wait for him to bring it up?" he asked.

"I want you to march into his office the first thing tomorrow morning and tell him."

Ray stared at Cindy and wondered what had happened to his sweet wife. He shrugged. "It's worth a try."

"No!" Cindy replied emphatically. "Tell him he has to do it."

———

While Ray and Cindy sat at the kitchen table, Corbin nursed his fourth shot of whiskey at The Office.

"One more for the road." He held up his glass to the new bartender, a large, bearded man in his thirties who could do double duty as a bouncer.

"No, buddy," the bartender replied. "I think you've already topped off for the night."

"Where's Ralph?" Corbin demanded. "He's never turned me down for a refill."

The bartender leaned on the counter and flexed his massive biceps. "Ralph went home early and left me in charge."

"Get him on the phone," Corbin said, his temper rising. "What's your name?"

The bartender pulled up the sleeve of his shirt, revealing a tattoo of the Greek god Zeus holding a thunderbolt in his hand.

"You can call me Zeus. And I'm not going to bother Ralph just because you want me to."

"Well, I'm going to call you Peter Pan." Corbin got up unsteadily from his stool. "And the next time I see Ralph, I'm going to let him know how you treated a regular customer who's been coming here since before you were born."

"Tell him whatever you want." "Zeus" stood up and folded his arms across his chest. "It's time for you to go."

Rage rose up in Corbin like gasoline thrown on an already raging fire. "Why, you stupid—"

Before he could get out another word, the bartender reached across the bar and grabbed the front of Corbin's shirt.

"If I have to come out from behind this bar, you're going to eat a mouthful of gravel in the parking lot," the younger man growled.

Corbin glanced to the side. Everyone else in the bar was watching. To Corbin's right was Kenny Pickett, the owner of a local used car lot. Corbin and Kenny had known each other for over twenty years. Kenny jumped up from his chair and came over to them.

"Calm down, Corbin," he said. "How about I drive you home?"

Corbin knocked away the bartender's hand, and the large man started to leave his spot behind the bar.

"Come on." Kenny lightly touched Corbin on the arm and urged him in the direction of the door. "Let's get some fresh air."

Corbin reluctantly complied.

"I've got this," Kenny said over his shoulder to the bartender.

Corbin and Kenny stepped outside.

"He doesn't know who you are," Kenny said. "Zeus has only been working here for about a month, and you haven't been coming in as often as usual."

"If I were twenty years younger—"

"He still would have tossed you out on your head. Corbin, you're a big man, but there's more teddy bear than grizzly bear inside you."

"That's not what Ray thinks," Corbin grunted.

"What's going on with Ray?"

Alcohol had loosened Corbin's tongue, and even though Kenny was only a casual friend, Corbin told him what happened.

"That's the way it is with kids," Kenny replied, shaking his head. "I sold my son a car at cost a few months ago, and he got mad at me when the engine blew because he didn't change the oil."

Corbin brushed his hair away from his forehead. "I'd better get going," he said.

"Are you sure you don't want me to drive you? You knocked down a pocketful of shots pretty quickly."

"Why do you say that?" Corbin asked, his voice rising in volume.

"Hey, it's just an opinion. You've always been able to hold your liquor."

"Where's my truck?" Corbin squinted his eyes. "I thought I parked beside the light pole."

"Is that it over there?" Kenny pointed.

Corbin followed Kenny's finger to the corner of the building. "Yeah, there it is. See you later." He turned away and began to walk unsteadily across the parking lot.

"Are you sure you don't want me to—"

"No!" Corbin waved off the question with his right hand.

Ray was sitting in the den doing his morning devotional when Cindy came in.

"Listen to this," Ray said. "'But seek first his kingdom and his righteousness, and all these things will be given to you as well.

Therefore do not worry about tomorrow, for tomorrow will worry about itself. Each day has enough trouble of its own.' It's in Matthew 6. If the trouble I'm going to face today is anything like what I went through yesterday, I'm going back to bed."

"It's too late," Cindy replied evenly. "I already made it."

Ray closed the Bible. "After sleeping on it and in the light of a new day, have you changed your mind about me talking to my father about a job?"

"No—but only if you agree it's the right thing to do."

"One big concern is that doing a stint with him will look bad on my résumé when I try to find a real job. The Simpkin firm is the best firm in town, and it's a short list of local lawyers I'd be willing to work for. This might mean a move away from Alto."

"Ray." Cindy put her hand to her mouth.

"We don't have to talk about that this morning," he added quickly.

Cindy nodded and moved quickly in the direction of the bathroom.

"I'll go see him!" Ray called after her.

Ray parked at the rear of the building and used his key to unlock the back door. Janelle was sitting at her desk, and she jumped when Ray came up behind her.

"You scared the fire out of me!" she said. "I knew it couldn't be your father coming through the back door."

"Yeah, he doesn't get here for at least another thirty minutes."

Janelle gave him a surprised look. "Didn't he get in touch with you?"

"About what?"

"He was arrested last night when he pulled out of the parking lot of The Office tavern. He refused a Breathalyzer, so they took him to the hospital for a blood test. He called me about an hour ago from the jail. They impounded his truck for the night. I assumed he'd already contacted you."

"No," Ray said, his shoulders slumping. "He didn't."

"He's going to catch a cab and come here as soon as they let him out."

On cue the front door of the office opened, and a disheveled Corbin Gage entered. His hair was sticking out all over his head, and he was wearing the clothes he'd worn the previous day. He stopped in his tracks when he saw Ray.

"What are you doing here?" he grunted.

"Why didn't you call me when you were arrested?" Ray shot back.

Corbin ignored the question.

"Janelle, can you take me home?" he asked. "I need a shower and change of clothes. I have a motion hearing at eleven, and I don't want to ask for a continuance."

"I'll drive you," Ray said to his father. "Janelle is your legal assistant, not your personal chauffeur. Is there anything you need to do before the hearing?"

Corbin looked at Janelle. "It has to do with the second request for production of documents I filed. You know, the ones asking for tax, bank, and corporate records for the other company owned by the defendant. Make sure the affidavit from the guy who used to work in the accounts payable department is on my desk. I can't remember his name. There are a bunch of exhibits attached to the affidavit that I need to go over."

"Anything else?" Janelle asked.

"Not that I can think of right now, but I don't trust my brain after spending the night in the drunk tank."

"Let's go," Ray said. "My car is out back."

"Why?" Corbin asked.

"Because that's where people who work here park their vehicles."

"What!" Corbin and Janelle both asked at the same time.

"I thought you were about to go to work with the Simpkin firm," Janelle said.

"There's no job over there for anyone named Gage," Ray replied. "Especially after a case filed against Colfax on behalf of two little boys with cancer landed on Nate Stamper's desk yesterday morning."

"Corbin," Janelle said, her voice rising. "You shouldn't—"

"No." Ray cut her off. "I told him what I thought about it yesterday at lunch, but I went about it the wrong way. I'll call you after I see how he's feeling."

"Don't talk about me as if I'm not in the room," Corbin said. "I hate it when people do that."

"Then let's leave," Ray said.

"What's behind your comment about working here?" Corbin asked when they were seated in Ray's car.

"It's simple. You owe me a job until I find another one, because you cost me the job I had. What's hard to understand about that? And I expect you to match my salary at the DA's office."

Corbin tried to process what was really going on, his mind weakened by a hangover and sleep deprivation.

"Isn't this what you wanted all along?" Ray continued. "For me to work with you? Well, now you're going to get it. All you have to do is agree to my terms, which are nonnegotiable."

"And if I don't?"

Ray glanced sideways at him. "Look in the mirror when you get home and decide if you need my help at the office while you get your life straightened out."

"You seem happy about all this."

"Not a bit. But maybe there's a chance this DUI will force you to admit that alcohol is a huge problem for you. If you care about yourself, Billy, and the law practice, you're going to admit the facts and do something about it."

They rode in silence for a few moments.

"Look, I went to the tavern because of what you said to me at lunch," Corbin said. "I haven't been drinking as much lately, and I guess I underestimated the effect it would have on me."

Ray kept his eyes on the road. "Dad, I spoke at Red's out of my own disappointment, and as I said in front of Janelle, I didn't communicate with you in a mature way. I'm sorry for that. But I'm not going to let you blame me for this DUI. You're sixty-two years old. It's time for you to take responsibility for your own conduct."

Corbin couldn't figure out why Ray seemed so assertive and confident.

"What's gotten into you?" he asked when they slowed to turn into the driveway of Corbin's duplex.

"I'm not exactly sure, but when I saw you walk through the door of the office today, something rose up inside me. Maybe it's because Mom prayed for me all those years." Ray turned off the engine and faced his father. "And there's no statute of limitations on prayer."

TWENTY-NINE

The cut below Corbin's eye had almost healed, but he didn't look good. His eyes were bloodshot and the skin on his face was sagging more than ever. He finished shaving, wiped his face with a towel, and checked to make sure he hadn't missed a spot. He leaned over to splash water on his face, and when he raised it up he felt light-headed. He rested his hands on the sink for a few seconds while he waited for the room to stop spinning. He moved slowly while getting dressed, then walked into the den where Ray waited.

"I feel like a new man," Corbin said, trying to sound optimistic.

"Where's your tie?" Ray asked.

Corbin felt his neck. He'd buttoned the top button of his shirt, but he'd forgotten to put on a tie. "On a rack in my closet," he said.

Returning to the bedroom, he saw the tie he'd selected lying on the bed. He picked it up and wrapped it around his neck without attempting a knot and came back out. "Let's go."

"I thought you might want a cup of coffee so I brewed a pot while you cleaned up. I called Janelle and told her we'd be on our way shortly. She has everything ready for your hearing."

Corbin grabbed the cup and saw a pile of dirty dishes in the sink. Some of the dried-on food was hard as concrete.

"I was going to clean the dishes last night," he said.

Ray walked away without responding. Corbin hesitated, wondering if he should fill the sink with water so the dishes could soak.

"Are you coming?" his son called out.

Corbin left the kitchen and found Ray waiting by the carport door. Corbin took a sip of the hot coffee. His mouth welcomed the slightly bitter drink.

"This is good coffee," he said.

"Do you want me to start making the morning coffee at the office?" Ray asked. "It could be part of my daily to-do list."

"Come on, Ray," Corbin said. "Are you serious about this job thing?"

"Did you look in the mirror like I asked you to?"

Corbin didn't answer. Ray backed up the car and turned it around so he could drive forward down the long driveway.

"You're right about one thing," Corbin said, taking another sip of coffee. "What happened last night is going to create all kinds of problems for me."

"I know. Are you ready to talk about it?"

Corbin looked out the car window. "Which part?"

"Wherever you want to begin."

"Do you think I can keep from losing my driver's license?"

"What would you tell a client in your situation?"

It was an easy question.

"That I can probably save his license if he agrees to pay a fine and take some classes about the dangers of drinking and driving."

"Sounds reasonable to me, unless Steve Nelson wants to be vindictive. In that case we'll have to work directly with the judge."

"You're going to represent me?"

Ray slowed as a car in front of them stopped to make a turn.

"I think I'm competent to handle a DUI charge. Of course we don't know the results of your blood test. How many drinks did you have?"

"More than two." Corbin sighed. "At least five or six over an hour and a half or so. I was sitting alone at the bar."

"Then you know that can make it tougher."

Corbin was feeling more remorseful and less defensive by the second. "Yeah, it was a stupid thing to do," he said.

"That's the most sober thing you've said today."

"And the bar association will probably be breathing down my neck wanting me to get treatment and threatening disciplinary action if I don't. But they can inspect my trust account and talk to my clients all they want to. My bank records are up to date, and I've not dropped the ball on any of my cases." Corbin paused. "Except for missing a deadline a few months ago in a low impact car wreck case. I settled directly with the client without notifying my malpractice carrier."

"Did the client have independent counsel to advise them on your offer?"

"No, but it was fair. More money than he could have gotten at trial."

Corbin remembered two other situations in which he could possibly be accused of abandoning representation. The cases were lingering problems he'd not resolved.

"Okay," Corbin said. "What were you making at the DA's office?"

Corbin knew Ray's salary when Jimbo Sanders hired him, but didn't know about raises. He was surprised at the low amount.

"That's not much more than when you started."

"True."

They reached the outskirts of town. Ray slowed as he reached the corner for Corbin's office. "Are you up to handling this hearing?" he asked.

Corbin drained the last drops of coffee. "I have to. The worst part is going to be facing the judge. I'm sure word of my arrest has made the rounds of the courthouse already."

"Probably, but it won't be a huge shock. Everyone figured it would happen eventually. I guess that's another reason why I've been so calm about it. I've been waiting a long time for something like this to happen. Now that it's here, I'm not surprised."

Corbin was still trying to digest Ray's comment as he got out of the car. As he entered the office, he realized that when he looked in the mirror he saw a different man than other people did.

———

Ray drove around to the rear of the office and called Cindy.

"What are we going to say to Billy?" she asked when Ray finished.

"That I'm going to work with Pops. He'll think it's a great idea."

"No, about your father's arrest for DUI."

"We won't say anything about it."

"Will that stop someone in his class teasing him about it on the playground?" Cindy asked, her voice rising with concern. "And there's no guarantee the newspaper won't mention it in the crime blotter."

Ray paused. "If that comes up, we'll deal with it then. There's no good way to explain it to Billy now."

"People are going to stare at me and whisper behind my back at the grocery store and church. How am I supposed to feel about that?"

"Uh, not good. But Dad's reputation as a man who likes to drink liquor isn't breaking news. I've dealt with it since I was a kid."

Cindy didn't answer.

"I'm sitting in the parking lot behind his office," Ray said after he waited a few more seconds. "I'll talk to you later."

"Bye."

Not sure what to make of Cindy's reaction, Ray chalked it up to information overload coupled with the hormonal dump that was part of pregnancy. He offered a quick silent prayer that the stress

Cindy felt wouldn't affect their unborn child. Losing the baby would be the ultimate blow.

———

Roxy sat at her desk grinding away on a brief in support of a motion for summary judgment that had little chance of success. Nevertheless, Mr. Caldweller would expect her to prepare a written argument that granting the motion was completely reasonable under the law and facts. As she worked she kept swatting away an inner voice that jumped up to object and disagree with each point she needed to make. It was a classic exercise of the selective logic an attorney has to apply when presenting a case—she had to avoid misrepresenting the evidence and judicial precedents to the judge and at the same time advance an argument Caldweller could deliver with a straight face. Even though the client would expect Mr. Caldweller to show up and argue the motion, Roxy wondered if the senior partner would ultimately send her into court for the suicide mission. Her phone buzzed, and she picked it up.

"Mr. Peter Spence is here for your lunch appointment," the woman said.

"He is?" Roxy asked in surprise.

"Yes."

Roxy pulled out her purse and checked her appearance. She hoped a quick touch-up to her face would remove the effects of working on the doomed motion. She smoothed her dress with her hands as she left her office. Sure enough, a smiling Peter stood as she entered the reception area.

"I thought we were going to see each other for supper tomorrow night," she said.

"I couldn't wait. Can you get away for an hour now?"

Roxy glanced at the young receptionist, who was vigorously nodding her head.

"You're not Mr. Caldweller," Roxy said to the young woman.

"And I'm not going to tell him where you are if he asks," she replied.

"It's okay," Roxy said. "I'm ahead of schedule on a project. I can slip away."

Peter briefly touched the back of Roxy's arm as he guided her toward the elevator. Even the simple contact made Roxy feel special.

"You took a big chance coming here unannounced," she said when they reached the bank of elevators. "You didn't know I could take a break."

"You're worth the risk."

Roxy rolled her eyes and smiled. "Have you been studying how to be romantic?"

Peter pointed to his heart. "I let this talk to me."

They stepped into the empty elevator. As soon as the door closed, Roxy threw her arms around Peter and kissed him.

"There," she said when they parted. "Did you see that coming?"

"No." He leaned toward her again, but the elevator stopped at another floor and two middle-aged men in dark suits got on.

Roxy touched Peter's lips with her index finger and whispered, "Your lips are red."

One of the men glanced over his shoulder. Peter rubbed his mouth with the back of his left hand. Roxy grabbed his hand and pointed at a red streak.

"See, there's my lipstick," she said in a louder voice.

Both of the men turned around and stared at them.

"It happens all the time," Roxy said to them with a sweet smile.

The door opened and the men got off. Roxy and Peter held back a second, then quickly stepped off.

"Do you think they'll report us to the building security guard?" Roxy asked.

"What has gotten into you?" Peter asked. "I like it, but it's, uh, different."

"It's your fault," Roxy sniffed. "You kidnapped me." She intertwined her fingers with his as they walked toward the parking deck. "Where are you taking me anyway?"

"A picnic. I wasn't sure how much time you'd have, so I picked up some food on the way over. I thought we could go to the park on the other side of Roswell Road."

They got into Peter's car and arrived at the park in a few minutes. The central feature of the area was a large playground set, deserted at the moment because the neighborhood children were in school. The only competitors Roxy and Peter had for the space were a few mothers with small children in strollers. He led the way to a quiet spot beneath a large maple tree and spread out a blue ground cloth.

"Where did this come from?" Roxy asked.

"A holdover from my camping days, but I threw it in the washer yesterday. It's clean."

It was a sunny day with a few scattered clouds that decorated the ground in splotchy shade. Peter had packed their lunch in a plastic laundry basket. It was a man's picnic, with plain paper plates and thin white napkins. The food was a loaf of artisan bread, a pack of smoked turkey from the grocery store deli, a broad sampling of condiments, and low-sodium potato chips. There was a large bottle of mineral water from a limestone well in Vermont.

"I thought we could make our own sandwiches," he said in an apologetic tone of voice.

"This is great," Roxy said as she stretched her legs out in front of her. "Let me fix your sandwich for you."

Roxy asked Peter questions and carefully constructed his

sandwich. It was a simple domestic act dropped unexpectedly into the middle of what had been a typical day of intense legal analysis.

"You know what I did last night while I sat on my patio relaxing after supper?" she asked after she handed him the sandwich and picked up a piece of bread for herself.

"No," he said as he chewed his first bite.

"I told God I was thankful for you. It popped out without me thinking about it."

"That's neat," Peter said as he swallowed his food. "I'd like things like that to be more and more a part of our relationship."

Roxy laid several thinly sliced pieces of turkey on the bread. "Along with what happened in the elevator?" she asked.

"Oh yeah." Peter leaned forward, but Roxy pushed him away.

"What's wrong?" he asked.

"You have yellow mustard on your mouth," she replied. "I like brown."

Roxy's phone, which was lying on the ground cloth beside the laundry basket, vibrated.

"I hope that's not from Mr. Caldweller," she said as she picked it up. A text message came through, and as Roxy read it her face grew pale.

"What is it?" Peter asked.

"It's from Ray."

Peter, who was reclining on his side, sat up straight. Roxy placed the piece of bread in her hand on a plate.

"And I've lost my appetite," she said.

THIRTY

It had been months since Corbin opened the door to the vacant office he'd occupied when he first came to work for Colonel Parker. It was on the other side of the reception area from Janelle's desk. Fortunately the cleaning crew kept the floor vacuumed and the furniture dusted.

Corbin ran his fingers along the edge of the desk where he'd written his closing argument in the million-dollar case against the logging company. He needed something positive to think about after his most recent experience at the courthouse.

Walking down the hallway, Corbin had approached two lawyers who saw him and stopped talking until he passed. Upstairs, Judge Perry's secretary didn't make eye contact with him while he waited to meet with the judge. The lawyer on the other side of the case, a friendly fellow from another town who didn't follow the local legal gossip, chatted with Corbin about a mutual acquaintance until the judge called them into his chambers.

Judge Perry was even more distant and condescending than usual and took under advisement a motion that should have resulted in an immediate ruling in Corbin's favor. Corbin could tell the other lawyer was surprised by the judge's reluctance.

After leaving the courthouse, Corbin caught a cab to the jail to see if he could get his truck. He knew the deputy on duty at the impoundment lot.

"We're supposed to wait twenty-four hours," the young man said when Corbin made his request.

"I just argued a case in front of Judge Perry. I'm sober and you're not legally required to keep a vehicle if the owner is able to operate it."

The deputy eyed him carefully.

"I'm going to my office," Corbin continued. "How far is that? Two miles?"

"Okay, Mr. Gage. But please don't do anything that will get me chewed out later."

Corbin held up his hand as if taking an oath. "I promise."

Driving to the office, Corbin felt slightly shaky. He couldn't decide if it was due to fatigue or residual problems from the previous night's binge. After talking to Janelle about what Ray would need to get up and running, he closed his eyes for a few minutes.

A knock on the door woke him up.

"I assume you want me to set up in your old office," Ray said.

"Uh, yeah."

Corbin dropped his feet to the floor and started to say something about his first day working for Colonel Parker, but it didn't fit the moment. He settled for a much more mundane question.

"How many boxes do you have?" he asked.

"Three more."

They walked in silence to the parking lot. Ray stacked up two boxes together, and Corbin grabbed one. Inside they set the boxes on the floor beside the desk.

"Well, I know the first thing I'm going to do," Ray said.

Corbin pointed to the empty computer stand. "Janelle already called the computer guy who takes care of us, and he's going to deliver and set up a machine later today."

"No. First I'm going to pray."

"Oh." Corbin stepped back toward the door. "I'll leave you alone."

"No. I want you to stay."

"But—"

"You don't have to join in, but I want you to hear what I have to say."

On a different day, Corbin would have ignored Ray's request and left anyway. But he was feeling vulnerable and didn't want to add another offense to the ones he'd already piled on Ray's plate.

"Okay." He shrugged. "Are we going to get down on our knees?"

It was Ray's turn to act surprised. "I hadn't considered that," he said, "but I think it would be a good idea."

There were two leather side chairs in front of the desk. Ray knelt in front of one, and Corbin lowered himself before the other. Corbin bowed his head, closed his eyes, and waited. Ray didn't speak right away, and after a moment Corbin cracked open one eye to peek. Ray's forehead was wrinkled, and he seemed to be deep in thought. Finally he began.

"God, the first thing I want to do is to dedicate myself and my time here to you. This isn't where I wanted to work, but now that I'm here, help me to do a good job for our clients and to serve Dad to the best of my ability through your grace. Send us the people you want us to represent and show us the best way to help them." He paused. "Regardless of what has happened between Dad and me in the past, I ask you to show us how to interact with each other in the future. Show us how to communicate in the right way, and let me be an encouragement to him. In Jesus' name. Amen."

Corbin had opened his eyes when Ray paused and watched his son's face during the rest of the prayer. When Ray said, "Amen," Corbin not only didn't know what to pray; he didn't know what to say. He slowly got up and extended his hand. Ray shook it, and Corbin left.

Janelle looked up from her computer when Corbin approached her desk.

"I'm going home," he said. "I'm about to crash from lack of sleep, and that will give you and Ray a chance to go over things without me interfering."

"Am I going to do all the work for both of you?" Janelle asked. "I realize Ray doesn't have any cases of his own yet, but that's going to change."

Corbin nodded and brushed his hair away from his forehead. "You're right," he said. "And you should pray about it."

Janelle's mouth dropped open.

———

Roxy and Peter ended up eating Chinese food at her townhome instead of going out for a nice dinner. Peter delivered the food.

"Whatever we don't eat can be divided for leftovers," Peter said as Roxy organized the different dishes on the kitchen table.

"There won't be any of the shrimp left," Roxy said. "Is that as spicy as it looks?"

"It had two peppers beside the name on the menu," Peter answered. "I'm going to fight you for that one."

"Most of the fight has been drained out of me," Roxy said with a sigh. "Just give me a taste."

Peter grabbed her plate and piled on half of the dish.

"Wait, wait," Roxy protested. "I want to partner the shrimp with fried rice and the chicken dish with baby corn."

They went out to the patio to eat. It took a couple of trips to transfer the food and drinks. Both Roxy and Peter were experts with chopsticks, and for a few minutes there wasn't any sound except the clicking of wood on wood.

"Did you hear anything else from your brother?" Peter asked after he swallowed a bite of chicken.

"We talked for a few minutes. He had to cut the conversation short because a guy showed up to install a new phone."

While they ate, Roxy summarized the conversation.

"My dad deserves whatever happens to him," she said, "but I feel sorry for Ray. Everything he's been working for professionally came crashing down. I wanted to give him some advice, but there wasn't anything to say. It was very frustrating."

"Did he ask for advice?"

"What do you mean?"

"Is that why he called you? To ask your opinion?"

Roxy paused. "Not really. But Ray has always leaned on me even though I'm the little sister. It's another odd aspect of our family dynamics. Part of it may stem from my mother having to assume so much responsibility because my dad was more focused on his next drink than on raising us."

"Remember our conversation the other day at the French restaurant?" Peter began.

"The one where I ended up bawling like a baby who'd lost her pacifier?" Roxy put up a hand. "I'm not in the mood to revisit your attempt to psychoanalyze my relationship with my father."

"Isn't that what you're doing right now?"

"Yes, but I'm finished."

She bit down on a red pepper that had sneaked into her mouth beneath a piece of shrimp. The pepper was so potent that it made her eyes water.

"A pepper is causing this," she said quickly as she wiped her eyes with a napkin.

Peter didn't respond.

"I'm serious," Roxy said.

Peter poured more tea into her cup. She took a sip but the tea did nothing to lessen the pepper's assault on her taste buds. Peter picked up a similar pepper with his chopsticks and popped it into his mouth. He chewed it, then calmly swallowed it.

"It has a kick," he said. "And the afterburn is worse than the initial heat."

"Tell me about it." Roxy was now fanning her face with her hand. "I'm going to get a glass of milk from the fridge. Do you want one?"

"No, thanks."

In the kitchen Roxy poured a glass of milk and took a quick sip. The impact of the dairy product was like magic to her throat. She finished the glass and returned to the patio.

"That cooled it right off," she said, then stopped at the look on Peter's face. "Are you okay?"

Peter put his hand to his mouth to stifle a belch and shook his head. "I'm not as macho as I thought. I guess I'd like some milk too."

Roxy hurried to the kitchen and returned with another glass, which Peter received gratefully.

"Talking about my father is like swallowing one of those peppers," she said. "That's why I want to avoid it."

"But every so often one is liable to sneak up on you. If that happens, what would be the milk to take away the hurt?"

"I'm focused on prevention."

Roxy knew Peter had something on his mind and suspected what it might be.

"Do you think that if I believed the right way about God it would take away the pain in my life caused by my father?" she asked.

Peter was balancing another big bite on his chopsticks. He returned the food to his plate.

"I don't know enough about God to make that claim. Would you like to meet with the pastor of Noah's church and talk to him about it? You could consider him an expert witness. I'd be glad to set it up."

"No!" Roxy answered more forcibly than she intended. "He's a stranger."

"And I'm not." Peter reached out and touched Roxy on the hand. "One of the things I want the most is for you to trust me with what's really going on in your heart."

Roxy stared at Peter and knew without another word being spoken that he loved her.

———

Corbin awoke from a three-hour nap. He wasn't refreshed, but at least he felt fully human for the first time since he'd ordered the final double whiskey at The Office the previous evening. His arrival at the tavern seemed like a week ago, not less than twenty-four hours. Thinking about the bar caused something else to wake up—the craving for another drink.

He was lying on his back looking up at the ceiling. He closed his eyes. And a feeling he'd never experienced before rose up from deep inside.

"No!" he called out. "I don't want it!"

Corbin let the surprising words linger in the air, then settle back onto his consciousness. He waited for the internal debate that would surely emerge. A statement like that could not go unchallenged. But nothing bubbled to the surface. Apparently competing voices were, for the moment, silent. He turned to his nightstand to check the time. The clock was resting on the Big Book he'd received at his first AA meeting. If he left in fifteen minutes, he could make it to the meeting at the Hopewell church.

Corbin got ready as quickly as if he'd overslept and had to rush to a calendar call. He'd showered when Ray brought him home, but he took another quick one. He shut his eyes and let the spray run off his face, then dried off and put on a casual shirt and blue jeans. The rapid-fire activity helped keep him away from the cabinet in the kitchen where the row of whiskey bottles waited for him. Corbin breathed a sigh of relief when he closed the door of the duplex behind him and got into his truck.

Even though time was short, he made sure he didn't exceed the speed limit on the way to the meeting. The last thing he needed was to be pulled over. Corbin knew a routine traffic stop might lead to the administration of a Breathalyzer test or a trip to the hospital for another blood test.

There were several vehicles in the church parking lot when he arrived. Max's car wasn't one of them.

As he got out of his truck, Corbin was amazed at his attitude. He wanted to go inside. He wanted to sit in a chair in a circle of support. He wanted to be with people who, like him, struggled with a craving that too often got its way. He walked in as the group gathered in a circle to recite the serenity prayer.

"God, grant me the serenity to accept the things I cannot change, the courage to change the things I can, and wisdom to know the difference."

"We're going to have a discussion meeting tonight," said the leader, a young woman in her thirties.

"I have something." Corbin raised his hand before she could continue.

"Usually we suggest a topic," the woman replied evenly, "but if you have something you want to share now, go ahead."

Corbin looked around the room. He'd faced many juries; he'd delivered many closing arguments. He'd appeared over twenty times in front of the Georgia Court of Appeals and six times at the Georgia Supreme Court. He'd argued three cases before the Eleventh Circuit Court of Appeals in a high-ceilinged, wood-paneled courtroom in Atlanta. But he'd never looked into the faces of a group of human beings and admitted a deep personal problem.

The eyes that looked back at him around the circle weren't poised to judge, criticize, or condemn. They simply waited to hear what he had to say. Corbin took a deep breath.

"My name is Corbin, and I'm an alcoholic."

THIRTY-ONE

Cindy was standing at the sink slicing tomatoes for a salad when Ray walked through the door from the garage. She wiped her hands on a paper towel, stepped over to him, and kissed him on the forehead.

"That's the best part of the day so far," Ray said. "Where's Billy?"

"Eating supper with Freddie's family. They're cooking hot dogs and roasting marshmallows over their fire pit. I thought it would be nice for you to decompress without him here."

While Ray talked, Cindy continued preparing supper.

He paused. "I wish I could see your face," he said.

"Maybe it's better you can't," she answered without turning around. "That way I can process our world getting turned upside down without having to hide what I'm feeling."

"You were right, though. If you hadn't told me to demand a job from my father, I'd be sitting here with nothing to do. After he left I talked to Janelle. She's worried she won't be able to handle the secretarial load for both of us."

"Janelle hasn't put in a full day's work in years. She doesn't know what she can do." Cindy opened the refrigerator and took out a glass container.

"What's that?" Ray asked.

"Homemade dressing." She held it up so Ray could see it. "Lemon dill. I hope you like it."

"I'm sure it's great." He shifted in his chair. "I also did an inventory of dad's open files. If you counted all the cases in the cabinets, you'd think his practice was booming."

"I assume there's a catch."

"Yeah. Over half of them are finished and should be closed. And of the ones he has left, I didn't find a single one that looked like a six-figure case. It's a bunch of small stuff, the kind of claims no other lawyer in town would touch. It would have been sad if I'd done an inventory like this last week, but now that we're both depending on revenue from the firm, it's downright depressing. The people he's representing need help, but that doesn't necessarily translate into profit."

"What about the case against Colfax?"

"It's too early to put a value on it. It could end up being more of a drain than anything else. Janelle told me he's agreed to fund the litigation himself. Regardless, it's going to be hard for him to pay my salary until I can generate some business on my own."

Cindy turned around and put both hands on her hips. "I know where you're going with this, Ray, and I'm going to stop you right now. Don't let him off the hook. That's what people have done for years. Part of the reason you're there is to make him honor a commitment for once in his life, even if it means he's going to have to sacrifice to do it."

"So I have to be selfish so he can learn not to be selfish?"

"Yes, and here's another one for you. Just because something *sounds* right doesn't mean it *is* right."

Ray knew he wasn't going to win the argument, so he dropped it. Financial reality would reveal itself.

Cindy's salad was a work of culinary art, with dark red smoked salmon on top.

"That looks awesome," Ray said. "Where did you get the salmon?"

"Beth Ann's husband shipped back a cooler full from a company fishing trip to Alaska and smoked it yesterday. It's sockeye."

It was the best salmon Ray had ever put in his mouth, and they ate in silence for a few moments.

Then Cindy spoke. "I went to the doctor today," she said.

"That's right." Ray tapped his fingers against his forehead. "I forgot. How are you and the baby?"

"Okay. Dr. Valance told me what I already knew—there's a chance she may put me on bed rest."

"I hope not. But if it happens, I should be able to take time off from work to help out."

"You've got two high-risk people in your life," Cindy said with a sigh. "I hate it that you might have to take care of me and your dad."

"I'd much rather do the former than the latter." Ray bit into a particularly succulent piece of salmon. "And I think taking care of people is what I'm going to be doing for a living."

———

The air smelled cleaner when Corbin stepped out of his duplex the following morning. He'd had a good night's sleep and felt physically recovered from his night at the jail. He straightened his tie and got in his truck. The DUI charge still hung over his head like a dark cloud, but that didn't mean he couldn't enjoy moments of sunshine.

Driving to work, he relived the AA meeting from the previous evening. It had been exhilarating, scary, and sad. Being honest about his addiction after forty years of denial was like taking the cap off a carton of spoiled milk and pouring the stinking sludge down the drain. As soon as the words "My name is Corbin, and

I'm an alcoholic" were out of his mouth, he knew he'd waited way too long to admit it. The subsequent venting of his recent problems and their effect on him brought a level of internal relief to a part of his soul that had lost hope of rescue. The reassurance his brief confession elicited from the other people in the group lifted Corbin up in a way he didn't think possible. He wasn't condemned; he was understood and affirmed for taking a first step toward recovery.

But fear followed closely on the heels of encouragement. He could fall in an instant. Another night of intoxication at The Office, a long lunch at Red's, or drinking a fifth of whiskey while sitting in his living room remained a future possibility. The statements by the people in the AA circle that sobriety was a daily battle were true, but their words didn't hold within themselves the power of change.

Before going to sleep, he'd felt especially sad for another reason—Kitty hadn't lived to see him genuinely reach out for help. Corbin quickly squelched the emotion that welled up from deep within. Lying in bed in his duplex wasn't the place to grieve over lost opportunities. There was only one place where that would be appropriate. And he wanted to have a better track record before making the short drive to her grave that he hoped would be the end of a long journey.

———

"Where are you now?" Roxy asked Ray when she answered his early morning phone call.

"Sitting in Dad's old office. You know, the one he used when Colonel Parker was still alive."

"Ouch. Dare I ask how you feel?"

"I wouldn't have called if I wasn't willing to answer that question."

Roxy was surprised by the calm confidence in her brother's

voice as he told her about the events of the past two days. Partway through the conversation, she got up and closed the door of her office so she wouldn't be interrupted or subject to an eavesdropper.

"You sound so, I don't know, so *normal* about everything," she said when he finished. "How is that possible? You lost a great job and ended up in a legal ICU unit watching our father's law practice die a slow, painful death."

"That is a super helpful way to put it," Ray replied. "Could you repeat it so I can tell Cindy exactly what you said?"

"Sorry." Roxy winced. "It's just the way it looks to me."

"If you're right, then all I can say is that God has given me grace to deal with what's happened. And I hope he doesn't cut off the flow."

Roxy paused for a moment. "I've been experiencing a kind of grace myself, mostly through Peter."

It was Ray's turn to listen. As she talked, Roxy found herself reinforcing in her own mind what had been going on between her and Peter and, in some way, God himself. She avoided any mention of her feelings toward Corbin.

"When am I going to meet this guy?" Ray asked. "And does any of this mean you're ready to reopen communication with Dad? You'd have to apologize, since he's still mad at you for the way you treated him when he stopped by to see you."

"No," Roxy said. "Not yet. But I do want you and Cindy to meet Peter."

"We could drive down to Atlanta, or the two of you could come here. With all that's happened in my life, I haven't done anything about Mom's estate."

Normally Ray's admission would have irritated Roxy, but today it didn't.

"That's okay. Let me think about the best way for us to connect. I think it should be you and Cindy first, then Dad."

"Yeah. He can fill a room by himself." Ray was silent for a moment. "I came in early this morning and pulled some cases I can start working on ASAP. I hear him now, so I'd better go."

"Thanks for calling," Roxy said as sincerely as she could muster. "I'm, uh, proud of you for the way you're handling all this."

"I'm certainly not copying your paper in eleventh-grade English on this one."

Roxy slowly lowered her cell phone.

———

Corbin poured a cup of black coffee and took a few sips before walking into Ray's office. He knew the first item on the morning agenda would be to tell Ray about the AA meeting.

"Good morning," he said. "I wanted to—"

"Hey," Ray interrupted, putting his hand on a stack of folders on the desk. "I went through all the open files and think I can help with these immediately. Will you sit down with me for a couple of hours to make sure I understand what to do?"

"When do you want to do it?"

"Right now if you have the time."

"Okay. Meet me in the conference room in ten minutes. Did you look at any of the files I keep in my office?"

Ray shook his head no.

"I'll pick a few of those for us to discuss too."

Corbin stepped over to Janelle's desk. She had her headset on and was transcribing dictation. Corbin cleared his throat and moved to the left so he was in her line of sight, but she didn't look up.

"Janelle!" he said.

The secretary lifted her hands from the keyboard and eyed him irritably. "Can't you see I'm working?"

"Yes, what are you typing?"

"A thirty-minute memo Ray dictated sometime between when I left last night and I arrived this morning. There's no way I can keep up this pace. And praying about it isn't going to change anything."

"Okay, okay," Corbin replied. "We're going to talk about the open cases in a few minutes and sort out your duties as well."

"You'd better."

Janelle returned the headset to its place, and Corbin retreated to his office. There were five phone messages on his desk; one was from Nate Stamper with a reference line for the Colfax case. Corbin picked up the phone to return the call, then changed his mind. Ray might end up doing a lot of legwork on the case. It would be good if he listened in on the initial conversation with opposing counsel.

Corbin gathered several files that were haphazardly scattered around his office. When he went into the conference room, Ray was already sitting at the table with a folder open in front of him. Corbin saw a repair invoice from a car dealership and knew which case it was.

"The plaintiff isn't going to make a good witness," he said. "He's an angry old man, and no jury is going to like him. There's not much money involved either. Maybe we should drop it."

Ray didn't seem to hear him. "I think we can convince a jury that ruling in the plaintiff's favor is good for society, not just for him. The reason a person goes to a mechanic is to get a car fixed, not have it come out worse than it was. And the car wasn't safe to drive. Someone could have been hurt or killed if the second mechanic hadn't fixed the problem. Everyone believes in safety."

"Nice work." Corbin nodded. "Call the second mechanic and see what he says about the car being dangerous."

"I already did," Ray replied. "I caught him early this morning before he had his arms in grease up to his elbows. He says a bad bump in the road would have caused a total loss of control in the steering mechanism."

Over the next three hours, they went back and forth about the open files. It had been so many years since Corbin had another lawyer to bounce things off of that he'd forgotten how valuable and mentally stimulating it could be. Most of the files ended up in front of Ray, who still had the zealous enthusiasm of a young lawyer running through his veins.

"Are you sure you want to assume primary responsibility for all of these?" Corbin asked, motioning to the stack.

"Yes. I also saw the past due bills on the corner of Janelle's desk when I came in this morning. How bad is the cash flow situation?"

"I'm working on it," Corbin replied vaguely. "With you here I can focus more on the business side of the practice."

Ray seemed unconvinced.

"I need to return a call from Nate Stamper about the Colfax litigation," Corbin continued. "Do you want to listen in?"

"Yeah, I guess there has to be a first time for me to line up against him on a civil case."

"And trust me," Corbin replied. "It won't be the last."

THIRTY-TWO

Corbin put the phone on speaker while the receptionist paged Nate.

"Well, Corbin," the defense lawyer began. "Thanks to you I've opened a brand-new Colfax file."

"And lost a good associate."

"Yeah, I regret that."

Corbin glanced up at Ray, who was staring straight ahead. "Is there no way around it?"

"Just a minute," Nate replied.

Corbin and Ray heard a door close.

"Should you tell him I'm on the call?" Ray whispered.

Corbin shook his head.

"It's not how I voted," Nate said when he returned. "But I'm not the only partner, and hiring decisions for associates have to be unanimous. It wouldn't be right for me to tell you exactly how it shook down, but—"

"Of course not. But I appreciate the sentiment."

Corbin looked at Ray, who shrugged. Nate was not wearing his black adversarial hat this morning.

"Look," Nate said. "I know you were in court when Judge Ellington issued the criminal fine to the company, but I can assure you this matter was investigated for months and months, and there isn't a connection between my client's business and the sick boys. We're sorry, but you're going to spin your wheels into the ground and not have anything to show for it. The Colfax corporate board was very upset about the disposition of the criminal case and didn't drop the matter after it was over. They hired a high-priced consulting company to perform a supplemental review of the situation. I wish we'd had their report when we went to the hearing in front of Judge Ellington, because it rebuts every major allegation in the state EPA file. Have you hired an expert yet?"

"I'm interviewing people."

"Are you relying on the presence of 2,4-dichlorophenoxyacetic acid in the company's new herbicide product?"

Corbin shifted uneasily in his seat. "It's a possibility."

"Well, I've read the public record information that's available and three peer review articles about 2,4-D and possible links to non-Hodgkin's lymphoma. The initial suspicions raised by the studies in Sweden, Kansas, Nebraska, and Canada have been disproved by subsequent research."

Corbin swallowed. He'd not mentioned any of this information in the complaint. All he did was allege that chemicals in the ground contaminated the drinking water in nearby wells used by the plaintiff families and caused the boys to contract cancer. Nate was talking as if he'd been looking over Corbin's shoulder.

The defense lawyer continued.

"Also, the area of Colfax's property where this occurred is over two hundred yards from where your closest plaintiff lives. It's too remote to be relevant. Who did the testing on their wells, and what did they find? You may as well tell me now because you know I have a right to the information."

Corbin looked at Ray, who had a questioning look on his face too.

"I appreciate the education," Corbin replied, "but I'd rather respond formally pursuant to a discovery."

"Suit yourself. It's on the way to you today. And neither Mr. Hathaway nor Mr. Simpkin suggested that I call you. I did this on my own to save everyone a lot of wasted time, energy, and money." Nate paused. "And embarrassment."

"You're already filing an answer?" Corbin asked, ignoring the final comment. "It's not due yet."

"Why wait? I'm going to push hard to move this case along. And we'll follow up with a Section 9-15-14 claim for costs and attorney fees." Nate's congenial tone was gone.

"You know where I am. You'll hear from either Ray or me."

"Ray's working for you?"

"He is and I'm glad to have him."

"Give him my regards," Nate said.

"Will do."

The call ended. Corbin pushed his hair out of his face.

"Please tell me you had the well water tested before you filed suit," Ray said.

"No, I was going to hire an expert who could advise me what to look for and how to do the test. I thought I could rely on the state EPA findings to get things going."

"Maybe, but their investigation had a different purpose. They proved a discharge of chemicals on the ground above safe levels. There wasn't any evidence of ongoing harm to the public, and Colfax stopped as soon as the state EPA got involved." Ray leaned forward. "We've got to prove a causal connection between a specific chemical or chemicals and two boys getting cancer."

"I know, I know," Corbin replied. He felt like Ray was cross-examining him on the witness stand. "Did you hear Nate send his regards? He still respects you. I could hear it in his voice."

"Don't change the subject. I've been in criminal, not civil, court for the past six years, but even I know it's hard for a defendant to get an award of costs and attorney fees against a plaintiff for filing a frivolous lawsuit. However, if we don't come up with something, that's exactly what will happen. And the Simpkin firm is going to churn this case like crazy—thousands of dollars a week in billing. Which judge has the case?"

"Ellington. I was able to sweet-talk June at the clerk's office into helping me out with the judicial lottery."

"Congratulations. But June can't maneuver us around what's coming."

"You're right." Corbin paused and cleared his throat. "Speaking of help, how are we going to prioritize our work for Janelle so she doesn't walk out on us?"

Corbin resisted the urge to slip over to Red's for lunch and order a cool glass of mountain water. Instead he convinced a reluctant Ray to join him for a sandwich at a local delicatessen. Corbin ordered a Rueben piled high with sauerkraut. Ray selected a ham and cheese.

"I assume you don't have to be in court today," Ray said. "If so, they'll be able to smell your breath before you cross the street in front of the courthouse."

"No." Corbin smiled. "And I always keep a few breath mints in my desk."

"In case you have a drink during the day and don't want to smell like a distillery?"

Ray had been moody since the phone call with Nate Stamper.

"I'm doing something about that," Corbin replied, trying not to become defensive. "I've been to several more AA meetings, including yesterday evening. Would you like to know what happened?"

Ray was about to take a bite of his sandwich, but lowered it. "I'm listening."

Corbin told him what he could without betraying the guidelines of the group.

"Before last night I was kicking the tires of AA but hadn't made a serious commitment. Admitting that I am . . ." Corbin hesitated, but he could see that Ray wasn't going to say anything to get him off the hook. "Admitting that I'm an alcoholic was a huge step toward recovery. But it's only the first step."

"What are the other eleven?" Ray asked in a friendlier tone of voice.

Corbin recited them, ticking them off on his fingers, but stopped one short. "I'm leaving one out," he said. "Maybe it will come to me in a few minutes."

"That's still impressive," Ray replied. "Have you had any cravings to drink today?"

Corbin nodded. "I wanted to sneak off to Red's but asked you to come here instead."

Ray took a sip of sweet tea and nibbled on a potato chip. "You know that if you really stick with AA it will help your DUI case."

"Spending the night in jail, along with worrying about you and Cindy cutting me off from Billy, is what got me motivated." Corbin took a bite from his sandwich, savoring the sharp tang of the sauerkraut. "When are you going to file an appearance of counsel on my behalf?" he asked. "And are you sure you want to do it? I'm sure Cameron Burke would take me on as a client."

Ray shook his head. "Cameron does a better job getting people to hire him than representing them when they do."

"It'd be different with me because I know what he should do."

"Let's make Cameron backup plan B," Ray replied. "Or maybe F. When it comes down to it, I believe I can work something out with either one of the judges."

"You're going to find their attitude shifts when you're no longer representing the state."

"Then it's a good idea to let me practice on you," Ray said and grinned.

Corbin grunted and picked up his sandwich.

———

All day Roxy's mind drifted in the direction of Alto as she wondered what was going on between her father and Ray at the law office. Finally, late in the afternoon, she popped a caramel into her mouth and called Peter to tell him about her father and brother joining forces.

"That's unexpected, right?" he asked.

"Totally. For it to work, they're both going to have to undergo massive change. My father will have to yield his will and Ray will have to find his."

"Could you repeat that last sentence?" Peter replied. "I'm not sure I got it."

Roxy laughed.

"Or you could laugh again," Peter said. "It's a sound I live for."

"I want to see you," Roxy blurted out. "Tonight."

"I thought you had to work late."

She bit down on the last morsel of caramel. "I know," she replied with a sigh. "But I'm getting to the place where if I don't see you every day my world isn't right."

"Could you repeat that sentence?" Peter replied.

Roxy did so, only a bit slower.

"You're putting a lot of pressure on me," Peter said. "I can try to move things around, but I'm not the only one affected, and—"

"No, no," Roxy cut in. "I don't want you to get into trouble. But I'm glad I let you know how I feel."

"Me too."

Roxy suddenly found herself on the verge of telling Peter she loved him, but stopped. That needed to be done face-to-face.

"So when will I see you?" she asked.

"Why don't I join you tomorrow for your morning run? I'll try to keep up."

"Great. See you in front of my place at six."

"Okay, but I'll be so excited that it will be tough to sleep."

"You're ridiculous," Roxy said, "but I like it."

"Bye."

Roxy lowered her phone with a smile on her face.

"Who's ridiculous but you like it?" a voice asked.

Mr. Caldweller was standing outside the open door of her office.

"Personal call," Roxy managed. "I finished the first draft of answers to interrogatories in the Spandale case a few minutes ago, and I'm staying late tonight to get a head start prepping for the depositions next week in New Orleans."

"That will have to wait," Caldweller interrupted her. "In an hour I'm going to have a conference call with Kennedy Goings."

Roxy sat up straighter in her chair. Her boss had received her summary of the Dr. Sellers interview, and Roxy suddenly wondered if she was in trouble.

"What's the purpose for the call?" she managed. Mr. Goings was the COO who supervised all litigation for one of the firm's biggest clients.

"Settlement of the case you've been working on."

"I thought we weren't going to explore that until mediation."

"Revenue from the drugs involved has dipped, and according to an e-mail I received from Goings this morning, it's making less and less sense to fund a lawsuit with money they can use to buy an extra month or so of peace with the generic manufacturers."

Roxy relaxed. At least it didn't sound like she was in trouble.

"Why do you want me on the call?" she asked.

"To tell them why they're wrong. You'll have the rudder of the ship, and I want you to assure him that the cost benefit analysis of pressing forward with the litigation is going to benefit the company more than rolling over now."

"What numbers should I use?"

"Ones that you can back up. Goings will grill you, and I think it will be more persuasive for him to hear the forecast from you than me. Your job is to accurately predict the cost of settlement and not overestimate the cost of continuing the litigation to get there. Don't box the firm into a negative revenue model, and give him the incentive to let us go forward."

Roxy's head was spinning. It was an impossible task. She didn't yet know what the plaintiff companies would agree to in settlement or how much time the law firm would bill to reach the optimal point of resolution. Mr. Caldweller was way more qualified to guess than she was.

Then she realized what the senior partner was doing.

He was setting her up to take the blame, whichever prediction proved wrong. A wave of anger rose up from within her. She tried not to let it come through in her tone of voice.

"Based on your experience, what do you suggest I say?" she asked lightly. "I don't want to be ridiculous."

"I thought you liked ridiculous."

Corbin was amazed at how much he found himself looking forward to another AA meeting. After he and Ray returned to the office after lunch, he kept checking his watch. The meeting at the local mental health center started at four, and the afternoon seemed to drag by slowly. Shortly before time to leave, his phone buzzed.

"There's a Dr. Westbrook on the phone for you," Janelle said.

Corbin quickly ran through a mental list of the doctors in town and came up blank.

"He said you sent him an e-mail," Janelle continued.

"Oh yeah, he's the guy in California I contacted about the Colfax litigation. Put him through."

While he waited, Corbin was glad he'd already talked with Nate Stamper and knew there wasn't time to spare getting organized.

"I appreciate you contacting me." Westbrook spoke in an accent that was more Maine than Malibu. "Tell me the status of the litigation."

Corbin quickly brought the chemist up to date. "I want to bring someone on board early to guide us through the initial stages."

"And you didn't think that was necessary before filing suit?"

It wasn't the type of question Corbin expected from a hired gun expert looking for a paycheck. His opinion of Dr. Westbrook went up several notches.

"Normally, yes, but the boys involved are sick, and I needed to move quickly. I believe the investigation performed by the state EPA officials fulfills that function."

"You may be right. Do you have a copy of their file?"

"I have the important parts."

"It sounds like you're more interested in hiring a consultant to advise you than a chemist who can testify as an expert in the case."

"I'd like someone who can do both."

The phone was silent for a moment.

"I'm interested, but I can't address issues of specific

causation—only whether the levels of a chemical in the water supply reach levels that could potentially result in harm to the users."

"What would you charge to do that?"

"Five hundred an hour with a three thousand retainer, billing thereafter on a monthly basis."

It wasn't an unreasonable fee, but it was just the beginning of a cash outflow Corbin wasn't sure he could sustain.

Westbrook continued. "Also, I think I can help you locate someone to connect the dots medically if the chemical levels are sufficiently high."

"Really?" Corbin perked up.

"Yes. I've worked with an internist who knows how to handle himself in a deposition. He's board certified and has a level of expertise in chemically induced diseases. We collaborated in two lawsuits involving benzene exposure, but I think this would be in his wheelhouse too."

Corbin couldn't waste time interviewing multiple experts.

"Okay," he said. "I'm interested in both of you. Send me your agreement, and I'll forward the information in my file along with the retainer. What should I do about testing the water?"

"I'll handle that once I'm on the case. A service I use can take the sample and deliver it to me. I'll run the tests here in LA."

"And send me the qualifications of the internist."

"Will do. I've not been to Georgia in years. How far are you from Atlanta?"

"About eighty miles. But we'll come to you if we take your deposition, probably via video so we can use it at trial."

"Whatever works for you and your clients."

Corbin picked up a hint of disappointment in the chemist's voice, but he wasn't going to pay travel time. Corbin would fly coach to Los Angeles . . . even if Nate Stamper would sit in first class.

THIRTY-THREE

By the end of the week Corbin had attended four AA meetings in five days. He'd experienced discussion meetings, Big Book study meetings, twelve-step study meetings, and speaker meetings. He'd especially come to appreciate the wisdom and insight of Jimmy Broome, who knew even more about alcoholism than he did alternators and transmissions. Corbin had stopped scoffing at the recommendation, first voiced to him by Max Hogan, that an alcoholic seeking recovery should attend ninety sessions in ninety days. Even though Corbin wasn't ready to take that step, the idea no longer seemed ludicrous. A 90-in-90 commitment was akin to learning a foreign language by total immersion—in this case the message of AA.

Corbin had gone the entire week without a drink. It wasn't the first time he'd reached five days of sobriety, but it was the first time he'd done so because he was trying to quit drinking entirely. But early on Friday he knew a high hurdle awaited him. After work on the final day of the workweek was his favorite time to unwind.

During his marriage to Kitty she could never plan a time for supper on Friday, as Corbin's arrival would unpredictably fall within a two- to three-hour bracket. She and the children kept their own eating schedule, and she'd save a plate of food for him, which he often didn't eat. Instead he'd collapse in a recliner in the den and doze off until waking up for another drink or two before going to bed. The tragic routine lost some of its pathos because of familiarity. Kitty, Ray, and Roxy structured their lives as if Corbin was out of town most Friday nights.

Corbin wasn't thinking about the past when he returned from lunch with Ray. He was anxious about the next few hours and the increased craving for a drink he could feel growing in his gut. He had a headache, and his hands shook if he held them out in front of himself. As the hours passed, the Friday afternoon hurdle was beginning to look like an insurmountable wall.

There was a knock on his office door.

"Come in," he growled.

Ray entered and Corbin lowered his hands below the level of his desk so his son couldn't see them quiver.

"I enjoyed lunch," Ray said. "I think that place is going to make it if they keep up the quality."

"Yeah, the cook knows how to fix vegetables the way people around here prefer them. What do you want?"

"I just got off the phone with the defense lawyer in the Peterson case. When I told him earlier today I wanted to schedule four depositions in the next month, he asked for a demand. The client gave me permission to take $10,000, so I called the lawyer back and started negotiations at $17,500. How does that sound to you?"

"You probably should have opened at $20,000, but it just means you'll have to go down slower. If you're able to squeeze $10,000 from the insurance company it will be a win."

A sharp pain shot through Corbin's head, and he couldn't keep from wincing. Ray stopped and stared.

"Do you have the Friday afternoon shakes?" he asked.

Corbin pushed his hands beneath his legs. "Headache," he

replied. "I'll take something in a minute. Let me know what happens in the Peterson case. It's been sitting in the file cabinet when I should have been working it. Good job." He waited for Ray to get up and leave.

"I know this can be your toughest day of the week," Ray said. "How can I help?"

Before AA cracked open the door of honesty, Corbin would have brushed Ray off. He started to fall back into his old paradigm of denial, then stopped.

"I don't know," Corbin said as he lifted a trembling hand to brush his hair away from his forehead. "There's a meeting at the church, but it doesn't start for a few hours."

"Do you think you should go to the hospital?" Ray asked in a soft voice.

"Why?"

"So you can enter a twenty-eight-day program."

Corbin had been toying with the 90-in-90 plan, but in the back of his mind he knew an inpatient program was a possibility. He shook his head. "I'm not ready for that. And I can't be away from the office."

"I'm here."

"For one week so far." Corbin shook his head ruefully. "You could run the DA's office, but you don't know enough about the civil side of a law practice to assume responsibility for all my cases. You've barely dipped your toe in the water."

Ray remained where he was.

"Aren't you going to say anything?" Corbin asked.

"This isn't an intervention, and you're not going to be persuaded by an argument. You've taken huge steps the past few weeks. And I hope you'll take the next one."

Corbin buried his face in his hands and closed his eyes. He

pressed his fingers against his pounding temples. When he raised his head, Ray was gone.

Corbin pulled open the drawer where he kept a bottle of pain-killers. He shook out two, then doubled the number to four. There was some cold coffee in a mug on his desk. He popped the pills in his mouth and used the stale coffee to wash them down.

———

Billy had a late Friday afternoon soccer match. During the drive to the sports complex, Ray couldn't get his mind off his father. He and Cindy had prayed for Corbin every morning that week, and even though the battle for his father's soul was fierce, he could truthfully report that Corbin Gage was fighting.

Cindy was standing alone on the sidelines, wearing a yellow sweater that was one of Ray's favorites. He sneaked up behind her and grabbed her around the waist.

She let out a scream and turned around, and Ray quickly released her. "Sorry—I wasn't trying to scare you."

"Then what were you trying to do?" she asked as she glanced around to see if anyone was staring at them.

"Let you know that I was glad to see you?" he offered. "You look so good I couldn't resist."

"A simple 'Hi, honey, you look nice' would have worked." Cindy lowered her voice. "And my body doesn't need a shock."

"I'm sorry," he said again. "That was a really stupid thing to do."

"And it's been a tough day," Cindy continued.

A cheer went up from the spectators as a player on the other team threatened to score a goal. Cindy and Ray paused to watch. Billy was in the middle of a scrum in front of the goal, and he kicked the ball into the clear.

"Great job!" Ray called out.

The teams flowed toward the center of the field.

"Why was it a tough day?" Ray asked.

"It started out good. I didn't get sick for the third day in a row, but then I saw Patsy Carpenter at the supermarket. Her parents want to sell their house on Roxbury Court. It's a cute three-bedroom with a big backyard, in the Westside school district. It's not on the market yet, but she said if we could work out a deal, her folks would save on the real estate agent's commission and pass some of that on to us. It made me dream for a minute, but then I had to remind myself that I can't."

The disappointment in Cindy's voice was tough to hear.

"I drove by the house on my way home," she continued, "and it's nicer than I remembered. They've spent money fixing it up on the outside, and Patsy told me they've replaced all the carpet."

"We don't like carpet," Ray offered.

"I don't like old carpet. But it would be a lot easier on a baby than hardwood floors. And it's just in the bedrooms. Tell me you wouldn't rather put your feet on carpet on a cold winter morning than on an unheated hardwood floor. And the kitchen has a new range and a nearly new refrigerator that will stay." Cindy sighed.

"How much do they want for it?" Ray asked.

"I don't want to tell you, and I was crazy to torture myself by looking at it. If things had worked out with the new job, it's within the budget we'd discussed. But once it hits the market I'm sure it will get snapped up."

She turned away and faced the playing field. Ray didn't know what to say or do. Their financial future was chained to a man desperately fighting to keep from slipping deeper into a pit of destruction, and what Ray thought might encourage her now seemed like more bad news. If Corbin went into an alcohol treatment center, there was no guarantee he would be able to function effectively as an attorney when he got out.

Roxy's words about their father's law practice being in the intensive care unit flashed through Ray's mind. He'd tried to keep a positive attitude all week, but in reality he knew there were only a handful of cases like the Peterson matter that might yield modest fees. Still, it was something positive to tell his wife.

"I made some progress today toward settling a lawsuit my father had on the back burner."

"Is it a big case?"

"Not really."

They watched the other team score a goal that put them ahead three to two. The coach took Billy out of the game.

"Why is he taking Billy out?" Cindy asked, throwing up her hands. "They're behind."

"He'll put him back in after halftime. Some of the substitutes haven't gotten to play at all."

A few minutes later the referee blew his whistle, signaling the half. The team huddled up around the coach.

"So who's going to come off the bench and help you and your father?" Cindy asked.

AA meetings usually ended promptly; however, Corbin stayed in the circle as the others got up to leave. Jimmy came over and sat beside him.

"Still got something going on?" Jimmy asked.

"Just what I shared earlier about Friday night being the toughest time of the week for me. I don't want to go home and face a house that's empty except for a TV and the liquor bottles in the cabinet."

Corbin waited for Jimmy to tell him to pour the liquor down the drain. To his surprise, he didn't.

"Where are you with Step Two?"

"The higher power stuff?"

"Yes. It's in there for a reason."

Corbin had a list of the Twelve Steps in his hand. He glanced down at the sheet of paper and silently read—*Came to believe that a Power greater than ourselves could restore us to sanity.*

Corbin looked at Jimmy, who didn't seem in a hurry to speak.

"What's your higher power?" Corbin asked.

"I met him in there." Jimmy pointed to the door of the fellowship hall that led toward the sanctuary. "Jesus is my source of strength."

"You're a member of this church?"

"And the person who asked the church board if this group could start meeting here."

"How long ago was that?"

"Eight years."

"You've been in recovery that long?"

"Longer. I hope to pick up my ten-year chip in a few months."

"Kitty was the religious one in the family. My son believes like she did, but my daughter, Roxy, and I—" Corbin stopped. "I just don't know about a power I can't see or feel."

Jimmy leaned forward. "Remember the other day when you told the story about taking your grandson fishing and making the choice to leave the moonshine in the truck? Floating in your boat, do you ever think about God creating the beauty you see or sending the breeze you feel?"

"No, I'm wondering what the fish are going to bite today."

"Spoken like a true fisherman." Jimmy smiled. "Jesus spent way more time fishing than most people realize. Maybe that's what you should check out in the Bible. It might help you connect with Step

Two so you can get to Step Three—'Made a decision to turn our will and our lives over to the care of God as we understood Him.'"

Corbin left the meeting. He tried to keep his eyes fixed on the road ahead as he passed The Office, but he couldn't help noticing out of the corner of his eye that the parking lot was full. The cars and trucks belonged to actual people, many of whom were long-time friends. They were real, the booze potent. An unseen power was less tangible than the air he was breathing.

He resisted the urge to turn around and go back. The Office wasn't the only place in town to satisfy a craving.

As he turned into the driveway of his duplex, Corbin knew what he was going to do as soon as he got inside.

THIRTY-FOUR

Roxy walked through the door and immediately kicked off her shoes in the foyer. It wasn't that her shoes hurt her feet; it was a symbolic gesture linked to stepping out of the mess Mr. Caldweller had dropped on her at work. She went into the kitchen and poured herself a large glass of wine. As she did, she thought about her father's decades-long Friday evening routine, but she quickly pushed the comparison aside. She plopped down on the sofa in the living room and swirled the wine around in the glass before taking a sip.

Her phone, which was on the sofa beside her, vibrated and she saw Peter's name and face. She placed the wineglass on a coffee table.

"I just walked through the door," she said. "Where are you?"

"Still at the office waiting for a conference call with a client in St. Louis. It's been the kind of day where I'm worried I'm going to mix up presentations and mention something in this call that was intended for a meeting earlier in the day. How are you?"

"I spent the afternoon serving as Mr. Caldweller's sacrificial lamb to one of our biggest clients. He made me guess what it's going to cost to continue defending a big lawsuit when we don't know everything the other side is going to throw at us. But that wasn't the tough part. I had to predict what the plaintiffs would agree to accept in settlement without the benefit of an initial offer from them."

"That sounds impossible."

"It is. The purpose was to divert any possible blame down the road away from Mr. Caldweller."

Peter was silent for a moment. "You speak Spanish, don't you?"

"I took it in high school and college, but I'm pretty rusty."

"Sometimes I listen to one of the Spanish TV stations to see what I can pick up."

"Why are we talking about this?"

"Why don't we move to Spain for a few years? I can do my work from anywhere in the world, and you can run along the beach every morning, then come back to our villa and sip fruity drinks the rest of the day."

Roxy laughed. "I was with you until you mentioned fruity drinks as the main part of my job description."

"Yeah, that kind of fizzled, didn't it? Listen, we both need a break. Would you like to drive up to Alto tomorrow? It would be a chance to get away from the city."

"Are you comparing Alto to the Spanish Mediterranean?"

"I can't say until I see it."

"We don't have to go to Alto to answer that question." Roxy stared at the glass of wine and thought about her last conversation with her father. "I assume this is part of your strategy to help me find emotional wholeness."

"I'm not trying to fix you. But I care about every molecule in your being."

"Now I really wish you were here," Roxy said. "But I'd hate to waste a trip if my father isn't going to see or talk to me."

"Could you call him and find out?"

She took a sip of wine.

"No, I'd rather not chance it," she said slowly. "However, we could still go so you can meet Ray and his family. Let me make sure he's going to be in town."

"Okay. It will be worth it just to spend a few uninterrupted hours with you in the car."

"Not if the return trip is a nonstop therapy session."

———

Corbin had a beautiful burgundy leather study Bible Kitty gave him on the first Father's Day after Ray's birth. At the time Corbin saw right through her agenda, and although he thanked her, the book ended up on a shelf where it had lived an orphan's life ever since. The leather was now cracked with age like an old man's face.

Corbin looked up *fish* in the concordance.

Over the next hour or so he read about loaves and fishes, nets full of fish, a gold coin in a fish's mouth, and eating broiled fish beside the Sea of Galilee. The most interesting story was the account in John 21 about a huge catch of fish. The number caught, 153, was specifically recorded in the text, just as a proud fisherman would do. The careful attention to detail surprised Corbin. It was the type of evidence he would present to a jury to convince them a witness was telling the truth.

In the study notes to the chapter there was a reference to Simon Peter's earlier denial of Jesus. Corbin turned back a few pages and read about the disciple's assurance of loyalty prior to Jesus's arrest, followed almost immediately by multiple denials that included curses. It was so raw and honest that it bolstered the credibility of what he was reading. Corbin could see it all playing out in his mind's eye.

He returned to the fishing story and read about Peter's restoration through repeated questions from Jesus. *Simon, do you love me?*

Corbin closed the book. He knew he'd been reading about events in the lives of real people. If that was true, what else about the life of Jesus deserved his attention? If Jesus knew where the fish were swimming beneath the surface of the water, was there a chance he knew about the turmoil swirling inside of Corbin's soul and what to do about it? Could Jesus reach across the centuries and provide the present-day power Corbin needed to change?

A tingle of affirmation suddenly ran down Corbin's spine. He wasn't expecting a physical reaction as evidence of a spiritual reality, but given his state of mind, he couldn't deny what he'd felt. Leaning back in his chair, he remembered Jimmy's words about a God who could be seen and felt. Corbin breathed in as if receiving a new revelation. Then in a soft voice, he prayed the first genuine prayer of his adult life.

"Jesus, will you be the God who helps restore me to sanity?"

———

"Roxy and her boyfriend, Peter, are driving up tomorrow," Ray said to Cindy when he returned to the den from the bedroom, where he'd taken the call.

The family was watching a movie and eating pizza for supper.

"Aunt Roxy has a boyfriend?" Billy looked away from the TV screen. "I didn't think she could have a boyfriend."

"What gave you that idea?" Cindy asked.

"Daddy said she was so bossy that no man would want to hang out with her."

"Uh, that must have slipped out when I was upset about something," Ray said. "It's not the truth."

"You talked like it was. We were at Gran's house after the funeral, and you were talking to Mr. Jones."

Barrett Jones was a high school classmate of Ray who knew Roxy well.

"Oh, we were talking about long ago when we were in school together. He knew I was joking."

"He didn't laugh."

"Are you watching this movie?" Ray asked irritably.

"I know what happens. This is the boring part."

Ray got up and went into the kitchen. Cindy followed him.

"After the movie is over we should help Billy fill out his application for law school," she said. "He did a very good job of breaking down your attempt to deny what you said to Barrett. Your credibility was shot."

"I'm not sure another lawyer is what this family needs."

"The way he idolizes you and your father, it could happen. Did Roxy say why she's coming?"

"She wants us to meet Peter."

"Really?" Cindy raised her eyebrows. "That sounds serious."

"Do you think she should run up a peace flag to Dad and invite him to dinner?"

"Dinner? Where?"

"Here, that's what Roxy wants."

It was Cindy's turn to show a hint of irritation. "Did you tell her you'd need to check with me about that?"

"You know Roxy doesn't like any of the restaurants here in Alto."

"What does the princess want me to prepare? Did she have a suggested menu?"

"We talked about it," Ray said, then stopped.

"And?"

Ray stepped over and started to wrap his arms around Cindy, but she pushed him away.

"Answer the question," she said. "Hugging me at the soccer field didn't go very well, and it's not going to work now."

Ray backed up. "I suggested steaks on the grill with baked potatoes, steamed broccoli, and a tossed salad. She said that was fine. I'll cook the steaks and help out with everything else except the salad."

"Why not the salad? You know how to cut up tomatoes and cucumbers."

"Okay, okay. Roxy is stopping off at Parson's butcher shop to buy the steaks, then swinging by the grocery store for the salad fixings. I think it's also a way for her to show Peter around town."

"Will you help straighten up the house?"

"Yes, Billy and I will do it. It's time that boy learned how to do some deep cleaning."

"I like the sound of that." Cindy smiled. "Do you know where I keep the vacuum cleaner?"

"That's a trick question." Ray scratched his head. "It's either in the hall closet or the room where you last used it and didn't put it away."

Cindy laughed. "You're right either way. When are you going to call your father?"

Ray glanced at the clock on the microwave. "I'm almost afraid to call him. You know what he loves to do on Friday night. But maybe tonight is different."

"Why?"

Ray checked in the den to make sure Billy was still watching the movie, then told Cindy about Corbin and AA. Her eyes widened as he talked.

"And that's the way I left him. Pressuring him was more likely to backfire than help, but I don't know what he did when he left the office. At least we haven't gotten a call that he's in jail."

"Do you think it's too late to pray for him?"

Ray shrugged. "It couldn't hurt. And if this dinner takes place, it's going to take more than a ten-second blessing before cutting into a steak."

———

Corbin spent a restless night tossed back and forth between bizarre dream scenarios without any hope of solution and the sensation of falling from a great height. When he got up to go to the bathroom, he didn't pour himself a drink. Instead he took a sip of water from the bathroom sink. Finally, around 5:00 a.m., he fell into a fitful sleep that lasted an hour past the usual time he got up in the morning. He opened his eyes to shafts of pale light peeking around the slats of the blinds in his bedroom. Where the light struck the opposite wall there were thin bands of rainbow color at the edges of the shafts. Corbin watched them, mesmerized, until the angle of the sun shifted and the colors disappeared. Greeting the day with a rainbow in his bedroom was much better than facing a bleary-eyed hangover.

Rolling out of bed, he brewed a pot of coffee. While he watched the dark liquid drip into the pot, he wondered how he would pass the time. There were dishes in the sink that needed washing, and the interior of the duplex reflected the general sloppiness of his life. He ran hot water in the sink so the dishes could soak. Taking his coffee outside, he sat on the front stoop of the duplex. From his hilltop location he could see down the hill and across the valley. The cars and trucks on the road to Alto looked like miniature vehicles as they passed by. He sipped the coffee and watched.

His phone, which was in the shirt pocket of his pajamas, rang. Seeing his son's name gave Corbin an idea about how he wanted to spend his day.

"Hey," he said before Ray spoke. "Any chance I can take Billy fishing? I know we didn't talk about it earlier, and if he has a soccer match, I'll understand—"

"He's going to help me clean up around the house and yard," Ray replied. "We're having some people over for dinner tonight, and he's going to learn how to do more than pick up his clothes off the floor."

"Will that take all day? Could he sneak away with me for a couple of hours? We could fish from the bank and not take the time to launch the boat."

"Maybe, but only if you agree to eat a steak and baked potato with a group at our house this evening."

"Who else is going to be there?"

"Roxy and Peter, her boyfriend."

Corbin set down his coffee cup. "Why are they coming into town?"

"To see us. She's going to show Peter around town, then end up over here around five thirty or so. We plan on eating at six thirty. If you take Billy fishing, he'll need to be home in time to clean up. You probably don't want to come to dinner smelling like worm guts and insect repellant either."

"The last time I saw Roxy, the conversation didn't go so well."

"I know, and I believe she'd like to put that behind her."

"Is that what she told you?"

"She wouldn't be that humble, but I know she regrets what happened."

Corbin looked across the valley. At that moment his resentment toward Roxy seemed the size of the cars on the road, but he knew it would swell to life size when seeing her face-to-face.

"Were you serious that I can't take Billy fishing if I don't come for dinner?" he asked.

"No, I think fishing is a great idea. It will help me motivate him to work hard this morning. But we really want you to come tonight."

"Let me mull it over. How about two this afternoon to pick up Billy?"

"Yeah, that should work."

"Okay. I might clean up my place too."

Ray was silent for a moment. "Dad, how are you doing this morning? You sound, I don't know, kind of different."

Several thoughts shot through Corbin's mind, but he wasn't sure which one to share, or whether he could verbalize any of them.

"I'm just sitting in front of my house drinking a cup of coffee," he said.

"Okay. See you later." Ray paused. "I love you."

The call ended, leaving Corbin staring at the phone in his hand.

THIRTY-FIVE

The closer Roxy and Peter got to Alto, the more uneasy she felt. She gripped the steering wheel tightly and tried to keep her focus on the road, but her mind kept drifting down paths her life had traveled years before. She thought about her mother, about growing up with Ray, about painful images of her father.

One night when she was twelve years old and couldn't sleep, Roxy had gotten out of bed to get a drink of water in the kitchen. She noticed a light on in the den and found her father passed out on the sofa. The odd position of his body and gaping open mouth caused the thought to flash through her mind that he might be dead. She crept closer. Suddenly he snorted and opened his blood-shot eyes. He lurched forward and reached for her.

"What are you doing sneaking up on me!" he called out.

Roxy screamed and ran from the room. The following day she nervously waited for him to scold her, but when he didn't say anything she realized he didn't even remember—which was scary in a different way. A parent out of control is a parent who can't be trusted.

Peter interrupted her thoughts. "Isn't that the exit for Alto?"

Roxy swerved off the interstate, barely missing a road sign. "Sorry," she said. "I was distracted."

"By what?"

"I'm picking up bad memories like lost radio waves," she said with a shudder.

"Do you want me to drive?"

"No, we're almost there."

As they reached the outskirts of Alto, Roxy pulled herself together and began pointing out places from her past.

"That's my elementary school," she said when they passed the redbrick building with the old-fashioned playground beside it.

"I bet you were the cutest girl in the whole school."

"I was a midget with skinny legs who acted like a know-it-all."

"Some things change, others don't."

Roxy laughed. Having Peter with her beat back the darkness.

They reached Willow Oak Lane. Roxy slowed at the end of the cul-de-sac. The grass had recently been cut, but there weren't any flowers in the beds. The house looked empty because it was.

"That's it," she said. "My mom brought me home from the infant nursery at the hospital, and that's where I lived until I left for college."

Peter looked intently out the side window of the car. "Which is your room?"

"The fourth window to the right of the door."

"Is that the window you climbed out when you were secretly meeting your boyfriend?"

"I didn't have a boyfriend."

Peter turned toward her. "Don't lie to me."

"I'm not. I was into sports and studying in high school. I didn't date anyone until college." She paused. "And none of those were serious relationships."

"Why not?"

Roxy knew what she wanted to say. She turned in the seat so Peter had her full attention.

"My father warped my view of men and soured me on guys so much that I doubted I could ever trust one. Then I met you and you've been methodically blowing up all the barriers I built to protect my heart."

"And I intend to knock down others," Peter replied, his eyes kind.

"Gently, I hope."

"Always."

She reached over and took his hand. "I never thought I'd bring a man to Alto, but the fact that we're sitting here proves how much I've changed. I should have asked you to be here when my mom died—"

Peter waited.

"And I wish she could have met you before she passed away," Roxy finished.

"I think sitting here with you is a lot like meeting her."

Roxy shook her head. "You've seen the physical similarities in the old photos at my townhome, but what's inside me is different. If you're brave enough, ask Ray if I'm like her. He'll tell you the truth."

———

Corbin and Billy fished from the bank at Hackburn's Lake and caught a few bream, but nothing like the monster fish Billy hooked on their previous outing. Still, the oval, flat fish fought with every ounce of their being. One ungratefully popped Corbin in the palm of his hand with its sharp dorsal fin when he took it off the hook to release it. A few drops of blood appeared. Billy looked worried, so Corbin applied a strip of gauze, held in place by an elastic bandage.

When he took Billy home, Ray saw the bandage and immediately started asking questions.

"It's nothing," Corbin said.

Ray leaned in closer, and Corbin knew what he was doing. The soft feelings he'd had toward Ray after their morning phone call evaporated as fast as morning mist in the middle of a Georgia July.

"Tell him, Billy," Corbin said. "What did I drink while we were fishing?"

"The bottled water from the bait store," Billy answered with a puzzled look on his face. "The water wasn't very cold, and I wish you'd bought me that fruit drink I wanted. I've never had that flavor—"

"Did either one of us drink anything else?" Corbin interrupted.

"No."

"Thanks for working so hard this morning so we could go fishing," Corbin said, rubbing the top of Billy's head.

"Sure, Pops. Are you going to eat supper with us?"

Ray spoke. "We're planning on it. Roxy bought plenty of steaks, and Cindy and I are set up to feed everyone."

"I don't think so." Corbin faked a yawn. "I've had a long day."

He could see the disappointment in Ray's face, but the bandage on Corbin's hand reminded him of the false accusation hurled in his direction seconds before.

"See you at the office on Monday," he said as he turned away.

He drove up the driveway to his duplex. Seeing the empty house, he felt a twinge of regret at stiff-arming Ray's invitation, but pride wouldn't let him change his mind at this point. Anyway, it would be less stressful for everyone if Corbin wasn't around when Roxy showed off her boyfriend. Cindy could relax, and Corbin wouldn't have to spar with Roxy, whose words on a good day were sharper than Ray's comments when he was in a bad mood.

Corbin wasn't fighting a craving for whiskey, but he really wanted a cold beer. It was a thought that had lurked in the back of his mind during the second hour he spent with Billy on the bank of the pond. In the refrigerator was a neat row of five cans nestled close together. Corbin grabbed one. Immediately the outside of the can was covered with a thin layer of frost that signaled the perfect internal temperature. Corbin popped the top. It was a sound like none other. He lifted the can and let the amber beverage flow smoothly through his mouth and down his throat. There was nothing like a cold beer at the end of a day.

"Ah," he said with satisfaction.

He sat down on the front stoop where he'd welcomed the day. He took two more long swallows that emptied half the can. The valley looked different in the late afternoon light. No longer poised in anticipation, it looked softer, more relaxed. The scene perfectly matched his mood. He wanted to savor the final bit of beer but gulped it instead. He stood up to get another can from the refrigerator when his phone rang. If it was Ray calling, he wasn't going to answer.

He took the phone from his shirt pocket and glanced at it. It was Roxy.

———

Ray went into the backyard. Roxy followed, carrying the raw steaks on a metal sheet. The red-hot coals were uniformly covered in gray ash. Ray laid the steaks on top of the grill. It wouldn't take long for them to begin to sizzle.

"How does Peter like his meat?" he asked.

"Medium, but less cooked is better than overcooked."

"I think I can handle medium." Ray glanced past Roxy toward the kitchen door. "Are you sure it's a good idea to leave Peter alone with Dad?"

"It's probably the best thing we could do. Dad's being the most social I've seen in years. He'd rather talk to Peter than us."

"Yeah," Ray chuckled, "I've heard those stories too many times to pretend that I'm interested."

"The thing about Peter is he's not pretending. He's wanted to meet Dad for weeks."

"Why?"

"Because he cares so much about me."

Ray glanced up. "I knew this was serious or you wouldn't have brought him to meet us," he said. "Has he asked you—"

"No, no." Roxy cut him off. "But he's really helped me come out of the shell I've been hiding in. He always knows what to say to me when my default is to shut down."

"I've never heard you talk like this."

"Believe me, it sounds weirder to me than it does to you." Roxy turned around toward the kitchen. "I'd better get back inside, if for no other reason than to satisfy my curiosity."

Ray wasn't sure what was happening in his sister's life, but any crack in her armor was positive. He eyed the steaks and resisted the urge to poke them with a long fork or lift up an edge to check how fast they were cooking. Scattered pops came from the coals as drops of melted fat fell through the grill. The kitchen door opened, and Cindy came outside.

"The potatoes are out of the oven," she said. "All I have to do is give the salad a final toss before putting it on the table. How's the meat?"

"It won't be long. The fire is hot. And I think someone has kidnapped my sister and downloaded someone else into her body."

Cindy smiled. "I won't file a police report if you won't. She's been very cordial, and I left Peter listening to your father as if he's a sage who spent his entire life in search of ultimate wisdom."

"What about the conversation around the dinner table?" Ray asked. "Who's going to steer that in a positive direction?"

"Not me." Cindy held up her hands. "I'm the nonlawyer in the family. The rest of you intimidate me."

"We'll let Peter direct the table talk. From what Roxy just told me, he's found the lost key to her soul and is on a mission to do the same for Dad. I want to watch him in action."

He turned the steaks over, revealing perfectly formed grill marks on the side exposed to the coals. "Unless anyone wants their meat burnt, these should come off in three to four minutes," he said.

Cindy left Ray with his thoughts. He looked up at the stars that were beginning to dot the night sky.

The back door opened a third time, and Billy came out, bringing a clean platter for the steaks. His hair was still wet from the shower and combed away from his forehead. He looked more and more like Corbin each day.

"Mama said you'd need this," he said, handing the plate to Ray.

"Thanks. Did you meet Peter?"

"Yeah, he and Pops are talking about you and Aunt Roxy."

"What are they saying?" Ray asked, raising his eyebrows.

"Stuff from when you were teenagers. I had a question for Pops about fishing, but he told me not to interrupt."

"There will be time for you to talk to him about fishing before he leaves." Ray handed the platter back to Billy. "Here, hold this while I take the steaks off the grill."

"I don't want to drop them."

"You won't. Anyone who can reel in some of the fish you've been catching can handle a platter of dead cow meat."

"Daddy, that's gross."

THIRTY-SIX

Even though it was slightly cramped, everyone sat around the table in the dining room. On the spur of the moment, Ray asked Billy to say the blessing for the food.

The little boy didn't hesitate. Bowing his head, he used the exact words in Ray's standard blessing.

"How much broccoli do I have to eat?" he asked as soon as he finished.

"It'll taste better because you prayed over it," Ray replied.

"Three pieces," Cindy said. "Which is two less than normal because you were willing to pray."

The serving dishes made it around the table, and everyone dug in.

"Did Roxy tell you we've gone to church together?" Peter asked Ray.

"Yeah, what prompted that?"

"I'm not sure how exactly to describe it, but I'm going through some kind of spiritual awakening. I didn't go to church at all when I was growing up, so this is all new to me, but I know it's real."

"I know what you mean," Corbin added under his breath.

Ray, who was about to put another bite of steak in his mouth, stopped. He could see the shock on his wife's and sister's faces.

"What did you say?" he asked Corbin.

"You heard me."

"But I don't know what you mean."

"That it's real."

"He's talking about God," Billy cut in. "I understand him."

"Yeah." Corbin motioned toward Billy. "That's right. Billy gets me."

With Peter's prompting, the conversation veered to Ray and Roxy growing up in Alto. It was a delicate subject, but Peter kept the focus positive by asking questions like, "What were some of the funny things you remember Roxy and Ray doing as kids?"

Corbin's story about an incident with a sprinkler and a water hose made Roxy smile. Ray couldn't remember the last time father and daughter had shared a molecule of common humor.

"Would it be okay if I asked a few questions about Mrs. Gage?" Peter asked.

"Kitty," Corbin replied. "She never would have let you call her Mrs. Gage."

Ray looked at Billy, whose eyes had suddenly widened.

"Maybe not now," Ray said, motioning with his head toward his son.

"Sure," Peter replied. "Billy, tell me about the lake your Pops mentioned, the one where you give names to all the big bass."

Everyone relaxed as Billy became the center of attention for the rest of the meal. As Ray listened he felt grateful for his son's unself-conscious influence on the adults. Even Roxy was relating to Billy more as a person than as an unformed juvenile. All this had to be due to what Ray labeled in his mind as the "Peter Factor." Roxy's boyfriend should have been the one nervous at meeting the extended Gage family, but he made all of them feel more at ease with one another.

"Who wants dessert?" Cindy asked. "I made a lemon meringue pie this morning while Ray and Billy were cleaning the bedrooms."

Everyone except Roxy opted in.

"It's already going to take an extra workout or two for me to take care of this meal," she said. "How about you, Cindy? Are you still working out a few days a week?"

Cindy was carrying the empty serving dish for the broccoli to the kitchen. She placed it in the sink and turned around toward the table.

"No, I'm pregnant, and the doctor wants me to take it easy during the first trimester."

The family-wide announcement was unexpected. Ray quickly glanced at Billy, whose eyes were suddenly fixed on his mother's abdomen.

"The baby is tiny right now," Ray said to his son. "But we're praying that he will grow and get bigger."

"Or she," Cindy added.

"Congratulations," Peter said.

"Uh, yeah," Roxy said with a perplexed look on her face. "Did the doctor clear you to have another baby?" she asked. "Because of your history—"

"Roxy!" Cindy cut in.

Ray raised his fingers to his lips and nodded toward Billy. Their son knew nothing about the multiple miscarriages.

"Oh, sorry," Roxy said.

Corbin, who was sitting next to Billy, put his hand on the boy's shoulder. "After dessert I'd like you to show me the school project you told me about. You know, the one about the impact of dams on fishing."

"Okay."

The room remained silent while Cindy cut the pie. Roxy left the table and brewed a cup of decaf from the Keurig.

Corbin swallowed a bite of pie. "I'll add my congratulations about the baby," he said thoughtfully to Cindy. "You and Ray are great parents, much better than I ever was. I've been thinking a lot about that recently, and I need to—"

"Pops," Billy interjected over a mouthful of pie. "You're awesome. Most of the kids in my class don't have a grandpa who takes them fishing and does fun stuff with them like you do with me."

Out of the corner of his eye, Ray saw Roxy shift in her chair as a dark cloud passed over her features.

Corbin ate another bite of pie. "Come on, Billy," he said. "Let's go to your room."

The remaining adults sat in silence for a few moments. Ray wanted to revisit Corbin's attempt at an apology but wasn't sure how to introduce it.

"Peter and I had better get going," Roxy said, looking at her watch. "Thanks for dinner."

"And to you for buying the steaks," Ray said.

Everyone stood.

"Are you going to say good-bye to Dad?" Ray asked.

"No, we've been civil to each other so far tonight. I don't want to chance a relapse."

"I look forward to seeing you again," Peter said. "Billy too. He's a great kid."

After they left, Ray and Cindy returned to the kitchen.

"Did you hear what my father was doing before Billy cut him off?" Ray asked her. "He was going to apologize for his mistakes as a father."

"That might work for you, but it's going to take a lot more than a few words over a piece of pie to get rid of that mountain for Roxy."

Ray wanted to say something about God moving mountains. But at that moment it would sound more like a platitude than a promise.

———

Roxy and Peter walked down the driveway to her car, and Peter opened the passenger door for her.

"I can drive," Roxy protested.

"Or you can ride," Peter replied.

Roxy slid into the seat, leaned her head against the headrest, and closed her eyes. Peter started the car and moved forward down the street.

"I'm exhausted," she said. "Being in the same room with my father wears me out worse than a three-hour case conference with Mr. Caldweller. And when he spouted out that lame comment about how Ray and Cindy are better parents than he was, pretending it was an apology, I thought I was going to throw up."

"Maybe there will be a time and place when he'll say what he needs to say directly to you."

"That's the point. Excuses aren't going to erase a lifetime of actions." Roxy sat up straighter and shifted so she faced Peter. "He put me through emotional purgatory for the first eighteen years of my life. That's not going to go away like a puff of smoke in the wind."

"Which road leads back to the interstate?" Peter asked.

"Oh, take a left at the next light. Sorry, I should have been paying attention."

"You pay attention very well," Peter replied. "Maybe too well."

Roxy bristled. "What's that supposed to mean?"

Peter reached the light, which was red, and stopped. "I don't want to make you mad, so I'll drop it."

"Are you saying I'm making a bigger deal out of this than I

should? You have no idea what it was like. Over dinner you wanted to hear funny stories from my childhood. You should have balanced it with stories about broken promises, yelling, and the number of times I walked in on my mother and found her in tears because Dad had done something that she wouldn't or couldn't tell me about."

"You're right," Peter said as he turned onto the highway that led to the interstate. "I can't get my mind around what you've gone through or what needs to happen to fix it."

"Fixing it is easy," Roxy said. "It's an abusive situation. When that exists you leave and don't come back. I made a mistake letting you talk me into begging him to come to dinner. I knew it wasn't right, but you and Ray ganged up on me."

"I wanted to meet him."

"Why?"

"So I can better understand you."

"Well, if you think I'm like him, you'd better drop me off at my townhome and never see me again."

Corbin made it through Sunday without a beer or shot of whiskey. It wasn't easy. He couldn't stay inside the house because the temptation from the kitchen cabinet and refrigerator was too great, so he spent most of the morning in his yard pulling weeds. Previously he'd left the weeds alone. He'd even welcomed them because they were green and offered a break from bare spots of clay that stubbornly resisted his best efforts to grow fescue grass.

Sunday evening he went to an AA meeting. To his disappointment neither Jimmy nor Max was there. It was a twelve-step meeting, and the discussion focused on Step Four—"Made a searching and fearless moral inventory of ourselves."

There were eighteen people present, and it was quickly obvious that most of them had spent a lot of time considering each word of the step. Their comments reminded Corbin of the way lawyers and judges analyzed an important section of a statute or law. As the discussion moved around the circle in his direction, Corbin became more and more uneasy. He knew he could pass and decline to participate, but he felt it would be a retreat from his recent breakthrough with steps one and two. A woman named Lynn, who was sitting next to Corbin, took a tissue from her purse before she spoke.

"This was the hardest thing for me to do," she said. "It was easy admitting all that was wrong in my life and what I'd done to other people. I did that when I was drinking. But I knew this would be different. I wasn't going to list my faults, then blame someone else for my problems. This time I had to hold the list beside my face while I looked in the mirror and accepted responsibility for everything on it. That's what I did, literally. It was painful but it was a turning point that helped me keep going."

"How long was the list?" the leader asked.

"Six pages," Lynn replied. "It was five years ago, but I still have it. Oh, and I've added more pages since then. This isn't a onetime thing. That's the reason for Step Ten—"Continued to take personal inventory, and when we were wrong, promptly admitted it." It sounds crazy, but by being weak, I've grown stronger."

Lynn finished, and the leader looked expectantly at Corbin. His mind was swirling with thoughts and images from his past, but none of them stayed still long enough for him to capture them.

"I'm not there yet," he said, then paused. "But I want to be."

To his surprise, everyone in the circle spontaneously clapped.

"What did I say?" Corbin asked when it was quiet.

"They don't call them the Twelve Steps for nothing," the leader replied, smiling. "And you just took a big one when you declared your intention to take the next step."

"I'm sixty-two years old," Corbin replied. "And I've been drinking too much for over forty years. A searching and fearless moral inventory could take awhile. I'm not even sure where to begin or end."

"We're all traveling down the same road," Lynn replied. "And we'll be glad to walk alongside you."

It was such an unselfish statement that it touched Corbin deeply. Heads all around the circle nodded. Corbin had seen some of the other men and women in other AA meetings during the past few weeks; others were total strangers. But he knew there was substance behind their silent support.

"Thanks," he said. "That's all I have to say."

THIRTY-SEVEN

Roxy woke up Sunday morning regretting the silence that had divided her from Peter during the drive back to Atlanta. She hadn't trusted herself to speak and suspected he didn't know what to say either.

She rolled out of bed for her morning workout. Usually Sunday was one of her favorite days to run because she didn't have to hurry off to the office, but today her feet felt heavy as she jogged toward the entrance to Piedmont Park. It was the coolest day of the fall so far, and she sped up to banish the chill from her bones and, she hoped, her soul.

Her best times of reflection often took place while her feet tapped out a steady rhythm. As the blood flowed into her legs her lethargy lifted. She breathed in air that wasn't as pure as what she inhaled in Alto, but felt cleaner to her. By the time she finished her run, she couldn't wait to call Peter and apologize. She was in such a hurry that she cut her cool-down time short. Unlocking the door, she went straight to the kitchen where she'd left her phone and tapped the number beside his face. While the phone rang she checked the clock on her microwave. Peter was also an early riser; she didn't have to worry about waking him up.

The call went to voice mail.

For an instant Roxy toyed with the idea of a voice mail apology. Then the beep that started the voice message process forced her to speak.

"Uh . . . ," she said. "I shouldn't have called. I'm sorry. Please call me."

Roxy returned the phone to the kitchen counter. She knew the message was laced with ambiguity. Was she sorry she called? Sorry for the way she'd acted? Sorry she didn't leave a message? Being at a loss for words or imprecise in her speech was out of character.

She trudged upstairs and found herself checking the phone every few minutes. Peter's face didn't appear.

Roxy muttered while she dressed, then called him again. She tapped her foot against the accent rug on her bedroom floor. "Answer!" she ordered him.

Ignoring her long-distance command, Peter didn't accept the call, and it again went to voice mail. This time Roxy was ready.

"Sorry for the earlier confusion. I'd just come in from a run. Hope you're having a good morning. Give me a ring. Maybe we can grab coffee."

Roxy felt better about the message until she replayed it in her mind. It sounded like something a college sorority girl would say to a boy she was chasing across campus to score a date. Agitated, she went downstairs to brew a pot of coffee. While she waited she thought about the previous evening in Alto and how angry she'd gotten at her father's hollow, vapid words. This prompted another spell of muttering.

The phone on her kitchen counter remained silent.

She went into the living room and turned on the TV. Sunday morning programming was a wasteland, and she channel-surfed, trying to find a show to distract her. She wanted to call Peter again, but there was no reason to do so. If he picked up his phone he'd see that she called. And if he wanted to call her he would.

The thought that he might not want to talk to her sent Roxy deeper into a funk. She drank a second cup of coffee and started a third. Desperately needing a large dose of endorphins to banish the blues, she toyed with the idea of going out for a second run. She glanced again at her phone to see the time and thought about what Peter might be doing.

And realized he would be going to church.

Fueled by anxiety and caffeine, Roxy bounded upstairs and changed clothes. As she brushed her hair, she noticed a hint of desperation in her eyes. She didn't want to lose Peter as a boyfriend. But there was more to it than that. Before meeting Peter, Roxy's soul had lived within an impregnable fortress constructed over many years of diligent effort. Repelling assaults from formidable adversaries had been proof of its invincibility. No one, not her father, not Mr. Caldweller, had been able to scale the ramparts.

She locked the door of her townhome, got in the car, and drove to the church.

———

"Are you ready?" Ray called down the hall to Billy's bedroom. "We need to leave in five minutes if we're going to make it to Sunday school."

"Can I wear my green shirt?" Billy replied through a partially open door.

Ray didn't have his son's wardrobe memorized. "Sure," he said.

He stepped into the single-sink bathroom he shared with Cindy and peered around her to straighten his tie. Sunday morning at their church remained as formal as an appearance in court.

"You look nice," he said.

Cindy, who still had two curlers on the top of her head and hadn't yet applied lipstick, raised her eyes.

"Are you kidding?" she asked.

"You have great natural beauty. I don't know why you bother to enhance it."

Cindy smiled and bumped him away from the sink with her hip.

"I'm feeling better in the mornings," she said. "And even if Roxy coiled up like a snake at the news, I'm glad I told your family about the baby."

"Yeah. It was an interesting evening. I lay awake last night for a while thinking about it."

"You did?" Cindy asked in surprise. "You usually fall asleep in less than a minute." She finished applying her lipstick and took the rollers out of her hair. "What were you thinking?"

"Mostly about Dad; wondering if he's really turning the corner with his drinking."

The two of them had moved to the kitchen when Billy appeared, wearing khaki pants and a green shirt with a largemouth bass leaping out of the water on the front.

"You know better than to wear that to church," Cindy scolded. "Take that off and put on your blue collared shirt."

"Dad said it was okay," Billy protested. "And Pops told me yesterday that Jesus went fishing all the time. He says the Bible tells exactly how many fish Jesus caught."

"Pops talked to you about Jesus?" Ray asked in surprise.

"And the Bible?" Cindy added.

Roxy arrived at the church. She'd been in such a rush to get there that she paused for a moment to gather her thoughts before getting out of the car. If Peter didn't show up soon, she would leave before the meeting started.

Making her way across the lobby, she saw a handful of people milling around. Peter wasn't one of them. There was a station set up for free coffee and tea in one corner of the meeting room. Roxy passed on coffee and fixed a cup of hot, decaffeinated tea. Another cup of coffee would make her so jumpy she couldn't sit still.

While she sipped the tea, people rapidly began to fill the room. There was still no sign of Peter. The band started tuning up. Roxy took her phone from her purse to see if he'd called, when someone tapped her on the shoulder. She turned around to see Heather Lansdowne.

"Roxanne, right?" Heather asked. "We met the other day at the deposition."

"Yes," Roxy said with a smile. "But I go by Roxy." She glanced over Heather's shoulder toward the entrance area.

Heather turned and looked too. "Are you waiting for someone?"

"My boyfriend."

"Want to sit with me until he gets here?"

Roxy hesitated. "Okay," she said.

To her relief Heather liked to sit halfway back from the front of the room. The service followed the same format. Roxy didn't make an effort to sing the unfamiliar songs and noticed Heather didn't join in either, which made Roxy relax even more.

The young minister continued his series of messages taken from the Sermon on the Mount. The focus of the morning was on loving your enemies. The verses contained noble aspirations that weren't practical. He expanded the definition of enemies to "the negative people in your life."

Roxy's mind drifted. She positioned her phone in her purse so she could see if Peter called.

As the minister built up to his conclusion, Roxy tuned in so she could tell Peter what he'd talked about if he asked her later.

"It's only possible to love the negative people in your life if you're experiencing the love of God on an ongoing basis. Are you experiencing God's love in your life? If you say no, can you give me a good reason why you wouldn't ask God to reveal his love to you? His love for the world is not only universal; it's profoundly personal. Let's pray."

Roxy obediently closed her eyes. Years of sermon listening in Alto had programmed her in how to process a religious meeting to its expected conclusion. It was like taking a bus ride to a designated stop where she could get off and resume normal life.

"Father God," the minister prayed, "reveal yourself today not only to those who are seeking you but also to the ones who've listened to this message without believing these words of Jesus are either practical or possible. Would you come now by your Holy Spirit and give them a glimpse of who you are and the incredible desire you have to love, save, heal, transform, and restore them?"

Suddenly Roxy had an unexpected mental picture of a giant teardrop poised above her head that burst and washed over her. The image was so vivid that she touched her hair to see if it was damp. The minister continued to pray that the congregation would receive grace to relate to their enemies and the negative people in their lives, but Roxy didn't go with him. Instead she pondered what she'd seen and wondered what it meant. She didn't feel any emotion, just intense curiosity. Nothing like that had ever happened to her before. The service ended and Heather turned to her.

"That was challenging," she said. "Especially to all the lawyers in the room."

"Not really," Roxy responded, touching her hair again. "The parties on the other side of cases aren't enemies. Maybe to our clients, but not for us. I stay personally detached."

An unbidden tear rolled out of her right eye and down her cheek. Heather, who was about to speak, stopped and stared. Roxy brushed it away.

"What's wrong?" Heather asked.

Roxy couldn't respond. She blinked her eyes as more tears cascaded down her face. Heather grabbed some tissues from her purse and pushed them into Roxy's hand. Other people sitting on their row began leaving, but when they saw the two women they moved in the opposite direction. Roxy bowed her head and tried to take steady breaths to keep from sobbing. She felt Heather lightly touch her on the back.

"Is there anything I can do for you?" Heather asked.

Roxy shook her head. She was past the point of embarrassment, a realization that released a fresh torrent of tears. Heather gave her another wad of tissues, and Roxy blew her nose. She wanted to leave, but knew she would attract more attention moving than she would remaining seated. Finally the tsunami subsided. Roxy wiped her eyes again and turned toward Heather.

"Sorry," she said.

"It's okay," Heather replied, wide-eyed. "Do you need me to do anything for you?"

"No," Roxy said, taking a deep breath that sounded like the beginning of a sob as she released it. "I'm ready to go."

The two women stood up. Roxy kept her eyes lowered as they left the room.

"Where are you parked?" Heather asked when they reached the elevators.

"On the second floor of the ramp."

"I'm in a lot across the street," Heather said. "Do you want me to—"

"There's no need," Roxy said, doing her best to offer a reassuring smile that she suspected fell far short. "I'll be fine."

"Okay," Heather said doubtfully. She took out a business card and scribbled on the back. "This is my cell phone number if you start feeling worse."

"I'm not suicidal," Roxy said, realizing the young attorney's concern. "I think most of my tears were from a good place."

The skepticism on Heather's face remained. Roxy could only guess what she looked like.

"We'll get together for coffee soon," Roxy added.

She took a few steps toward the parking deck, then paused and looked over her shoulder. Heather was watching her. Roxy waved her hand.

And fled.

THIRTY-EIGHT

Corbin sat in his car for a few extra moments before entering the office. He'd spent the morning like a tennis ball, bouncing back and forth between competing paradigms. On the one hand he was clinging to the threads of hope picked up at the AA meetings. On the other, he found himself inexorably drawn to ingrained patterns of thinking and behavior. Before leaving for work, he barely avoided choosing a shot of whiskey over a cup of coffee.

It had been three weeks since he'd taken a draw from the law firm, and he'd left a stack of bills on the kitchen counter. Another stack waited for him inside the office, where he'd stuffed them in the top left-hand drawer of his desk. And now he had to come up with three thousand dollars to send Dr. Westbrook to get the Colfax litigation going. It was enough to convince him to return home and drink himself into oblivion. But difficult circumstances were familiar territory, and Corbin knew grinding his way forward was the only option on the table.

He entered through the back door and made his way to Janelle's desk. The secretary was staring at her computer screen and glanced up when he approached.

"I've heard from two bill collectors already this morning," she said. "If we don't pay the medical record copy service, they're not going to fulfill our requests to the local doctors' offices in future cases. That will shut us down and make it—"

"Pay it," Corbin said.

"And the other one is for our computer research service. They've extended us three months and restructured the contract. If you don't make a minimum payment, they're going to pull the plug."

"Pay it."

"And if I heard your dictation correctly, you want to wire three thousand dollars to Dr. Westbrook in the Colfax case. If you do that, it's going to be tough to make payroll on Friday. Are you holding back a week on Ray? We can squeak by if I only pay him one week instead of two."

"We didn't talk about that. I told him I'd pay him biweekly. I'll let you know. Any good news?"

"Not yet," Janelle replied. "But the day is just getting started."

Corbin went into his office, and a few minutes later Ray knocked on his door and entered, some letters in his hand.

"I went by the post office on my way into work to get the morning mail," he said.

"That's Janelle's job. She usually waits until ten o'clock in case something comes in later."

Ray held up the envelopes. "I didn't open these," he said, "but when they're marked Final Notice and Past Due on the outside, there's not much doubt what's inside."

"I'm working on it," Corbin replied defensively. "Juggling the bills is part of running a solo law practice."

Ray pressed harder. "Has it always been like this or has it gotten worse?"

Corbin's attempt at calm evaporated. He pointed his finger at Ray's chest.

"You marched in here the other day and demanded that I hire

you when you lost your job at the DA's office. So until you're willing to assume shared responsibility for the bills of this firm, I don't want to hear anything from you about it. Is that clear?"

Ray's face reddened, and Corbin waited for a counter explosion. Instead his son turned and walked away. Corbin took several deep breaths, then buzzed Janelle.

"Where's Ray?" he asked.

"I don't know. When he left your office he headed straight toward the back door. What happened?"

———

Roxy returned from her morning run and was drinking a Gatorade in the kitchen when her phone vibrated and an unfamiliar number appeared. Doubting a known caller would attempt to reach her this early in the day, she thought about letting it go to voice mail, but then she answered anyway.

"Hey, it's Peter."

"Where have you been?" she asked sharply. "I called you more times than I can remember yesterday and didn't hear a word from you."

"I left my phone in my pants pocket, and it got washed. Right now it's sitting in a bag of rice to dry out, but I think it may be a goner. I had to spend the day at the office with a long conference call to a client in Mumbai. My team and another group in Chicago had to brainstorm solutions. We bounced ideas back and forth and wrote some patchwork code on the spot because it was a rush job. Do you believe me?"

"If I didn't, it would take too long to cross-examine you and get to the truth."

"Great. I'm sitting in my car in front of your place and wondered if I could see you for a few minutes.

Roxy wiped her face with a towel. "I haven't taken a shower or—"

"Don't worry. I'll keep my distance."

She went into the foyer and let Peter in. His eyes looked tired.

"Why are you up so early if you worked late?"

"So I could catch you before you went to the office. I want to apologize for putting so much pressure on during the trip to Alto. I have no business pretending to be a counselor or amateur psychologist. Not that you need one, but once I saw how upset I made you, I knew I had to—"

"Enough," Roxy said. She held up a hand to stop his flow of words. "I reverted to an eight-year-old on Saturday and pitched a tantrum in the car."

"Still, I'm sorry. And it was worse that we didn't talk yesterday."

"Yeah, I went to the church hoping I'd see you there."

Peter's eyebrows shot up in surprise.

"And I had the biggest emotional meltdown yet," she continued with a sigh.

As she told him what happened, Roxy toyed with the idea of leaving out the teardrop vision, but the rest of the events at the church wouldn't make sense without it.

"So I'm standing next to a woman I barely know, bawling my eyes out. It was a great morning."

"I wish I'd been there."

"You like watching me cry?"

Peter stepped closer, took her hand, and looked into her eyes. "I don't enjoy watching you cry unless the tears are good," he said.

"And you believe those were good tears?" she asked.

"Don't you?"

Ray circled around to the side of the office building and leaned against the painted brick. Having his face rubbed in the firm's financial struggles at the post office, then listening to his father stonewall him with unsubstantiated promises of payment, was a tough way to begin the day. Nothing about his father surprised him, but the impact of his current irresponsibility on his own family hit him hard.

To cool off and clear his mind, he decided to walk over to the courthouse. He didn't have any business to take care of, but he stopped at the clerk's office to review the file in the Colfax litigation. Date-stamped five minutes before his arrival was the answer and counterclaim filed by Nate Stamper. Ray flipped through the paperwork. It contained standard denials of everything except that Colfax was a corporation doing business in Rusk County. The rest of the allegations were "vigorously denied and strict proof thereof demanded." The counterclaim for costs and attorney fees would only become a problem if Corbin and Ray weren't able to at least present a case that would get them past summary judgment and in front of a jury.

Thinking about the cost of obtaining expert witness testimony brought Ray back to how he felt when he left the office—where was the money going to come from?

Still not ready to go back, Ray walked over to the courtroom. He slipped in unnoticed and took a seat. It was a criminal calendar call and motion day, and Brett Dortch was standing in the spot Ray had occupied for the previous six years. Judge Ellington was presiding on the bench. Steve Nelson was nowhere to be seen. Not surprisingly the DA had passed off his duties to Brett without any mentoring.

Ray settled in. Brett was doing his best, but the ability to handle a calendar call and respond to the infinite variety of unexpected issues in motion practice required the skill of an orchestra conductor, and Brett was still learning to read sheet music. Ray watched as a hearing on a motion to suppress evidence painfully unfolded before him. Only Judge Ellington's seasoned hand on the rudder of justice kept the state's case from crashing into the rocks.

After the case was finished, the judge called the next case, then suddenly slumped over onto the bench. Ray jumped to his feet as the elderly bailiff made his way over to the judge.

"Someone call 911!" the bailiff shouted out.

Ray made the call as he rushed toward the front of the courtroom. The panic-stricken bailiff was holding Judge Ellington's head in his hands.

———

Corbin heard the siren but remained at his desk. The local hospital was six blocks away, and it wasn't unusual for an ambulance to scream by the office. But the siren didn't fade into the distance. It was soon joined by another. Corbin stepped over to a window that faced the street and moved aside the blinds. Both ambulances were parked next to the courthouse, which could mean a lot of things. The possibility of violence by an irate litigant or criminal defendant flashed through his mind. He left his office and went into the reception area. Janelle was already standing in the open front door.

"Any idea what's going on?" Corbin asked.

He brushed past Janelle and stood on the sidewalk to get a better view. The absence of police vehicles calmed his first fears. While he watched, medical personnel exited the side door of the courthouse with a figure on a stretcher and loaded it into one of the ambulances. The siren was still screaming as it left the area. Corbin was about to turn away and go back inside when he saw Ray come out the same door of the courthouse as the stretcher.

Corbin crossed the street without checking for oncoming cars, and a honking horn caused him to jump out of the way of an approaching vehicle. The driver raised one of his hands in exasperation, but Corbin ignored him and walked rapidly toward his son.

"It's Judge Ellington," Ray said. "He collapsed on the bench."

"Any idea what's wrong?"

"I'm not sure, but it looked serious. The EMTs put him on oxygen, and from what I could tell he wasn't responding to their questions."

———

Roxy knew she was going to be late for work and didn't care. Peter waited while she showered and dressed, then they drank coffee together on her little patio.

"If I'd been at church maybe none of that would have happened," Peter said.

Roxy shook her head. "I've been more of a crybaby around you than I have in my entire life. One sympathetic look from you when the tears started to flow would have breached the dam."

"It sounds like it had already been breached."

"True," Roxy agreed. "It was totally embarrassing."

Peter took a sip of coffee. "So while you were getting dressed I thought some more about your tears and what they might mean."

"Decided to play counselor and amateur psychologist after all?"

"If you don't want to hear—"

"Ignore me," Roxy interrupted. "I'm acting like this because I'm feeling insecure and vulnerable, which is exactly opposite of how I want to feel. I'm listening."

"Are you sure?" Peter looked skeptical.

"Yes. I mean it," she reiterated, speaking rapidly. "And I won't get mad if you say it has something to do with releasing the pain caused by my father that I've kept bottled up all these years and softening my heart so I'm willing to consider that God loves me even though I'm not sure he exists."

"Yeah," Peter said, wide-eyed. "That's what I was going to say, only you did it a lot better."

"Well, let's do this," Roxy said as she shifted in her chair with nervous energy. "I'm ready."

"For what?"

"To move on to the next thing. Currently I'm stuck wondering when I'm next going to burst into tears. What if it happens in court? Or worse, in a trial strategy meeting with Mr. Caldweller? It'd be easier to explain an emotional breakdown to a judge than to him."

"What is the next thing?" Peter asked, the amazed look still on his face.

"I don't know." Roxy threw up her hands in exasperation. "But you got me started down this road with your incredible, sensitive comments, and you can't leave me like this. It's not right!"

THIRTY-NINE

Corbin and Ray returned to the office together. The sight of Judge Ellington leaving the courthouse on a stretcher made Corbin pensive. The same thing could unexpectedly happen to him at any time. He listened as Ray told Janelle what happened.

"If he's had a heart attack or stroke, what will they do about the cases on his docket?" she asked.

"Judge Perry will take them," Ray said, then turned to his father. "Including the lawsuit you just filed against Colfax."

Ray's comment jerked Corbin back from thoughts about his own mortality. The demise of the claim for the two boys was a more imminent possibility.

"All the more reason why I need to get an expert on board as soon as possible," Corbin said, trying to sound more confident than he felt.

At noon Corbin's stomach growled. He was hungry but there was something he wanted more than food. The beast within was off its leash and out of its cage. A glass of mountain water along with a bowl of red beans and rice at Red's sounded better than an aged steak topped with sautéed mushrooms accompanied by a glass of fine red wine. Corbin licked his lips. His mouth felt bone dry.

He got up from his desk and went into the reception area. The door to Ray's office was closed, and Janelle was already on her lunch break. Corbin had his hand on the handle for the front door when a voice stopped him.

"Could we have lunch together?" Ray asked, sticking his head out the door of his office.

"I have plans," Corbin said.

"If they include red beans and rice, I'm up for that. And I have some good news."

Corbin had to conduct a split-second evaluation of the situation. If he blew Ray off it would send a clear message that Red's bootleg liquor still held the reins, which would affect his access to Billy.

"Sure," he said. "I should have checked with you anyway."

Corbin tried to mask his grumpiness as they walked down the street. Ray talked about several cases he'd been working on since returning from the courthouse, including one that he hoped to settle by the end of the week.

"I saw your note that we might be able to recover $10,000 total," Ray said as they waited for a light to turn. "I talked to the insurance adjuster and believe she's going to offer $40,000. That means our fee will be $10,000."

The news was good enough to slightly improve Corbin's mood. They arrived at Red's and sat in a booth Sally usually served. The waitress appeared with two regular waters and raised her eyebrows at Corbin.

"Anything else to drink for you gentlemen?" she asked.

"I'll have sweet tea," Ray added.

"Naw, I'm good," Corbin grunted.

"I can see that," Sally replied. "Ready to order your food?"

After she left Ray rested his arms on the table and leaned forward. "Thanks for letting me spoil your party," he said.

"What party?" Corbin replied, feigning ignorance.

Ray gave a slight smirk that made Corbin wish his son was still young enough for a spanking. They sat in silence until Sally returned with the food. Ray bowed his head and said a blessing, which made Corbin think about the prayer he'd uttered sitting on the front steps of his duplex.

"I prayed the other day," Corbin said. "It's part of my work on the second step of AA."

"Can you tell me more?"

Corbin relaxed and shared with Ray what he'd been learning. Repeating it outside the walls of an AA meeting room made it seem more tangible. Ray listened as intently as a juror in a murder trial, which encouraged Corbin to keep going. He finished the bowl of red beans and rice without noticing whether it was a good batch or not.

Ray had a questioning look on his face.

"Go ahead and ask me," Corbin said.

Ray took a sip of water. "Dad, do you remember your first drink?"

Corbin didn't have to search the ancient files of his memory to locate what had been a life-altering moment.

He nodded. "Yes, I do. I was barely fifteen. A friend and I snitched a bottle of whiskey from his father's liquor cabinet and went behind a barn to try it out. When the liquor hit my brain, it was like a light switch flipped on—a switch I didn't know existed." Corbin paused as in his mind's eye he returned to the scene. "I felt fully alive for the first time in my life. I saw things more clearly; I could talk without getting tongue-tied; I believed I could do anything I wanted to do. I've always hoped the next drink would take me back to the place that whiskey took me. Sometimes it did. Most of the time it didn't."

———

During the walk back to the office, Ray couldn't get his father's words out of his head. He repeated them to Cindy as soon as the two of them were alone at the kitchen table later that evening.

"It was a very strange feeling," he said. "As if I was talking to the real man for the first time in my life. He's spent our entire relationship hiding behind a curtain, pretending. Today at the lunch table he gave me a peek of who he is and what's made him that way."

"Like the Wizard of Oz."

"I wish it were that benign."

"I didn't mean to make light of it," Cindy replied. "What's next?"

Ray leaned back in his chair. "I'm not sure. Today I forced my way between him and a stiff shot of moonshine at Red's, but that's not possible on a 24–7 basis. I can only hope that he'll continue with AA."

"Hasn't he stopped drinking?"

"I think so, but I think it'll be better if he tells me about his progress on his own terms. Otherwise it will seem like I'm pressuring him."

"Isn't that what we've been doing with him and Billy? And why you grabbed him before he slipped out of the office to drink at lunch?"

"Yeah," Ray admitted.

"And both of those were the right thing to do. Don't get too passive. For a lawyer you sure do try to avoid conflict."

"'Cause I'm a peacemaker," Ray said, then leaned forward to give Cindy a quick kiss. "And a lover."

She rolled her eyes. "Then show me your love by helping me clean up the kitchen. I ran out of energy late this afternoon but wasn't able to grab thirty minutes for a short nap."

"Sit in the den and relax while I work," Ray said, standing up.

"I'm a submissive wife," Cindy replied with a smile. "You won't get an argument from me."

———

Instead of heading home at five o'clock, Corbin drove to the hospital to check on Judge Ellington.

"He's in ICU," the volunteer at the desk told him when Corbin asked for the room number. "No visitors except close family members are allowed."

Corbin took the elevator to the ICU, which was on the third floor of the small hospital. He knew the judge had a son and a daughter who were in their thirties, both of whom lived in the Atlanta area. As he stepped off the elevator, he saw a man who resembled the judge, and introduced himself. It was indeed Judge Ellington's son, there with his wife.

"How is he?" Corbin asked.

"Too soon to know," the man replied. "He had a cerebral hemorrhage. The neurosurgeon says it depends on the amount of bleeding, where it's located, and whether they can get it under control. My mom's with him now."

Corbin stayed for a few minutes then left. He was walking down the hallway when he heard someone call his name. Corbin stopped, and Jimmy Broome came up to him.

"What brings you up here?" Corbin asked.

"Judge Ellington."

Corbin told Jimmy what he'd learned about the judge's condition. "How do you know him?" Corbin asked when he finished.

"He's one of the main reasons I started going to AA. It was part of my sentence when I had my second DUI. I was looking at six months of jail time that would have cost my job and who knows what else. I'd been to AA a few times before the arrest, and my sponsor came with me to court. The judge knew him and gave me one last chance. So far I haven't blown it."

"Who was your sponsor?"

Jimmy mentioned a man Corbin knew slightly.

"I didn't know he was an alcoholic."

"He's been sober for over thirty years. He agreed to sponsor me when I was less than thirty days into the program."

Jimmy had to be at least fifteen years younger than Corbin, but in some ways he seemed older and wiser. An idea crossed Corbin's mind.

"Would you consider being my sponsor?" he asked.

"Why would I want to do that?"

Corbin jerked his head back in surprise. "Because I asked you, I guess."

"That's not why you get a sponsor. There's only one reason for that."

Corbin thought for a moment. "Because I want to stop drinking."

"Yeah, that's why AA exists. To help one alcoholic at a time find the path to sobriety. If that's what you want, I'd be honored to sponsor you."

Corbin heard a sound behind him, and they moved out of the way as a man about Corbin's age was rolled by on a gurney. There were tubes coming out all over the man's body. An IV was attached to his arm, and there was an oxygen tank affixed to the rolling bed.

"I'm not as sick as that guy," Corbin said when the man continued down the hall. "But I know I'm going to need help to beat this thing."

"You're both right and wrong," Jimmy replied. "You're right that you need help, but you're wrong about your condition. Like the rest of us in AA, you're way sicker than you realize."

"Okay." Corbin nodded.

"Okay, what?" Jimmy asked, looking directly into Corbin's eyes.

Corbin took a deep breath and exhaled. "I'm powerless over alcohol and my life has become unmanageable. I want to stop drinking."

Jimmy smiled and took his cell phone out of his pocket.

"Great. As your sponsor I'm here for you 24–7. What are all your contact numbers?"

Roxy made it through the day without manifesting the emotional meltdown she'd feared. That included a two-hour meeting with Mr. Caldweller during which two other women, a paralegal and an associate more junior that Roxy, fought back tears when confronted with their failures in a recent round of discovery disputes in a hotly contested case. Caldweller had prepared a PowerPoint presentation that illustrated their mistakes. It was a brutal beatdown that grew worse as each slide came into view.

"The public thinks trial is the focal point of litigation," Caldweller growled when he finished going over the final slide. "But discovery is where the main battles are fought and the war is won or lost. And it's a war of attrition. Our client pays us to make the other side pay more to their lawyers than they pay us. Can you remember that in the future?"

"Yes, sir," the associate responded, her voice quivering slightly.

"You'd better."

Roxy listened stoically. When Caldweller's attention turned toward her to discuss the Boren litigation, she found herself strangely calm. She went over what she'd done in discovery per his instructions to make things tough for the other side in hopes that the case could be settled.

She could feel the animosity radiating toward her from the female associate who'd just been chewed out. Caldweller listened without interrupting until Roxy finished.

"That's what I'm talking about," he said to the room. "How many of you were taking notes?"

No one raised a hand. Caldweller paused as if gathering momentum for a volcanic eruption. Even Roxy found herself holding her breath. The senior partner put both hands on the table and scanned the room.

"That's all for today. You can leave."

Everyone stood up, and then Caldweller spoke again.

"Roxy, stay for a minute. I have another matter to discuss with you."

FORTY

The following morning Ray again went by the post office to pick up the mail. Included in the stack of bills and letters was the answer filed by Nate Stamper in the Colfax litigation. Ray knew what it contained and didn't bother to open it. Back at the office the phone rang. Janelle wasn't there yet, so he answered it.

"Gage Law Offices," he said.

"Ray? Is that you?"

"Yes."

"It's Branson Kilpatrick. I thought I'd leave a message, but I'm glad you answered. Tommy and Larissa are taking Mitchell to Emory today for an evaluation. Your dad told me to let him know if there was any change in his condition. The local oncologist thinks he might be a candidate for some kind of special treatment program and wants him to see a specialist at the children's hospital. What's it called?"

"Egleston."

"That's it. Anyway, they're going to admit him this afternoon and keep him for a couple of days."

"Okay."

"Is there anything else going on with the case? I know it's early, but this has got us so torn up that any bit of news would be welcome."

Ray hesitated. He wasn't sure if he should answer or let his father provide an update. "Will you be available later?"

"Off and on. I have a full day on the mower, mostly on the east side of town."

While he listened Ray decided what to do.

"It's progressing faster than I expected," he said. "Colfax's lawyer filed paperwork with the court yesterday, and my dad is talking to an expert in California about testing the well water to find out what made the boys sick."

"If they've stopped dumping, will it still be in the system?"

"I'm not sure."

"All right. At least Judge Ellington is the judge on the case. He's a fair man."

"Uh, that may change." Ray told him about the judge collapsing at the courthouse. "I haven't heard anything about the judge's condition this morning. We'll have to wait and see."

"I probably won't mention that to Tommy just yet. Oh, and Millie Watson keeps asking me what I think is going to happen. She doesn't want to bother you, but it might be a good idea for all of us to have another meeting at your office as soon as it's convenient."

"I agree," Ray said.

The call ended and another one came in. This time Ray let it go to voice mail. He walked over to the filing cabinet where his father kept the Colfax litigation. There were several folders; none had much in it. He found the research his father had performed via the Internet about chemicals that could cause non-Hodgkin's lymphoma. Reading over it, Ray remembered Nate Stamper's comment that the information relied on in the complaint had been discredited by recent research. Now Ray wished he'd taken more of an interest in the technical aspects of the criminal case instead of simply submitting into evidence the work performed by the attorney general's office. He looked over the retention agreement forwarded by Dr. Westbrook, the California expert. Corbin hadn't yet signed it, probably because he couldn't pay the three-thousand-dollar retainer.

Ray logged onto his computer. Within thirty minutes he identified fifteen cases in which Dr. Westbrook appeared in court as an expert witness, all for the plaintiff. That last fact made Ray uneasy. One of the marks of a hired gun witness, whether for the plaintiff or defense, was a history of providing testimony for only one side.

Dr. Westbrook also enjoyed traveling. He'd successfully marketed himself to law firms from California to New York, and even appeared in a recent trial in Puerto Rico. Ray followed a link to more information about the Puerto Rico case, which led to a list of motions filed by the parties both prior to and after a verdict in favor of the defendant corporation. One of the motions was for sanctions against the plaintiff's lawyer. Dr. Westbrook's name appeared in the description of the motion. Ray opened the motion and read it. When he saw the basis for bringing the matter before the court, his mouth dropped open.

———

Corbin stopped off to eat breakfast on his way to the office. He rarely ate a full breakfast, but it seemed like a good idea to have something more than coffee in his system as he faced what he hoped would be a full day of sobriety. The special of the day was a mega breakfast burrito filled with some of Corbin's favorite foods. He was reading the ingredients for the second time when the waitress returned to take his order. She leaned over and followed his gaze.

"It's better in person than in the photo," she said.

"And more dangerous to my arteries than a pint of pure

cholesterol. I'll take one egg over easy with dry wheat toast and one strip of crisp bacon."

"There are three pieces of bacon in an order."

Corbin glanced at a nearby table where two husky young firefighters had taken a seat. "Give an extra piece to each of them."

Corbin handed the menu back to the waitress. The door to the restaurant opened and Max Hogan came in. Unlike their encounter weeks earlier, this time Corbin wanted to talk. He waved his hand. Max saw him and hesitated. Corbin made a more insistent gesture, inviting his former drinking buddy to come over.

"Are you meeting someone?" Corbin asked.

"No."

"Then sit with me. I'd like to talk to you."

Max remained standing. "Is it about AA or drinking?"

"Yes. I've been going to a bunch of meetings, mostly at the Hopewell church, and last night Jimmy agreed to be my sponsor."

"He's my sponsor too," Max replied, looking past Corbin. "But things aren't going well right now. I slipped."

Corbin didn't know how to process the news. Within seconds he felt angry, sad, inadequate, and bewildered. "What happened?" he managed.

"What do you think?" Max shrugged.

"Sit down anyway," Corbin replied, trying to sound nonchalant. "I'm the last person in Rusk County who has the right to give you a hard time about taking a drink."

"And if you're trying to stop, I'm toxic."

"Shut up. I'm buying your breakfast, and it hurts my neck to keep looking up at you."

Max slid into the opposite side of the booth and made full eye contact with Corbin. "You still look like a drunk," Max said. "Are you messing with me?"

"No, and I'm still better looking than you ever dreamed of being."

Max smiled slightly. Corbin waved the waitress over.

"Changed your mind about the burrito?" she asked.

"No, but my friend is joining me and needs a menu."

For Corbin the next thirty minutes were akin to an out-of-body experience. Max didn't want to talk about his "slip," but seemed willing to listen to Corbin talk about his short journey in AA. Corbin didn't hold anything back, including his epiphany on the front steps of his duplex and the desire for change he could feel stirring inside him. He barely noticed his food when it came and was surprised when he looked down at his plate and it was clean.

"It sounds like you're starting to build a good program," Max said when Corbin paused. "And I hope it works out for you."

"Are you giving up?" Corbin asked. "I mean, you sound like you'd still like to be sober."

Max shook his head. "I don't think I can handle the ups and downs of making it a day, a week, a month, then falling off the wagon."

"Have you had a drink today?"

It was the kind of question only appropriate for an alcoholic at eight thirty in the morning.

"No," Max said.

Corbin leaned forward. "Look, I'm barely out of the gate myself. We could start this thing together."

Max looked down at his plate of half-eaten scrambled eggs and hash browns with chopped onions. "You don't want to tie yourself to me."

"Who said anything about that? If we do that we'll both drown. Let's finish breakfast then go to the meeting at the Serenity Center. They have one this morning at nine. I went last week."

"Don't you have to go to the office?"

Corbin shrugged. "Ray can handle any calls that come in. And this is important."

Max didn't respond. He continued to pick at his food. Corbin was out of ideas and words. Then he had an unusual thought. He closed his eyes as if blinking for a few seconds and prayed.

———

Mr. Caldweller waited until the room cleared before he spoke. "I heard back from Kennedy Goings about the conference call the other day."

Roxy braced herself. She'd tried her best to walk the tightrope between convincing the client to continue funding the litigation by giving a lowball estimate of future costs and tossed out her best guess at the amount it would ultimately take to settle the case. After the call ended she crossed her fingers that a postmortem risk benefit analysis by the company's accounting department wouldn't generate a negative report of the law firm's recommendation.

"He's given us the go-ahead based on your analysis."

"There's no way we can guarantee settlement close to the amount I gave him. So much can happen between now and then—"

"It's going to work out," Caldweller cut in. "Your estimate was dead on with the one I prepared but didn't disclose."

Roxy allowed herself to breathe. But her boss wasn't finished.

"That's not all I wanted to talk to you about. I was on a conference call last night with the firm partnership committee, and your name came up."

The tightness in Roxy's chest returned.

"We're considering you for equity status."

Roxy didn't try to hide her shock. "Me, a partner?"

"Don't look so surprised. You know how we operate around here. It's Darwinian to the core, and you're a survivor. Nothing is final yet, but you're on the short list of candidates who will be considered at the London retreat. If approved, you can expect a move within the next year, most likely to New York, but San Francisco is an option, as is Munich. I lived in four cities and two different countries over an eight-year period before landing here. You speak German, don't you?"

Roxy's head was spinning. "Uh, barely conversational. It's not at a level for legal analysis."

"That wouldn't be expected so long as you could make yourself understood to staff and in social settings with clients."

"With practice, I'm sure I'd get there."

"Don't start watching German TV quite yet. Anyway, expect phone calls or e-mail inquiries from attorneys on the partnership committee over the next few days."

"What are they going to ask me?"

"Nothing you can't handle," Caldweller replied with a slightly forced smile. "Anticipating what you'll need to know or say without warning is part of the process. You've worked with me long enough to know what it's like to be grilled."

"And fried."

Caldweller's smile broadened. "That's one thing I like about you. Beneath that steely face of yours is a sense of humor that will keep you from going insane from the pressure we experience on a daily basis."

"Minute by minute."

"That too. Now get back to work. I expect a research memo on my desk in the morning about the motion filed by the defendant in the Catalonia case."

Corbin left the AA meeting with a smile on his face. He'd always considered the practice of law as an opportunity not only to make money, but to help people in need. Tossing out a lifeline to a fellow drunk like Max Hogan made him feel even better. In virtually every AA meeting Corbin had heard the phrase "by the grace of God and fellowship of AA," but it took on a new meaning when Max walked into the room, where he was welcomed without condemnation. Jimmy wasn't there, and on the way to the office Corbin called him and left him a voice mail with the good news.

"I went to an AA meeting this morning," Corbin announced to Janelle when he entered the office.

"I hope it went well," the secretary replied with a slightly puzzled look on her face.

"Better than that," Corbin replied. "I'm really starting to get what it's all about."

"To stop drinking?"

"Yeah, that's the main thing, of course. And I'm still taking baby steps." Corbin stopped and smiled. "That's why they call them the Twelve Steps."

Janelle's expression metamorphosed into incredulity. "Uh, I need to get back to work," she said.

"Sure."

"Oh, and Ray needs to talk to you."

Corbin stepped over to Ray's office, knocked on the door, and opened it before his son responded. "I'm here," he said cheerily.

"I'll come over to your office," Ray replied, a somber expression on his face. "I have something important to show you."

FORTY-ONE

Ray had spent much of the morning as he waited for Corbin to arrive completing his investigation of Dr. Westbrook. When his father knocked on the door, Ray was in the midst of a frustrating search for another chemist they could hire as an expert. Corbin went on to his office, and Ray collected his information and entered the reception area.

"He's in a weird mood," Janelle said. "He claims he went to an AA meeting this morning, but he's acting more like he had a couple of drinks before he left the house."

"I hope he doesn't want a drink after he hears what I have to tell him about the expert he was about to hire in the Colfax litigation."

Janelle pursed her lips together. "He's your father."

Ray wasn't sure what Janelle meant by that, but didn't want to ask a question to find out.

Corbin had his back to the door and was humming a tune Ray didn't recognize. Ray cleared his throat, and his father turned around.

"You know Max Hogan, don't you?" Corbin asked.

"The guy who runs the payday loan service? We investigated him a couple of times while I was at the DA's office but couldn't get anything to stick. If you've got a possible civil suit against him, I'd like to take a look at it and—"

"No, no," Corbin interrupted with a wave of his hand. "He's

the one who got me interested in AA, and this morning I was able to return the favor."

"I'm not following you."

"It's okay," Corbin replied. "I shouldn't talk about it anyway. Janelle said you wanted to see me about something important. What's on your mind?"

Ray placed the information he'd uncovered about Dr. Westbrook on the edge of the desk. "Read this. Bottom line, we don't want to hire Dr. Westbrook as an expert in the Colfax litigation."

"Why not? He knows what we need and will give it to us if the testing on the wells pans out."

"That's part of the problem. Dr. Westbrook gave an opinion last year in a toxic tort case in Puerto Rico that was great for the plaintiff, until the defendant proved Westbrook's assessment was based on falsified evidence. It resulted in sanctions against Westbrook and the law firm that hired him."

Ray waited while his father read the information.

"It's on appeal," Corbin said when he finished. "What if this was a defense-minded judge looking for a chance to beat up on the plaintiff's lawyers and using Westbrook as the club? Every one of these allegations was contested during the hearing before the judge."

"There were two chemists who proved that Westbrook's findings were fabricated."

"Testified, not proved. And who hired them? Corporate defendants are always able to throw more money at a case than a plaintiff."

"But—"

"I see your point," Corbin cut in. "And we can't wait for an appellate court to decide what it thinks about Dr. Westbrook. I just don't want you to have a mindset that jumps too quickly to agree with a big corporation or insurance company. You have to be mentally tough to be a plaintiff's lawyer."

"You're tougher than I am." Ray couldn't keep from smiling. "Janelle said you were in rare form this morning, and now that I've seen you, I agree. Whatever you and Max Hogan did buoyed you up. I just hope it wasn't a round or two of Bloody Marys."

"No," Corbin replied. "I'm committed to sobriety, one day at a time. That's what I told the AA group this morning at the Serenity Center on Maxwell Street."

"That's great," Ray said, not wanting to overreact. "You know I'm supporting you."

"Thanks. But don't say anything to Cindy or Roxy. I could always slip."

Corbin hesitated as if he had something else to say. Ray waited.

"I guess that's it for now," his father continued. "Since you uncovered the problem with Dr. Westbrook, take a stab at finding another chemist. Also, we need a medical expert. Westbrook claimed he knew someone, but maybe we should steer clear of him too."

"Yeah, I'll spend time on it today."

Ray stood up. He still felt there was something unsaid. Corbin turned around toward his credenza and picked up a file. Ray didn't leave.

"Would it be all right if I said a prayer?" Ray asked.

"Yes," Corbin replied quickly. "I'd like that."

Ray closed his eyes and began to pray. After a few seconds he peeked and saw his father with his head bowed and his eyes closed. His mother would have given anything in the world for a moment like this. Ray's voice threatened to crack, but he steadied it and said, "Amen."

"That was good," Corbin said, touching his chest. "It's like I could feel it in here."

The phone on Corbin's desk buzzed. He answered it and listened.

"Let me see what Ray thinks," he said and lowered the receiver.

"It's Cecil Scruggs from the newspaper," he said. "He wants to talk to me about the Colfax case."

"I'm not sure that's a good idea," Ray replied.

"Are you kidding? This is my first shot at the jury of public opinion. By suppertime tonight everyone who reads the newspaper or knows someone who does will say we're David going out to fight Goliath."

"You're not worried about tainting the jury pool?"

"One article isn't going to do that, but it will plant a seed I can water when the case ends up in the courtroom."

"We have a long way to go before that day. And now we have Judge Perry standing in our way."

"Trust me. I've known Cecil for years. I can guide him down the right path."

———

Roxy returned to her office in a state of shock. During her entire time at the firm, she'd been mentally preparing for the rejection she knew might come. The sudden possibility of grabbing the gold ring of success didn't seem real.

Sitting in front of her computer screen, she pulled up the firm's internal directory and calculated the chance an associate with her years of experience had of achieving partnership status. There were over two hundred lawyers who had been with the firm the same length of time as she had. None of them were partners. That meant she was up for promotion in the first batch of her class. It was stunning.

She then spent over an hour analyzing the track records of a select group of younger partners. It was an amazingly diverse yet brilliant group. It shocked Roxy to think she might be joining them. She wanted to call Peter with the news but decided it would be best to tell him in person.

Can we meet this evening? she texted him. I have big news.

What's it about?

Later.

8 at the teahouse on Ponce de Leon?

Great.

The teahouse was a former private residence converted into a boutique watering hole. The rooms were set up with a few tables in each one, so the number of competing voices would be limited. It was a great place to talk.

Roxy found Peter with a small china teapot in front of him at a table in the corner of a former bedroom.

"How long have you been here?" she asked as she slid into a chair. "I'm not late, am I?"

"No, they just brought it out. I thought you'd want something with low caffeine, so I asked for coconut pouchong."

Roxy poured a cup of the slightly sweet tea made from long green leaves, then took a sip. "Perfect," she said.

She took another sip that tasted even better than the first. The tea shop was truly half a world away from the sticky sweet iced tea brewed in Alto.

"What's your news?" Peter asked. "Is the firm considering you for partner status?"

Roxy almost dropped her cup. "How did you—" She stopped. "Did someone performing a background check already contact you?"

"Is that a possibility?" Peter raised his eyebrows. "It's an international law firm. You're not going undercover with the CIA."

"You're right. That won't happen, but how did you guess?"

"Just piecing together what you've said about your interactions with Mr. Caldweller over the past few months. He respects you. If you've gone to that level with him, the next step logically follows."

Roxy told him about the conversation. "I'm still not sure what to think," she said when she finished.

"It's a tough decision," Peter replied slowly.

Roxy was puzzled by his tone of voice. "What do you mean?"

Peter tilted his head to the side and studied her for a moment. "Whether or not you're supposed to become a partner. It's one thing to work as an employee. You're an outsider. If you become a partner then you're more closely linked with the personality and character of the firm. You have to decide if Frank and Donaldson is enough like you that it makes sense for you to become part of them."

"Are you saying that because I might have to leave Atlanta?" Roxy asked, bristling. "Our relationship is a huge deal to me, and I don't—"

"I know," Peter interrupted. "But I'm thinking on a different level. Can you really see yourself treating people the way Mr. Caldweller has treated you?"

"It's toughened me up."

"Sure, but what's excited me recently is watching you soften."

Roxy's eyes watered. "If you're trying to make me cry again, it's not going to happen," she responded, even as her voice trembled slightly.

Peter refilled her teacup. As he did, Roxy focused on his hands. They were rock steady, and he didn't spill a drop. But more importantly Peter knew how to hold her heart.

"Okay," she said. "That's a base level question I need to be brave enough to ask myself. But if they offer me partnership status and I turn it down, I will probably have to leave the firm. If that happens, I'll have to start over someplace else."

"That's what you're doing anyway, isn't it? In areas of your life that are at least as important as where you work."

"You've lost me."

Peter pointed up. Then he took out his phone and showed her a picture he'd taken of Roxy, Ray, and her father standing in the kitchen at Ray's house.

"So not only do I have to deal with Mr. Caldweller, I also have to please God and make my family love one another?"

"Yeah," Peter replied with a smile. "And throw making me happy in there too."

Roxy took a sip from her cup. "This is good tea, but to do all that I may need something with more caffeine."

———

Ray was worn out. He'd talked to four chemists, all of whom were evasive about the connection between 2,4-D and non-Hodgkin's lymphoma. He'd exchanged e-mails with two professors with multiple PhDs who claimed to be experts in just about anything that had been developed by Western civilization since Galileo, and a Harvard graduate who promised she could bring a high level of pathos and sympathy to her courtroom testimony about chemical compounds. The retainer fees ranged from two thousand to twenty thousand dollars, all nonrefundable.

"Did you see the article on the front page of the newspaper?" Cindy asked as soon as he walked through the door.

"No."

She pointed to the paper that was lying on the kitchen table. Ray picked it up and read the headline.

LOCAL ATTORNEY FILES LAWSUIT TO SHUT DOWN COLFAX
FERTILIZER PLANT

"What?" he blurted out.

"Keep going," Cindy replied flatly.

Ray couldn't believe the alarmist spin Cecil Scruggs placed on the case. The reporter's emphasis wasn't on the sick boys, but on the number of jobs that would be lost and the devastating effect on the local economy if Colfax curtailed or ended its operations. But the worst part was a reference to Ray.

Former Assistant District Attorney Raymond Gage has joined forces with his father's firm and will be actively involved in the case. Upon learning about this development, District Attorney Steve Nelson expressed concern that confidential information obtained by Gage during his time at the DA's office has been improperly utilized in the civil case. Nelson is exploring the need to file a complaint with the State Bar of Georgia and the State Attorney General's Office.

"This stuff from Steve Nelson is ridiculous!" Ray cried out.

"If someone knows the truth," Cindy replied. "How many people would that be? Maybe five?"

"And the reporter gives no context for why the DA's office was involved in the first place. Judge Ellington found Colfax criminally liable for damage to the environment. That's not mentioned."

"Did you finish the article?"

"No."

Ray turned to the interior page where the article continued. Included was a paragraph about abuse of the legal system by plaintiffs' lawyers filing spurious lawsuits, and a quote from Guy Hathaway at Colfax. Hathaway said he couldn't comment specifically about the allegations of the lawsuit, but revealed the company might open a plant in Honduras, which would lessen the need for the Rusk County facility.

Ray closed the paper and tossed it onto the table. "That couldn't have been worse if it had been written by the marketing department at Colfax."

"No kidding. I've already had one call from a friend whose husband works there, asking why you and your father would try to bring down the company and throw a bunch of people out of work."

"Who was it?"

"I'm not going to say because I don't want you to get mad at her. But if one person called, you know a bunch more are thinking the same thing."

"Yeah," Ray sighed. He told her about the loss of Dr. Westbrook and his daylong efforts to find a replacement.

"We need to pray about this," Cindy said.

"I already tried that," Ray replied. "And things have gotten worse, not better."

———

Corbin left the office ignorant of the contents of the newspaper article he had hoped would be discussed around dinner tables all across town. The Rusk County jury pool was about to be contaminated, not educated. Stopping at the grocery story, he passed a sales box for the local newspaper and bought a copy. He stood outside and read it as the door automatically opened and closed for people entering and leaving. As soon as he saw the headline, Corbin forgot about buying groceries, returned to his car, and called Ray.

"Yes, I read it," Ray said as soon as he answered the phone.

Corbin was so mad he could barely talk. "When I get my hands on Cecil Scruggs, I'll squeeze his scrawny neck until his head pops off!"

"I don't doubt you would," Ray replied. "And they'd add murder to your DUI charge."

"This isn't funny!"

"And I'm not laughing," Ray said. "It took Cindy thirty minutes to calm me down, and I've had more time to digest the news than you have. There's no doubt Ben Hixson gave Scruggs his marching orders and told him the angle to take."

"The publisher? He lives in Birmingham. His company owns scores of these local rags all across the South."

"Yes, and there's got to be a money reason behind what he's doing. Maybe Colfax donates fertilizer to Hixson's favorite golf course."

"I'm still not in a joking mood."

"Look, at least it happened early in the litigation. There will be time for people to forget the article by the time the case comes up for trial. We know where we stand and can be careful. No more interviews."

"If the paper has an agenda, they won't let people forget about it. And it won't matter if we keep quiet. They can continue to spew propaganda and make it impossible for us to stay in town. If a lie is repeated often enough, people begin to believe it. Our business depends on folks trusting us."

Ray was silent and Corbin knew he'd raised a point his son hadn't considered.

"And how do you think the Kilpatrick family and Millie Watson feel right now?" Corbin continued.

"I called them and they're coming to the office first thing in the morning to talk things over."

"Are you going to try to convince them to drop the case?" Corbin bristled. "I refuse to be bullied!"

"That's not my decision."

"And I don't want you in the meeting!"

Ray was silent again. "That's your call too," he said softly. "Bye."

Corbin threw his cell phone down on the passenger seat. He should have known that poking Colfax would produce a hornets' nest reaction that wouldn't be limited to what happened in the controlled environment of the courthouse. But he didn't need Ray running for cover at the first sign of battle. Corbin started the car's engine.

He needed a drink.

FORTY-TWO

Roxy was sitting in her living room with her shoes off listening to music when her phone lit up. She pulled out her earbuds and answered the call.

"What's up?" Ray asked.

"Do you really want to know?"

"Only if it's good."

"I think it is. You'll have to decide."

She started telling him about the partnership opportunity with the law firm. A few sentences into the conversation, she realized how hard it must be for Ray to absorb her news after watching his own future blow up in his face.

She cut it short. "That's it."

"Congratulations," Ray said, without any hint of jealousy. "I'm sure you'll nail the interviews and get the offer."

"If I do, I'm not sure I'll accept."

"What? Why would you turn them down?"

"That's harder to explain."

As she told him about what had been going on in her personal life, Roxy felt her tongue loosen. Some people would have preferred a face-to-face conversation, but she felt more comfortable talking over the phone about her emotions and the new thoughts that had entered her world.

"That's amazing," Ray said when she finished. "I wish Mom could hear you."

The tears that had launched numerous unexpected assaults on Roxy over the past weeks climbed over the wall and attacked once again. She sniffled and wiped her eyes.

Ray continued. "And I believe there's a good chance she did. She's part of the 'cloud of witnesses.'"

Roxy's lower lip trembled. "What do you mean?" she managed.

"It's a verse in Hebrews," Ray said, "about our running our earthly race, surrounded by a great cloud of witnesses who've gone before us. I'm not sure if it's selective or general, but I'd like to think they are able to somehow enjoy our earthly triumphs."

Roxy nodded her head even though Ray couldn't see her. "I hope so too," she said. She grabbed a tissue from a container beside the couch, wiped her nose, and added it to the small pile at her feet.

"I had another reason to call," Ray said. "It has to do with the case Dad filed against Colfax."

Roxy wasn't surprised to hear that the wheels had fallen off the lawsuit before it left the garage. "Better to cut and run now," she said.

"He's not going to do that, at least not without an opinion from a bona fide chemist. I spent all day trying to track one down who could give us trustworthy guidance, and came up empty. Do you have any recommendations for an expert witness service you trust or suggestions that will point me in the right direction?"

"Logistics like that are handled by our clients or a subgroup of the firm in our LA office that performs the kind of background check you did on this Westbrook character. But I can't ask them to work on a case for another law firm. Like all of us, their time is scrutinized under a microscope."

"Okay. Dad is meeting with the plaintiffs in the morning. He doesn't want me in the room because he's afraid I'll pour cold water on the case."

"It needs an ice bath." Suddenly Roxy had an idea. "Ray?"

"Yeah."

"There's a chemist in Chicago who might be able to help. I interviewed him recently as a shadow expert in a big case. Maybe I can talk to him off the record for a few minutes. Isn't the compound you're focused on a relative to DDT?"

"Yes, it's called 2,4-D; it's also a cousin to Agent Orange that the military used for defoliation in Vietnam."

"Can you send me the data from the attorney general's investigation?" she asked.

"Sure."

"What is the next step you want to take?"

"Test the water in the wells for the families with the sick children."

"Who's going to run the test? What's the protocol?"

"We don't know."

Roxy rolled her eyes. Ray wouldn't last thirty seconds in a strategy session with Mr. Caldweller.

"I hate to waste a call with the chemist," she said.

"I could send water samples along with the information from the AG's office," Ray offered hopefully.

"You want me to ask the guy in Chicago to run the tests?"

Ray didn't answer, and Roxy was silent for a moment. Her old level of compassion for her brother when he was in a tight spot resurfaced.

"I get it," she said. "You're desperate and need my help."

"Not if you don't want to," Ray said defensively.

"I do," Roxy replied. "I'll try to reach him in the morning. And

I'm not going to hold it over you when I'm finished. Those days are behind us."

———

Corbin sat in his car but didn't leave the parking lot. He watched people enter and exit the grocery store. One large man came out with a big smile on his face and a twelve-pack of beer in each hand.

"Somebody's having a party in the middle of the week," Corbin muttered.

He started the car's engine and turned onto the main road through town. He wasn't sure where he was going, but knew at some point The Office tavern would be on his itinerary. His early morning effort to drag Max Hogan out of the pit of AA failure now seemed utopian. He stopped at a red light and noticed that his hands shook slightly if he took them off the steering wheel.

His phone vibrated. When the light didn't turn green, he picked it up.

"Thanks for answering," Jimmy said. "Have you gotten the shakes yet?"

"What are you talking about?"

"Then the answer is yes," Jimmy replied. "After I got your message about driving a stake in the ground at the AA meeting this morning, I knew the counterattack would come soon."

"It's been a rough day on several fronts," Corbin replied.

The light changed, but instead of continuing, Corbin pulled into a nearby parking lot for the convenience store where he often bought beer. The owner kept the coolers as close to freezing as possible, and the effect on the beer boosted business.

"Where are you now?" Jimmy asked.

Corbin told him. "But I just stopped here so we can talk."

"Lock the doors."

Feeling silly, Corbin obeyed. "Done."

"What's Step One?" Jimmy asked.

"We admitted we were powerless over alcohol—that our lives had become unmanageable."

"Does that seem more true now than it did this morning at the meeting?"

"Yes," Corbin admitted. "Because I'm alone."

"Corbin, you're not alone," Jimmy replied. "I'm here on the phone, and God is there with you. What's Step Two?"

"Came to believe that a power greater than ourselves could restore us to sanity."

"Is that true?"

Corbin looked out the windshield as two girls who didn't look old enough to buy alcohol walked out of the store with several bottles of cheap wine under their arms. He had a sudden urge to roll down the car window and warn them.

"Corbin, are you there?"

"Yes, I believe."

"Where do you stand with Step Three?"

A copy of the Twelve Steps was on the floorboard on the passenger's side of the truck. Corbin leaned over and picked it up.

"Made a decision to turn our will and our lives over to the care of God as we understand him."

"That's the point where you get plugged into the power source of help," Jimmy said.

Corbin didn't question Jimmy's sincerity, but that didn't keep doubts from dancing around inside his head.

Jimmy continued, "Your job is to make the decision; God's job is to provide the power."

"Yeah, I know," Corbin said halfheartedly.

"Is that how you talk when you're trying to convince a judge about something?"

Corbin felt backed into a corner, but wasn't mad about it. "No."

Jimmy didn't say anything. Corbin knew he was waiting on him.

"Okay," Corbin said, taking a deep breath. "Right now I'm making a decision to turn my will and my life over to the care of God as I understand him. And for me that means Jesus Christ."

Corbin had spoken that name in a profane way many times. To say it as an act of surrender was a new experience.

"What are you going to do now?" Jimmy asked.

Corbin paused. He'd expected at least a little bit of affirmation from his sponsor.

"I guess I'll go home," he said. "And I'm not going to have a drink."

"Good. Call me as soon as you wake up in the morning. Don't worry about the time. I want tomorrow to be another successful day of sobriety."

Corbin left the convenience store. A mile farther down the road he approached The Office tavern. He braced himself for the inevitable desire to turn into the parking lot. But tonight the flashing neon lights didn't reach out and wrap their colorful fingers around his soul.

He continued down the road without looking in the rearview mirror.

———

The following morning Ray worked on non-Colfax matters until Corbin arrived. He left the door of his office open and stepped out into the reception area as soon as he heard his father's voice.

Corbin, a cup of coffee in his hand, looked him in the eye. "You can join the meeting with the Colfax plaintiffs," he said before Ray could speak.

"And I need to let you know what else I've been working on."

"Go ahead," Corbin replied.

Ray raised his eyebrows and glanced at Janelle, who spoke up.

"If you two start keeping secrets from me, this firm won't last six months." She turned to Ray. "Most of your brain cells may still be functioning, but if Corbin doesn't tell me everything, who's going to remind him when he forgets?"

"Okay, okay." Ray told them about his conversation the previous evening with Roxy. "After I talked to her, I called Branson Kilpatrick and Millie Watson and asked each of them to bring some well water with them this morning. I want to send the samples to the chemist so he can run a few tests and give a preliminary opinion about what's in the water and potential harmful effects."

"He's not going to do that kind of work for free," Corbin replied skeptically. "And we'll have to tell the other side about him in responses to interrogatories. If his results come back adverse to us, that's going to be another hurdle we have to overcome."

"For now we can designate him a shadow expert. Roxy is going to take care of all communication. Which means—"

"Her communication with him won't be discoverable because she's not a counsel of record on the case," Corbin finished. "Good work."

"Two Gages on a case is plenty," Janelle interjected. "Three would be, I don't know, too many."

Thirty minutes later, Janelle buzzed Ray and let him know that Branson Kilpatrick and Millie Watson were waiting in the conference room. Both clients had grim expressions on their faces when Ray entered and sat down. Corbin was seated at the head of the table.

"My phone has been ringing off the hook since the newspaper article came out," Branson said. "I've lost five of my best customers. Four of them are management folks at Colfax, and the other one is the sales manager for the company that services their copy machines. And I know this isn't the last of it."

"My mother chewed me out horribly," Millie said, her eyes slightly red. "She accused me of trying to collect a bunch of money off Josh getting sick. I tried to explain what the lawsuit is about, but she wasn't hearing any of it."

Corbin tapped his fingers against the tabletop as he listened. Ray could feel the tension building.

"Branson, what's Mitchell's status at Egleston?" Corbin asked.

"We don't know yet. They're still running tests."

Corbin turned to Millie. "And how is Josh?"

"Getting ready for the next round of chemo as soon as the doctor gets it approved."

Corbin balled his beefy hand up in a fist. Ray braced himself for what he knew would come next—a slam to the table followed by verbal outrage directed at Colfax, Cecil Scruggs, and anyone else who deserved it. Instead his father took a deep breath and let it out.

"Do you have the water samples Ray asked you to bring?" he asked.

Branson and Millie each put a gallon jug on the table.

"We didn't know how much you needed, so we brought a lot," Branson said. "I wrote the name of the well on the bottom of the jugs in permanent marker, along with the date and address."

Corbin looked at Ray, who took it as his cue and explained

the problems they'd had locating an expert. As he was finishing, Janelle stuck her head into the room.

"Roxy called and told me to let you know the chemist will test the water. She also said to send him the information from the attorney general's office."

"Great," Ray replied, then turned to the group. "Your jugs of water are about to take an overnight flight to Chicago."

FORTY-THREE

Roxy hung up the phone. She'd agreed to pay Dr. Sellers twenty-five hundred dollars out of her own pocket to test the water in the Colfax case and evaluate the data from the Georgia Attorney General's office. When she made the call, she'd not had the nerve to ask the chemist to work for free. After all, it wasn't his family that was stuck in a legal ditch.

"The relationship between 2,4-D and non-Hodgkin's lymphoma, especially in children, is subject to debate," Sellers said when she explained what she wanted him to do.

"That's what I understand."

"Over what period of time did the exposure take place?"

"I'm not sure about that either. My brother is going to send the data from the environmental impact study conducted by the state EPA prior to filing criminal charges against the company. Maybe there will be an indication of duration in that information, or they may have to work their way backward based on the date the company started testing 2,4-D as a component in its herbicide/insecticide product."

"Duration of exposure along with degree of saturation will be important factors. The compound doesn't leach out of the soil quickly, but it will be tough to prove enough toxicity to significantly contaminate well water unless multiple tests were performed."

Roxy wished she could present the chemist with a persuasive

factual scenario, but she couldn't. Everything he said was a missile that the defense lawyers would launch at her father and Ray.

"I'm just the go-between," she said.

"I understand. Should I send my report directly to you?"

"Yes, that way it's off the books for the lawsuit." Roxy paused. "In case I have bad news."

"Exactly."

"Okay, I don't mind doing it. It fact, I'm curious. Most chemists cook up compounds for the betterment of mankind, but when they mess up it can be a public health nightmare. And I'm inherently suspicious of anything in the DDT family."

"How much time will you need to prepare a report?"

"A few days at the most. I'm in between projects, and all I'm teaching this semester is a graduate-level seminar class."

"Thanks again."

Shortly before lunch Roxy received a call from an unfamiliar lawyer who worked in the Dallas office of the firm. Suspecting it might be related to her future partnership status, she took a few seconds to compose herself before accepting it. Forty minutes later she hung up the phone, relieved at how well it had gone, and confident it had tipped the scales in favor of her becoming a partner.

Of course, the next call might have the opposite effect.

———

"I'm on my way to the bank," Corbin announced to Janelle. "Then to lunch. Where's Ray?"

"He left for a doctor's appointment with Cindy. Is she okay?"

Corbin held his hands out in front of his abdomen.

"She's pregnant?" Janelle's eyes widened. "I thought they weren't going to try for another child."

"Keep the news to yourself until Ray mentions it."

Corbin walked briskly to the bank and made a small deposit into the law firm operating account. The teller, a young woman in her thirties who was normally very friendly, treated him like a stranger.

Her attitude left Corbin puzzled; then, as he walked out of the bank, he remembered that her husband worked at Colfax. The shunning had begun.

Corbin continued down the street to the sandwich shop Kitty liked so much. When he entered a couple of people glanced at him and turned away. Corbin ordered his sandwich to go and left with it in a white paper bag. Not wanting to eat at the office, he walked down the street, not sure where to stop. When he reached the local library, he sat on a bench at the edge of a small, carefully manicured patch of grass. Because it was the middle of the day, the fall air was pleasant, and the sun felt good on his face.

Corbin took small bites of his sandwich. He didn't particularly want to rush back to the office. For now, at least, the pull of alcohol was muted, and he could enjoy being alive. He was overdue at the doctor's office for a checkup. One reason he'd stayed away was to avoid a lecture from Dr. Fletchall about limiting his consumption of liquor. Now he could tell the sharp young internist that he was on the path of sobriety, one day at a time.

Corbin glanced down the sidewalk and saw Maryanne Christopher approaching. He'd not seen her since the day she tracked him down at Red's after Kitty's funeral. Seeing her, Corbin's first thought was that her husband worked in management at Colfax. To avoid making eye contact, he glanced down at a few blades of grass fighting for life through a tiny crack in the concrete.

"Hey, Corbin. Enjoying this beautiful weather?"

He looked up. Nothing in Maryanne's face revealed a hostile agenda.

"Yeah, I don't usually have a little picnic in the middle of the day. How are you doing?"

"Fine," Maryanne replied. "I saw the article in the newspaper about the lawsuit you filed against Colfax."

"About that," Corbin began. "It's nothing personal against the folks that work there, and I don't believe there's a real danger that the company will close up and move to someplace in Central America. I mean, it's been here for over seventy years."

Maryanne interrupted him. "That's not why I brought it up," she said. "I saw through the real purpose of the article by the time I reached the third paragraph."

"You did?"

"Give me credit," she replied with a wry smile. "I'm not going to talk about it openly, but if the company did something that made those boys sick, it should make it right. No, the first thing that popped into my head was what Kitty asked me to tell you when I visited her in the hospital."

Corbin had tried to forget the conversation, but Maryanne's words brought it back. "That you should believe for me until I believed for myself?" he asked.

"Yes."

Corbin nodded and scooted over to one end of the bench. Maryanne joined him on the wooden slats.

"I don't know about you, but I've continued to think about her words," Maryanne said. "I think she wanted me to continue praying the prayers I heard her pray for you."

Corbin ached with regret that he never heard Kitty pray for him. Then he felt worse because he knew how he would have reacted if he had.

"Is it okay to say that to you?" Maryanne asked. "I don't want to offend you by making it sound like there's something wrong with you."

Corbin was able to chuckle. "I'm not offended," he said. "I've been thinking a lot recently about what's wrong with me. How would she pray?"

Maryanne repeated phrases that had a familiar ring to them.

"That sounds like Kitty," he said.

"It should. I kept the journal for our prayer group and wrote down what each person prayed."

"Well, I have some good news for you," Corbin said.

And sitting on a bench in front of the local library, Corbin told Maryanne about coming to believe in a power greater than himself.

———

Ray and Cindy left the ob-gyn appointment. To their relief the doctor saw no need to put Cindy on bed rest or restrict her activities more than normally expected for this stage of a pregnancy.

"So far, so good," Ray said when they reached their vehicles and prepared to go their separate ways.

"Yes, and next visit they'll do the ultrasound that should tell us whether it's a boy or a girl. What was the nurse saying to you when you left the examination room?"

"Oh, she knows one of the little boys we're representing in the Colfax case. She moonlights occasionally at the hospital in the oncology unit. She couldn't say anything specific, of course, but she told me Josh is a good kid, a real fighter. I needed to hear something positive. The fallout from the newspaper article has been almost 100 percent negative. A man who works at Colfax fired us this morning. It was the best car wreck claim in the office."

"How did your dad take the news?"

"He doesn't know yet, but it's not all bad. I settled a case that will plug a few financial leaks and keep the boat from sinking immediately." Ray paused and pointed behind them at the doctor's office. "And if the nurse is right about Josh being a fighter, the least I can do is fight for him."

FORTY-FOUR

Roxy checked her watch as she waited for Peter. Normally punctual, he was ten minutes late and hadn't sent a text letting her know why. This time Roxy wasn't going to accept the cell phone in the washing machine excuse. Looking up she saw him walk rapidly into the restaurant and glance about. She waved him over to the table.

"Sorry," he said as he sat down. "I was here on time, but I had to stay in the car to finish an important call."

"It's all good now that you're here," Roxy said.

He reached across the table and squeezed her hand. A waiter brought a water for Peter, and Roxy ordered a glass of wine. Peter stared at her across the table.

"What is it?" she asked, shifting in her chair.

"The phone call in the parking lot. A senior vice president in Boston wants me to consider stepping into upper-level management. I'd still get to do some of the hands-on stuff I like, but I'd also oversee a subgroup that will focus on new products in the communications industry. It's one of the hottest areas going, with tons of professional upside."

The logical side of Roxy's brain enthusiastically tracked with Peter's news. The emotional side rapidly rose up in alarm.

"That's great but scary," she said as both sides sprang into action. "It's a lot like my conversation with Mr. Caldweller about becoming a partner."

"Believe me, I know." Peter paused. "This new job could put me in London for at least a year, then to Boston. We both like to run long distances, but we mean a few miles, not different continents. All I could think about was that I'd go crazy if I couldn't do things like meet you for dinner on short notice, or go for Saturday morning runs at the crack of dawn, or see you for no reason at all except that I want to be with you."

As Peter talked Roxy's eyes got bigger and bigger. She wasn't sure she had room in her heart for a man with such a huge level of commitment to her.

"Do you know what this means?" Peter asked.

Roxy's heart began to pound, and her mouth suddenly felt dry. "Uh, that we have a lot to talk about when it comes to our jobs?"

Peter laughed. Roxy felt her face flush, a reaction she'd successfully avoided since the eighth grade.

"What's so funny?" she asked irritably.

"It's my fault," Peter said. "I said the wrong thing at the wrong time. I'd make a terrible lawyer."

"What did you want to say?" Roxy asked.

"That I love you, and the only move I want to make is to be closer to you. So yes, we need to talk about our jobs and what they mean for our relationship."

Roxy allowed herself to exhale. As she did, excitement rose up in her heart. "And I love you too," she said.

"Good." Peter smiled. "I'm glad we agree."

Roxy smiled back, surprised to find herself feeling more secure than she'd ever felt in her life. She relaxed.

And let Peter's love and kindness wash over her.

Corbin went to the evening AA meeting at the Hopewell church. Both Max and Jimmy were there. It was a speaker meeting featuring a gracious older woman from Savannah. Her topic was how to make a searching and fearless moral inventory, admit to God the wrongs committed, then make amends to those harmed by them. As he listened to the woman's soft, rolling accent, Corbin was reminded of the wealthy women in his hometown. He wondered how many of them hid a secret addiction to sherry and twelve-year-old bourbon. Looking at the speaker's carefully coiffed white hair and nicely tailored outfit, he had trouble imagining that her inventory would require more than a single sheet of paper. But it did.

Corbin began to feel overwhelmed by the scope of what a searching and fearless moral inventory required. Even more daunting was the prospect of trying to make amends to those he'd hurt. His strategy had been to ignore the wrongs he committed and hope those affected by them would do the same.

"Steps Four, Seven, and Eight are like everything else in a good program," the woman said as she came to the end of her talk. "They're done one day at a time by the grace of God and the fellowship of Alcoholics Anonymous. Thanks for listening."

After the meeting, Jimmy came over to Corbin. "Well?" he asked.

"You know the answer," Corbin replied. "I'm thinking this is impossible. How long was your list, and what happened when you tried to make amends? That could get messy."

"I never counted pages. All I've cared about is whether I'm being honest or slipping into alcoholic double-talk. You start your list where God and your mind take you. It can be recent; it can be forty years ago."

"That's my time frame."

"And you can't control how people react when you make amends. We've spent too many years believing the lie that we can control ourselves and others. That's not true whether you're drunk or sober. In making amends you say what you need to say, pay what you need to pay, confess what you need to confess, return what you need to return, forgive what you need to forgive, etc. And leave the results up to God. I compare it to a seed. You plant it with the hope that it will take root and grow up into something beautiful."

Corbin looked at Jimmy with increased respect. "How did you get to be so smart?"

"I've had good sponsors," Jimmy replied with a smile. "And I know how we alcoholics think."

When he got home, Corbin sat on the front stoop and watched the stars pop into view. It was a clear night, and this far from town there wasn't much competition from artificial light. Soon the sky filled with shiny pinpoints of white. Corbin surveyed the multitude.

"That's not even close to the number of wrongs in my inventory," he said to the expanse above his head.

And in that instant an unexpected thought flashed through his mind.

But the light shines in the darkness.

Startled, Corbin looked to his right in a reflex reaction to see where the idea came from. He'd never heard, or claimed to hear, the voice of God. But with piercing succinct clarity the words etched themselves on his soul. He leaned back and stared again at the stars, thousands of lights shining in the darkness.

Now they looked like friends, not enemies.

Ray lay on his back awake, his head resting on the pillow. Cindy was breathing peacefully beside him. He slipped out of bed and made his way into Billy's bedroom. A shaft of light from the street came through the window and illuminated Billy's form enough that Ray could see the outline of his face. Ray knelt on the floor and rested his hands on the spot at the foot of the bed where the light touched the bedspread.

Praying at night was something Ray had done sporadically since he and Cindy brought Billy home as an infant from the hospital. But the origin of the practice went back to Ray's own childhood when his mother would slip into his room from time to time and do the same for him. In spite of her best efforts at being quiet, it wasn't unusual for him to wake up as she knelt beside his bed. When he was a little boy, he would sit up in bed to receive a reassuring hug before drifting back to sleep. As he grew older he would pretend to remain asleep and let the comforting wave of peace she brought to the room flow over him. It was impossible to explain but wonderful to experience. Ray longed to bring the same reality to Billy.

And recapture it himself.

The upheaval in so many areas of his life following his mother's death had taken its toll. Ray began to mentally check those areas off. As he did, his anxiety increased. Some things were good, especially Cindy's pregnancy and the glimmer of hope about his father's alcoholism. But the existence of hope not realized carried its own levels of tension and stress. And the things that were bad generated a long list with much less obvious solutions. Ray let out a long sigh.

"Are you okay?" Billy asked.

Ray glanced at Billy, who was lying on his side, watching him. "I'm sorry. I didn't mean to wake you up."

"Why are you praying?" He sat up.

Ray got up from his knees, sat at the end of the bed, and told Billy about his grandmother.

"She used to do that when I spent the night with her," Billy said.

"I'm sure she did."

"I liked sleeping at her house."

"How do you like this room?"

"It's good too." Billy yawned. "When I'm really tired, I can sleep anywhere."

It was true. Ray had seen Billy nap through thunderstorms and fire engine sirens.

"Good night," Ray said, getting up from the bed.

"Good night, Daddy. I love you."

"I love you too."

Ray left the room. He stopped at Billy's door and glanced back at his son. Somewhere between the bed and the door, the peace Ray longed for returned. He closed his eyes to savor it for a moment. Maybe the mention of his mother's prayers was enough to summon it back. Maybe he could capture her faith and pay it forward.

A cool, damp drizzle was falling when Roxy left her townhome for her morning run. She didn't go out in a downpour, but a few drops of moisture hovering in the air were a natural spritzer that refreshed her as her body heated up with exercise. Only a handful of runners joined her in Piedmont Park. The moist air motivated her to quickly increase her tempo, and her feet beat a rapid staccato across the grass and onto one of her favorite paths. She scaled back to cruising speed, and her mind turned to Peter. Now that she had someone to love, she wanted to do it right just like everything else in her life. But there was someone standing in the way.

Her father.

When she was in college, she'd looked up the personality traits of adult children of alcoholics and tried to convince herself she didn't have the typical defects. She wasn't afraid of authority figures, nor did she struggle with guilt when she stood up for herself. Criticism didn't freak her out, and she wasn't attracted to alcoholics or friends with addictive personalities.

But in the solitude of her morning run, Roxy knew there were flaws that dogged her: isolation, an overdeveloped sense of responsibility, a tendency to judge herself and others harshly, the inability to trust, and fear of commitment.

She knew Peter wanted what was best for her. He'd proven that beyond all reasonable doubt. And his desire that they be an emotionally healthy couple was every sane woman's dream.

The morning mist began to clear, and there were cracks in the cloud cover, holding hope for a clearer day. Roxy reached the turnaround point in her run and began to retrace her steps. This path was familiar. The one leading to the healing of her heart remained unknown.

———

"I heard this morning that they're going to transfer Judge Ellington to a rehab facility," Janelle said when Corbin arrived at the office.

"Is he communicating yet?"

"No, but he recognizes his wife and grandson."

Corbin thought of what it would be like to be lying in a hospital room with Billy standing beside his bed. "Schedule an appointment for me with Dr. Fletchall," he said.

"Have you paid your bill? The last time you wanted to see him, they wouldn't give you an appointment because of an outstanding charge."

"Uh, no."

"Do you still want me to call?"

"I guess not."

Ray came in carrying the morning mail. "This is for you," he said, handing Corbin an envelope from the DA's office. "I've sent out plenty of those."

Corbin stuck the envelope in his pocket.

"Aren't you going to open it?" Janelle asked.

"Just so you can satisfy your curiosity?" Corbin replied.

"I'll find out eventually," Janelle sniffed.

"And then you'll have an answer to your question." Corbin turned to Ray. "Anything else in there?"

Ray handed Corbin another envelope. It was from Simpkin, Brown, and Stamper.

"It's probably the settlement documents in the Morrison v. Pegrim case," Corbin said as he wedged a thick finger under the seal and ripped it open. "Those are way overdue."

He read for a moment, then looked up at Ray. "It's a motion to dismiss filed by Nate Stamper in the Colfax case. It's set for hearing in front of Judge Perry."

"On what grounds?" Ray asked.

"Lack of subject matter jurisdiction and failure to state a claim upon which relief can be granted."

"That's bogus," Ray replied with a wave of his hand. "It's just a delaying tactic."

"That's not all," Corbin continued. "There's a notice of association of co-counsel. They're bringing in another law firm to assist with the defense."

"Who is it?"

"Frank and Donaldson," Corbin replied grimly as he handed the papers to Ray.

"Frank and Donaldson," Janelle repeated with a puzzled look on her face. "Isn't that where Roxy works?"

FORTY-FIVE

"Come into my office," Corbin said to Ray. "We need to talk." As soon as the door closed, he continued. "I thought all they did was pharmaceutical work."

"That's what Roxy does," Ray replied. "Have you ever looked at the firm's website? It's like a map of the world. They handle all types of complex litigation, from medical patents in France to commercial zoning in Singapore. If there's a client with deep pockets, Frank and Donaldson is poised to jump in. One thing is clear. Colfax is taking the lawsuit seriously and doesn't trust Nate Stamper to take care of it."

Corbin read the notice more carefully. He'd never heard of Theodore Daughbert, the lawyer mentioned in the pleadings.

"I don't recognize the name of the lawyer they've associated," he said. "Roxy works with a guy named Caldwell or something like that."

"Her supervisor is Caldweller, and the firm has at least five hundred partners. This guy may not even be in the Atlanta office. They could bring him in by special leave of the court."

Corbin and Ray stared at each other for a moment.

"Do you think I should call Roxy and ask her what she can tell me about this Daughbert guy?" Corbin asked. "I wouldn't be asking anything about the case, only what she knows about him."

"No," Ray replied. "And there's something related to Roxy's career you don't know."

———

There was an e-mail from Dr. Sellers in Roxy's inbox. The chemist had received the water samples from Alto and promised to have a report to her within the next few days. Roxy typed a brief reply that she'd mailed the check for his services the day before. After she finished dealing with forty-eight other pending e-mails, she began working on preparation for a deposition scheduled the following week in Toronto. Unless he dumped the task on her at the last minute, Mr. Caldweller would fly up and take the deposition. Her job was to make sure there weren't any surprises.

At noon she got up to stretch and take a break. Her phone vibrated. It was a text from Peter that contained a link to a website that sold gourmet caramel-covered apples. Roxy smiled as she clicked on the link. The sight of the golden brown apples made her stomach growl. She took a caramel from her stash in the desk drawer and began to unwrap it. There was a knock on her door, and she quickly dropped the caramel and closed the drawer.

"Come in," she said.

It was Mr. Caldweller, accompanied by a fit-looking lawyer in his forties with neatly trimmed brown hair.

"Roxy, this is Ted Daughbert," Caldweller said. "He came down from Chicago to consult with a client yesterday. His return flight isn't until later this afternoon, and I thought the three of us could do lunch."

"I'd like that," Roxy replied, standing up to shake Daughbert's hand.

The man had the firm grip of an athlete.

"Ted is a new member of the partner committee," Mr. Caldweller said while they waited for an elevator to respond. "He was going to call you, but when this came up he decided to take care of two matters at once."

"Byron tells me you're a serious runner," Daughbert said in an accent that sounded Midwestern.

Hearing someone refer to Mr. Caldweller by his first name was always a bit unnerving to Roxy. "I enjoy it."

"Year round?"

"Yes, the winters are usually mild here, and it takes a really bad day to keep me inside. How about you? Do you train crossfit?"

"Yes, how did you guess?" Daughbert asked in surprise.

"Roxy has uncanny instincts," Caldweller grunted. "It can be unnerving."

"Your handshake," Roxy said. "It wasn't hard to tell that you've been in the weight room. And pumping iron by itself is boring. Like the law firm, I'd expect you to diversify."

Daughbert laughed. The elevator reached the ground floor, and they got out.

"I'm into core strength more than anything else," Daughbert said. "With resistance workouts thrown in."

"I'll break up a run with a few sets of Kipping pull-ups every so often," Roxy replied. "There's a horizontal bar station on one of the routes I take."

"Stop it," Caldweller cut in. "I don't like people talking about things I know nothing about."

"I'm convinced exercise makes me a better lawyer," Daughbert said as they entered the parking deck. "It doesn't just keep me in shape; it flushes the toxins out of my brain."

"Toxins are Ted's specialty," Caldweller said to Roxy. "He's developed a nice niche defending chemical companies from environmental and toxic tort claims."

"Somebody has to protect companies like Monsanto," Daughbert said with a smile. "They're always getting harassed by rogue members of the plaintiffs' bar looking to swipe a few bills from their pockets."

"Their very deep pockets," Caldweller added.

They reached Mr. Caldweller's vehicle, a white Mercedes with an interior like a corporate jet.

"Byron tells me you have a chemistry degree and know how to use it," Daughbert said as he held the door open for Roxy to get into the passenger seat.

"It helps," Roxy replied, "but I don't try to turn myself into an expert witness."

"I do," Daughbert said crisply. "Otherwise the other side's witness works me over instead of the other way around."

"Don't let Roxy fool you," Caldweller said. "She does the same thing without getting bigheaded about it."

An uneasy silence descended on the car.

"What kind of case brought you to Atlanta?" Roxy asked in an effort to get the conversation rolling.

"A cancer claim against a fertilizer company."

Roxy felt the blood drain from her face. She stared straight ahead, glad that the Chicago lawyer couldn't see her expression. He continued.

"A sole practitioner in a little town north of here filed a state court action case alleging a fertilizer company contaminated the groundwater and caused a couple of kids to contract non-Hodgkin's lymphoma. I've reviewed all the data, including a study by the Georgia EPA, and there's nothing to it. No legitimate science supports the allegations in the complaint or a causal connection to the illness.

"I handled a similar case last year in Illinois filed by an aggressive law firm who put up a decent fight before caving in. They spent at least a hundred thousand dollars in expenses and two or three times that in attorney time before we kicked them out of court. By the time I'm finished with the lawyer in this case, he'll wish he'd stuck to fender benders and DUIs."

While Daughbert talked, Roxy gripped the straps of the seat belt across her waist and forced herself to breathe evenly.

Caldweller spoke up. "People who claim computer research evens the playing field between big firms and small outfits don't see the whole picture," he said.

Roxy remained silent as the conversation veered toward technology and the practice of law.

"Have you spent time in Chicago?" Daughbert asked Roxy as they approached the valet stand for the restaurant.

"Uh, yes. I was there not long ago meeting with a chemist serving as a shadow expert."

"Who was it?"

"Willard Sellers."

"Yeah, I've used him several times. He's sharp." Daughbert paused. "Now that you mention him, he might be a good choice to bring into the fertilizer case."

"No!" Roxy blurted before she could stop herself.

The valet opened the door, and Roxy slipped out before Caldweller or Daughbert could ask her to explain her over-the-top reaction.

"Let me handle it," Ray said to his father. "Roxy is going to freak, and I don't want—" He stopped.

"Me to mess it up?" Corbin finished the sentence.

"It's hard for her to hear anything from you," Ray replied. "Especially something that will make her feel vulnerable."

As soon as he spoke the words, Ray regretted them. What he'd said was true, but it was truth packed in deep layers of recrimination.

"You're right," Corbin said after a few moments passed. "But at least tell me what you're going to say."

"There's not much I can say. We're on opposite sides of a huge lawsuit, and there has to be a total wall of separation for any relevant communication. Roxy will have to notify the expert in Chicago that she's out of the picture. Then we can only hope nobody at Frank and Donaldson finds out she did anything to help us."

"It's a big firm." Corbin nodded confidently. "Unless her boss is asked to assist in the case, there's a good chance it won't ever come up."

"How can you be so sure? You've never worked for an international law firm."

"Neither have you," Corbin shot back.

Ray checked his watch. "I don't want to call her at the office. I'll wait until this evening."

"I think you should call her now," Corbin replied. "But what do I know? I'm just a simpleminded country lawyer."

"Who needs to put a DUI charge behind him," Ray replied, changing the subject. "Let me read the plea offer."

Corbin took the envelope from his pocket and gave it to Ray, who read the letter.

"This is a relief," he said. "Steve isn't going to give you special treatment."

"I want special treatment."

"Not the kind I'm talking about. He's going to let you plead to reckless driving. That's a break. But you'll receive the same punishment as if you pleaded guilty to DUI."

"I won't do it."

"Remember, Dad, you are in fact guilty." Ray continued reading. "You'll have to pay a thousand-dollar fine, no jail time other than the night you were arrested, complete drunk driving school, and serve three months' probation."

"That's a hefty fine. Three hundred dollars would be better. You sound more like a prosecutor than a defense lawyer," Corbin said grumpily.

"Do you want to fight this or put it behind you? You'll have until the day before you're scheduled to appear in court to accept the deal, then it will disappear. As your lawyer I'm recommending you take the offer."

"Let me think about it," Corbin said.

Ray tossed the letter onto the desk in disgust.

"Okay, I've thought about it. I'll take the deal," Corbin said. "May you be able to persuade all your clients to take your advice as quickly as you did me."

"And may I never defend you in another DUI case."

———

Roxy made it through lunch without having an overt panic attack; however, she suspected any good first impression she'd made on Ted Daughbert had vanished like the dirty plates at the end of the meal. Every time she looked at the litigator, she imagined him standing in the same courtroom as Corbin Gage. Whether done with a three-inch surgical scalpel or a five-foot broadsword, the result would be the same—death to her father's case.

"Are you okay?" Mr. Caldweller asked her at one point. "Do you have a headache?"

"No, sir."

"Well, you're not holding up your end of the conversation. Ted isn't interested in my old war stories. He'd like to hear a few of yours."

"Uh, which one do you suggest? You know everything I've done," Roxy said, then suddenly realized it wasn't true. "I mean, almost everything."

"Tell him about the motion for sanctions you argued last year in front of Judge Palmore." Caldweller turned to Daughbert. "He's a federal judge in the southern district who hates lawyers. By the time Roxy left, he was tossing out compliments like candy at a birthday party."

Roxy forced herself to retell the incident, but her conduct now seemed self-serving and petty. Daughbert listened politely, then glanced at his watch.

"Byron, I'd like to have a bit of time back at the office before my flight. I have a few ideas on the fertilizer case that I want to run by our local counsel. I also need to give him his marching orders for the next week or so."

"Sure. I hope you enjoyed the food."

"It was sufficiently paleo," Daughbert replied with a wink at Roxy.

"All I saw were hunter-gatherer items on your plate," she managed to respond.

Mr. Caldweller gave a short huff in reply.

Riding in the car on the return trip, Roxy wondered if Daughbert would stop by for a final interview chat before leaving town. He'd already had one chance to see the name *Roxanne Gage* on the door without asking if she was related to Corbin Gage, counsel for the plaintiffs in the spurious lawsuit against Colfax Fertilizer Company. Given a second chance at name identification, Daughbert was much more likely to connect the familial dots.

As soon as she was safely inside her office, Roxy closed the door, logged onto her computer, and deleted all her e-mail communication with Dr. Sellers. She then called him on her cell phone. She popped a caramel in her mouth while she waited and hoped he would answer. Instead she got his voice mail and left him a message to call her private number. She wasn't exactly sure what she was going to say to the chemist, but she hoped inspiration would come in the heat of the moment.

———

Corbin left without telling Janelle where he was going. A legal pad in his hand, he walked across the street to the courthouse. Going to the main courtroom, he peeked inside. It was empty and was church-sanctuary quiet until the old wooden floor creaked beneath his feet. He sat on one of the back benches.

Inside the front pocket of his shirt was a copy of the Twelve Steps. The sheet of paper had been folded and unfolded so many times that the creases made a permanent grid. Corbin got up and walked down the aisle to the front of the courtroom, stopping in the familiar spot where he'd stood on countless occasions before a human judge. Glancing over his shoulder to make sure he was still alone, he cleared his throat and in his best courtroom voice read all Twelve Steps out loud:

1. "We admitted we were powerless over alcohol—that our lives had become unmanageable.
2. Came to believe that a Power greater than ourselves could restore us to sanity.
3. Made a decision to turn our will and our lives over to the care of God as we understood Him.

4. Made a searching and fearless moral inventory of ourselves.

5. Admitted to God, to ourselves, and to another human being the exact nature of our wrongs.

6. Were entirely ready to have God remove all these defects of character.

7. Humbly asked Him to remove our shortcomings.

8. Made a list of all persons we had harmed, and became willing to make amends to them all.

9. Made direct amends to such people wherever possible, except when to do so would injure them or others.

10. Continued to take personal inventory and when we were wrong promptly admitted it.

11. Sought through prayer and meditation to improve our conscious contact with God, as we understood Him, praying only for knowledge of His will for us and the power to carry that out.

12. Having had a spiritual awakening as the result of these Steps, we tried to carry this message to alcoholics, and to practice these principles in all our affairs."

Corbin then laid his copy of the Twelve Steps on the bench as if presenting it to a judge. He stood in silence, his head bowed. After a few moments he opened his eyes and glanced around. Nothing in the courtroom had changed. He didn't feel any different.

But he believed the Judge who mattered had heard his testimony.

FORTY-SIX

R ay called the DA's office. The receptionist who answered the phone insisted on chatting with him for a couple of minutes.

"We really miss you over here," she said.

"Who's included in that 'we'?" Ray asked.

"Yours truly and most of the police force. The detectives knew when they brought you a case you'd handle it properly."

Ray was tempted to uncork a bottle of gossip, but resisted. "Is Brett available?" he asked.

"Yes." The receptionist lowered her voice. "He keeps asking me for files you worked on so he can see what you did in the cases."

"I did the same thing when I started working for Jimbo."

"No, you didn't," she responded with a short laugh. "All Jimbo could teach you was to act political and chew tobacco."

"And I wasn't interested in either."

"I'll put you through to Brett."

While he waited on hold, Ray did a quick internal check to see if he missed the DA's office. By the preponderance of the evidence he could say no.

"How's it going?" he asked when Brett picked up the phone.

Ray was unprepared for the floodgate his polite comment opened. For over thirty minutes he answered a steady stream of questions about how to function as an assistant DA.

"That's it for now," Brett finally said. "Thanks so much. Is it okay if I run stuff by you later?"

"Sure."

"Okay, bye."

"Wait a minute," Ray quickly interjected. "I called you."

"Right. What can I do for you?"

"I'm calling about my father's DUI charge. Do I need to talk to Steve about it?"

Brett was silent for a moment. "No, I'll be the one in the courtroom when it comes up. However, I can't modify the terms of the offer without Steve's okay. And I don't think he's going to budge."

"That's not why I called. My father will take the deal. When is the next calendar call so we can enter the plea and get this behind him?"

"I'm sure I can tack it onto the end of the calendar on Thursday."

"Pencil it in. That way there won't be a bunch of people gawking at him."

The call ended. Ray left his office and walked across the reception area toward his father's office to tell him, but Janelle intercepted him.

"He's not there," she said.

"Where is he?"

"I don't know."

"Is Thursday morning around eleven clear?"

"Yes. The first thing he has is a deposition after lunch."

Roxy spent an anxious afternoon dreading a follow-up visit from Ted Daughbert and hoping for a return call from Dr. Sellers. Neither occurred. She was in her car leaving the parking deck when her phone vibrated and she saw Ray's name. She pulled into a vacant space and answered the phone.

"Your firm has been associated by Simpkin, Brown, and Stamper to represent Colfax in the lawsuit Dad filed," Ray said without any preamble. "I didn't want you to get blindsided—"

"Too late," Roxy cut in. "I had lunch today with Ted Daughbert, the litigation partner from Chicago who's on the case."

"Oh no," Ray replied, his voice deflated.

"It wasn't a total disaster. He didn't make the connection with me and should be on a plane back to Chicago by now."

"Whew. Why did he have lunch with you?"

"He's a member of the partnership review committee. Mr. Caldweller was also there."

"How did the case come up?" Ray asked. "Wait, you can't say anything about it."

"Correct, and I'm going to be hanging over a cliff by a thread for who knows how long, worrying that someone at the firm is going to connect one Gage lawyer to another."

"What if this Daughbert guy asks you to work on the case?"

It was a possibility Roxy should have considered, but in the midst of the day's turmoil she hadn't.

"Let's hope he doesn't," she said, tight-lipped. "But we have a more immediate problem—Dr. Sellers. I've hired an expert to help you in litigation my firm is defending."

"Right."

"And that's not all. Daughbert knows Sellers and may be contacting him too."

"Wait, what's the connection between them?"

"Daughbert's specialty is chemical exposure litigation, and he's used Dr. Sellers as an expert in the past."

"Seriously?"

"Yes, and he's litigated at least one case with similar facts that didn't go well for the plaintiff. And that's more than I should probably tell you."

Ray was silent for a moment.

"I've been stressed out all afternoon," Roxy continued. "I have a call in to Sellers, and as soon as I hear from him I'll tell him to deal directly with you about the results of his testing."

"Okay, but what if Daughbert follows through and contacts Sellers too?"

"Sellers will have to disqualify himself. When he does, I'm going to ask him to keep my name out of the conversation."

"But Daughbert will figure out—"

"Yes! He probably will!" Roxy exploded. "And not only will I not become a partner, I won't have a job!" She was so mad she wanted to throw the phone onto the floorboard of the car.

"I'm sorry," Ray said.

"It's just another way our father is trying to destroy our lives! We both told him to drop this case. It's a loser that has already cost you a job you'd worked hard to get, and now it's about to blow up my career. And I'm not moving back to Alto to work at Gage and Gage!"

"It's not Gage and Gage. I just needed a place to land until I can figure out my next step."

Roxy wanted to keep on venting, but she realized she had the wrong person on the other end of the phone.

"It's not your fault," she said, trying to calm down. "And I should have been more upset over what happened to you. I mean, you have a family to support and a baby on the way. But here we are, and I don't know what else to do."

"Would it be okay if I called Dr. Sellers directly?"

"Of course; you're going to have to finish up with him on the substantive stuff for the case. I am completely out of the loop. But don't expect any good news. He's not a hack who massages a report to please the folks paying his bill."

"And he's doing this gratis."

Roxy didn't correct him. After the call ended, she sent a text to Peter telling him she needed to see him. To her relief he immediately responded and told her where to be in thirty minutes.

———

Corbin attached his boat trailer to his truck. He'd wanted to call Cindy and invite Billy to join him for a quick fishing trip before suppertime, but knew that would defeat the purpose for his excursion. Corbin needed to be alone. He needed to be away from the liquor bottles in the kitchen cupboard that had been calling his name ever since he came home early from the office. He needed to be in a secluded place where he could think clearly without interruption. He needed to be in a place where he could pray.

Leaving his fishing gear and tackle box on the shelves in the carport, he drove slowly down the driveway and turned in the direction of Braswell's Pond. Backing the trailer up into the edge of the water, he released the winch and climbed into the boat. All he took with him were a legal pad and a pen. He didn't start the engine, but paddled to the middle of the pond and dropped the anchor. As soon as the wake caused by the boat subsided, the water was glassy smooth.

Ponds and lakes had always been places of peace for Corbin in the midst of the constant storms of his life. Being on the water settled his thoughts and calmed the constant churning of his soul. Today no mason jar in a cooler distracted him. Taking out the legal pad, he wrote Ray's name at the top of the first page. Then he turned over a few sheets and wrote *Roxy*. Turning over a few more sheets, he wrote another name. Then he bowed his head. After a few moments he raised it. And started to write.

Corbin left the pond in time to make it to the evening AA meeting at the Hopewell church. He was glad to see Max's vehicle in the parking lot. It was a Big Book meeting, and the topic was chapter 4, "We Agnostics." As the female leader read several excerpts, Corbin realized how far he'd come in his spiritual understanding and belief. Sentences he would have completely identified with a few weeks earlier no longer described his status.

One unique feature of the Big Book's presentation on all topics was the use of "we." When referring to a doubter, the text was inclusive—"We know how he feels. We have shared his honest doubt and prejudice. Some of us have been violently anti-religious." The Big Book didn't point fingers; it held out its arms. Then the leader read a passage that stunned Corbin—"We looked askance at many individuals who claimed to be godly . . . And who could comprehend a Supreme Being anyhow? Yet, in other moments, we found ourselves thinking, when enchanted by a starlit night, 'Who made all this?' There was a feeling of awe and wonder . . ."

"That exact thing happened to me the other night!" Corbin blurted, then put his hand over his mouth. "Sorry to interrupt."

"That's okay," the leader responded. "Do you want to tell us about it?"

Corbin related his experience on the front steps of his duplex.

"Have you read chapter 4?" the leader asked when he finished.

"No."

"You might want to," the leader said. "It will confirm what happened."

A man in the circle spoke up. "I don't want to jump ahead, but would it be okay if I read from the last pages of the chapter?"

"Sure," the leader said. "There's no harm in knowing where the discussion will end."

The book made its way around the circle to the man.

"The chapter ends with the story of a minister's son who lost his faith and came to the point of suicide," the man said. "Then he cries out in frustration and an answer comes."

He flipped several pages and cleared his throat. "'Who are you to say there is no God?' This man recounts that he tumbled out of bed to his knees. In a few seconds he was overwhelmed by a conviction of the Presence of God. It poured over and through him with the certainty and majesty of a great tide at flood. The barriers he had built through the years were swept away. He stood in the Presence of Infinite Power and Love . . . Even so has God restored us all to our right minds. To this man, the revelation was sudden. Some of us grow into it more slowly. But He has come to all who have honestly sought Him.'"

Corbin knew he was listening to truth, not because of natural discernment honed in the courtroom, but because the inner witness who spoke to him in front of his house confirmed the words at the deepest level of his being.

"That's right," he muttered.

Jimmy, who was sitting on the opposite side of the circle, looked at Corbin and nodded his head.

"One of the things I get from that chapter," Jimmy said to the group, "is the relentless nature of God in seeking us out. I mean, who but God would want to hang out with a bunch of drunks? And who but God has the power to change us?"

When the meeting ended, Corbin walked over to Jimmy. "I worked on my inventory this afternoon," he said, feeling proud of himself. "The toughest part was getting started."

"And it's even tougher not to quit too early."

"That's encouraging." Corbin frowned.

"And when you think you're finished, there's always Step Ten, the continuing inventory. Life doesn't stop."

"Any other good news for me?"

"Yeah," Jimmy said, smiling. "Once you committed to the program, you're like my rottweiler with a chew toy. He'll clamp down with those big jaws and dare me to try to take it away from him. I pity the person who tries to talk you out of what you're gaining here."

Corbin smiled.

"And you must be one heck of a lawyer."

Corbin's smile broadened.

"When you've not been drinking, of course."

FORTY-SEVEN

Two days later Ray ended a morning call with Dr. Willard Sellers. The past forty-five minutes had been a cram course in the chemical makeup of 2,4-dichlorophenoxyacetic acid, its characteristics, its solubility, and its toxicity. But the conversation had been more roller-coaster ride than college lecture. Ray's elation at the chemist's confirmation that 2,4-D was clearly present in the well water dissipated when he told Ray that, based on current research, the concentration did not rise to a level that created a health hazard.

"This doesn't mean it wasn't higher in the past," the chemist added. "2,4-D finds entrance into the water table as runoff, direct entry, or by leaching through the soil. Coarse, grainy soils are the most amenable to leaching."

"This part of Georgia is red clay country," Ray said.

"Which means the soil is more impervious to penetration."

"How long can 2,4-D remain in the water table?"

"It has a relatively slow half-life of over three hundred days in most subterranean environments. Given the levels I found in the samples, which by the way were consistent with each other, I cannot state there has been a health hazard within the past year, if ever. It appears the company began developing the new herbicide product

about eighteen months ago. Prior to that do you have any indication they were manufacturing anything except nitrogen-based
fertilizers?"

"No," Ray said.

"Then I wouldn't be able to draw a causal connection between
the presence of 2,4-D and a potential health risk."

Ray racked his brain for something else to ask that might give
him a glimmer of hope. His thoughts didn't find a place to land, so
he retreated to a fallback question.

"What am I missing?" he asked.

"Nothing unless you uncover additional data. Have you
deposed anybody who works for the company?"

"Not yet. We wanted to know where we stood first on the well
samples."

"I understand. Sorry I couldn't be of more help. Oh, and please
give my regards to your sister. I enjoyed meeting her a few weeks
ago."

"I will, and as I told your assistant when we scheduled the call,
there's no need to contact Roxy about your findings."

"That's noted in my file."

"And send your bill to me."

"Ms. Gage took care of it."

"She did?" Ray asked in surprise.

"Yes."

After the call ended Ray stared across his office without bringing anything into focus, which was exactly how he felt about the
Colfax case. After a few moments, he shook his head to clear it,
then walked across to his father's office to deliver the devastating
news in person.

Corbin listened to Ray without expressing any emotion. "Roxy paid the guy's fee? How much was it?"

"I didn't ask him. But it makes sense that he wouldn't work for nothing. I guess she felt sorry for us and wanted to help us out."

"What's next?" Corbin asked.

"I think you should apologize to Roxy for putting her promotion in jeopardy—"

"No, I mean for the case. What are we going to argue at the hearing on the motion to dismiss next week, and where are we going to find an expert?"

"You don't care about what happens to Roxy?"

"Yes," Corbin replied irritably. "But everything bad that happens in her life isn't my fault."

He immediately regretted his words, but before he could correct them, Ray spoke.

"As to the motion, we'll stand on the allegations in the pleadings and tell the judge we have the right to conduct discovery to determine the exact nature of the wrong committed and its impact on the boys. The pleadings state alternative theories of recovery that can't be adjudicated without evidence. We don't have any evidence, but that's not the issue. At least not yet."

"You seem pretty confident."

"About that I do."

"Do you want to argue the motion?"

"Why me?" Ray asked in surprise.

"Because we both know what Judge Perry thinks about me. He's less likely to go rogue on you." Corbin checked his watch. "Especially after he accepts my guilty plea in about an hour."

"I'll get ready."

"No." Corbin shook his head. "I'll take my medicine alone. Your time is better spent trying to find a chemist who can help us.

I thought we were wasting our time with Roxy's expert. I'm sure he always testifies for defendants."

"I asked him that. He's split about sixty-forty between defense and plaintiff." Ray paused. "Are you sure you don't want me beside you?"

"No," Corbin grunted. "Everything bad that's happened in my life is my fault."

When it was time for him to leave for the sentencing hearing, nervous butterflies woke up and fluttered around inside Corbin's stomach. He climbed the steps of the courthouse without looking at the lawyers who passed him on their way out. Solitude and isolation were friends in his moment of humiliation. He didn't know if any of the lawyers stared at him or not.

Reaching the courtroom, he cracked open the door. He'd hoped placement of the case at the end of the morning calendar would result in an empty courtroom; to his dismay he saw a number of people sitting together on one of the front pews. It wouldn't surprise him if Cecil Scruggs from the newspaper was among them.

Judge Perry was on the bench. Brett Dortch and an unrepresented criminal defendant stood in the open space before the judge. Using measured steps Corbin walked down the aisle and slipped into a seat across the aisle from the one where the people were sitting. Dortch glanced over his shoulder, saw him, and held up a single finger, which Corbin took to mean he was up next. He cast a furtive glance to the side and did a double take. He recognized everyone in the opposite row.

They were all from Alcoholics Anonymous.

There was Jimmy. Next to him was Max Hogan. All in all there were four men and two women. Corbin was stunned. His nervousness was replaced by bewilderment.

"Mr. Gage," Dortch said. "Come forward, please."

With a glance toward his AA supporters, Corbin stood.

"Are you here to enter a plea in your case?" Dortch continued.

Corbin faced the judge and was greeted with a look of disdain and disgust that made Corbin angry. Judge Perry was a sanctimonious hypocrite. The fact that he was about to pass judgment on Corbin was an insult. He wanted to shout out, "No!" and walk out of the courtroom. But the eyes on his back helped keep him sane. He cleared his throat.

"Yes."

He stepped through the bar and stood straight as the assistant DA read the charges. The judge flipped through the papers in front of him as if uninterested.

"How does the defendant plead?" Judge Perry asked without looking up.

Corbin waited for Dortch to say something about the plea agreement, but the assistant DA remained mute. Corbin pulled the plea offer from his coat pocket and handed it to Dortch.

"Is this your recommendation?" the judge asked the assistant DA.

"The State has no objection to reduction of the charge to reckless driving and entry of sentence as stated in the letter you received, but we will, of course, yield to the Court's discretion," Dortch said.

"Let me take a look at it," the judge said.

Corbin handed it to him, and the judge quickly scanned it.

"Mr. Gage, how do you plead?"

"Guilty to reckless driving," Corbin responded.

The judge tapped his pen against the bench several times. Corbin stood ramrod straight. Judge Perry could reject the offer and send him to jail, but Corbin wasn't going to beg for mercy.

"Plea accepted."

"And the sentence?" Dortch asked.

Corbin felt the hair on the back of his neck rise up. He suddenly had the feeling that came over him in his younger days when a fight was about to break out in a bar, a potent mixture of excitement and fear.

"A thousand-dollar fine, credit for jail time served, completion of driving school program within thirty days, and three months' probation, along with a $150-per-month probation fee."

Corbin exhaled. But the judge wasn't finished.

"I further order you to contact the Lawyer's Assistance Program and undergo an evaluation. You will cooperate with their recommendations and report back to the Court confirming your compliance. Is that clear?"

"Yes."

"Anything else, Mr. Dortch?" the judge asked.

"No, Your Honor. That completes the morning calendar."

Without another glance at Corbin, Judge Perry left the bench. Corbin turned toward the group sitting on the bench.

"How did you know to come?" he asked, holding his arms open wide.

Jimmy spoke. "I called your office the other day and spoke to your son. He told me the date and time, and I asked him not to mention it to you. We were here in case the judge had a question about what you're doing to stay sober."

Several people nodded.

"I don't know what to say," Corbin said.

"That you'll be here for another alcoholic someday would be a nice start," one of the women replied.

"Yes, I will," Corbin replied.

And he meant it with all his heart.

———

387

Roxy finished a forty-five-minute phone call with another member of the partnership committee. The lawyers on the committee apparently charged a huge amount of time to internal firm business. Otherwise they wouldn't devote so much energy to the process. The woman who interviewed Roxy worked in the Denver office. Her emphasis was more on convincing Roxy of the benefits of partnership than grilling her about her qualifications. Roxy knew the firm left nothing to chance. The woman's call was part of the process, and Roxy quickly realized she was being manipulated. Also, the call reassured her that the surreptitious contact with Dr. Sellers about the Colfax litigation remained secret.

She'd previously arranged to slip away for a longer than usual lunch date with Peter and was closing down her computer when there was a knock at her closed door.

"Come in!" she called out.

It was Mr. Caldweller. He had a thin folder in his hand, which he held tightly. Roxy had a sinking feeling that a last-minute project was about to be deposited on her desk and abort her lunch date. The senior partner closed the door behind him.

"May I sit down?" he asked.

"Yes," she replied, slightly puzzled at his politeness.

Caldweller sat across from her desk with the folder still in his grasp. "Did you talk to Colleen Dankins?" he asked.

"Yes, we finished up a few minutes ago."

"Did she give you the hard sell on why you should become an equity partner in the firm?"

"I guess you could say that."

"But you figured that out within a few minutes of the conversation, didn't you?"

Surprised that Caldweller so readily confirmed her unspoken suspicions about firm strategy, Roxy wasn't sure how to respond.

"It doesn't matter," Caldweller said with a quick wave of his hand. "I have something more pressing to talk to you about."

He handed her the folder, and she opened it. At the top of the first page were the words *Severance Agreement*. Employment litigation wasn't an area of expertise for Roxy, but she knew that past experience didn't limit Caldweller's present expectations. She read the first few lines of the document, then stopped.

"This has my name in it," she said.

"That's right. It's the best I could do for you under the circumstances. Either sign it and take what we're offering, or your departure from the firm will be categorized as termination for cause."

"But why?" Roxy started, then stopped.

"Do you really have to ask that?"

Roxy knew but was having trouble believing it.

"You crossed the line in the case filed by your father," Mr. Caldweller continued with more tenderness in his voice than Roxy could remember. "If you'd come to me first, I might have given you the okay to contact the chemist in Chicago, and when the firm was retained, there would have been a tactful way for you to back out. By not doing so, there's nothing I could do to protect you. The firm has a zero tolerance policy for acting contrary to the interests of our clients."

"I didn't know—"

"But you knew you were over the line from the first step you took."

"Yes," Roxy admitted. "I didn't think it through."

"Which is another requirement for everyone who works here as an associate or partner. Ted Daughbert was livid when he spoke with the chemist in Chicago and made the connection with you and the lawsuit. It made it worse that we discussed the case before and during lunch, and you didn't speak up. Daughbert went to the top of the firm ladder in New York and wanted you canned on the spot. I lobbied for what I could get."

Roxy would receive three months' salary so long as she agreed not to "disparage the firm" and kept the terms of her departure confidential. Most of the rest was boilerplate language. There was no effort to restrict the geographic area where she might seek other employment. That meant she could go to work for another law firm in Atlanta if the right job came along.

She took a deep breath and stared at Mr. Caldweller.

FORTY-EIGHT

Ray was in the middle of a phone interview with yet another potential expert when his cell phone vibrated and Cindy's picture popped into view. He had to let her call go to voice mail while he continued listening to the chemist, a woman with impressive credentials who seemed genuinely interested in working on the case. Dr. Kimberly Clayton didn't flinch when Ray brought up the results from Dr. Sellers's tests for 2,4-D in the well water.

"That's important, but it's not the final word," Dr. Clayton replied. "There are issues related to airborne transmission as well. Based on what caught the attention of the state officials, that is a factor linked to exposure and could result in manifestation of a disease process quicker than if it only occurred from a single source."

While the chemist talked, Ray's phone vibrated again to signal receipt of a text message. It was from Cindy, and he opened it.

At the doctor, please pray.

Reading those five words erased everything Dr. Clayton had said to Ray over the past thirty seconds.

"I'm sorry, could you repeat that last part?" he managed.

"About the research into phenoxyacetic arrays?"

"Uh, yes."

Ray tried to concentrate on the chemist's words, but it was no use. As soon as he could interject a comment, he did.

"Thank you very much," he said. "Is it okay if I call you later to finish our conversation?"

"I'm leaving the office in an hour to attend an environmental conference in Sao Paulo, Brazil, and won't be back for a week. Some of the things being done to the rain forest are criminal."

"Yes, I'm sure that's true."

"And it's my policy to charge for multiple phone consultations. I hope that's not a problem. My assistant will send you a sample contract and financial requirements."

"Great," Ray replied absentmindedly, then ended the call.

He immediately called Cindy, who didn't answer. Ray hurriedly left his office.

"Cindy is at her ob-gyn's office," he said to Janelle. "There's some kind of problem, and I'm on my way over there."

Ray drove as fast as he could across town to the doctor's office and unsuccessfully tried to reach Cindy twice on the phone. He saw her car when he swerved into the parking lot and jumped out. Once inside the office, he dashed up to the receptionist.

"Cindy Gage?" he asked, slightly out of breath. "Where is she?"

"With the doctor," the young receptionist replied nonchalantly.

"I have to see her!"

"She'll be out after she finishes," the woman replied, glancing down at the cell phone in her hand. Ray could see there was a game running on the screen. "Have a seat."

"I'm her husband," Ray replied with as much bridled intensity as he could muster without yelling. "And if you don't tell me where she is, I'm going to search this building until I find her."

The woman's eyes got big. "Let me check," she said, getting up quickly from her seat.

Ray fumed as the seconds passed. A very pregnant woman came in and stood behind him. He didn't step aside. The receptionist returned.

"A nurse will be out in a minute to take you back to see her."

Ray moved over. In a few moments the door opened, and a woman in blue surgical scrubs appeared.

"Mr. Gage?" she asked. "Come with me."

"How is she?" Ray demanded.

"She's with the doctor."

It wasn't an answer, but Ray suspected it was all he would get. They turned a corner, and the nurse opened a door.

"They're in here."

Ray stepped inside. Covered by a white sheet, Cindy was propped up in bed with her doctor beside her. Dr. Valance saw Ray and moved toward the door.

"I'll leave you alone," he said.

Ray went over and grabbed Cindy's hand. Her eyes were red and teary, but she gave him a weak smile.

"It's a girl," she said. "I started bleeding at home and came right in. Dr. Valance doesn't think I'm in imminent danger of a miscarriage, but she wants me to keep off my feet for a few days."

"A girl?"

Cindy smiled. "The tech caught her in a position that left no doubt. Dr. Valance was in the room too. She confirmed it."

"Why didn't you call me to come home and drive you?"

"Because it would have taken twice as long."

Ray sat on the end of the bed. "How do you feel now?" he asked.

"Happy, relieved, excited, scared, thankful, worried—how many emotions can a woman simultaneously experience?"

"My brain would explode."

Cindy touched her abdomen. "All I want is for our daughter to keep getting bigger and bigger."

Ray stayed with Cindy for another thirty minutes before the nurse told them it was fine to leave.

"I can drive," Cindy said when they reached the parking lot.

"No!" Ray shot back.

"How are we going to get my car home?"

"I think I can find someone to help."

Cindy got in the passenger seat and leaned back. "While you're chauffeuring me around, I'd like you to take a detour. It's not too far out of the way."

"Are you sure that's a good—"

"Arguing with me causes so much stress," Cindy replied, closing her eyes for a moment.

"Okay, okay. You win."

Cindy smiled. "Just hearing those words from your lips makes me feel better."

Ray followed Cindy's directions across town and into an older residential neighborhood of larger homes. When she told him to turn onto Willow Oak Lane, he pulled into the short cul-de-sac and stopped.

"If we're on a secret house hunt, there aren't any For Sale signs on this street."

Cindy reached over and touched his hand. "Last week I asked the Realtor to contact the bank about your mother's house."

"Even as a foreclosure it would be way over our price range." Ray paused. "And I'm not sure I'd want to live there even if we could."

"Why not? It has a nice floor plan and a great yard for Billy and the new baby. And the possibility of bringing the flower beds back to life makes me want to get my hands dirty. Think about how thrilled your mother would be."

Instead of answering, Ray drove slowly forward until they were directly in front of the house. Cindy told him the price range the real estate agent thought might be acceptable to the bank.

"That's way less than I would have thought," Ray admitted, "but it's still above our range."

"I could sell my hair," Cindy said, running her fingers through her closely cut blond locks.

Ray smiled. "I love your hair, but you're no Rapunzel."

"Then how about this. I floated the idea of a lease purchase to the Realtor and told her how much we could pay in rent with part of it going to the purchase price if we could close within two years. She thinks the bank might go for it."

"What were the figures?"

When Cindy told him, Ray's eyes widened. "If the bank would consider that—"

"You'd agree?"

"Maybe. Let's get you home before I need to go to the doctor and be treated for shock."

———

"I've learned a lot from you," Roxy said to Mr. Caldweller as she signed the severance agreement.

"There is more than one way to interpret that."

"Yes, and I'll leave it to you to decide which one to choose."

Caldweller shook his head. "I didn't want to lose you," he said. "You're as tough and smart as any associate, male or female, I've worked with. It takes much more than brains to be a successful litigator, and you have the intangibles to succeed no matter where you go."

Roxy was surprised that she didn't feel any emotion as her boss spoke honestly and without a manipulative agenda.

"Would you give me a good professional reference in the future?" she asked.

Caldweller hesitated and Roxy knew it was due to concern that he might get into trouble for saying something nice about her. The older lawyer's fear was his own burden, but it had a profound impact on Roxy. If a senior partner at the firm couldn't feel secure, why would Roxy want to voluntarily choose to live in the same gilded cage?

"That's okay," she said before he responded. "I don't want to put you in an awkward position. If I'm as good as you say, I should be all right."

Caldweller stood. "You know the drill," he said.

"I'll log off my computer, pack up my personal belongings, and leave immediately."

"I'm not going to send the office manager back to watch you."

When an employee left abruptly, someone normally made sure they didn't engage in an act of vengeful sabotage on the way out the door.

"Can I make a copy of the severance agreement before my copier key is canceled?" Roxy asked.

"I'll do it for you," Caldweller said, holding out his hand.

"My key is already revoked?"

"Yes."

Roxy handed him the document. When Caldweller left he seemed a little bit older, his shoulders slightly more stooped. It was a sad sight.

Roxy got a couple of empty boxes from the supply room. When

she returned to her office, a copy of the severance agreement lay on her desk. She loaded up the boxes with her diplomas, a few photos, random personal items, and a half-empty bag of caramels. There wasn't much physical evidence from her stay; the main takeaway was the invaluable knowledge and experience gained from surviving in a merciless legal boot camp.

Roxy held her head high and looked straight ahead as she carried the boxes from the office. She didn't encounter anyone on the way to the elevators. Her former coworkers had their noses firmly planted on the Frank and Donaldson grindstone. The receptionist was on the phone and didn't pay any attention to her departure. As far as she knew, Roxy was simply tidying up her office. Roxy stood alone in the middle of the elevator and watched the doors close on what had been the center of her life.

———

Corbin got off the phone with Ray, leaned back in his chair, and thought about Billy having a little sister. It was hard to imagine a female version of Billy with his strong, solid build. Then a memory of Roxy as a skinny, rambunctious three-year-old popped into his head. Maybe a female prototype for Ray and Cindy's baby already existed; however, the world wasn't ready for a duplicate Roxy. Hopefully the melding of Ray and Cindy would yield a mellower version.

Thinking about Roxy, Corbin knew he owed his daughter an apology. Before he could talk himself out of making the call, he dialed her number. Not surprisingly, given her demanding schedule at work, she didn't answer, and he left a brief voice mail simply asking her to call him back. He then phoned Ray.

"Hey, I had another thought," he said. "Since Cindy should be taking it easy, why don't I pick up Billy as soon as he gets home from school and take him fishing for a few hours?"

Ray checked with Cindy and then gave Corbin the okay.

"Tell him we'll pick out the worms together," Corbin said.

———

Roxy waited for Peter to arrive at the restaurant. He was a few minutes late, and she assured him in a text message there was no need to hurry. She watched the restaurant workers scurrying about. There was now a big difference between them and her. They had a job; she didn't.

Roxy had never been fired from a job and wasn't sure how she ought to feel. The tears that had been lurking in vast secret reservoirs behind her eyelids stayed safely contained. She wasn't sure what would happen when Peter arrived. He walked rapidly through the door, saw her, and a huge smile creased his face.

And the tears sloshed over the brink of the dam.

Roxy took out a tissue and dabbed her eyes. Peter came over and gave her a hug and quick kiss.

"What's wrong?" he asked.

"It's a mix of wrong and right," Roxy replied. "Sit down. I need a sip of water."

An anxious look in his eye, Peter settled in across from her at a table for two. "Drink up and talk," he said.

Roxy sipped the water and felt more composed. "What do you want first? The wrong or the right?"

Peter hesitated. "The right."

"Good. That's shorter." Roxy smiled. "When you walked through the door and saw me, the look of love on your face made me tear up for a second."

"So the good made you sad?"

Roxy rolled her eyes.

"Okay," Peter said. "That probably ruined the mood, which goes to show that I'm an ordinary guy discovering what it's like to hang out with a beautiful, sensitive woman."

"Your mood meter is fine," Roxy replied. "Do you want to know what's wrong?"

"Does it have to do with me?"

"Mostly me, but it affects us."

"All right," Peter said. "I'm listening."

Roxy told him about losing her job. She remained surprisingly dispassionate. No tears appeared.

Peter listened until she finished. "Is that all?" he asked.

"Yes, although I'm sure I left out a few details."

Peter nodded his head. "So where's the bad news?"

"Even though they called it a severance agreement, I was fired," Roxy replied patiently.

"Based on everything I know about you and the job at the law firm, I think this is not only good news, it's great news. With all the changes taking place in your personal life, it was only a matter of time before your basic incompatibility with the firm's culture made it impossible for you to keep working there. Better to leave now than try to extricate yourself after you've been locked into partnership status."

Roxy's mouth dropped open. "How long have you believed this?"

"Uh, I'm not sure. It took a ton of willpower not to warn you about considering an equity offer when it first came up, but I was worried you'd think I was jealous of your success or trying to control you."

Roxy started to disagree, then realized he was right. "Thanks," she said. "If you'd said something then I wouldn't have listened."

"I'd rather provide confirmation than direction."

The waitress brought their entrées, a pair of salads featuring grilled salmon.

"Do you think it's time you started being more open with me about what you think?" she asked.

Peter swallowed his first bite. "I can do that."

He took another bite. Roxy waited, her salad untouched.

"Go ahead," she said.

"I am." Peter pointed at the salad with his fork. "They cook this salmon on a charred wooden plank. It's delicious."

"I mean talk to me about my life."

"Okay. I think that your being between jobs will be a great chance to settle things as much as you can with your family. It's weird, but sometimes I feel your father is hanging around us even though I know he's eighty miles away."

Roxy bristled but immediately reminded herself she'd asked him to be honest with her. "What do you think I should do?"

"First, eat your salad. Then we'll talk. For once you don't have to rush back to work, and I'd rather be here with you than anyplace else on earth."

FORTY-NINE

C orbin and Billy pushed away from the shore of Hackburn's Lake. The cooler at their feet contained a Styrofoam container of fresh worms for the bream to bite and bottled waters for the two fishermen to drink.

"Before I go after any bream, I want to see if any bass are biting," Billy said.

"Sure," Corbin said as he fiddled with the boat motor. "But if you want big bass, Braswell's Pond is the place to go."

Corbin pulled the cord, and the motor sputtered to life. He quickly steered the boat to a weedy part of the lake where bass occasionally hung out and let the boat drift quietly into position.

"What lure do you want to use?" he asked Billy.

"A plastic worm."

Corbin glanced up at the sky. It was cloudy, and the water was murky. "We'd better use a darker color, maybe the purple one. I'll put it on a hook so—"

"Can I try?" Billy asked.

Correctly rigging a plastic worm on a hook so that it performed properly in the water wasn't easy. It wasn't just a matter of piercing the artificial body and tossing it overboard. It required a special hook that enabled the fake worm to duplicate a real worm's underwater movements.

But Corbin didn't argue. He handed Billy a worm and a hook, then watched. The boy held the hook correctly, maneuvered the worm onto it, then held the finished product up in the air.

"What do you think?" he asked.

"That if I were a bass, I wouldn't look any further for an early supper."

Billy knew two different knots to attach a lure to his monofilament fishing line. Corbin silently approved the boy's choice.

"Where should I cast it?" Billy asked him.

Corbin pointed to a spot past the reedy area. "See if you can get it in there, let it sink, then work it across in front of the brush."

On his first cast Billy sent it too long and started to quickly reel it in for another.

"No, give that one a chance," Corbin said. "Use it to practice your retrieve."

Bass fishing wasn't passive. The lures had to be continually cast out and brought back to the boat.

"Try to picture what the worm is doing underneath the water," Corbin said. "And then imagine a big bass pouncing on it like a lion on its prey."

No bass pounced on Billy's first cast and retrieve. Nor the second, third, or several others. Corbin was pleased that Billy didn't complain.

"Ready to move to another spot?" he asked.

"No, I want to try to the right. I thought I saw a swirl over there a minute ago."

Corbin moved so he wouldn't be in the way. Even so, Billy's line shot close to his left ear.

"Careful," Corbin said.

"Sorry, Pops," Billy replied with a grin. "I don't want to catch you."

The line hit the water, and Billy let it sink before beginning his retrieve. Suddenly a fish hit so hard that the force jerked the rod out of Billy's hand. Corbin tried to grab it as it skidded across the bottom of the boat past his feet. His hand ended up caught in the space between the reel and the line, causing the rig to dangle on his wrist. Billy jumped up, and the boat tipped precariously to one side.

"Sit down!" Corbin roared.

Wide-eyed, Billy plopped into the bottom of the boat. Corbin dislodged his wrist from the rod, which was bent double by the pressure from the fish. As soon as his wrist was free, the line skimmed out as the fish dominated the drag on the reel. Corbin tightened the drag slightly, but it kept going out.

"Get beside me," he said to Billy.

The boy carefully moved onto the seat right next to Corbin, who handed him the rod.

"It's all yours. You've hooked him good or we'd have lost him already."

As Billy fought the fish, Corbin tried to remember the weight limit of the line on the reel. It would be a shame if the line snapped because it wasn't strong enough.

"Who do you think it is?" Billy asked, pulling back on the rod and managing to turn the reel a few times as the fish rested.

"I don't know," Corbin replied. "It fights like General Lee."

General Lee was a legendary bass Corbin caught several times in Braswell's Pond before Billy was born. Long since dead, the fish was the standard by which he evaluated all big-time bass. After fifteen minutes passed, the fight settled into a stalemate.

Corbin kept a close eye on Billy's hands and arms to see if he showed any signs of tiring. "How are you doing?" he asked.

"If you're asking me to give you the rod, I don't want to," Billy replied.

Corbin laughed. "All right. I'll keep my mouth shut."

Finally the fish began to weaken. Billy cranked on the reel, slowly pulling the fish toward the side of the boat. Corbin reached for the landing net and held it over the spot where he guessed the fish would surface. When it did he leaned over and scooped it up in the net, which sagged from the size and weight of the bass. It was a monster fish. Corbin was about to swear but caught himself. The hook had pierced the corner of the fish's mouth. The plastic worm was gone.

"Hand me the tape measure," he said to Billy, who'd already opened the tackle box.

"Here's the tape and the scale."

"Hold the net."

Billy put his hands around the pole for the landing net. Corbin could tell it took all the boy's strength to keep it steady. Corbin held up the fish so he could measure and weigh it. Multiple scars received from a long life were visible on its body.

"Ten pounds, seven ounces," Corbin announced. "And he's fifteen and a half inches around the middle."

The fish had a gaping maw of a mouth. It was so large Billy could put his fist inside it. He then gently touched the torn place where he hooked the fish.

"That will heal up in no time," Corbin said. "And he'll be mad and hungry for a week."

"What's his name?" Billy asked.

"We've never caught this fish before, so you get to name him."

Billy thought for a moment. "Do you think he's the biggest, best fish in the lake?" he asked.

"No doubt."

"Okay," Billy replied. "I want to call him Pops."

Corbin and Billy both held the fish as they released it back into the water. After fanning its gills for a few seconds, it slowly swam off.

An hour and a half later, Corbin listened to Billy excitedly tell Ray the fish story while they sat at the kitchen table. Cindy was resting in the bedroom.

"Why did you want to call him Pops?" Ray asked when the boy finished.

"When I saw him, it seemed like that was his name." Billy shrugged. "I couldn't think of anything else."

"You should have seen him," Corbin added. "He was a beast. He had scars from suckers, parasites, maybe even a boat motor."

"That explains it," Ray said. "You and that fish sound like twins."

———

Roxy felt like she was drifting in space, untethered to anything stable. She drove home from lunch and stared at the four walls of her townhome. The sense of security she felt in Peter's presence evaporated as the distance between them increased.

Unable to stay cooped up inside, she put on her exercise clothes and went out for a second run. This time she didn't push herself for training purposes, but set an easy pace that she could maintain as long as she wanted. She ventured beyond her usual routes into new territory and tried to enjoy the new sights. As she cooled down in the kitchen, her phone vibrated. It was an unknown number.

"Ms. Gage?" a male voice asked. "This is Dr. Willard Sellers."

"You need to call my brother—" Roxy began.

The chemist interrupted her. "No, I tried to reach you at the law firm a few minutes ago and found out you're no longer employed there. I hope this doesn't have anything to do with the conversation I had yesterday with Mr. Daughbert. Initially it wasn't clear why he was contacting me, but when I connected the dots, I realized the two of you were acting at cross-purposes in the Colfax Fertilizer matter."

"That's a mild way of putting it."

"So there's a direct connection between your leaving the firm and Mr. Daughbert's contact with me?"

Roxy couldn't see any need to deny the basic facts.

"Yes, but it's not your fault. I stepped out of bounds. It was inadvertent but that didn't change the result." Roxy hit on an apt analogy. "It was like a chemical reaction that can't be stopped once it starts."

"I'm very sorry this happened."

"And I appreciate that, but it may work out for the best. I'm just not sure about my next step."

"Of course." The chemist was silent for a moment. "I told Mr. Daughbert I wasn't in a position to render an opinion for his client."

"And he wasn't happy about it."

"He was somewhat abrupt."

Roxy didn't want to prolong a conversation that was becoming more painful by the second. "Thanks again for calling," she said. "It was very thoughtful."

"If I can ever be of assistance in the future, don't hesitate to contact me."

The call ended, and Roxy stared at her phone. She would never forget the unexpected role Dr. Willard Sellers played in her life.

———

Sunday morning Corbin attended the service at the Hopewell church. He sat with Jimmy and his family in the middle section of the sanctuary. It was the first time since his wedding day that

Corbin had walked through the doors of a church with a sense of positive anticipation. He noticed a few sideways glances in his direction as they settled into their seats.

"Do people suspect I'm here because of AA?" he asked in a low voice.

"If they do, it's not because I told them. Would it matter?"

"Maybe."

"Well, it's probably because you're a new face. Church folks are like cows in a pasture. Anyone unfamiliar arouses their curiosity."

Corbin chuckled and relaxed. With his guard down, he was surprised how much he enjoyed the service, and mentioned it to Jimmy as they stood to leave.

"Yeah, church is way better when you're not mad at God," Jimmy said. "And it gets even better when you no longer believe he's mad at you."

"That makes sense."

"Care to join us for lunch?" Jimmy continued.

"No, thanks. I'm going to swing by and see my son and his family. They'll be interested to find out where I've been this morning."

"Good choice."

———

Cindy stayed home from church. Ray and Billy were leaving the sanctuary when Corbin called.

"Can I pick up lunch and bring it to the house?" he asked.

"Dad?" Ray responded. "Where are you?"

"In town. Would you like some fried chicken from the Chicken Box?"

Billy, who was standing close enough to hear the conversation, began to vigorously nod his head. "I want three legs, Pops," he said in a loud voice. "And they have those potato things with orange stuff on them."

"Billy is asking for three drumsticks and an order of potato wedges with the Cajun seasoning," Ray relayed. "But we need some healthy sides too."

"Everything they serve is heart healthy," Corbin replied.

Ray was puzzled by his father's Sunday morning exuberance. He stepped a few feet away from Billy. "Don't get mad," he said in a low voice, "but have you been drinking?"

"No. I went to church with my AA sponsor and really enjoyed it."

Ray almost dropped the phone. "Okay, grab some chicken and come over," he said. "But don't rush. I need to give Cindy a few minutes' notice. Oh, the broccoli casserole at the Chicken Box is good and so are the collard greens. You might also see if they have okra and tomatoes."

"I don't like okra," interjected Billy, who'd inched closer. "It's slimy."

Ray was quiet during the short ride to the house. Several people at church had given him the cold shoulder, and the only explanation could be ongoing animosity caused by the newspaper article about the Colfax case.

Billy broke the silence. "Pops has been different since he banged his head and had to go to the hospital," the boy said.

"How so?" Ray asked.

Billy didn't immediately respond. Having brought up the subject, he now seemed at a loss for words. "I don't know," he said. "Just different."

"Good different or bad?"

"Good," Billy said. "I mean, Pops and I get along great, but sometimes you and Mama and Aunt Roxy act mad at him. But he's trying to be nicer, and I think you should be nice to him too."

"Okay," Ray replied. "I'll do better at lunch."

Cindy's eyes widened when Ray told her Corbin was on his way to eat lunch with them after attending church. "Where did he go?" she asked.

"I didn't ask, but it may have been Hopewell. That's where one of his AA meetings is held."

While Cindy got dressed, Ray and Billy straightened up the house. It was a pointless exercise, since his father wouldn't notice, but Ray knew Cindy cared.

As soon as Corbin came through the front door, the aroma of freshly fried chicken permeated the atmosphere. Billy followed his grandfather into the kitchen like a starving puppy. They unloaded the dinner, spread it out on the kitchen table, and sat down.

"Ray says you went to church this morning," Cindy said to Corbin.

"At Hopewell, and I plan on going back."

"Let's pray and eat," Ray said.

"Pops, will you pray?" Billy asked.

Everyone looked at Corbin, who closed his eyes and bowed his head. "God, thank you for this food and for my family. I really mean it. Amen."

By the time Ray finished eating a single chicken breast, Billy had deposited three pristine chicken leg bones on his plate and polished off most of the potato wedges.

"This is the best food I've eaten in a long time," the boy said, licking his fingers.

Cindy raised her eyebrows. "Use a napkin, and if all it takes to make you happy is fried chicken, maybe your father can bring it home more often."

FIFTY

R ay had cleared the table and was preparing to slice a water-melon when his phone on the kitchen table vibrated. Cindy picked it up.

"It's Roxy," she said.

"Answer it while I wash my hands," he replied.

"We just finished lunch," Cindy said to Roxy. "Your father is here too." She listened for a moment, then handed the phone to Ray.

"Put me on speakerphone," Roxy said. "That way I won't have to repeat myself."

Ray placed the phone in the middle of the kitchen table. "Billy is here too. Is that okay?"

"Sure, but I doubt he'll be interested in my news."

Billy gave Cindy a questioning look. She pointed in the direction of his room, and he left.

"Go ahead," Ray said. "We're here."

"I had to resign my job," Roxy began. "The terms of my sever-ance agreement are confidential, but this is what happened."

While Roxy talked, Ray kept glancing at Corbin, who looked defeated but not defiant.

"That's it," Roxy said when she finished. "And Peter and I are going to come up to Alto next weekend."

"Why?" Ray asked.

Roxy ignored his question. "I'll let you know our schedule. Have you made any progress in lining up another expert?"

Ray thought about Dr. Kimberly Clayton. "Maybe. And you need to send us a bill for the amount you paid Dr. Sellers."

"We'll discuss that later," Roxy said. "I gotta go."

"I'm sorry about your job," Corbin began. "If I'd known this was going to—"

"She already hung up," Ray said, picking up his phone. He glanced at Cindy, who was staring hard at Corbin.

"Are you going to offer Roxy a job?" she asked.

"What?" Corbin's head jerked back. "There's no way she would want to join us. I mean—"

"She's too good to work with you and Ray?"

"I don't think that's why she's coming up next weekend," Ray said, hoping to diffuse the tension. "It's not a job interview."

Cindy went into the kitchen. With the lighthearted mood of the dinner squashed, Corbin left a few minutes later. After he was gone, Cindy propped her feet up on the sofa in the living room while Ray finished cleaning up the kitchen.

"Do you feel like this Colfax case is cursed?" Cindy asked when he joined her. "It cost you a job you've wanted for over two years, and now it's ruined Roxy's career. Who knows how many hours she's slaved at that law firm for a chance to make partner."

"She seemed pretty calm about it. I've heard her more upset about much less important stuff."

"Maybe something good will come from all the pain we've been through trying to help those boys." Cindy sighed. "It's cost our entire family a lot too."

Even though Ray was going to present the argument against Colfax's motion to dismiss the complaint, Corbin would attend the hearing. He put on his best blue suit, straightened his tie, and ran his finger over his face and neck to make sure he'd dispatched any remaining gray stubble. When he went into the kitchen to brew some coffee, he had a sudden strong urge to have a shot of liquor. He opened the cabinet door and surveyed the different kinds of whiskey. Each one had its own unique flavor profile. One of his favorites was a ten-year-old blend that was so smooth it made moonshine taste like turpentine. He touched the bottle then slammed the cabinet door so hard he almost hit his fingers.

Arriving at the office Corbin smelled coffee as soon as he came through the rear door.

"Good morning," Ray said. "Why are you decked out in your best suit? Have you decided to argue the motion?"

"No, but I want to be there."

"I thought you didn't want to antagonize Judge Perry."

"I know I said that, but if I don't go, I'll pester you about exactly what happened."

"It's fine with me. I came in early to fine-tune my argument."

"Let me hear it."

Corbin went into Ray's office. It wasn't a complicated issue, and Ray did an excellent job of explaining why it was legally incorrect for the judge to throw out the case at this early stage in the proceedings.

"What are the odds the lawyer from Roxy's firm will show up?" Ray asked when he finished.

"Less than 10 percent," Corbin replied. "They'll save him for the big stuff: depositions, motion for summary judgment, and trial."

"Trial? I'm confident about today, but I have serious doubts that we'll make it to a jury."

"Don't go in with a defeatist attitude. Nate Stamper and Judge Perry will smell your fear."

"That should help me relax," Ray said, smiling. "And I think the chance of you letting me do all the talking in court this morning is less than 1 percent."

Ten minutes before the hearing they walked across the street to the courthouse. Corbin felt more nervous than if he were the one planning to argue the case. They went to Judge Perry's chambers.

"He's going to hear the motion in the courtroom," the judge's secretary told them.

"Why?" Ray asked. "There aren't going to be any witnesses."

"All I know is that's what he told me to tell the lawyers."

Corbin looked at Ray and shrugged. He waited until they were alone in the hallway to speak. "You know what to say if Nate tries to put on any evidence."

"Yes, yes. He can't turn it into a motion for summary judgment without prior notice that gives us the opportunity to present testimony and affidavits of our own."

They entered the courtroom. Nate Stamper was already at the table used by the defense counsel in civil cases. He turned around and saw them but didn't acknowledge their presence. Another man was beside him.

And it wasn't Guy Hathaway from Colfax.

"Who's that with Nate?" Ray whispered as they walked down the aisle.

Corbin shrugged. "Probably somebody from Colfax's corporate headquarters."

They reached the wooden bar and crossed into the open area before the bench.

"Good morning, Nate," Ray said.

Nate shook Ray's hand. Corbin held back.

"This is Ted Daughbert," Nate said. "You received a notice that his firm is going to be co-counsel in the case."

Corbin narrowed his gaze as he studied the man responsible for Roxy's termination from Frank and Donaldson. Daughbert shook Ray's hand.

"And I take it this is the lawyer Gage the elder?" Daughbert said, moving closer to Corbin. "It's quite an accomplishment, convincing two of your children to follow in your steps."

"You know Roxanne?" Nate interjected in surprise.

"We met once," Daughbert replied. "She used to work for our firm."

"When did she leave?" Nate asked.

"Recently," Daughbert said, keeping his eyes fixed on Corbin.

Daughbert looked physically fit, but Corbin was confident a well-placed blow from his meaty fist to the younger lawyer's chin would render him unconscious.

The judge and a court reporter entered the courtroom. Corbin sat down, and Ray organized his paperwork. While the court reporter set up her machine, Judge Perry ignored the lawyers and flipped through the file.

"I'm ready," the court reporter said.

"Kilpatrick et al and Watson et al v. Colfax Fertilizer Company," the judge said. "This is the hearing on defendant's motion to dismiss the complaint. Proceed for the defendant."

Nate Stamper remained seated as Daughbert stood and introduced himself to the judge. Stone-faced, Corbin watched and listened.

"Welcome to Rusk County, Mr. Daughbert," Judge Perry said. "Go ahead."

"Thank you, Your Honor."

Daughbert spoke without notes. He had a clear voice and relaxed approach. It was a style Corbin knew worked well with both judges and jurors, who could quickly be turned off by attorney arrogance or bombast. However, the law wasn't on Daughbert's side, and the defense lawyer didn't come up with any deceptively creative spin in support of the motion. Other than not wanting to miss an opportunity to bill his new client, it didn't make sense why he'd made the trip to Alto.

"Even forecasting the evidence in the light most favorable to the plaintiffs, there isn't a sufficient recitation of provable facts to establish proximate cause for the damages alleged, and the complaint should therefore be dismissed."

Daughbert sat down, and Corbin breathed easier. The out-of-town lawyer's argument was a trial court version of the big bad wolf's threats against the brick cottage.

"I'll respond on behalf of the plaintiffs," Ray said as he stood to his feet.

Ray left his notes on the corner of the table in case he needed them and also spoke extemporaneously. Several sentences into his argument, he cited three appellate court decisions that provided judicial precedent to deny the motion. One of the cases involved a toxic tort, a nice touch.

"I'm familiar with the Vicenza case," the judge interrupted when Ray mentioned the tort case. "What happened when it was remanded to the trial court?"

"I don't know," Ray replied. "Its relevance this morning is the Court of Appeals ruling on the standard to follow in considering a motion to dismiss the complaint in a case like this one."

"Your Honor, I know what happened," Daughbert said.

"Please tell Mr. Gage," the judge replied.

Daughbert turned toward Ray. Corbin caught a glint of malice in the defense lawyer's eyes.

"A subsequent motion for summary judgment was granted based on affidavit testimony and affirmed on appeal."

Ray turned to Judge Perry.

"Which is different from the procedural posture of our case today," he said. "There aren't any affidavits in the record from either side."

Ray waited for a moment, and when Judge Perry didn't respond he continued his argument without seeming to be flustered. He continued to score points.

He concluded by saying, "Based on the consistent interpretation of the rules by the courts since the adoption of the Civil Practice Act, we respectfully ask you to deny the motion so that discovery can begin."

Corbin felt proud. Ray had held his own with Daughbert from a presentation standpoint, and he'd left no doubt about the status of the law in Georgia. Still, Corbin needed to hear the right words from the judge's lips.

"Gentlemen," the judge said, "there's no need for me to take this under advisement or request supplemental briefs. I'm ready to rule."

Corbin felt the tightness in his chest relax. Judge Perry glanced at Corbin and Ray, then looked at Daughbert and Stamper.

"I'm going to grant the motion to dismiss the complaint. Counsel for the defendant will prepare a proposed order."

Corbin was on his feet.

"There's no need for me to hear from you, Mr. Gage," Judge Perry said icily.

"We request detailed findings and conclusions of law in your order," Corbin sputtered.

"That's not necessary," the judge said in the direction of the defense lawyers. "Keep it simple."

Judge Perry left the bench. Red-faced, Corbin turned to Ray, who raised his finger to his lips. But Corbin wasn't going to be muzzled. He faced Daughbert and Nate Stamper.

"You know he's wrong!"

"Whatever your personal opinion, the judge made his ruling," Daughbert replied evenly. "And that's the law of the case."

"It won't be after the Court of Appeals gets hold of it!"

Nate stepped closer to Corbin and Ray and spoke in a conciliatory tone of voice. "Corbin, we know you have the right to appeal. We're just doing our job."

Corbin wasn't going to back down. "Which is going to delay treatment for two boys who may die," he said. "And if they do, it's going to be on your head! And yours!" He gestured at Daughbert.

"Come on," Ray said, touching his father on the arm. "Let's go."

Corbin shrugged off the contact. Ray left him and began walking up the aisle. After a final glare at the two defense lawyers, Corbin followed him.

FIFTY-ONE

"If I thought I could get away with it, I would have punched Daughbert," Corbin said to Ray as they crossed the street in front of the courthouse. "He needed to be knocked all the way back to wherever he came from."

"That would have been a mistake on a lot of levels, especially on the heels of your DUI," Ray replied, trying to keep his voice calm.

"Where's your passion?" Corbin challenged him. "Don't you care what just happened?"

Ray stopped on the sidewalk in front of the office and faced his father. "Of course I care. But talking like a madman isn't going to change anything or make me feel better. If it helps you, go ahead and vent. But don't expect me to jump in the mud pit with you. We're different."

Corbin grunted and pushed past Ray into the office.

Ray held back and didn't follow for a few moments.

"What happened?" Janelle asked him with an apprehensive glance at Corbin's office. "He stormed in like a tornado and slammed the door."

"The judge dismissed the case."

"I can't say I'm surprised." Janelle shook her head. "All of my friends have been giving me a hard time ever since the newspaper story. The whole town is against us."

"Including Judge Perry." Ray shrugged. "If there's a follow-up article, it will be a huge political boost for him. No one will have the nerve to run against him when he comes up for reelection next year."

"Will you file an appeal?"

"Sure, but what good is that going to do the clients? The Court of Appeals won't consider the case or issue a decision for at least nine months to a year. At that point the boys will either be in remission or dead. And a death claim for a minor child may have sympathy value, but it would be tough to justify the economic basis for a big verdict, especially with a judge who is going to fight us as hard as the other side. He could grant their motions and deny ours so many times that the case could bounce back and forth with the Court of Appeals like a tennis ball and drag on for years and years before we finally get in front of a jury."

The forecast of the future was discouraging.

"If there's going to be an article in the newspaper, someone should notify the clients. You don't want them reading about it first."

"He should do it." Ray gestured toward Corbin's door. "He's had much more interaction with them than I have. But first he needs to calm down. He was ready to punch the defense lawyer from Roxy's old firm."

Ray told Janelle about Roxy losing her job.

"Do you think she might come to work here too?" Janelle asked, her eyes wide. "There's no way I can work for three lawyers."

"No, she'll probably try to find a spot with another firm in Atlanta."

Ray went into his office and closed the door. He considered calling Cindy to break the bad news to her, but it didn't seem right to drag her down. In front of him on his desk was a list of experts to interview. He pushed it to the side. That task had gone from the top of his list to the bottom. He forced himself to work on another case in order to take his mind off their courtroom fiasco. After an hour passed, it was time to suggest that Corbin contact the Kilpatrick family and Millie Watson.

"Have you heard anything from him?" he asked Janelle.

"No, all his calls have gone to voice mail."

Ray stepped across the reception area and knocked on the door. There wasn't an answer. He entered and found Corbin lying on the floor beside his desk with his hands folded across his chest.

"Dad!" Ray called out in alarm.

Corbin opened his eyes and turned his head. "Yes?"

"Why are you on the floor?"

"Because I feel like I've been knocked out. I wanted a drink but decided to lie down instead."

Ray wasn't following the logic of his father's thought process; however, resisting the urge to drown his disappointment in alcohol was a positive step. He held out his hand and helped him to his feet. Corbin pushed his hair off his forehead and sat down behind his desk.

"We got bushwhacked by politics and public opinion," he said.

"That's what I told Janelle. And we need to talk with the clients before they find out about it in the newspaper."

Corbin let out a low groan.

Ray still wasn't sure his father's mind was functioning properly. "Do you think you should go to the doctor?" he asked.

"I should, but not today." Corbin fumbled through some slips of paper on his desk and plucked one out. "Here's Millie Watson's number," he said with sigh. "I'll call her and Branson. What do you think I should tell them?"

Ray thought about the long road he knew lay ahead if they continued the litigation. The end of the road was the edge of a cliff.

"We both know where this is heading," he said.

Corbin put his head in his hands. It was a simple act of defeat and resignation that made Ray sad. He'd rather see his father fighting mad than reduced to surrender. He held out his hand.

"Let me make the calls," he said. "I'll lay it out for them. Appeal is an option, but as a practical matter nothing is going to happen soon, perhaps ever."

"We could—" Corbin started, then stopped. "No, you're right. I wanted to take one last swing for the fences in a case that really mattered."

"I know you did."

Ray took the slip from Corbin's hand. When he did he noticed a slight tremor. "And I respect you for it," he added.

———

Roxy woke up Monday morning and stretched like a contented cat when she realized she wouldn't have to face Mr. Caldweller. There was lightness in her soul during her morning run. Later she sat with her legs crossed in front of her laptop as she studied the profiles of firms on her short list of future employers. Many firms don't publicize an opening, but she knew they would create a position to land a lawyer they believed could come in and immediately contribute. Her phone vibrated.

"Hello," she said.

"Ms. Gage, this is Willard Sellers. Do you have a few minutes to talk?"

"Yes, I'm at home this morning."

"Once again, I'm sorry about your job. I know you told me to contact your brother directly about the water samples he sent me, but I did some more tests and found something I wanted to discuss with you first."

"What?" Roxy uncrossed her legs and sat up straighter.

"I ran a different array of tests and discovered a very high level of perchloroethylene, or PERC."

"The chemical used in dry cleaning?"

"Yes, but that's not its only commercial application. It's also used to degrease and clean machinery."

Roxy's mind was racing. "The water you tested came from wells that aren't near any dry cleaning establishments. Is there a possibility the fertilizer company used PERC on its machinery and didn't dispose of it safely?"

"That's what I thought. PERC is a known carcinogen; however, limited concentrated use to clean machinery probably wouldn't produce the type of long-term contamination needed to provide a causal connection with the development of non-Hodgkin's lymphoma."

"Oh." Roxy's excitement evaporated.

"But the levels in the wells present an immediate public health risk on multiple levels, and the people in the area should be warned and corrective action taken."

"Of course."

"I'd like to forward you the data."

Roxy hesitated. "You'd better send the information directly to my brother. I need to stay out of the loop."

"Fine, but I knew you'd appreciate the issue and wanted to give you a heads-up."

The call ended. Roxy stared at her computer screen, but she could no longer stay focused on the phony smiles of the lawyers who worked at a boutique litigation firm in Buckhead.

———

Corbin left the office for the noon AA meeting at the Serenity Center. He sat glumly during the discussion of the Twelve Traditions that provided guidelines for governance of AA groups. The first tradition emphasized the primacy of common welfare and unity. At least Corbin felt safe from community condemnation sitting in the circle.

When the meeting ended, Jimmy came over to him. "Are you fighting an urge to drink?" he asked.

"I did earlier and resisted, but if you're picking up on something, it has to do with pressures at work."

"Okay, just remember the Twelve Steps aren't only a strategy to stay sober."

Someone called Jimmy over, leaving Corbin to ponder his sponsor's words as he returned to the office.

"Come here!" Ray said when he saw him. "I've got to show you something."

They went into the conference room where papers were spread out on the table.

"This came in from Roxy's chemist."

"What is it?"

"The results of more tests on the water samples. He's found something worse than 2,4-D."

Corbin listened while Ray gave him a crash course on PERC.

"Would it cause non-Hodgkin's lymphoma?" Corbin asked when Ray paused.

"Dr. Sellers can't say. We don't know how long it's been in the groundwater."

"We can ask Tommy Kilpatrick to check with the guy who still works at Colfax in product development. He's the one who gave us the material safety data sheets. Maybe he can find out about duration."

"Let's do it."

Corbin retrieved the file he needed from his office and returned to the conference room. He picked up the phone, then stopped.

"Does Tommy know what the judge did this morning?"

"No, this came in shortly after you left the office, and I've been reading the research papers Dr. Sellers recommended. Millie Watson doesn't know about the dismissal either."

Corbin phoned Tommy and put the call on speakerphone so Ray could listen. Before Corbin could say anything, Tommy spoke.

"I'm glad you called," he said. "We just found out that Mitchell has been accepted for the trial program with the new chemo meds at Egleston. The big question is whether our insurance company is going to authorize it."

Corbin and Ray looked at each other across the table.

"That's great," Corbin replied. "But I need to let you know we had an unexpected setback this morning in court. It might be reported in the newspaper, and I wanted you to hear the truth from me."

It was one of the tougher messages Corbin had delivered to a client in a long time.

"But it's not all bad," he said, then explained the new findings from Dr. Sellers. "Do you think Carl can find out when and how often they've used cleaning solvent on the machinery during the past few months?"

"I don't know." Tommy spoke slowly. "He took a big risk getting me the stickers from the barrels. And even if he does this, will it change the judge's opinion?"

"Not immediately," Corbin replied. "But Ray and I are working on a way to leverage this into the case."

"Okay," Tommy replied. "I'll see what I can do. Have you talked to Millie?"

"No."

"This is going to hit her hard. Lance is getting out of jail today, and she's gone to pick him up. We've invited them over for supper to celebrate."

"I'll wait to call her," Corbin said. "But don't hold off on contacting Carl." He replaced the phone in its cradle.

"What's our strategy to leverage the new information?" Ray asked.

"You were so excited when I got here, I figured you'd already come up with a plan."

———

An hour later Ray was putting the finishing touches on a memo organizing Dr. Sellers's findings when Corbin burst into his office.

"Carl says they cleaned the entire line at plant 4 with some type of potent solvent within the past two months. A month before that they did the same thing at plant 3."

"Does he know what they did with the cleaning residue when they finished?" Ray asked.

"They dumped it down a drain that leads to the creek at the rear of the company property. Carl says those drains are supposed to be for nontoxic discharge like gray water from sinks or showers."

"If that's the time frame, it happened after the state EPA cited Colfax for the solid waste stuff it dumped on the ground."

"And shows the complete disregard the company has for environmental rules and regulations. This is much worse than the violations that got them into trouble when you were in the DA's office, and explains the dead fish Billy and I saw in Braswell's Pond."

"However, it doesn't establish the kind of sustained exposure needed to make our clients sick."

Corbin slapped his hands together. "Maybe, but it gives us a chance to run a convincing bluff. How are you coming with that memo?"

"I'm almost finished."

"Turn it into a letter to Nate Stamper"—Corbin paused—"with a copy to that lawyer at Frank and Donaldson whose name I don't want to mention. Give them the data from Dr. Sellers and tell them we're going to file a complaint tomorrow based on newly discovered evidence of PERC contamination and appeal the dismissal of the old complaint relying on 2,4-D to the Court of Appeals. Then draft a letter to the attorney general's office and let them know that what we've uncovered is a huge threat to public health. Whatever happens to our lawsuit, the State is going to have to do something immediately about contamination of the water in every area of the county that may be affected. We'll give a copy of that letter to the newspaper. Once it hits the street, the attitude of the whole town is going to shift 180 degrees."

For the second time that day, Ray was impressed with his father. "Okay," he said. "What are you going to do?"

"Uh, go back to my office and see if I can think of anything else."

Ray dictated the letter to the attorney general's office and sent it to Janelle. He typed the letter to Nate Stamper and Ted Daughbert himself. As each word formed on the computer screen, his sense of vindication increased.

Corbin had stirred up a hornets' nest when he filed the complaint. So far only people named Gage had been stung. That was about to change. He printed out the letter and took it into his father's office.

"This is good, but add a sentence that we've confirmed use by Colfax of PERC-related products."

"Should I call Nate and let him know it's coming?"

"No."

Ray changed the letter, then ran it along with the pertinent data from Dr. Sellers through the scanner so he could forward everything to the two defense lawyers as an e-mail attachment. He tried to imagine the reaction from the other side. A few minutes later Janelle brought him the letter for the attorney general's office.

"Is it safe to drink city water?" she asked. "This is scary."

"I don't know," Ray replied. "But don't say anything about this to any of your friends. Let the government handle it."

"I don't think you're right not to—"

"Janelle." Ray held up his hand.

"Okay," she sniffed. "But I'm going straight to the grocery store as soon as I leave work to buy distilled water before there's a run on it."

"Good idea."

Ray took the second letter and sent it to the attorney general's office with a copy to the defense lawyers. Finally he asked Janelle to fax a copy of the letter to the newspaper.

"Mark it to the attention of Cecil Scruggs," he said, then paused. "And also send one to the news desk at the *Atlanta Journal Constitution* in case the local folks try to bury it."

Ray returned to his office. Now all he could do was wait.

FIFTY-TWO

Corbin and Ray didn't hear anything by noon, and they walked down the street to Red's. The owner of the restaurant personally escorted them to an empty booth. Ray went to the restroom, leaving the two older men alone.

"Thanks," Corbin growled. "We've been getting the cold shoulder all over town the past few days since the article came out about our lawsuit against Colfax."

"Who believes anything you read in the newspaper?" Red shrugged. "But don't get them mad at me. I don't need an investigative reporter snooping around my back door. Speaking of that, do you want any mountain water? I have a first-class batch, smooth with a steady burn."

"No, thanks, I'm going to AA."

Red's eyes widened, and he swore under his breath.

"And no one in town would believe *that* if it made it into the paper either," Corbin said. "But there may be something else coming out about Colfax in the next few days."

Still muttering, Red returned to the cash register. Ray returned to the table.

"I just blew Red's gasket," Corbin said.

"What do you mean?"

Corbin told him. "And it felt good," he said when he finished. "No, it made me feel stronger. Someone at a meeting recently said that each person we tell about our commitment to sobriety is like driving a nail into the coffin of alcoholism."

Ray's eyes watered.

"What?" Corbin asked.

"You have to ask?" Ray replied as he quickly wiped his eyes with a napkin. "I get choked up every time I think about watching you eat a bowl of red beans and rice with onions sprinkled on top."

Corbin chuckled. Even though he and Ray were swimming in a swirl of pressure and uncertainty, they didn't talk about the case as they ate. Instead they focused on the object of their common love—Billy.

"I wish we'd had more times like this lunch over the years," Corbin said. "And it's my fault that we haven't."

Ray's eyes reddened again.

"Don't cry," Corbin said with a grin. "I'll buy your lunch."

———

"I can't handle this!" Janelle exploded as soon as they walked back through the door. "You set off an atom bomb, then leave me to deal with the radiation fallout."

"Calm down and tell us," Ray said.

"Calm down! How can you—"

"Then don't calm down," Ray interrupted. "Tell us as hysterically as you want."

Janelle blinked her eyes. "Millie Watson called, crying her eyes out, when she heard the case had been dismissed. There are reporters demanding to talk to you, a government lawyer from Atlanta is going to serve a subpoena on us, and Nate Stamper has phoned three times and yelled at me when I told him you weren't available."

"That's a good sign," Ray said to Corbin. "Where do you want to start?"

"Millie," Corbin replied.

"Send all our other calls to voice mail," Ray said.

"What if someone barges in and demands to see you?"

Corbin pointed to the out-of-date fishing magazines stacked on the low table in the reception area. "Give them something to read."

They went into the conference room, and Corbin phoned Millie. She didn't answer, and Corbin left a message trying to reassure her.

"I've talked to Tommy Kilpatrick," he said. "And we're going to get together soon and go over the case."

"I'll call Nate," Ray said.

"What are you going to say?" Corbin asked.

"I'm going to listen."

Ray placed the call, and the receptionist with the British accent crisply asked him to hold for a moment. Ray fidgeted nervously as the time to transfer the call dragged on.

"Ray?" Nate's voice came on the line.

"Yes, and I have you on speakerphone with my father."

"Good, because you both need to hear this. You know what's coming."

"No, you tell us," Ray replied evenly.

"Colfax is going to sue you individually, along with your clients, and by the time this is over you won't be able to find a job picking up trash along the roadside."

Corbin pulled the phone closer to him and spoke. "Then we'll be working alongside your client, who will be cleaning up all the toxic trash it has dumped on the land and in the streams of this county. The truth is going to come out."

"Why don't we sit down and discuss the situation?" another voice responded.

"Who is this?" Corbin asked.

"Ted Daughbert. I'm patched into the call while driving back to Alto from Atlanta. I've been on the phone with Colfax's home office this morning, and there may be a creative way to resolve this situation if we work together."

Corbin was mentally prepared for Nate's belligerent onslaught. He didn't know how to respond to Daughbert's slick conciliatory statement.

"I don't know," Corbin replied warily.

"That's why we should talk. Is there a chance you could get your clients into the office for a meeting later this afternoon?"

"A meeting with you?"

"Not directly if you don't want them to, but so they would be immediately available for feedback."

Corbin looked at Ray, who shrugged and nodded.

"Okay. That shouldn't be an issue," Corbin said.

"Let's make it four o'clock. Notify Nate if the time needs to change."

The call ended.

"I don't trust him," Ray said.

"Of course not," Corbin replied. "Neither do I."

Corbin asked Ray to get in touch with the attorney general's office while he rounded up the clients for the four o'clock meeting. Branson Kilpatrick answered when Corbin called and was skeptical of any benefit from a meeting with the defense lawyers.

"I agree," Corbin said. "But all we have to do is listen. In fact, I'm not going to put you in the same room with them."

"Should we bring Mitchell?"

It was something Corbin hadn't considered. The skinny, bald-headed young boy would be graphic silent witness.

"Yes, if he feels up to it."

"I know it will be easier for Millie and Lance to bring Josh. That way they won't have to find someone to watch him on short notice."

"Okay. Come a few minutes early so I can answer any questions you think of between now and then."

"Oh, and what should we do if someone from the newspaper contacts us?"

"Refer them to me. That's the smartest thing to do when there is pending litigation."

The call ended. Corbin had been ignoring the requests for statements and interviews from the press that were filling up his voice mail. Janelle buzzed him to let him know another reporter was on the line.

"Aren't you going to talk to any of them?" she asked.

"Not yet."

"Even Cecil Scruggs?"

"Especially Cecil Scruggs."

"Give me something to say."

Corbin thought for a moment. "Tell them our office can't comment on pending litigation."

"That makes you sound like one of those lawyers on TV."

"Good. Tell the same thing to any TV stations that call."

Corbin went into Ray's office to receive an update on the conversation with the attorney general's office.

"Because of the immediate health risk, it's going to be expedited," Ray said. "They're getting in touch with Dr. Sellers directly."

"Our hand is off the tiller with the State," Corbin said. "Does Cindy know what's going on?"

"No, but I should tell her about the meeting this afternoon so she can pray."

Prayer talk about practical matters still sounded odd to Corbin, but remembering the AA meeting earlier in the day, he didn't say anything.

"What about Roxy?" he asked. "Should we notify her?"

"I'd love to pick her brain about what Daughbert has in mind, but I don't see how we can justify talking with her. She has a conflict based on her prior employment with Frank and Donaldson. Her hands are tied and her lips sealed."

"Yeah," Corbin replied. "We're on our own."

The Kilpatricks were the first people to arrive. Seeing Mitchell walk slowly into the conference room made Ray wonder if they should have brought their clients with them to court for the motion in front of Judge Perry. But Ray was now convinced the judge had made up his mind before the lawyers opened their mouths to argue.

The Watson family came in a couple of minutes later. Millie introduced her husband, Lance, to Ray and Corbin. Josh, a slightly built boy who looked even sicker than Mitchell, clung to his father, whom he'd not seen for six months.

Everyone gathered in the conference room, and Corbin summarized what was going on.

"So why do you think the lawyers for Colfax want to meet?" Tommy asked.

"Anything I say would be a guess," Corbin said. "And there's no use talking about a future we can't see. Just remember they can't make you do anything, and don't be intimidated by threats."

Branson spoke. "Lawyer talk is like what happens before a professional wrestling match. It's all for show."

"Yeah, that's usually true," Corbin said with a slight smile. "But I hope not today."

"Do you think they want to talk settlement?" Tommy persisted.

"That's possible," Corbin admitted. "If so, remember their first proposal is just to get the discussion started. It's not the best they'll do."

The phone in the middle of the table buzzed, and Ray picked it up and listened to Janelle, then nodded to Corbin. "They're here."

"Okay," Corbin said to the group. "We'll talk to them in my office, then come back and tell you what they say."

They entered the reception area. Ray saw Ted Daughbert and wondered what he thought about a small law office with old fishing magazines on the coffee table and the firm's only secretary sitting at one end of the room.

"Are your clients here?" Daughbert asked.

"Yes." Corbin gestured toward the conference room. "They're in there. We'll talk in my office."

Colonel Parker always said no one shakes hands before a knife fight, and Corbin led the way into his office. Ray took up the rear. The scenario had a surreal feel to it. They brought in extra chairs. Corbin sat behind his desk, with Daughbert, Nate, and Ray in a semicircle across from him.

"We don't think any new evidence you've allegedly uncovered is going to change the outcome of your claim," Daughbert began. "But I'm not going to make you listen to the reasons why I believe that's true. We're here to put an end to the litigation. Do you want to hear our offer?"

As Daughbert spoke, Ray's heart climbed higher and higher into his throat.

"Go ahead," Corbin said, brushing his hair away from his forehead.

"I've spoken with Colfax corporate in Richmond. They are sympathetic with your clients' medical situation and want to address it. The most humane way to do so is to provide optimal care for the two boys."

Ray knew his father hadn't yet calculated the amount of money needed to fund treatment. No matter how much Daughbert offered, they'd have to hire someone to research the issue.

"And we're not going to do that via a monetary offer," the lawyer continued. "Colfax would rather spend its money fighting the lawsuit than pay it to you and your clients."

"Then we don't have anything to discuss," Corbin said, his face suddenly getting red.

"Yes, we do," Daughbert replied, glancing down at a piece of paper in his hand. "I'm authorized to offer employment at Colfax to Thomas Kilpatrick and Lance Watson at their previous positions beginning the first of next week, so long as the necessary documents are completed. Because they've previously worked for the company, they won't be subject to any waiting period before triggering eligibility to add dependents to the company's major medical health benefit program. Each of them will receive a pay raise sufficient to cover the increased cost of dependent coverage. Their employment will be guaranteed for five years to ensure adequate time for the boys to receive the care they need. Hopefully they'll be in remission at the end of the contractual employment period."

"The treating oncologists want to put Mitchell Kilpatrick into an experimental program at Egleston Hospital in Atlanta," Corbin said. "Will that be paid?"

"Egleston Hospital?"

"It's the children's hospital at Emory Medical Center," Nate said.

Daughbert nodded. "For a facility like Egleston, approving treatment won't be a problem. We'll include language in the settlement documents to cover that possibility. And because the group health program is largely self-funded, the company can administer it for the best interest of the patient without having to answer to an insurance company until any excess coverage kicks in."

As he listened, Ray was seeking to uncover hidden traps like a dog searching for its favorite treat. "How much has to be paid on a claim to trigger the excess coverage?" he asked.

Daughbert kept looking at Corbin.

"Two million dollars for each boy, which as you know from your preparation in the case will more than cover the average cost of care during the critical first two years of treatment for non-Hodgkin's lymphoma in children."

Corbin spoke. "Our clients have out-of-pocket costs for deductibles, and we have expenses of litigation that we've incurred here at the firm. We want those paid too."

"Not happening," Daughbert replied matter-of-factly. "And our proposal is nonnegotiable. I came here to make you and your clients a fair offer that meets their needs. If they don't accept it today, it's withdrawn as soon as I leave this office."

"I can't recommend that to my clients," Corbin said, his voice rising in volume.

"I understand, but you have an ethical obligation to communicate it to them."

Ray braced for an explosion from his father. None came.

"One other thing," Daughbert said. "You will agree to issue a press release stating that the litigation has been resolved to the satisfaction of your clients without the payment of monetary damages. We'll draft the press release. All other terms of the settlement will be confidential, and if breached will result in loss of the benefits outlined."

"What if someone at Colfax mentions the settlement?" Ray asked. "The plant managers will have to know about the employment agreements."

"No, they won't. Your clients will be given a person to contact at human resources in Richmond who will ensure the terms of the employment agreements are followed."

"What if they make a mistake on the job that would normally result in firing?" Corbin asked.

"They will remain employed, although perhaps in another capacity. Colfax is committed to making this work and will have to trust your clients to do their part. Otherwise they'll get stuck in a room doing the most boring job in the plant. Hopefully that's not what they want."

Ray had to admit it was a creative proposal. Corbin stood up.

"Wait here while we talk with them," he said.

Corbin led the way across to the conference room. Ray tried to grab him so they could retreat to the rear of the office and go over things first, but Corbin had the conference room door open before Ray could stop him. They stepped inside to a roomful of anxious faces.

FIFTY-THREE

Corbin turned to Ray before he addressed the group. "If I leave anything out or misstate something, jump in and correct me."

Ray sat down beside Branson to listen. In a calm voice Corbin repeated what they'd heard. When he mentioned the employment contracts for Tommy and Lance, Ray heard Millie gasp.

"They'd take him back even though he's been in jail?" she blurted out.

"Yes, and unlike everyone else who works on the manufacturing floor, he'd be protected by an employment contract. I've not seen the actual document, but the real reason for the job is to provide health insurance for the boys in return for dropping the lawsuit."

He explained the proposal without interjecting emotionally charged terminology and included Daughbert's statement about it being nonnegotiable.

"Do you think they're bluffing?" Branson asked.

Corbin looked at Ray.

"No," they both said at the same time.

"It's not that sort of situation," Ray added.

"I don't like being pressured about making up our minds," Tommy said. "It sounds suspicious."

"I agree," Corbin replied. "But that's what is on the table."

He then explained the confidentiality provisions and gave additional details about the employment contracts.

"Part of their motivation is to make the company look good," Corbin said. "They're going to get a ton of negative publicity about polluting the water, and I guess they figure it makes good business sense to get us off their backs in what sounds like an act of generosity."

Branson muttered but didn't say anything.

"We'll take it," Millie said, then immediately glanced at Lance. "Won't we?"

"Yeah." Her husband nodded slowly. "I don't see any other way."

"Remember, we haven't researched the average cost of treatment," Corbin cautioned.

"I have," Branson said. "And what the lawyer said sounds about right. I mean, the treatment is going to work or . . ."

No one wanted to complete the sentence.

Corbin turned to Tommy and Larissa. "Questions?"

"We won't get any cash for all they've put us through," Tommy said. "And you won't get paid if we don't get any money."

"That's correct. The contract you signed with me states that no attorney fee is charged unless we collect money from Colfax."

"Are you okay with that?"

Corbin again looked at Ray, who simply nodded. Rarely had such a simple gesture been more unselfish.

"Our job is to represent you," Corbin said. "If you believe accepting Colfax's offer is in your best interests, that's what matters, and we'll help make it happen, including help with all the work needed to finalize the settlement. This law firm is a business, so we have to make money, but Ray and I will have to trust that we'll make it up on other cases."

Tommy turned to Larissa. "What do you think?"

"I agree with Millie."

"Then I guess we're in too," Tommy said.

"Does everyone understand they can't talk about this with anyone?" Corbin asked. "And by that I mean family members, friends, people who live in another state, etc."

"I can keep my big mouth shut for the boys," Larissa said.

"All of you should keep that in mind," Corbin said. "What we're about to do is for them."

Heads nodded around the room.

"Any other questions?" Corbin asked.

No one said a word. Corbin and Ray left the room.

—

It took two hours to crunch out the additional details. To Janelle's relief all the typing was done by clerical workers at Daughbert's office in Chicago. At one point during the process, Ray and Nate were alone in Corbin's office.

"Colfax is cleaning house," Nate said. "Guy Hathaway is gone, and I heard other heads at the local plant will roll."

"If they're responsible for this mess, it needs to happen."

"Yeah." Nate paused. "And I'm sorry the way this all came down for you. You know, for your job at the firm."

Corbin and Daughbert returned. Ray realized that even if Nate wanted to continue the conversation and renew the offer to come to work at Simpkin, Brown, and Stamper, Ray wouldn't accept it. That ship had sailed.

After the documents were signed and everyone left the office, Corbin and Ray returned to the empty conference room. Corbin plopped down, leaned his head back, and closed his eyes.

"I'm beat," he said. "Now that it's over, I admit I'm too old for this type of litigation."

"You're 100 percent right," Ray replied.

Corbin opened his right eye. "You didn't have to agree so quickly or with such enthusiasm."

"If you can't tell your law partner the truth, who can you tell?" Corbin grinned.

"We're still not finished," Ray said. "We need to make one more call before we go home."

"Roxy?"

Ray nodded. Using the speakerphone, he punched in his sister's number.

"I need to give you an update on the Colfax case," Ray said when she answered.

"You can't because—"

"Don't worry," Ray interrupted. "It's settled and what I'm going to tell you will be in the press release prepared by Ted Daughbert. He left our office a few minutes ago."

"Daughbert was at Dad's office?"

"Careful what you say," Ray replied. "You're on speakerphone, and our father is listening."

"Yes, Daughbert was here," Corbin said. "And he didn't comment on the décor."

While Ray talked Roxy was clearly trying to figure out how the case was resolved.

"I know they're going to provide health care benefits for the boys," she said. "I'm just not sure how it's going to be justified."

"My lips are sealed," Ray said, "but we wanted to thank you for connecting us with Dr. Sellers. His report was crucial."

"And suicidal for my job prospects."

"Roxy," Corbin said. "I'm sorry that—"

"Save your apology for this weekend, if that's where you're going," Roxy interrupted. "Peter and I are coming up to Alto on Saturday, and I'd rather hear it from you in person."

———

Ray and Cindy sent Billy into the backyard to play while they finished straightening up the house prior to Roxy and Peter's arrival.

"Lie down on the sofa in the living room," Ray said. "You can give orders from there." He finished in the kitchen, then moved into the living area.

"Are you sure we shouldn't fix dinner here?" Cindy asked. "Putting your father and Roxy together in a public place like a restaurant is a recipe for a short meal. At least here one of them could go to another room to cool off."

"He insisted," Ray replied. "And he's going to pick up the tab. He hasn't taken us to a nice place to eat since we got married."

"When did he do that before we were married?"

"Never," Ray agreed as he knelt down to retrieve some of Billy's military action figures from their hiding place beneath a recliner. "I guess these guys were planning a sneak attack."

"What is Roxy's plan for this trip?"

"She didn't say, but my guess is Peter has asked her to marry him, and she wants to tell us in person."

"Impressive. I didn't know you thought about things like that when it came to your sister."

Ray crawled across the floor, where he located more action figures hiding behind the entertainment center.

"Peter has her number," he replied, looking up at her. "Just like I have yours."

Cindy picked up a coaster and cocked her arm as if to throw it.

"No," Ray said. "Don't exert yourself. I'll come closer so you can bop me on the head."

The doorbell rang and he got up to answer. His father stood on the doorstep, wearing a crisply laundered shirt and freshly pressed pants.

"I thought we were going to meet you at the restaurant," Ray said.

"There's a change in plans," Corbin replied. "I want to make a stop on the way."

"Where?"

"You'll know when we get there. Where's Billy?"

"In the backyard."

Corbin headed toward the kitchen, then stopped. "Cindy, will you be okay if we take a short walk and have to stand for a few minutes?"

"Yes, so long as I can take it easy."

Corbin left to see Billy.

"What do you think he's up to?" Cindy asked.

"I don't know," Ray replied. "After all the uproar about the Colfax case settled down a little, we had a good week. Once the press release went out, we had three people contact us about decent cases. Nothing huge but better than most of the other open files in the office."

"So should I talk to the Realtor about Kitty's house?"

"Yes." Ray smiled. "I think that's a great idea."

He was straightening up the guest bathroom when the doorbell chimed again. This time Cindy beat him to the door and let Roxy and Peter inside. The first thing Ray did when he went into the living room to greet them was check out Roxy's left hand. Sure enough, a large, shiny diamond, surrounded by a ring of smaller ones, glistened on her ring finger. Cindy stood beside her, beaming.

"You were right," Cindy said.

"I knew it!" Ray said. "Congratulations!"

"No job yet," she said, "but I've said yes to something, and someone, way more important."

Ray shook Peter's hand and gave Roxy a quick hug.

"I saw Dad's truck," Roxy said. "I thought he was going to meet us at the restaurant."

"Change of plans," Ray replied, "and I don't know what they are. I'll get him. He and Billy are in the backyard."

"Don't say anything to him about this," Roxy said, pointing to the ring. "Let's see how long it takes him to notice."

Corbin was standing on the ground beneath a tree as Billy climbed higher.

"They're here!" Ray called out. "Billy! I hope you're not going to have to take another shower before we leave."

Billy scrambled down and jumped to the ground from a limb that seemed way too high. He popped up and ran over to Ray.

"Pops and I are planning a fishing trip," he said. "There's a private pond he knows about that's about two hours away. We're going to camp out and fish."

Corbin spoke. "Someone in, uh, the group I go to told me about it. He's going to set it up with the owner. Supposedly the pond is home to some enormous bass that need to be caught and given proper names."

"Sounds good," Ray replied.

"So I can go?" Billy asked.

"We'll talk it over with your mother. Go inside and wash your hands."

Corbin and Ray returned to the living room. Peter shook Corbin's hand. Roxy nodded in his direction but held back.

"Congratulations," Corbin said to Peter. "I look forward to getting to know you better as a son-in-law."

"What? How did you notice?" Roxy asked, holding out her hand.

"I may be old," Corbin said with a smile, "but I'm not blind."

Billy returned from washing his hands.

"Can Billy ride with me?" Corbin asked Ray.

"Okay," Ray replied. "The four of us will take our car."

"Buckle your seat belt," Corbin said when he got into the truck.

"Pops, I always buckle my seat belt," Billy replied.

They backed out of the driveway. Making sure Ray was behind him, Corbin drove slowly away from the house.

"Daddy said we're going to eat steak," Billy said.

"That's right. And I want you to order anything else you want on the menu."

"Even dessert?"

"Yes. I hear the coconut cream pie is awesome."

They drove toward the center of town. When they reached the church, Corbin slowed down and put on his blinker.

"It's Saturday," Billy said. "There's nothing going on at the church."

"I know. We're going to Gran's grave. Is that okay with you?"

Corbin waited for a car to pass so he could make the turn. Billy's face was serious.

"You don't have to get out if you don't want to," Corbin continued. "You can wait in the truck."

Corbin entered the cemetery and parked beneath a large oak tree. He opened the glove box and took out a thick envelope.

"What's that?" Billy asked.

"It's why we're here."

Corbin got out, and Billy joined him. They began walking toward the grave. Partway there, he felt a touch as Billy took his hand. Corbin glanced over his shoulder and saw that everyone was following.

They reached the grave. The mounded dirt had almost sunk to ground level, and the plot was now covered by newly sprouted rye grass. Ray, Roxy, Cindy, and Peter joined them. They stood in a semicircle facing the gravestone.

Corbin cleared his throat. "It needs flowers, doesn't it?" he asked.

Roxy already had a tissue in her hand and held it to her eyes.

"But that's not why I wanted to come here today," Corbin continued, holding up the envelope. "I came to leave this. You all know something about the journey I've been on in recent weeks. And coming here is a huge step. I've tried to make a fearless moral inventory and admit to God the exact nature of my wrongs"—his voice cracked—"against her. I've asked God to forgive me, and I've made a list of the things I'd say to her if she were standing here with us."

Corbin released Billy's hand, stepped forward, and placed the envelope on top of the gravestone. He'd written *To Kitty* in large letters on the outside.

He heard Roxy gasp out a sob. Tears were streaming down Cindy's face. Ray and Peter watched, wide-eyed. Billy sniffled.

Corbin cleared his throat again. He had to say this with the level of earnest conviction he felt in his heart.

"Kitty, I humbly ask you to forgive me. Everything I need to make amends for isn't on those sheets of paper, but it's a start. And I'm praying for God to show me more."

Corbin stepped back. He wasn't sure what to expect, but a heavy burden lifted off his soul. He turned to his children.

"Ray, I'm working on another list for you. And Roxy—" Corbin stopped as suddenly his own tears broke through. He paused for several seconds. It took every ounce of willpower for him to continue. "There's no way a sheet of paper can make up for the pain I've caused you. But I want to do the best I can if you'll—"

In a flash Roxy stepped across the few feet between them and fell into his arms. Corbin held her as she sobbed against his chest. His own tears streamed off his face onto her shoulder. Both Ray and Peter were now wiping their eyes.

And that's the way they remained until the fountains were dry.

Roxy stepped back. Corbin glanced down at Billy, who rubbed his eyes with his broad little hands. The boy gazed up at Corbin with a look of pure innocence that transported Corbin back to his own childhood, before the ravages of his devastating choices wreaked havoc on the lives of those he should have loved. The boy's simple look gave Corbin hope that restoration was possible. He gently stroked the top of Billy's head, then leaned over and kissed it. He straightened up and faced Roxy.

"Thank you," he said, looking at her tearstained face. "But this is just the first step. I know rebuilding trust is going to take time and has to be based on changes in my life that are real."

Then he turned to Ray and Cindy. "And thank you for filling the gap Kitty left. The good in her lives in both of you."

Cindy's lower lip trembled as she faced the gravestone in silent homage to the godly influence of a woman who'd gone to her reward. Ray seemed to stand up a bit straighter and taller. They remained in a semicircle as the late afternoon sun shot through the bare limbs of the trees that stood in silent witness.

Then Billy reached out and took Corbin's hand. The boy joined his other hand to his mother, who took Ray's hand in hers. One by one, they came together. Hand in hand, heart to heart. The semi-circle became a circle.

No longer a house divided.

Discussion Questions

1. Discuss some things about Kitty that make her special.
2. How are Ray and Roxy alike—and different? What are some of the common characteristics of adult children of an alcoholic?
3. Can we ever love another person enough to change them into who we want them to be? (See page 139.)
4. Corbin did not consider himself an alcoholic. What were some signs that he was?
5. What was your response to Peter's comment to Roxy—"I don't want the woman I love to carry such a huge weight of past pain into our future relationship"?
6. Was it a surprise to you that depositions can be more contentious than a trial? (See page 218.)
7. Do you remember the line on page 233—"And there's no statute of limitations on prayer"? What do you think about that, and how might it affect your life if it is true?
8. What do you think about Corbin, and how did your opinion of him change throughout the book? Answer the same question for Ray and Roxy.

9. What did you learn about Alcoholics Anonymous from reading the story? What do you know about its history? Without revealing any confidential information, have you known someone who was a member of AA? What was his or her experience?

10. What do you think can be the relationship between AA and Christianity?

11. How would you define the "Peter Factor"? (See page 296.)

12. If you were to recommend the book to someone, who would it be and why? Which character(s) influences your answer?

13. If you could ask Robert Whitlow, the author, one question about the book, what would it be?

ACKNOWLEDGMENTS

Writing a novel is both solitary and collaborative. Thanks to my wife, Kathy, for protecting my solitude, to LB Norton, who corrected my mistakes, and to Ami McConnell, my longtime editor, for her guidance and suggestions. Special appreciation to my friend Pat for his insight that kept the story true to its mission.

CONFESSION IS GOOD FOR THE SOUL, BUT IT COULD
MEAN DEATH TO AN AMBITIOUS YOUNG LAWYER.

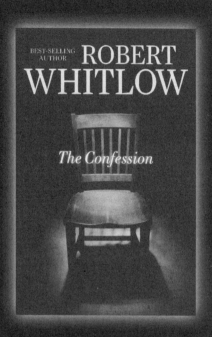

BEST-SELLING
AUTHOR **ROBERT**
WHITLOW

The Confession

"Christy Award winner Whitlow's experience in
the law is apparent in this well-crafted legal thriller.
Holt's spiritual growth as he discovers his faith and
questions his motives for hiding his secret is inspiring.
Fans of John Grisham will find much to like here."

—*Library Journal*

AVAILABLE IN PRINT, E-BOOK, AND AUDIO.

THOMAS NELSON
Since 1798

"Writes in the tradtion of John Grisham, combining compelling legal and ethical plotlines . . . but Whitlow has explicit spiritual themes."

—*WORLD Magazine*

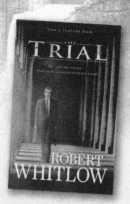
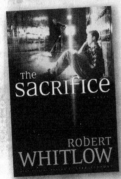
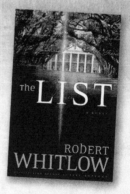

About the Author

Robert Whitlow is the bestselling author of legal novels set in the South and winner of the Christy Award for Contemporary Fiction. He received his J.D. with honors from the University of Georgia School of Law where he served on the staff of the *Georgia Law Review*.

Visit him online at www.robertwhitlow.com

Twitter: @whitlowwriter

Facebook: robertwhitlowbooks